WHITE CORRIDOR

Also by Christopher Fowler

FULL DARK HOUSE
THE WATER ROOM
SEVENTY-SEVEN CLOCKS
TEN-SECOND STAIRCASE

For more information on Christopher Fowler and his books,
see his website at: www.christopherfowler.co.uk

WHITE CORRIDOR

CHRISTOPHER FOWLER

Doubleday

LONDON · TORONTO · SYDNEY · AUCKLAND · JOHANNESBURG

TRANSWORLD PUBLISHERS
61–63 Uxbridge Road, London W5 5SA
A Random House Group Company
www.booksattransworld.co.uk

First published in Great Britain
in 2007 by Doubleday
an imprint of Transworld Publishers

A CIP catalogue record for this book
is available from the British Library.

ISBN 9780385610674

Addresses for Random House Group Ltd companies outside the UK
can be found at: www.randomhouse.co.uk
The Random House Group Ltd Reg. No. 954009

The Random House Group Ltd makes every effort to ensure that the papers used
in its books are made from trees that have been legally sourced from well managed
and credibly certified forests. Our paper procurement policy can be found at:
www.randomhouse.co.uk/paper.htm

Typeset in 10/13pt Sabon by
Kestrel Data, Exeter, Devon.
Printed and bound in Great Britain by
Clays Ltd, St Ives plc.

2 4 6 8 10 9 7 5 3 1

For Jim Sturgeon
(1944–2007)
The real Arthur Bryant

ACKNOWLEDGEMENTS

I owe a debt of gratitude to Simon Taylor at Transworld for appreciating the Bryant and May mysteries and shepherding them towards readers who do likewise. The same goes to Mandy Little, my ever-perspicacious agent, to Kate Samano and Claire Ward for their expert styling of words and pictures, and to Anna Kenny-Ginard for restoring my faith in publicists.

A special tip of the hat goes to the many local press and website reviewers who love books and bring them to the attention of their readers. I couldn't do it without you. This one is also for Peter Chapman – the groom who was also the best man.

Visit www.christopherfowler.co.uk for more . . .

'In the depths of winter, I finally learned there was in me
an invincible summer.'
Albert Camus

'The old know everything, including all the secrets of the young.'
Gary Indiana

WHITE CORRIDOR

NOTICE

THE PECULIAR CRIMES UNIT WILL BE SHUT
FOR ONE WEEK COMMENCING
MONDAY 19TH FEBRUARY

THIS AFFECTS THE FOLLOWING UNIT
PERSONNEL BASED AT MORNINGTON
CRESCENT

Raymond Land, Acting Unit Chief
Arthur Bryant, Senior Detective
John May, Senior Detective
Janice Longbright, Detective Sergeant
Dan Banbury, Crime Scene Manager/Information Technology
Giles Kershaw, Forensic Scientist/Social Sciences Liaison
Meera Mangeshkar, Detective Constable
Colin Bimsley, Detective Constable
Oswald Finch, Unit Pathologist
April May, Office Manager

IF YOU HAVE ANY QUERIES CONCERNING
YOUR DUTIES DURING THIS PERIOD, PLEASE
CONTACT RAYMOND LAND IMMEDIATELY

*WILL SOMEONE ALSO MAKE ARRANGEMENTS TO
FEED CRIPPEN AND EMPTY HIS LITTER TRAY*

I

SECOND HEART

'Concentrate on the moth.'

The creature fluttered against the inside of the upended water glass as the women leaned in to watch. It was trying to reach the light from the amber street lamp that shone through the gap in the curtains. Each time its wings batted against its prison, the Shaded Broad-bar *Scotopteryx chenopodiata* shed more of the powder that kept it in flight, leaving arrow imprints on the glass.

'Concentrate hard on the moth, Madeline.'

In the early-evening drizzle, the Edwardian terraced house at 24 Cranmere Road was like a thousand others in the surrounding South London streets, its quiddity to be a part of the city's chaotic whole. There were shiny grey slates, dead chimney pots and shabby bay windows. The rain sketched silver signatures across the rooftops, leaving inky pools on empty pavements. At this time of the year it was an indoor world.

Behind dense green curtains, five women sat in what had once been the front parlour, narrowing their thoughts in the over-heated air. The house was owned by Kate Summerton, a prematurely grey housewife who had reached the age at which so many suburban women fade from the view of men. As if to aid this new invisibility, she tied back her hair and wore

TV-screen glasses with catalogue slacks and a shapeless fawn cardigan.

Her guests were all neighbours except Madeline Gilby, who worked in the Costcutter supermarket on the Old Kent Road and was disturbingly beautiful, even when she arrived still wearing her blue cashier's smock. Kate had known her for almost three years, and it had taken that long to convince Madeline that she possessed a rare gift beyond that of her grace.

The small brown moth batted feebly once more, then sank to the tablecloth. It was losing strength. Madeline furrowed her brow and pressed pale hands to her temples, shutting her eyes tight.

'He's tiring. Keep concentrating.'

The Broad-bar made one final attempt to escape through the top of the glass, and fell back. One wing ticked rapidly and then became still.

'That,' said Kate, adjusting her great glasses, 'shows the true intensity of the directed mind. The energy you generated is not measurable by any electronic means, and yet it's enough to interfere with the nervous system of this poor little creature. Of course, the test is hardly very scientific, but it suffices to demonstrate the power you hold within you.'

Madeline was astonished. She gasped and smiled at the others.

'You have the gift, dear, as all women do in different degrees,' said Kate. 'In time, and with our help, you'll be able to identify the auras of others, seeing deep inside their hearts. You'll instinctively know if they mean you good or harm, and will never need to fear a man again. From now on, you and your son will be safe.'

Kate was clear and confident, conscious of her middle-class enunciation. As a professional, she was used to being heard and obeyed. She turned to the others. 'You see how easy it is to harness your inner self? It is important to understand that, in a manner of speaking, all women have two hearts. The first is the muscle that pumps our blood, and the second is a psychic heart that, if properly developed, opens us to secret knowledge. You can all harness that heart-power, just as Madeline is doing. Males don't possess this second spiritual heart; they have only flesh and bone. They feel pain and pleasure, but there is no extra dimension to their feelings, whereas we are able to find deeper shading in our emotional spirituality. This is the defence we develop against those who hurt us and our children, because most men do eventually, even if they never intend to. They are fundamentally different creatures, and fail to understand the damage they cause. With training, we can open a pathway illuminated by the pure light of truth, and see into the hearts of men. This is the breakthrough that Madeline has achieved today, in this room.'

Madeline was unable to stop herself from crying. As a child she had been lonely and imaginative, used to spending long afternoons with books and make-believe friends until boys discovered her nascent beauty. Then the nightmare had begun. Now, there was a chance that it might really be over. For the first time since she had met Kate, she truly believed that her power existed.

'That's it, let it all out,' said her mentor, placing a plump arm around her as the others murmured their approval. 'It always comes as a shock the first time. You'll get used to it.'

Madeline needed air. She left the suffocating parlour and passed quickly through the herb-filled kitchen into the garden, where she found her son kicking sulkily at the flower beds that held etiolated rosebushes, each with a single despondent pink bloom.

'It's cold out here, Ryan. You should stay indoors.'

'Her husband smokes.'

'Even so.' Madeline rubbed her bare arms briskly, looking about. The Anderson shelters and chicken sheds of postwar London had been replaced with rows of flat-pack con-servatories. New attics and kitchens thrust out along the terrace, the residents pushing their property boundaries as if halfheartedly trying to break free of the past. 'I'm ready to go now. Come and get your jacket. We'll go home.'

As the neighbours gathered in the hall with their coats,

Mrs Summerton removed the tumbler from the parlour table, crushing the moth between her thumb and forefinger before it had a chance to revive, flicking it into the waste bin. She had started her refuge over twenty years ago, when alcohol abuse had been the main problem. Now it was drugs, not that men needed to take stimulants before battering their partners. Madeline had come to her with a black eye and a sprained wrist, but had still been anxious to get home on that first evening in order to cook her husband's dinner. Seeing the gratitude in her protégée's eyes convinced Kate she was doing the right thing, even if it meant performing a little parlour trick with a moth. Madeline was a good mother, kind and decent, but badly damaged by her relationships with men. If she could not be taught to seek independence and protect herself by traditional means, it was valid to introduce more unconventional methods.

Mrs Summerton said her good-byes and closed the front door, then checked the time and went to change, remembering that someone new was coming to the shelter tonight. She only had room for eight women, and the new girl would make nine, but how would she ever forgive herself if she sent her home without help? Besides, the new girl came from a wealthy family; her fee could finance the refuge for months.

Mr Summerton stayed in the kitchen reading his paper. He had coped with the house being turned into a women's shelter, had even enjoyed it for a while, but now it was best to stay out of the way. His wife was honest down to her bones, he had always known that. She had made a few mistakes in her overeagerness to help, that was all, but now she was exploring strange new territory, enjoining the women to discover their innate psychic powers and leave their husbands – encouraging suspicion and hatred of all men, of which he disapproved.

Still, she was a force of nature when she made up her mind, and he knew better than to raise his voice in protest. There had always been too many women in the house: Kate's friends, their daughters – even the cat was a female. His mother had once warned him that all women go mad eventually, and he was starting to believe it. Overlooked and outnumbered, he sipped his tea and turned to the sports pages.

Madeline walked home in the rain, clutching Ryan's hand too tightly. 'Why are we walking?' asked the boy. 'It's bloody freezing.'

'Don't swear,' his mother admonished. 'I haven't got enough for the bus fare. It's not very far, and the exercise is good for you.'

'That's because you gave all your money to her.'

It was true that Mrs Summerton charged for her services, but you couldn't expect her to do it for nothing. Kate had made sense of Madeline's life. During her lonely childhood years, she had been sure that some secret part of her was waiting to be discovered. But instead of gaining self-knowledge she became beautiful, and the curse began. Boys from her school hung around her house, laying their traps and baiting their lies with promises. She had even seen that terrible crafty gleam in her own father's eyes. She trusted easily, and was hurt each time. Beauty made her shy, and shyness made her controllable.

Now, at thirty years of age, she was finally discovering a way of standing up to the men who had always manipulated her. She owed Kate Summerton everything.

'Is she a lady doctor?' asked Ryan.

'Not exactly. What makes you think that?'

'You went to see her when you hurt yourself.'

Madeline had told her son that she'd fallen in the garden, and he seemed to believe her. 'She was very kind to me,' she said.

'You were ages in there,' Ryan probed, watching her face in puzzlement. 'I was stuck in the smoky kitchen with her horrible daughters and her boring husband. What were you doing?'

'Mrs Summerton was helping to teach me something.' She was unsure about broaching the subject with her son. He was at the age where he seemed simultaneously clever and childish.

'You mean like school lessons?' Ryan persisted. 'What was she teaching you?'

Madeline remained quiet until they had turned the high corner wall of Greenwich Park. Winter mist was settling across the plane trees in a veil of dewdrops. 'She was showing me how to deal with your father,' she said at last.

2

THE SHAPING OF MEN

Johann Bellocq stretched up on the staircase to the sea, and pulled another of the ripe orange loquats from the overhanging branches of the tree. Biting into them was like biting flesh. The juice ran down his chin, staining his blue nylon shirt, dripping darkly on to the hot steps. His stolen bounty held the sweet taste of sin. He spat the large stone at the landing below, watching it skitter and bounce into the storm drain, then loaded his pockets with all the sticky fruit he could touch on tiptoe. He was a tall, slim boy, and could reach into the dusty leaves for the most tender crops hidden from the flies and the harsh glare of the sun.

Summer had come early to *la petite Afrique* that year, encouraging his mother to keep the shutters closed, not that she needed much persuasion. She rarely allowed sunlight into the villa, so the rooms remained cold and damp-smelling deep into summer. Even when the mistral came, drawing dry north-easterly winds across the hills, she would not air the house. Thick yellow dust silted beneath the doors and across the window ledges, but she stubbornly refused to unseal the rooms. To allow nature in was to admit pagan forces, a blasphemous act of elemental obeisance that would disturb the pious sanctity of her home and unleash the powers of godlessness upon the three of them.

His mother was entirely mad.

Johann skipped up the steep staircase, noting the sun was low over the cliffs above. He had no watch, but knew instinctively that his mother would be waiting to punish him cruelly. Today, though, he did not care.

He had just passed his twelfth birthday and was growing fast, already handsome, with a maturity beyond his age. Soon his grandfather would die, and he would be bigger than she. He could afford to bide his time.

He had stolen a transistor radio from one of the girls on the beach, and tuned it to a station that only played songs by the old French singers: Michel Delpech, Mireille Mathieu and Johnny Hallyday. He hated English bands, despised Culture Club and Queen, the arrogant *regardez-moi* prancing and posturing. He'd hidden the radio in the exhausted little orchard behind the house, where his mother would never find it. Pop was the Devil's music, and led to licentiousness, which was an old-fashioned word meaning sex. She would allow nothing in their home that might run the risk of destroying his innocence, because when boys discovered sex it turned their heads from God.

His stroke-afflicted grandfather, who lived with them, had ceased voicing his opinions, and spent his days drifting in dreams. Marcel's wife was dead, and he was not far behind. She had suffered cruelly with stomach cancer. If God was so merciful, why would he take two years to destroy a woman who had visited the little village church three times every Sunday and never uttered an unkind word in her life? Doubtless the old man would have liked to have asked his daughter this question, but knew all too well what she would say: God had tested her faith and found it wanting.

The house was tucked beneath umbrella pines and surrounded by twisted pale olive trees, their tortured roots thrust above the dry ground like ancient knees. Here the plants seeped pungent oils as a protection from the heat, as well as sharp-scented nectars that formed the bases for the area's perfume factories. No wooded aromas permeated the house, however. Perfume was the smell of sin, and was worn by the painted whores who paraded along the Avenue de la Californie after dark. Johann's mother washed the edges of the doors and windows with disinfectant to keep the smell from entering.

Inside the little single-floored house, all was bare and white and pious. The rooms were scoured with bleach, the floors and steps with cleaning alcohol, the windows with paper and vinegar. In every room was a large pine crucifix, no other adornment. In the kitchen, a wooden table and three chairs; in the bedrooms iron bedsteads, narrow and rickety, topped with dented copper knobs, and above each bolster, a lurid picture of Our Lady, beatific and tortured, eyes rolled to Heaven. In his room, his mother had placed a faded Victorian sampler on the dresser, picked out in brown and white. Its stitched letters were a warning: '*Dieu Voit Tout.*' God sees everything.

Johann hated the house, and longed to burn it to the ground. Soon the fierce cyan of the Alpine skies would turn to grey, and winter would settle across the region, sealing them away from the world until spring. He would be left at the mercy of his mother. During the rare times when his grandfather was awake he provided protection, but he was sleeping more and more, and could no longer be relied upon as a guardian.

Once, when Johann was seven years old, they had taken a holiday at Lac de l'Ascension, and his mother had pointed up into the dark sky, where rolling clouds had parted to release a shaft of sunlight down to the surface of the lake. 'That,' she told him, 'is the pathway which leads directly to God. It is His way of watching all life on earth. He looks for those who flagrantly commit sin beneath His gaze, and punishes them.'

'How does he do that, Mother?' asked Johann.

'By poisoning their lives, so that everything they touch sickens and dies,' she replied, as if it was the most obvious thing in the world. His mother saw signs, symbols and portents in everything. When she recognized some secret harm in her son, she called him to the shadowed passage where she waited with the slender leather whip that striped the backs of his knees, branding his guilt into place until the marks remained through the suntan of summer. He had come to realize that her religious fervour was a form of illness, a disease of the brain that infected her every action. While his classmates met after school to play football, he was sent to the priest for further teaching. He spent his weekends in church, or at the seminary helping in the vegetable garden. He was never allowed to mix with the children from the village. To be left with others was to encourage the Devil, who gleefully made work for idle young hands. The Devil, like the dirt, the dust and the sun, was the enemy outside, and had to be kept beyond the door.

How he longed to let the Devil in, just to see what he would do. He wanted to talk to his grandfather, to understand why the old man's daughter was so much stricter than any of the mothers in the village, but the yellow-faced old man in the wicker chair was growing feebleminded, and the time was fast approaching when he would have no remaining power of speech.

One Saturday morning in early October, just before the weather turned, Johann slipped the great iron latch and ran off down the hill towards the village. His mother allowed him no money, but he had already planned to do without; he would hitch a lift with one of the lorry drivers who drove vegetables down to the city. Once aboard, he knew he would be safe, for she would have no way of finding him. He hung around the dusty grocery store waiting for a delivery, and his patience was rewarded when a truck pulled into the depot.

One look told him that the driver would never allow him on board. He waited until the lorry had been loaded, and was trying to climb into the back when his mother arrived at the store on her bicycle, and spotted him.

This time, his mother whipped him with the oiled birch she kept in the shed, in order to impress the fullness of her love upon him. After that he was kept at home, where he could be watched by God and his family. Her intention was to keep him pure and untouched by evil, but her prescription had the opposite effect. The boy became sly and dark. Subterfuge came naturally to him.

He remained in the little house for five more years, waiting for an opportunity to free himself, and when the chance finally came, he seized upon it with the full violence of his trapped spirit.

It was a storm-ravaged morning in late autumn, soon after his grandfather had been placed in the gravelled cemetery behind the dry-stone wall that also served as the village's *petanque* pitch. He stood in the middle of his mother's bedroom, knowing exactly what had to be done. Raising the ceramic pitcher she kept on her dresser, he hurled it with all his might on to the floorboards, and when he heard the approaching thump of her stick, went to wait for her in the corridor, where she kept the leather strap.

Beating an old lady should be easy if you have the stomach to do so, he thought. *If she has done everything within her power to deserve it. But it's not if God can see you. If He witnesses your fall from grace, you are damned for eternity.* His mother stood before him, her small sharp teeth bared, the whip raised, about to strike him down – and then a miracle occurred.

Earlier that morning the first snowstorm of the season had ridden over the mountain peaks and across the *haute route* above the village, whitening the tarmac. In seconds the sky had grown dark, as if someone had thrown a sheet over the sun and God was blinded from His view of mortals. The silent blizzard dropped over the house and all around them. Now, Johann thought, he could do whatever he needed to survive. Hidden inside the caul of falling snow, protected by the purity of nature, he snatched back the whip and beat his unrepentant mother to her knees.

He did not stop when the sky suddenly cleared and he could once more be seen by the Almighty, because he decided that God should see what he had done. *If I am to be damned, it is how I will live,* he told himself. He looked up into the pin-sharp panel of azure that had appeared inside the banks of clouds, and openly defied his Maker. *See what I have done. I defy you to save me.* God saw all, and once He did there could only follow judgement, trial, repentance and suffering.

Johann walked to the front door, kicked it back and stepped out into the front garden. In the sky above, the white corridor that had opened through the vaporous mountains shone all the way up to the heart of the sun.

3

GOOD MORNING, ARTHUR

'The urge has come over me to speak to you about carpet slippers, Mr Bryant,' Alma Sorrowbridge told her former lodger. 'You wander in from the garden with half of London on your boots and tramp it all over my spotless kitchen floor, and it does my head in.'

'I thought you wanted me to get into the great outdoors,' grumbled Arthur Bryant, lowering his library book with reluctance. He wore his tweed overcoat and pyjama bottoms to the table, in protest over Alma's restrictions on the bar heater, which had been faulty ever since he had tried to fix it with a toasting fork.

'Yes, but I didn't expect you to bring it back in with you. I thought you might come to Regent's Park with me, instead of digging holes in the garden looking for – whatever old rubbish you expect to find out there.'

'Old rubbish? Relics, madam!' Bryant peered over his pages and scowled. 'You have no idea of the history upon which you stand, do you? I don't suppose you know that near this site, Sir Edmund Berry Godfrey was slaughtered in most vexing circumstances.'

'I read the papers,' Alma bridled.

'I doubt you'd have been reading them in 1678, when his

body was discovered among the primroses near Lower Chalcot Farm. He had been strangled until his neck broke, and a sword run through him, yet spatters of candle wax placed him miles away at Somerset House. His three murderers eventually confessed to having brought him to this lonely spot by horse and sedan chair. We live in Chalk Farm, a corruption of Chalcot Farm, within the cursed circle of Mother Shipton, the area's most famous witch, who said that once the farmland was hemmed in on all sides by London houses, the streets of the metropolis would run with blood. She proved correct, for the area became famous for its fatal duels. And so I dig through London clay, the most recalcitrant material imaginable, in the hopes of finding evidence of those deaths. And once I find it, as I surely will, it will end another chapter of my biography.'

'Here, am I in this book you're writing?' asked Alma, suddenly suspicious.

'You most certainly are. So I should watch your step, especially when it comes to forcing me on route marches and making me eat your bread-and-butter pudding.'

'You're a stubborn old man,' Alma decided, folding her arms. 'A proper walk would do you the world of good.'

'I am not being dragged around a park to feed ducks and admire crocuses while you hand out evangelical leaflets to uninterested passers-by,' snapped Bryant. 'Besides, I'm already planning a trip of my own this week which will require the commandeering of your decrepit Bedford van, and I intend to drive with the windows closed specifically to avoid breathing in the odours of the so-called countryside.'

'But your lungs is filled with London soot. When you cough it's like a death rattle. You've got clogged phlegm in your tubes.'

'I am trying to eat a boiled egg, if you don't mind,' Arthur Bryant complained. 'I can't imagine how long you cooked it. The yolk isn't meant to be this colour, surely.' He shut one eye and peered into the eggcup as if half expecting to find baby chicks nesting inside. 'And your toasted soldiers are rudimentary, to say the least. You're meant to use fresh bread.'

'You can't make proper toast with fresh bread. You've never complained before, and you've been eating them for over forty years.' Alma bristled.

'That's because I used to be your tenant, and was scared of you. We all lived in fear of making the place untidy, only to have you come charging forward with your squeegee and your lavender polish. Well, now you're my tenant, and I can finally take revenge.'

Arthur Bryant had conveniently forgotten that it was he who had persuaded his long-suffering landlady to part with her beautiful Battersea apartment, in order to live with him in a converted false-teeth factory set back from North London's Chalk Farm Road. The area was peppered with warehouses, sheds, huts, and light industrial manufacturing plants that had now been transformed into expensive loft-style homes. The difference was that Bryant's place was the only one not to have been converted, for it still looked like a factory. He was too old and twinge-prone to start renovations himself, and as Alma could no longer be tempted up a ladder with a claw hammer and a mouthful of tacks, they were forced to make the best of things, carrying out odd bodge-jobs as the need arose. If the situation became desperate (as it had last month, when part of the kitchen ceiling fell down, mostly into Alma's casserole), Bryant would head for the Peculiar Crimes Unit to make sad kitten-in-a-boot eyes at his colleagues, who could be relied upon to rally around at the weekend armed with tools and planks and electrical tape to aid a poor helpless old man. It was shameless, but a perk of being officially classed as elderly, and he knew he was sufficiently loved to be able to get away with it.

'It would be nice if you could put the book down long enough to eat,' Alma suggested.

Bryant's great watery eyes swam up from his copy of *The 1919 Arctic Explorer's Handbook Volume II: Iceberg Partition*. 'This is fascinating stuff,' he told her. 'Maggie Armitage sent it to me.'

Alma harrumphed and made a face. Bryant's theatricality was catching. 'That woman is godless,' she complained.

'Quite the reverse. As a practising white witch she's more aware of true religion than most Christians, whose experience usually only extends to miming "O God Our Help in Ages Past" during weddings and christenings.'

'Well, I hope you're going into work today, and not just sitting around reading.' Alma disapproved of such pointless activities. 'I'm planning on a spot of hoovering.' She shifted him to clear away the breakfast things.

'Just in time, I'd imagine. There was a rumour the BBC was coming around to film a documentary about the insects inside your hall rug.'

'Are you insinuating I don't keep a clean house?' asked Alma, mortified. 'All these years I've been looking after you, with your spilled chemicals and your disgusting experiments. Who fed rotting pork to carnivorous plants on top of his wardrobe during the heatwave of 1974?'

'That helped me catch the Kew Gardens Strangler, if you recall.'

'You boiled my tropical fish in 1968, and filled my bedroom with mustard gas.'

'In order to track the Deptford Demon, as well you know. I didn't realize your aunt was sleeping in the house at the time.'

She could have mentioned that the ancient detective had also grown plague germs in her baking trays and ruined her best kitchen knives by putting stab wounds in sides of beef to determine methods of death. He had also rewired the toaster to see if it could be made to electrocute anyone walking across a wet kitchen floor in bare feet, and had been able to answer in the affirmative after nearly setting fire to a Jehovah's Witness.

'You filled my sink with sulphuric acid last Christmas, and if I hadn't been wearing rubber gloves to do the washing up, I'd have ended up in hospital. Took the finish right off my plug, but did I complain?'

'You most certainly did, madam, and the fact that you bring it up at the drop of a hat reminds me how long you bear the grudge.' He rose and collected his battered brown trilby from the table.

'I wish you wouldn't leave that thing over the teapot; it's unsanitary.'

'Most probably, but it keeps my head warm. When you've as little hair as I have, such small comforts are appreciated.' He smoothed the pale nimbus of his fringe back in place. 'I might remind you that I am still the breadwinner in this household, attending to police work for six decades with an unbroken record, despite your regular attempts to poison me. I could have taken holidays but was too conscientious.'

'Too scared of missing out on a good murder, more like.' Alma sniffed. 'It's not natural, all this morbidity, especially at your age.'

'It's not morbidity, it's my job. In my field there's no substitute for firsthand experience. You knew what to expect when you took me in.'

'I knew you was on the side of law and order; I didn't expect you to experiment in my lodgings with meat and germs and explosives.'

They bickered to such an extent each morning that they might as well have been married. The plump Antiguan land-lady (she still thought of Bryant as her tenant) attempted to reform Bryant by tricking him into church attendance, goodwill whist drives and assorted charity events, but he invariably saw through the subterfuge and reminded her that his adherence to paganism precluded any chance of a late conversion.

'Will you be home in time for dinner tonight?' Alma asked, waggling a cake slice between thick brown fingers.

'That depends on the form of culinary witchcraft you're intending to inflict upon me.'

'I'm baking a mutton pie with sweet potatoes, callaloo and cornbread.'

'If I'm back in time, I'll join you for supper. I don't suppose another hour in the oven will adversely affect the texture of your concoctions.'

Alma folded her arms against her chest. 'You're a very rude man, Mr Bryant. I don't know why I put up with you.'

'Because you know the quality of your life would be

immeasurably poorer in my absence,' said Bryant, pushing his luck. Still, Alma could hardly disagree. The old detective had always brightened her days with surprises, even if many of them had proved disagreeable. If he appeared with a bunch of daffodils, there was a good chance that a neighbour would call indignantly to demand their return to the front garden from which they had been torn. The thing about Bryant was that he always meant well. Alma was filled with a patient and loyal adoration for him that defied sense or logic.

'I thought you said the unit was quiet at the moment. Do you have to go in?'

'Raymond Land is thinking of holding a retirement party for our medical examiner, and wants me to help him arrange it,' he explained. 'It could take a while, as I have to plot out a number of unpleasant practical jokes for the evening's festivities.'

Oswald Finch, the only member of London's Metropolitan Police Force who was older than Bryant and still gainfully employed, had finally made good his promise to leave the Peculiar Crimes Unit, although why he thought he would be happier in Hastings than in a mortuary mystified Bryant. Everyone assumed that the irascible pathologist was to be replaced by Giles Kershaw, the Eton-educated junior staff member whom Finch had trained to take over unit operations at the Bayham Street Morgue.

Bryant buttoned the shapeless brown cardigan he had worn for the past twenty years, dragged his horribly moth-eaten Harris tweed coat over the top of it and finished the ensemble with a partially unravelled scarf in an odd shade of plasticine-mauve. The February weather had been unseasonably warm, but he was taking no chances. As he left the house, he hoped the week ahead would prove to be a busy one, for although he tired more easily these days, hard work made him feel alive. Retirement was an option only suitable for people who hated their jobs. Arthur loved working with his partner John May, and revelled in the fact that they performed a service no one else in the city could offer. No one had their arcane depth of knowledge, or was able to use it in the cause of crime prevention.

Across the decades they had continued to close cases few could understand, let alone solve. The Peculiar Crimes Unit was less of a secret now than it had been, but few really appreciated how it operated, or even what it did. It had been founded in a spirit of invention and experimentation, along with Bletchley Park and the Cabinet War Rooms, and Bryant hoped it would survive as long as London remained confounded by impossible crimes.

He tightened his scarf around his throat and, whistling an off-kilter air from *The Pirates of Penzance*, set off towards the Tube station.

4

PECULIARITIES

'Mr Bryant is so old that most of his lifetime subscriptions have run out.' Leslie Faraday, the increasingly portly liaison officer at the Home Office, poked about on his biscuit tray looking for a Custard Cream. 'He's only alive because it's illegal to kill him.' He wasn't used to being summoned to work so early, and needed tea before he could concentrate. 'If we made him redundant he'd not be entitled to a full pension, technically speaking, because he's working beyond our recommended statutory age limit. How would he be expected to survive?'

'Sentimentality can't be allowed to stand in the way of modern policing procedures,' replied Oskar Kasavian, peering from the window into the tiled Whitehall courtyard. Faraday took a quick peek to see if the new supervisor in charge of Internal Security cast a shadow, as his cadaverous pale form had created office rumours of supernatural lineage. 'We're not here to provide the inefficient with a living.'

This last remark confused Faraday, who believed that this was precisely the purpose for which Whitehall had been created. 'Quite,' he said, 'but surely we must take into account his long and illustrious career working with John May. One doesn't force admirals into retirement simply because they no longer go to sea. We benefit from their experience.'

'Old generals are the cause of military disasters,' said Kasavian, drumming long fingers on the windowpane. 'The elderly are weak precisely because they live in the past.' It was his absence of humanity others found so perturbing, as if Countess Bathory and Vlad the Impaler had mated to create the perfect bureaucratic hatchet man. 'It would be prudent to act before someone causes a criminal outrage that could have been prevented by the PCU.'

'You sound as if you have something in mind,' said Faraday, who preferred to allow others to put forward their ideas, so that he could appear blameless if they failed.

'Clearly, I should have treated my last attempt to close the unit as a warning. The detectives have a few friends in senior positions – including, it seems, the Lord Chancellor – who are eager to protect the unit whenever it is threatened with closure. Therefore, we need recourse to a higher power.'

'Higher than the Lord Chancellor?' Faraday looked as if he could not imagine such a thing.

'Naturally, I have someone in mind,' said Kasavian, looming over the civil servant with threatening proximity. 'Leave all the arrangements to me.'

'The trouble with Arthur Bryant is that he treats us all as though we're uninvited guests gate-crashing his private world,' complained Raymond Land, the acting head of the Peculiar Crimes Unit, as he adjusted his navy-blue golf-club tie. 'That's what I resent most of all, the sheer lack of respect.'

Land had failed in his attempt to be transferred to another division following the unit's success in capturing the murderer dubbed 'the Highwayman' by the national press. He reluctantly accepted the fact that he would probably be stationed in Mornington Crescent for ever, but it didn't stop him from vilifying the chief engineer of his fate. Land had arrived at the unit in the early 1970s, expecting to while away a single summer of lightweight criminal cases that fell below the radar and beyond the interest of his superiors. Instead, he had found himself thrust blinking and ill-prepared into the limelight of a series of sensational high-profile murder investigations. He blamed Arthur Bryant and John May, the founders of the unit, for poking him above the parapet of visibility, but managed to enjoy the national attention for a while.

However, during the Thatcher years, things began to go wrong for the PCU; a number of investigations were mishandled and the unit's funding was cancelled. Suddenly, Raymond Land realized he was being scapegoated for a division now considered to be unreliable and unworthy of public trust. Arthur Bryant's much-publicized willingness to hire psychics, necromancers, eco-warriors, numerologists, clairvoyants, crypto-zoologists, chakra-balancers and all manner of alternative therapists placed him in the firing line when his techniques failed. Over the years, only the gentle arbitration of his partner John May had mollified the Whitehall mandarins.

The simple fact remained that Land was a bureaucratic phantom working in a highly unorthodox specialist police division, which made him redundant, the kind of man who needlessly checks his e-mails on trains and complicates things by interfering. He appreciated order, hierarchy, structure, accountability. What he got was a unit that behaved with the unruliness of a backpackers' hostel. The PCU got away with murder because few of their suspects ever did. In short, they achieved results, and so long as the statistics continued to add up, they would continue to be funded in spite of their procedural irregularities. Thus, Land found himself paying for a success he had never wanted, while the engineers of his fate continued their wayward course through London's criminal world, causing indignation and admiration in equal measure.

'On Bryant's insistence we worked right through Christmas,' he told his wife, who had actually enjoyed the unusual yuletide peace in the house, 'because he thought he'd found another victim of the Deptford Demon, a case that was supposedly solved in 1968! So now I feel entirely within my rights to do what I'm about to do.'

'And what is that, dear?' asked his wife, who was only half listening and longed for him to return to the office so that she could get on with painting the kitchen a disagreeable shade of heliotrope that she had spotted in the latest issue of *Homes & Gardens*.

'I'm closing the unit down for a week,' he explained in irritation. 'A compulsory holiday. We've no outstanding investigations underway at the moment. It's the perfect time to reorganize our operational systems.' Land loved the idea of reorganizing things. He fantasized about clean paper-free offices where colour-coded computer files were backed up and alphabetized, as well as being catalogued by subject, theme, date and importance. Arthur Bryant was as likely to arrange papers by the colour of his correspondents' eyes as by a nationally recognized system. Sometimes he wrote up his notes in naval code or medieval cryptograms. Land was convinced he did it just to be annoying.

'I don't think Mr Bryant will like that very much,' replied Mrs Land, eyeing the kitchen cabinets with ill-concealed impatience. She knew that if her husband stayed home, they would never get painted. 'You've always said he only manages to stay alive because of his work. You can't shut down the unit without his approval.'

'Bryant isn't the only important member of staff, Leanne. We can all be conscientious. We each have our part to play. No one is more valuable than anyone else.'

'That's not strictly true, though, is it, dear?' said his wife, who enjoyed needling him. 'I mean, there would be no unit without Arthur and John. They founded it, didn't they, and they continue to set its policies, whereas I've always thought of you as more of a middle manager. You excel at expediting things. You handled shipments in that tinned-fruit warehouse in Wapping when you were younger, remember?'

Land narrowed his lips, his eyes and the zip on his windcheater with annoyed determination. 'I'm going to the office,' he snapped. 'And I won't be back until late.'

Leanne smiled to herself and headed for the paint cans under the stairs.

* * *

John May thoughtfully examined his mail as he sipped his first strong black coffee of the day. He looked down from his kitchen window into the narrow cobbled street, the planked porters' crosswalks bridged at angles between the warehouse buildings of Shad Thames. The sky was ocean green. A sliver of cloud held a tinge of jade. The weather was darkening, the temperature falling; the wind had changed direction, sweeping down from Norway into the estuary and along the Thames. He re-read Monica Greenwood's letter with a sinking heart, knowing that she was gone, and that he had to let her go.

In spite of everything, I still love my husband . . . best not to see each other for a while . . . don't want to hurt your feelings . . . you know how special you will always be to me . . . my duty is to remain with him.

He folded the pages with precision and placed them in a drawer. He had known Monica long before she had become the wife of a former murder suspect. She was an artist, stifled by a passionless academic husband, and yet she had returned to him. May's vanity was dented. The women in his life had provided him with more heartache than any man deserved. His wife, his daughter and now Monica, all gone. Only his granddaughter April had been saved. She was working under his watchful eye at the unit, her agoraphobia held in check for the first time in years. The barriers between the pair had finally fallen, the circumstances surrounding her mother's tragic death laid bare and forgiven. April was all he had left now. He would let nothing bad ever happen to her.

John May always felt old in winter. He was three years younger than his partner – and looked considerably more youthful – but his bones were just as tired. During the shortest days he questioned his motives for continuing. Suppose something happened to Bryant, as he knew it eventually would? Arthur veered between untapped reservoirs of strength and fault lines of frailty. How much longer could either of them draw enough stamina to continue fighting for the unit?

May grew annoyed with himself; self-doubt felt weak, but it expanded with age. The young were confident because they did not know any better. And for once it was he, and not Bryant, who needed a decent investigation in which to become absorbed. It was the best way to reconcile himself to the loss of such a wonderful woman.

As he shaved and dressed, he became more infuriated about the way in which the PCU was treated. The unit regularly suffered budget cuts and redundancies because it was a specialist investigation agency. As the nation converged on a single set of public services, the experts were being lost to countries that still held their seniors in high regard. He and Bryant were too old and too attached to London ever to consider leaving, and that made them obvious targets. After all this time the job should have got easier. Instead, they were now fighting for everything they had once been able to take for granted.

Our time must come, he told himself, although he had to admit that it was getting a little late.

The backlit fascia of the Mornington Crescent all-night taxi office bathed Detective Sergeant Janice Longbright in an unflattering shade of canary yellow. She shoved up the new roller-shutter covering the entrance of the Peculiar Crimes Unit with a strong right arm and locked it in place. The shutter had been added at the insistence of Raymond Land, after a gang of local thugs had rammed the door with a stolen builders' van. Mornington Crescent, once an area of rough-edged gentility, of brown brick terraces bordered by damp green canals and soot-blackened railway lines, of dirt-grimed walls and windows and battered street signs, was becoming another London no-go zone of drunks and crazies, where keeping a watchful eye was no longer enough to protect you from harm.

Figures for robbery, burglary, drug offences, fraud and theft were falling across the Western world, but here sexual attacks, acts of terrorism and brutal murders were on the rise. Small crimes could be thwarted by improved technology, but that left something stranger and more menacing on the streets. Bryant and May had insisted on staying at the epicentre of violent

crime in the national capital, arguing – rightly, as it turned out
– that they were as badly needed as any other emergency
service.

The difference lay in the PCU's operating methods. Un-
shackled from the endless backup procedures of the
Metropolitan Police, they were able to occupy a unique place in
the city's investigative system. London remained a security
nightmare despite its reliance on CCTV cameras, but the Met
coped well with mopping blood, drying tears and calming
fears; taking care of commonplace crimes was their job. Once,
streets like Islington's notorious Campbell Bunk had existed in
gruelling poverty, beyond the boundaries of order and safety.
Now, at least, the path was clear for specialist units like the
PCU to investigate the misdemeanours that would have gone
undiscovered in such areas.

Bryant told every prospective member of staff that their
agenda knew no borders of class, age or race. Their remit was
to settle sensitive cases with abstruse thinking, their purpose to
prevent public panic and moral outrage. In recent years, the unit
had become adept at handling the investigations the Met no
longer had time to consider in depth. The Home Office now
called the shots, and their demand for paperwork had increased
until younger, more energetic staff were wasted in the daily
untangling of office life that took place behind the crescent
windows above the Tube station.

As Longbright straightened her seamed nylons and gathered
the weekend's post from the mat, Crippen, the unit's moth-
eaten feline mascot, shot past her into the street, searching for
somewhere to micturate. *Arthur's been to the office on a
Sunday again and locked the cat in without putting its tray out,*
she thought. *Doesn't that man ever rest?*

She clumped up the bowed stairs in her film-star heels,
savouring the emptiness of the unit, wrinkling her nose at the
smell of Bryant's stale pipe tobacco. *How long will the calm last
this time?* she wondered. Peace was both desired and dreaded,
for although most of them welcomed a break from the long
hours, it turned Bryant into a tyrant, as he stalked about the

corridors getting on everyone's nerves and under everyone's feet.

That, she supposed ruefully, was the trouble with the Peculiar Crimes Unit; you never knew what you were about to get. Recently they had spent an unnerving week clambering about on the city's rooftops looking for a man who had become known as the Highwayman, only to discover that the unusual nature of his identity probably meant the guilty would never be properly punished. If anything, the Highwayman had become even more popular with teenagers in the weeks that followed his arrest. You still saw T-shirts bearing his logo on the market stalls of Camden Town. When ordinary people started glorifying cruelty and throwing rocks at the police, maybe it was time to find another job. Except that Longbright's mother had worked at the unit before her, and had charged her with its protection. Janice felt possessive about the place, and knew that as long as she was needed here, she would face any challenge the detectives set her.

Sorting through the morning's mail, she turned on the lights and began the day.

5

OUBLIETTE

The winter sun seared the back of Madeline Gilby's bare neck.

Only in the café's shade were the chill tendrils of the season felt. She closed her book, pushed the blond fringe from her eyes and slid Euros across the palm of her hand, tipping them to the light in order to count them; the denominations were still confusing. The boy looked up at her anxiously from across the tiny wrought-iron table. Above them, swallows dropped to the eaves of the building, then looped out across the dark sea. Placing the money for the bill in the little white dish, she returned to her novel.

'Put the book down,' said Ryan. 'You're always reading.'

'You've got nothing to worry about, all right?' she said for the third time, setting the paperback aside. 'We've enough to get by. I've told you, let me take care of the cash. You're ten. You can start worrying properly in about eight years' time, when we have to stump up for your student loan.'

'I'm not going to university,' said Ryan. 'I'm going to get a job and help you.'

'Over my dead body. Finish your croissant.'

'I'm not hungry.'

'You wanted an ice cream half an hour ago.'

'That's different.' Ryan stared dolefully at the picked-apart croissant. 'Only the French could invent bread that explodes when you try to eat it.'

Madeline looked into the sky. 'I wanted a child, I got Noel Coward,' she complained.

'Who's Noel Coward?' Ryan asked.

'A very funny man who lived a long time ago – to you, anyway.' She reached across the table and stole the remains of the croissant. 'If you're not going to eat it, I will.'

'How long do we have to stay here?'

'It's a holiday, Ryan, you're meant to be having fun.' She tore off a buttery flake and chewed it, watching him. The blue bruise over her right eye was fading. The grapevines in the trellis above them patched their shoulders in green and yellow light.

'I don't know anyone.'

'Then go out and make a friend.'

'There's no one here my age. They're all in school.'

'Yeah, it's not exactly high season. You'll be at a new school as soon as we've found a place.' She squinted up at the deceiving sun, then resettled her sunglasses. 'Meanwhile we have to make the best of it. Besides, we'll only stay for a few more days, until the cheque comes through.'

'What if it doesn't?'

Madeline sighed. 'It will. Your father is required by law to pay up. It's called a divorce settlement, and it should have been cleared by now. So we just sit tight until it arrives.'

'If you hadn't left Dad—'

'If I hadn't left him I'd be in A and E with my arm in a sling or worse, so drop it, OK?' She softened, aware of his growing alarm. Her lies about the origins of her cuts and bruises had made him realize the truth. 'I'm sorry, baby, I don't mean to shout at you, it's just – everything at the moment. Look, I can pay the bill without managing to get us thrown in jail, and if the sea's too cold to go swimming we'll take a walk, all right?'

They descended to the steep pebbled beach and strolled across banks of rank-smelling olivine seaweed, passing through pools of shadow cast by the cypress trees that grew behind the walls of secretive villas. Out of the sunlight, the air was chill.

'Who do you think lives there?' asked Ryan, jumping in an impossible attempt to see through the railings.

'Rich people, honey, no one we're ever likely to meet. They hide behind their high walls and don't talk to people like us. Actually, I don't think they're here out of season. All the windows are shuttered, see?'

'Then where are they?'

'At other houses, in other countries.'

'What do they need more than one house for?'

'Good question. To get away from each other, I guess.'

She thought about the world she had left behind. Back in Elephant and Castle, Madeline's days had been split between her supermarket shifts, working afternoons in East Street Laundromat and evenings in The Seven Stars, a deafening bar popular with the area's young professionals. Jack, her husband, changed oil and tyres at the local MOT centre, answering to a boy ten years younger than himself. The marriage had failed years earlier, largely because Jack could never control his drinking or his unfocused anger, and after one remorseful fight too many she had pushed for a legal separation. Things had soured between them when her promised support payments failed to materialize.

When Jack's brother turned up in the bar to tell her that she was a headcase, and accused her of trying to destroy their family, the escalation of hostility was so unnerving that she had grabbed Ryan from school, borrowed some cash from her mother and booked an easyJet flight in the nearest Internet café. They had ended up in the South of France because a flight to Nice was affordable and available, but living here was almost as expensive as London, and she was running low on funds.

All she could do was wait for the cheque to clear in her bank account, knowing that Jack would try to cancel it when he realized where she had taken Ryan. They had caught a train east, along the coast, looking for somewhere cheap to stay, and disembarked at the first tiny station they reached, the village of Eze-sur-Mer.

High above them – an hour's walk into the Savaric cliffs –

was the other Eze, an ancient *village perché* consisting of shops selling tasselled velvet cushions and Provence tablecloths in the colours of sea and sunshine. Low-ceilinged galleries were filled with lurid daubs of boats at rest, postcards and fridge magnets. Far below, away from tourists searching for a taste of the old country, there was barely anything to indicate a town; a single restaurant called La Vieille Ville, a closed bar, a modest little hotel without stars, commendations or any other guests, and stepped parades of shuttered villas built on the forested scree beneath the cliffs. At the only café, the passing of a car was enough to make the proprietor step out and watch with his tea-towel over his shoulder.

It was the perfect place to hide away, a town as lost from recollection as any oubliette.

Mme Funes, the stick-like proprietor of L'Auberge des Anges, had a permanently puckered look on her face that might have been due to excessive sunlight or general disapproval of the world. She wore a dead auburn wig that made her resemble the corpse of Shirley Bassey, and was always to be found lurking behind the bar within clawing distance of the cash register. Whenever Madeline addressed her, Mme Funes headed off any attempt to speak French with a barrage of tangled English that was presumably less offensive to her ears. Her grey-skinned husband possessed a similar air of resurrection, and had the habit of peering through the hatch of the kitchen like a surprised puppeteer whenever Madeline passed. His presence in the kitchen obviously had nothing to do with cooking, as *daube de boeuf* and *salade niçoise* were the only specials to appear on the blackboard.

Before dinner, Madeline and her son risked further disapproving looks by venturing out to the little village park, where they sat watching distant cruise ships pass between San Remo and Nice like floating fairgrounds. The temperature, so long as you stayed in sunlight, remained at eighteen degrees centigrade. The flower beds were immaculately trimmed, banks of pink and saffron petals ruffled around the stems of attenuated palms in a colour combination that seemed to exist only in France. As distant church bells rang, a solemn procession passed their bench, something to do with the patron saint of bees. Fat paper statues were solemnly held aloft in displays of orange and yellow artificial flowers, a reminder that the customs of other countries would forever remain mysterious to outsiders.

Ryan watched in amazement as purple bougainvillea petals were scattered by a troop of surpliced choristers following a giant paper bee perched on a honeypot, in a blessing ceremony that appeared to dovetail artisanship and religion. Moments after the priests and children had been lost from view, Madeline realized that her handbag had been taken from beside her feet.

'It's got everything in it,' she said, scanning the surrounding grass. 'My passport, my paperback, all our remaining money.'

'Why would you do that?' Ryan accused.

'I didn't trust the hotel, I thought it would be better with me. Help me look.'

They were still searching the ground when she raised her eyes and saw the bag held in a tanned fist. Its owner gave a tentative smile, and despite his white teeth, she had an impression of darkness. She thought perhaps he was a delivery man, because he wore a scuffed brown-leather satchel across his chest.

'You are looking for this?' he asked in good English. He was younger than she, but only by a year or two – perhaps twenty-eight. Mediterranean colouring, black cropped hair, black eyebrows almost touching green eyes, curiously baby-faced. He was slender, dressed in jeans, a navy-blue bomber jacket and pristine white trainers, entirely unthreatening, yet there was something studied in the way he regarded her.

'Thank you, I thought I'd lost it.' She took back the bag and instinctively drew Ryan to her side. The park had emptied now, and the evening felt suddenly cooler.

'It looks very nice here, very safe, but you must still be careful,' he told her. 'Thieves come over the border from Italy, and there are gypsies. They will take anything, especially during a saint's parade.'

'I'll remember that—'

'Johann. My name is Johann Bellocq.' His smile faded, and he turned, walking away as abruptly as he had appeared.

'Let's go and eat.' She patted Ryan on the head, but looked back at Johann Bellocq as they crossed the deserted main road.

6

LAST DAY TOGETHER

The sky above the unit glowed with an eerie sulphurous light. Behind the cardinal tiles of Mornington Crescent station, the detectives had arrived for the start of a dark, miserable week.

'We're a public service; you can't just shut us down willy-nilly,' complained Bryant, cracking his briar pipe down on the mantelpiece in an effort to unbung it.

'I'm not doing this out of caprice,' Land told him. 'Your IT chap, Mr Banbury, wants to upgrade the PCU's computer system and link it to the Met's area-investigation files. Apparently it's not going to cost anything because he's down-loading some dubious piece of software to do so.' He eyed the mountainous stacks of books bending Bryant's shelves. 'It all sounds very dodgy, but I harbour a fantasy about you running a paper-free office.'

Bryant blew hard into his pipe bowl, scattering bits of burnt tobacco on to Land's head. 'Come off it, Raymondo, you know there's no such thing. Be honest, you just fancy a few days off with your feet up. I need another decent case for my biography. Just think how disappointed my readers would be to find an entry saying February nineteenth: all murder investigations stopped due to Acting Head Raymond Land's need for a lie-down.'

'That's another thing I've been meaning to speak to you about,' said Land. 'Your biography. I read your account of the business you've chosen to call *Seventy-Seven Clocks*—'

'What were you doing reading my notes?' asked Bryant, appalled. 'That's a work in progress.'

'Too right it is. Murderous barbers and starving tigers? You've made most of it up. You can't go around doing that.'

'I may have ameliorated some parts for dramatic effect,' Bryant admitted, 'a bit of creative licence. It would have been a rather boring case history otherwise.'

'But you're passing it off as fact, man! All right, it's true that a painting at the National Gallery was vandalized, and that an upper-class family was ultimately to blame, but the whole thing reads like some cod-Victorian potboiler, and to paint yourself as the hero of the hour is an outrageous falsification. We'll become a laughing stock if anyone reads about this. What were you thinking of?'

'The royalties, obviously. You really shouldn't take these things so seriously. The public likes a good story.'

'That's all very well, but such fevered imaginings could destroy the credibility of the unit,' snapped Land. 'You'd be lost without the PCU. You've nowhere else to go.'

'I say, that's a bit below the belt. Actually, I have got somewhere to go, and I'm thinking of taking John with me.' Removing a packet from his pocket, he stuffed his pipe with a mix of eucalyptus leaves, Old Navy Rough Cut Shag and something that looked like carpet fibres from an Indian restaurant, before waving Land from his office. 'Off you toddle. Play some golf, enjoy yourself, the place won't burn down without you.'

'It did before,' Land reminded him as the door was shut in his face.

Moments later, John May arrived, flicking off his elegant black raincoat and dropping into the opposite chair. 'What did Land want?' he asked.

'Oh, some rot about shutting down the unit for computer work, I wasn't really listening,' Bryant replied nonchalantly.

'You know how he's been ever since he found out about his wife having an affair with the ball-washer at his golf club.'

'I don't think you should make so many off-colour jokes about him becoming a cuckold. You're only getting away with it because he doesn't know what it means.'

'That's the beauty of the English language. One can wrap insults inside elegance, like popping anchovies into pastry. You're right, I shouldn't mock, but it is such fun. Are you feeling all right? You're as pale as the moon. I think you need a bit of a holiday.' Bryant tried to contain a mischievous smile.

'Oh, no, not me, I'm happy here.' May usually felt much younger than his partner, but today he was tired and out of sorts. He had always prided himself on his ability to embrace change, and had at least retained a walking pace beside the growth of modern police technology, adopting new techniques as they arrived. Bryant, on the other hand, loitered several metres behind each development, and occasionally drifted off in the opposite direction. As a consequence, his knowledge of the Victorians was greater than that of the present Second Elizabethan era. He knew about Bazalgette and the development of drains, the last night of the Vauxhall Pleasure Gardens and the cracking of Big Ben, the cholera epidemic of 1832, the fixing of the first London plaque (to Lord Byron, in 1867), the great globe of Leicester Square and the roaring lion that had once topped Northumberland House, but could not remember his computer password, the names of any present-day cabinet ministers or where he had left his dry-cleaning.

'You haven't had a holiday in years,' Bryant persisted. 'Unless you count accompanying your ghastly sister and her husband to traction-engine rallies. Raymond seems intent on closing the unit down for a few days, and Janice can run a skeleton staff for us, so how would you like to come on a jaunt with me, all expenses paid?'

May regarded his notoriously cheap partner with suspicion. 'What do you have in mind?' he asked. 'I still have hideous memories of that clairvoyants' dinner-dance in Walsall where all the toilets overflowed. They didn't see that coming, did they?'

'This will be more fun, I promise. A trip to the country. It will do you good to breathe something you can't see for a change. Down to the Devon coast.'

'You detest the countryside. And it's February,' May reminded him. 'It'll be freezing, and there's supposed to be bad weather on the way. What do you want to go there for?'

'The International Spiritualists' Convention at Plymouth Civic Centre. It should be more fun than it sounds. There'll be talks, dinners and demonstrations, not to mention the odd punch-up when the neo-Wiccans get plastered on porter at the free bar and pick a fight with the Druids. We have trade stalls and parties, an awards ceremony, and we always put on a spectacular show for the closing night.'

'Next you'll be trying to convince me that the people who attend aren't utterly barking.'

'At least they're never boring, and they're from all walks of life. We get judges, shopkeepers, call girls, all sorts. I'm conducting a panel on the incorporation of spiritualism in investigative techniques.'

'For God's sake don't let Faraday or Kasavian find out about that,' warned May. He knew how eagerly the Home Office ministers were looking for reasons to shut the unit down. 'How are you intending to get there? Your old Mini Cooper's not up to the journey, for a start.'

'I'm taking down the stage props for the closing show, so I'm borrowing Alma's van. She uses it to ferry the North London Evangelical Ladies' Choir around, and seeing as most of them tip the scales at eighteen stone, it should be up to the job. Janice and Dan can keep an eye on things here, just to make sure that Land doesn't get up to anything underhand. We'd only be gone for a couple of days, you know.' He attempted to look pathetic. 'It's a long journey for a lonely old man. I could really do with someone to share the driving, or at least handle the map-reading.'

'There's no need to pull the homeless-puppy routine with me,

Arthur; it doesn't wash any more. I don't mind coming with you. If Banbury's going to be pulling up floorboards and relaying server cables I wouldn't want to be here anyway. Besides, you're not allowed to drive alone on motorways since that business with the travelling circus.' Seven years earlier, Bryant had accidentally rear-ended a Chessington Zoo truck and released a startled lion into the slow lane of the M2. 'When are you planning to leave?'

'First thing in the morning.' Bryant dragged out a much-folded map and pinned it on the crowded wall behind him. 'I've already plotted our route, although this Ordnance Survey map was published before the war, so it may contain inaccuracies.'

'Good God, it won't have motorways marked if it was published in the forties.'

'I meant before the Great War. 1907, actually.'

'That's no good,' said May, 'I'll print something from the Internet.'

'No, you won't, the system's down.' Dan Banbury sauntered in, eating an iced bun. He always seemed to be eating or drinking. 'Raymond told me the unit would be empty this week.'

'He didn't think to warn any of us,' Bryant complained. 'Anyone else here?'

'Full complement,' said Dan through a mouthful of sugared dough. 'They're milling around in the hall, waiting to be told what to do.'

DC Colin Bimsley came from a long line of spatially challenged law enforcers. Like his father and grandfather before him, it was enthusiasm rather than expertise that kept him in the field. Despite perforated eardrums, flat feet and an inner ear imbalance that found him periodically lying on his back, he was determined to bring honour to his family. On the plus side he had a heart of oak, being humane, decent and fair-minded, as strong as concrete and, barring the effects of an occasional self-inflicted head wound, quick to react. True, his brain sometimes lagged a little behind his body, and his hand-eye coordination was virtually non-existent, but to any woman who valued fidelity and reliability over smart-arse remarks, he was a godsend.

All of which made it quite unfathomable that DC Meera Mangeshkar could remain so stubbornly resistant to his charms. His compliments were greeted with sarcasm, and his attempts to lure her out for a drink were met with unforgiving dismissal. The diminutive Indian officer was ambitious and determined, hard in mind and body, and following a career path as pre-ordained as a logic board. Bimsley's shambling heroism impressed her no more than his offers to take her down Brick Lane for a curry with his mates. But they were shackled together now, sharing an office at the unit, and there was no alternative but to make the best of things. John May had planned it this way; he drew the best from staff by placing them in the proximity of opposites.

Wary of her threat to stick him with a harassment charge, Colin Bimsley entered the office quietly and began leafing through the week's activity folders. Meera raised her head from her paperwork, regarding him suspiciously. 'What?' she asked finally.

'I didn't say anything.' Bimsley looked startled. His fellow DC rarely instigated any conversation.

'Exactly; you're being too quiet. You're up to something.'

'I can't win with you, can I?' He sighed. 'If I speak, you always tell me to shut up.'

'Yeah, well, I don't trust you.'

'You don't trust anyone, Meera.' He knew she had spent time on some of the capital's poorest estates, in Peckham, Dagenham, Deptford and Kilburn. It would be hard not to become cynical after a daily diet of gunshot wounds and stabbings committed in chip shops and at bus stops, where drug feuds were as liable to be settled at family weddings and christenings as on the street. Even so, there were days when she seemed barely able to contain her anger. 'But if you did decide to trust someone,' he said, 'you could tell me anything.'

'Thanks, Colin, but if it's all the same to you I'd prefer to eat my own colon first.' Her head lowered almost to the page as she returned to studying witness statements.

Be as nasty as you like, he thought. *My back is broad. And I'll persevere until the day I find out what makes you tick.*

Next door, April rose from her dead computer screen and walked to the window of her office. The sky was animated with roiling clouds, dark and volatile, filled with glimpses of amber and emerald. The streets around the Tube station were almost deserted. Camden was one of the most crowded, dangerous and interesting boroughs in London; the rush hour lasted around the clock and the pavements were never free of life, but there was something different about today. Raymond Land had come around telling everyone they were on paid leave for a week, but she could not trust herself to go home. Having conquered her agoraphobia with her grandfather's help, she was loath to allow it the opportunity of returning within the confines of her safe, small flat.

'Are you OK?' John May stuck his head around the door. 'May I come in?'

'Of course.' April still felt like an interloper at the unit, despite her involvement in an investigation that had finally closed a decades-old cold case. She knew there had been suggestions of nepotism, that she had only secured the job because she was the granddaughter of the unit's co-founder, but she was already winning the trust of her colleagues, and the work was fascinating.

In the filing cabinets opposite were secret details of cases no other unit in the country had the ability to unravel. The PCU had earned the right to handle the kind of investigations no one in the Metropolitan Police force had the faintest interest in solving. They had captured demons and devils, phantoms and monsters; not real ones, of course, mostly deluded loners who believed themselves to be invulnerable to the law. Individuals who had stolen, blackmailed and killed for tenebrous, private purposes: to protect themselves, to hide truths, to destroy enemies. Murder, Arthur Bryant insisted, was invariably a squalid, sad business driven by poverty and desperation, yet the cases passed to the Peculiar Crimes Unit had often been marked by paradox and absurdity. Sometimes they were the dream cases other detectives fantasized about resolving, but Bryant and May chose their staff with care, employing novices who were knowledgeable social misfits, in the same way that computer companies sometimes hired the very hackers who had attacked their clients from behind bedroom doors.

'Arthur and I are taking a trip to Devon. You can come with us if you want. There's plenty of room.'

'No, I'm still settling in here.'

'Will you be all right on your own?'

'I'll be fine, I promise.' She gave him a reassuring smile. 'I have a lot of reading to catch up on. Someone needs to hold the fort. I'm working my way through Uncle Arthur's journals.'

'Don't believe everything you read in them,' May warned. 'He has a habit of greatly exaggerating our successes.'

'And libelling everyone else. One police chief is described as "a human leech with a mind genetically resembling old Stilton". I can't imagine these accounts will ever see the light of day.'

'For God's sake don't tell him that. He thinks he has a bestseller on his hands. Remember to call me if you feel the slightest anxiety, won't you?' He hovered awkwardly in the doorway. 'I know I haven't always been there for you in the past, but now that you know part of the reason why—'

'It's fine, Granddad,' April assured him. 'You don't have to say anything.'

But after her grandfather had left the office, his turn of phrase began to puzzle her. *Part of the reason?* He had finally been honest about her mother's death, but was there more she had not yet learned about her blighted family?

7

PATHOLOGY

Oswald Finch was peering gimlet-eyed through the crack in the door like some grizzled old retainer considering whether to admit a tradesman into a mansion. Bryant wrinkled his nose at the sour reek of chemicals drifting through the gap. He looked up from his desk and gave a start.

'Good Lord, Oswald, you frightened the life out of me; it smells like something has died. Don't lurk outside like some grotesque from *Gormenghast*. Come in and stop scaring people.'

The ancient pathologist creaked into the room and lowered himself gingerly on to a bentwood chair. 'Piles,' he explained, grimacing into a tragedy mask. 'I'm at the age where my diary is marked with more hospital appointments than social events. Of course, doctors can do miracles now. Do you know, I've hardly anything left that I started out with. Nothing is in its original place. The doctor who opens me up is in for a shock. My intestines lose several feet every year.'

'Well, I'd love to discuss the state of your internal organs all day, but as you can see I'm pretending to be busy.' Bryant ostentatiously flicked over one blank page to examine another. 'What do you want?'

Finch sniffed noisily and looked around with disapproval. 'The state of this place. A little order wouldn't kill you. What's in those petri dishes?' He pointed to a row of plastic bowls arranged on the windowsill.

'It's rat excrement. I scraped some from the heel of that woman found dead beside the canal at York Way. The canal rats feed mostly on discarded junk food, but those samples contain grain. There's not much loose grain in King's Cross, so I guessed she was moved from somewhere else and dumped after dark. The rats had fed on a particular type of red split lentil used in Indian cooking. We tracked the ingredient to a factory in Hackney.'

'I still don't understand,' Finch admitted. 'What's it doing on the windowsill?'

'Oh, Alma told me it was good for growing mustard and cress. I love ham-and-cress sandwiches.'

'You are quite astonishingly disgusting. No wonder I never come up here from the morgue.'

'Too much paperwork, no doubt.'

'No, too many stairs. I was wondering if you'd heard anything about the equipment I was supposed to be getting. I've been promised new tanks, a small-parts dissection table fitted with a decent stainless-steel drain and a second mobile instrument cart for seven months now, and the cover is still off my extractor fan. Plus, one of my refrigeration cabinets is on the blink. I suppose it was you who left several wine boxes and a tray of sausage rolls in there.'

'They're for your send-off.'

'Ignoring the fact that it is unsanitary and illegal to keep foodstuffs in a refrigeration unit reserved for body parts, the sausages are past their sell-by date.'

'So are you, old bean. I thought you'd be pleased.' Bryant narrowed his watery eyes in suspicion. 'You haven't become a vegetarian, have you?'

The pathologist looked troubled. 'I have the awful feeling that by retiring at this late stage in life, I may find myself with no purpose. I can't just wither away in Hastings.'

'No choice, old sock. Your retirement's been accepted and processed. You can sit on the pier and throw stones at the seagulls.'

'But I like seagulls.'

'After a few months of watching them you won't. Just think of all the fun that lies ahead.' Bryant stapled some papers together and sniffed. 'Personally, I've always found Hastings to be positively suicide-inducing, but I won't be living there. I'm sure you'll discover some advantages; it'll be as quiet as your morgue, and you won't have me pulling hideous practical jokes on you any more.'

Finch gloomily picked something unpleasant from his nails. 'I suppose that's true. I worked it out the other day. Over a period of more than forty years, you've played a mean-spirited trick on me at least once a week, which comes to well over two thousand japes, jokes, hoaxes, wind-ups and pranks played out with a straight face against my person, while I am trying to carry out the serious business of ascertaining causes of death to make your department look good. You tricked me into cutting up my credit cards over the phone, nurturing a rare mollusc that turned out to be a mildewed mango seed, calling my wife to accuse her of conducting a fictitious affair with a limbo dancer and telling my son that he'd been adopted following his rescue from a Satanist cult. You super-glued my office door shut, put gunpowder in my cigarette filters, sewed prawns into my jacket pockets, dropped a live eel down my toilet, relabelled my sandwich box with plague bacillus warnings, hid whoopee cushions in my cadaver drawers and retuned my radio to receive fake "end of the world" bulletins. No wonder I've never had any respect around here. Poor Raymond Land, I've finally come to understand exactly how he feels.'

'You'd better sit down, Oswald, you've gone scarlet. You don't want to have a heart attack the week before your retirement, eh? Everyone knows that your sense of humour petrified as soon as death's dark caul wrapped itself around you. Besides, you know I only play jokes because I respect you. You'll be sorely missed.' Bryant had secretly petitioned the Home Office to have Finch's pension increased. 'At least we've got young Giles Kershaw to take over the position. I was thrilled to nominate him in your place.'

'I've been meaning to talk to you about that. I'm afraid I turned down Kershaw's application.'

'What on earth did you do that for?'

'In my opinion, he doesn't have enough experience.'

'But he'll be devastated, Oswald. The job was all but promised to him.'

'Then it will teach him not to be so ambitious,' said Finch. 'These overbearing young graduates come along thinking the world owes them a living, when they have to pay their dues.'

This wasn't like Oswald. Bryant assumed that the pathologist was out of sorts because the reality of his long-pending resignation had finally sunk in. Everyone knew he was happiest when he was elbow-deep in somebody's chest. Physical and mental health problems had a way of crowding in when one's purpose in life was removed, and Finch's purpose was to provide resolutions to unfortunately truncated lives.

'You're looking done in, old friend,' said Bryant gently. 'Why don't you go and put your feet up?'

'I don't trust you when you're nice to me,' Finch complained. 'Besides, I can't. It's my last week, and the workload will be starting up again.'

'I haven't seen any cases come in this morning.'

'That's because the unit's officially shut from today, so Faraday has been instructed to release me to the Met, to help out with their overload. That means I'll be dealing with Sergeant Renfield, God help me. I daresay I'll be kept busy right up until the moment of my departure.'

'Then you should have shared your work with Kershaw. I think I'd better have a talk with him. You've made a wrong call there, Oswald. He's a bright lad and deserves to go far, even though that upper-class accent makes him sound as if he's being strangled. He did a great job on that business with the Highwayman. I hope you haven't disappointed him too much.'

'What about me? I was having a farewell party on Friday, but now there won't be anyone here to see me off.'

'Never mind,' said Bryant jovially. 'We'll post your cake to Hastings.'

8

CONTROL

The morning sky was such an impossibly deep shade of blue, it seemed as if the earth's atmosphere was barely thick enough to protect them from the cruel infinity of space. Madeline and Ryan sat at an outside table at La Vieille Ville and enjoyed the sun's warmth on their faces. The scent of pomegranates and jasmine blossom hung in the warm air. In the kitchen behind them, Momo the chef was stirring the bouillabaisse he prepared for the village's housebound residents once a week.

'I think I could live here.' Madeline pushed back her book and rested her chin on her hands. 'Clean air, birds singing, lots of flowers, no litter. Do you like it?'

'There's no one to play with. We're stuck here without a car. There's nowhere to go. You're always reading.' Ryan stirred the long spoon about in his ice cream. His complaints had become a refrain over the past few days. During the winter season, the trains only called at the little station once an hour, turning every outing into a day trip, and day trips became expensive.

'You would like to go somewhere?'

Madeline looked up and saw the young man who had rescued her handbag at the parade. He was wearing the same clothes, even down to the leather satchel at his side.

'There is a very beautiful building on Cap Ferrat, the Villa

Rothschild. It has many gardens and a waterfall, and is open to the public. I have a car.' He pointed back at a blue open-topped Peugeot. 'We could drive there.'

She saw Ryan's face brighten and realized how much he still missed his father. The boy had mostly seen his good side, and was young enough to be able to forget the bad. Jack Gilby had portrayed himself as a hero to his son, turning her into a villain in the process.

'Can we go, Mum?' Ryan was already pushing his ice cream aside and rising from the table.

She regarded the young man with a cool eye, but he did not move beneath her critical gaze. 'That's a pretty underhand trick, Mr Bellocq,' she told him as Ryan began tugging at her hand.

'Please, call me Johann.' He gave a tentative smile, anxious to be accepted.

As they drove, he thought back to the first time he had seen her, standing on the empty railway platform with a map and a backpack, the boy's hand held tightly in hers. Her floral dress was English and cheap, her trainers disproportionately large for her thin bare legs. After he had spoken to her, he'd realized that she was everything he had ever wanted in a woman. Down here, away from the mountain villages, there were only blank-eyed American tourists and pompous English couples in ridiculous straw hats. The permanent residents were elderly and sour, too rich to concern themselves with being pleasant. This one was different. There was an innocence, a vulnerability about her. She had been hurt by a man and left without money or confidence. She would not sneer at him as others had done. The boy was the key – he needed male companionship; otherwise, he would get on her nerves and drive her away from the village.

He had broken into the garage of a locked-up summer home in Rocquebrune and taken the Peugeot, carefully repairing the door behind him, knowing it would be weeks, possibly months, before anyone noticed it was missing. The holiday villas of the wealthy provided him with everything he needed. From Marseilles to Monte Carlo there were thousands of poorly protected properties, and each fell under a different police jurisdiction. Half the time, the prefectures failed to maintain proper contact with one another. People travelled during the winter months, and the gendarmeries were short-staffed. It was the time of *le chômage saisonnier*, the seasonal unemployment that kept this part of France empty for six months of the year. The perfect time to live a little beyond the law.

He turned to smile at the boy in the passenger seat, sensing that he had already won the battle for his mother's heart.

'I don't know, he seems like some kind of exile. From the way he speaks English I suppose he's French, but there's another accent. Did I tell you he has pale green eyes? Hold on, I'm lighting a cigarette.' Madeline tucked the mobile under her right ear and dug for a throwaway lighter. Her one extravagance was a weekly phone call to her half-sister in Northern Spain. She and Ryan would have gone to visit, but Andrea had married a taciturn mechanic from Bilbao whose eyes had followed Madeline a little too closely when she last stayed there.

'Well, he stands out, I suppose. There aren't many people out on the streets down here, or in the houses by the look of it, and Jack's settlement cheque hasn't come through yet so I'm pretty much stuck here . . . Of course I look! I go to the bank in Beaulieu every other morning, but there's nothing.' She checked to make sure that Ryan was not within listening distance. 'Well, I don't know, he's a typical Mediterranean type, I suppose, rather good-looking, a little younger than me, and I have the feeling he's just as lonely. Far from home. I know, of course I've got Ryan, but I need adult company as well. No, I don't know if I'd go out with him, he hasn't asked me. It's just that – I always seem to be running into him. It's a small village, there aren't that many places you can go, but even so. I hardly ever see the same people twice in London. It just seems a bit odd that we keep bumping into each other.'

Perhaps he just fancies you, Andrea had suggested. *You're finally free to do what you want. Jack knows that if he comes near you again, the police will be on him. Maybe you should go on a date with this guy.*

The problem was, she had forgotten how to be single. Besides, she had Ryan to look after, and the boy was already getting stir-crazy. She stepped back from the balcony into the neat little room, hemmed between the sheer granite cliffs and the glittering green sea, and wished there was someone she could ask for advice. The afternoon at the Villa Rothschild had passed like a hazy waking dream. Johann had paid the admission fee for the three of them, and they had walked through the Japanese garden beyond the pink *palazzina* villa that straddled the cape, watching Ryan run after iridescent dragonflies.

The exotic themed gardens – nine in all – that surrounded the former home of the Baroness Ephrussi de Rothschild were trained into the form of a vast land liner that crested the outcrop of land. To complete this illusion, they had once been crewed by twenty gardeners in white sailors' outfits with red pompom hats. The place was absurd, vulgar, ostentatious and beautiful, filled with grottoes and pergolas, temples and water-falls. Tall pines and cypress trees, ancient agaves and tunnels of bamboo fended off the glare of the low afternoon sun, hemming the cadenced emerald lawns with jewelled shadows that crossed the grass like a rising tide. The cicadas all ceased at the same moment, leaving only the sound of sea wind in the treetops.

She had looked across at Johann and found him staring at the pulsing fountains, lost in thought. His eyes were deep and dark, set close to his brow, as serious as a statue's. If he realized she was studying him, he gave her no sign of it. They walked beside each other as Ryan ran ahead, but the silence between them was far from easy. 'Come.' He smiled. 'There is a gift shop. I will buy you some postcards of the beautiful gardens, for you to remember me whenever you look at them.'

He knew she was watching, but was careful not to show emotion. It was important to make her understand that he was a gentleman, and that meant being in control. He had not felt like this around a woman before. Madeline was unlike any of the girls he knew from the villages. He saw things in her eyes none of the others had: strength and grace and acquiescence. She had made mistakes and overcome hardships, but there was nothing of his mother about her, only kindness.

Most importantly, she was ready for him. He had never been close to anyone since he was a child, but he knew how to make himself appealing. It was as much about hiding bad traits as displaying good ones, and essentially, she must not learn of his predisposition towards breaking the law, which meant arranging their conversations in such a way that she would see nothing wrong.

If he managed to keep up the subterfuge, he wondered if there was a chance that she might become more than just a conquest. Her pale skin had tanned, drawing out freckles, even in the days since he had been watching her. He had seen the full repertoire of her wardrobe now: one summer dress, a couple of T-shirts and a pair of faded jeans. He wanted to hold her, to reassure her that life could be good once again. In turn, he knew she would not disappoint him. He looked up into the sun-swept sky and tasted salt, felt cool sea breezes in his hair. If he was to do this, to finally become close to a woman and share his life and his secrets, it meant hiding them for a while longer.

He was not sophisticated when it came to the subtleties of expressing affection, but he had seen films and watched enough television to provide passable imitations of various emotional states. The next evening, he asked her back to his room for a drink, but when she made an excuse and shied away, he realized he had made a mistake. It was too soon to exclude the boy from a meeting. Persisting, he invited the pair of them to join him for a pizza – it was a Sunday night, and there was nowhere else open in the village – and she accepted, although she insisted on paying her share of the bill. She was determined not to owe him anything.

The conversation was easier to control when Ryan was seated there between them. He could deflect her questions and ask something about the kid. The challenge would come, he knew, when they finally met *à deux*. He just wanted to do what was right, what she deserved.

On Monday night it rained, and Mme Funes offered to take Ryan along with her sons to see an animated movie playing in English at the little side-street cinema in Beaulieu.

It could have been the night for him to make his move, but he resisted. Instead, he took them both to Monte Carlo.

9

THAW

The statue was of a man in a tall top hat with a bird on his arm.

Given its spectacular setting, it was a surprisingly modest and slightly ridiculous monument. Flags covered with red and white harlequin diamonds hung from either side of Monte Carlo's slender square, and parades of *palmiers* were swathed in tiny white lights. In the centre of the park, water cascaded with immaculate symmetry into stepped fountains. The arcing lawns were blade-perfect, the flower beds as plucked, scented and primped as nightclub hostesses. The view pointed in one direction between the palms frosted in luminescence, towards the icing-and-marzipan splendour of the casino, its base encrusted with polished Lagondas and Maseratis. Only the gawping tourists lowered the tone; untidy and loud in Mambo shorts and Nike socks, they snapped each other standing beside gull-wing sports cars. The tiny, densely built principality of Monaco stood between cliffs and sea, its secret money and tainted glamour lending it a faintly sinister air.

Madeline looked on in awe as a pair of angular fashion models in white mink coats paraded before a crouching photographer.

'Don't be fooled by all of this,' said Johann. 'I read that the average resident here has seven bank accounts, but you won't see any of them around town. They're up in the hills. This is just a display for tourists.'

But it was obvious to Madeline that Monte Carlo was geared to amusing thin white rich people. As she passed a silver Baby Bentley, its licence plate carrying the blue and white Monaco coat of arms, she felt herself shrinking into insignificance. The policemen looked like male models, and the streets were as clean as expensive restaurants. Down in the bay, elderly couples watched television on gleaming yachts in the world's most expensive floating trailer park. This was Old Europe at its richest and creepiest, attracting serious wealth while simultaneously fish-eyeing the tourist classes, pocketing their money while making them feel like grateful nonentities.

Ryan had taken to holding their escort's hand as they walked. Shafts of sunlight slanted between the green cliff peaks, tilting the town even further towards the sea.

'I don't think this is my kind of place,' said Madeline. 'I don't feel comfortable here.'

'I like it.' Johann pointed up to the lampposts. 'See the cameras? Everything that happens here is filmed by the security system. There is no crime. They see everything.'

'I suppose that's a good thing,' said Madeline doubtfully.

The cameras simultaneously protected and threatened. Johann liked that. They watched for petty crime and bad behaviour, but missed the fact that he had broken the law. It was the beauty of Europe: so many countries with different rules and moral codes, butted up against one another, and none of them communicating. Paradoxically, he felt safer here than anywhere else, knowing that the technology was more efficient than those who operated it.

'Let's go back.' He took up the hands on either side of him and led them back to the underground car park where the shining floors squeaked and the walls played music.

Madeline watched the passing lights through the windscreen as they passed out of town toward Cap-d'Ail. 'What happened to your other car?' she asked, touching the polished dashboard of the silver Mercedes.

'There was a problem with the gearbox.' He did not take his eyes from the road. Ryan was asleep in the back.

'Really? It seemed fine to me.' She knew quite a bit about cars; Jack had always discussed his work with her. 'Where did you get this?'

'My brother has a half share in a secondhand-car dealership. He lends me vehicles from time to time.' The lies came easily. They always had.

'I thought you said you were an only child, Johann.'

'I call him brother. Our family adopted him to raise as their own.'

'Does he live near by?'

She was asking too many questions. Impatiently, he floored the car and allowed it to glide around the angle of the cliff road. 'He is in Ventimiglia.'

'He must trust your driving ability.'

She was thinking things through; he could see something going on behind her eyes. He changed the subject. 'Why did you not pick Spain for your holiday? I thought the English preferred the Spanish coast.'

'A certain type of English, I think.' She looked back at the sleeping boy. 'Maybe I should have taken Ryan there. He'd have had more friends, and we'd have been able to save money. Things are expensive here.'

'I have money. I can lend you some.'

'No, it wouldn't be right.'

'It is only money. You must not misunderstand my purpose, Madeline. I mean, it would help you to stay. I will miss you if you go.'

'I didn't mean – it's very kind of you to offer, Johann.' She placed her hand on his and smiled. The barrier between them thawed a little further.

'Tonight I take you to El Morocco. You like couscous?'

'I don't think I've ever had it.'

'Then I show you what you are missing. Then we put Ryan to bed and I take you for a drink.'

'Only at my hotel.' It was not a refusal. This time he was

unable to keep the smile from his face. Perhaps he worried too much about hiding his feelings. Where was the harm? He could feel she was genuinely starting to care about him. He allowed himself to dream about her a little.

It was a dream that did not include the boy. He had always imagined that true love would arrive in the form of a young virgin, not a single mother as old as himself. He knew he would have to adjust. Nothing was ever what you expected. That was the beauty and the terror of life.

Smiling to himself, he pushed down on the accelerator, and the Mercedes crested the curve of the Moyenne Corniche with a wealthy roar.

10

EMBARKATION

Very early on Tuesday morning, John May arrived at his partner's house in Chalk Farm to find him already outside, trying to close the doors of Alma's van.

'There's a mile of string tied around this engine,' he said, peering beneath the bonnet of the old white Bedford. 'It looks like it's holding the distributor cap on.'

'Your obsession with reliability is misguided,' Bryant replied cheerfully, opening the passenger door and checking the musty interior. 'My father used to make deliveries all across London in one of these, right through the 1950s. It took them ages to catch him.' This was the sort of annoying remark Bryant was wont to make, in that it obscured as much information as it illuminated. 'Do you think it will hold the Garden of Eden?'

'I'm sorry?' May looked up from under the hood. His partner's conversation always left you feeling you'd missed something.

'The closing night show is taking comparative religious myths as its theme. We need to get a hardboard Garden of Eden in the back, along with several apple trees, a horn of plenty, two plastic gazelles and a partial view of a mountain built for Alma's church production of *The Sound of Music* that's still covered in goat pellets. We're staging the fall from grace without a volcano, as our Adam had to be taken to the infirmary suffering from smoke inhalation last time we ignited it. It wasn't my fault; the ventilation in St Peter's Holborn is a disgrace. I suppose I made the production a touch too theatrical. When the snake turned into Satan accompanied by the detonation of an Ariel Bombshell, the ladies in the front row looked as if they'd just given birth.'

The news that Bryant had re-enacted the Creation in a city church came as no surprise to May. At this time of the year, and at a time in life when most men were fantasizing about spending their afternoons in a soft armchair, Arthur was more likely to be found organizing a conference for ufologists or leading a hunt across the East End in search of the Dagenham Strangler. He seemed able to draw on reserves of strength that powered him through the winter and propelled him towards another spring, much as a vehicle low on petrol might charge a hill in order to coast the next down slope.

'At least you won't need to pack costumes.' May chuckled.

'Oh, we will. There's Ganesh and Shiva, Buddha and Mohammed, plus robes, hats and props for their followers. We take a quick canter through all the major myths and legends. We usually manage to incorporate Arthurian and Celtic tales, too, if we've room to take the dragon. Sometimes we chuck in a bit of Hans Christian Andersen. It's all for charity, you see, Children in Poverty. We get the local school to help out, although never the Catholic ones, as they're not keen on having their Lady of Grace sharing the stage with half a dozen trolls and an elephant-headed god covered in sparklers. Those who take their religion too literally can be very narrow-minded about such things. We try to show that whether you're pagan or Protestant, you can still learn something from those who draw strength from faith.'

'Are you telling me you've discovered faith in your old age?' asked May.

'Good heavens, no.' Bryant readjusted his spectacles and squinted up at his partner with watery wide eyes. 'I just like a nice bit of theatre. Doesn't everyone?'

'When are we leaving?'

'Just as soon as we get these doors shut and I remember where I left my hearing-aid batteries. We should be able to reach Plymouth by late afternoon, which will give us time to unload the van and set up for the start of the convention tomorrow morning. It only lasts two days, climaxing with the awards ceremony and the show on Thursday evening. We can either stay overnight and set back first thing Friday morning, or leave on Thursday night. Can I trust you to be captain of our supply team? I've got enough to do just sorting out my pills.'

'What do I have to do?'

'Alma has manufactured a hundredweight of sandwiches for us to take along, and some of her special "thick" pea-and-ham soup that might come in handy for fixing radiator leaks. She'll give you the full list of comestibles.'

'Good heavens, we're not going to the North Pole, Arthur.'

'Just as well, because it's not there any more,' said Bryant gloomily. 'Global warming. I read in the paper that it's melted clean away. I don't suppose I'll see a frozen landscape again in my lifetime.'

'You're wrong about that, Mr Bryant.' Alma Sorrowbridge had come into the yard behind their home waving a copy of the *Daily Mail*. 'Blizzards, it says here, turning very nasty. Look at the forecast – the coldest winter in fifty years. It's snowing in Somerset, and going to get worse. The gritters are going on strike and the roads will be like ice. Decent people will freeze to death in their beds.'

'Always the bearer of cheering news, aren't you?' Bryant sighed, slamming the van doors with finality. 'She just wants me to cancel the trip because she doesn't approve of my multifaith approach to spiritualism. That, and the fact that last year we made a chapter of her evangelists' gospel choir share their dressing room with a pair of Brahmins and some Hasidic Jews.' Bryant neglected to mention that the choir had brought a family bucket of pork ribs into the dressing room and had almost started a war.

'The doctrine of salvation by faith is the essence of gospel teaching,' said Alma hotly. 'It's Protestant, not Pick 'n' Mix. I don't approve of throwing all these religions together with non-believers.'

'There's no such thing as a non-believer,' Bryant stated. 'Everyone believes in something, whether it involves alien visitations or simply being nice to each other and repairing a fractured world with good deeds, a cabalistic lesson you might learn the next time you consider torturing me with your culinary experiments. Now be so kind as to go and finish packing my warm clothes.'

It was a little after eight fifteen when they embarked on their journey. John May had agreed to come along partly because his partner was not to be trusted with the driving, but also because he had never shown any interest in Bryant's enthusiasms, and had decided it was about time he did.

'I've planned our route,' said Bryant, settling into the passenger seat and pulling the collar of an enormous astrakhan overcoat up around his ears. 'We need the A38, possibly via Bittaford and Moorhaven, assuming those villages are still there after two world wars. Perhaps we should stop and buy a more recent map. Do you think I should put a satellite navigation system in my Mini Cooper?'

'You are the last person in the world to be trusted with SatNav,' May retorted. 'Remember what happened when you borrowed Dan Banbury's car?'

'Oh, er, vaguely.' Bryant sank further into his overcoat, recalling his flustered response to the insistent electronic voice warning him to turn right. It had led him into a closed street where work on the London Underground system was under-way. Bryant surprised the railway workers by shooting Banbury's vehicle into a trench filled with exposed electrical cabling for the Northern line. He had managed to shut down the City Branch during rush hour, and none of the electronic readouts in Banbury's car had worked properly since.

'So what's our route?' asked May.

'We make our way to Hammersmith and eventually get on to the M3 as far as Winchester, then head for Salisbury and Yeovil on the A30, switch to the A303 past Exmouth and Newton Abbot, skirt the southern edge of Dartmoor on the A38 and hit Plymouth by teatime. If we're running ahead of schedule, we could visit my Auntie Dolly in Weymouth. She just had her telegram from the Queen, and still does her own shopping, although some of the things she comes back with take some explaining.'

'All right, I'll handle the M3 and you can take the back roads. Let's find a garage first. No doubt you'll want to stock up on boiled sweets.'

'No, I've taken to buying them wholesale. I've got a pound of Rhubarb and Custards in the back, some Jelly Tots, and a half of Chocolate Limes. Do you want a Pear Drop?'

'No, acetone takes the roof off my mouth. You think Janice can manage looking after the PCU? We've never left her in charge before.'

'She'll probably be better than you or I,' Bryant told him. 'We'll only be away for a couple of days. What could go wrong in that time?'

'What about April? Do you think she'll be all right? I mean, now that we've talked about her mother's death.'

'I don't see why not. For heaven's sake, stop fretting about everyone.' Bryant's thoughts were generally so abstracted that he found it hard to empathize with other people's personal problems. 'April can call you if there's anything on her mind. Put your foot down, I have my heart set on a pint of scrumpy tonight.'

May turned the ignition key. There was a grinding noise beneath the hood, then a peculiar squeaking sound.

'Wait!' Alma came running out. 'Open the bonnet!' May did as he was told, and the landlady reappeared from beneath the hood with an armful of mewling kittens. 'They were keeping warm under there. I'm minding them for a neighbour.'

This time, the van started.

'I'm sure I'm going to regret this,' muttered May as he pulled out into the peristaltic column of traffic passing slowly through Chalk Farm.

'Look at it this way,' said Bryant, leafing through pages of villages that no longer existed. 'For the next three days you won't have to think about solving a single crime.'

II

REVELATION

'Come with me, I want to show you something.'

'Are you sure it's safe?' Madeline asked. 'Isn't it private property?'

'A rich old guy used to own it, but he died. Now some Swiss property developers want to turn it into a hotel, but the mayor won't allow them. He's probably holding out for a bribe, and until he gets it, the place stays empty. Give me your hand.' He outstretched his arm and hauled her on to the granite wall beside him. 'Be careful of this plant,' he warned, indicating the purple bougainvillea that had overgrown the garden of the chateau. 'It has pairs of sharp thorns.' He placed his hands around her waist and lifted her into the long grass. 'The ground slopes down to the sea. Hold on to me.'

The sun had just sunk behind the cliffs, and Ryan had passed out in his hotel room, exhausted after a day spent racing up and down the shingle beach with Johann. Madeline allowed Johann's hand to stay on her waist even after she had steadied herself.

The chateau's vermilion tiled roof had partially collapsed. Olive trees and agaves had broken through the plaster on the ground-floor walls. The grand old house had clearly been empty for many years. Between the pines and date palms Madeline could glimpse an indigo triangle of ocean. Rotting tangerines littered the grassy slope. Their sharp citrus scent made her mouth water.

'Over here, you have to see this.' Johann pushed back the branches and allowed her to climb through. There, in a small clearing behind the chateau, was a white stone summerhouse, its roof decorated with stencilled fleurs-de-lis clipped from green tin. A band might have played there on warm summer evenings. He climbed up the steps of the rotunda and swayed from side to side, his head tilted. 'Listen, you can almost hear the accordion playing.'

'I don't hear anything.' She laughed, joining him.

'No, really, there is music all around us. There are ghosts in the trees. Look.' He pointed upwards, and she smiled in surprise. 'Fireflies. They always gather here at dusk.'

'How do you know this place?' she asked.

'I came here as a child. I was forbidden to visit the chateau – the old man was still living here then. He was a wealthy member of the old Monaco family, a genuine Grimaldi, but—' He tapped the side of his head. 'Crazy, you know? One day I found a crack in the wall and climbed through. My mother could not find me. It became my secret place. Everyone needs such a place, where they can be alone with their thoughts.'

In London Madeline had hardly ever been alone, passing her days in the steam of tumble dryers and her nights in the warm beery fug of the bar, rushing from the launderette to pick Ryan up from school or coming in at midnight to release her neighbour from guardian duty. She had never made enough time for herself. Now, though, perhaps there was a chance. She picked up his hand and held it in hers. They sat beside each other on the dusty bandstand floor, and he lightly touched the nape of her neck with tanned fingers. Great grey-blue clouds hung low, leaving a golden ribbon of light above the line of the sea. Their backs prickled with cold. He wanted to give her his jacket, but she refused.

'Let's go back, Johann.'

'It is early yet. I think one day I will come to your hotel and you will have moved back to England.'

'Then let's not go to my hotel. Ryan will be fine for a while. Let's go to your place.'

His hesitation made her wonder if she'd been too forward, but she had not felt a man's touch for a long time, and she sensed a need in him matched by her own. Finally he seemed to reach an agreement with himself and rose, hauling her to her feet. They climbed back to the car, and headed away from the Basse Corniche into the hills.

High in the Savaric cliffs the roads were covered with plumes of gravel, stones washed down from the rocks above. Gradually the route narrowed, until it was little more than the width of a car. Johann stopped before a tall steel gate, tucking the Mercedes beneath the overhanging pine boughs, and helped Madeline out. The long-stemmed birds-of-paradise surrounding the house had lost their tough orange petals, but the plant borders had been meticulously maintained. No lights showed in the single-storey building of peach stucco that lay ahead.

There was something clandestine about his behaviour, and she was compelled to ask, 'Are we supposed to be here?'

'It's fine, really, it's not a problem. The house belongs to an old friend who only stays between June and September. The rest of the year it's empty. He let me have the keys. Come on.'

He had trouble remembering where the lights were, and then only turned on one of the lamps in the lounge. The walls were covered with stag antlers. There was a pair of leather wing-backed armchairs and a bearskin rug on the floor that she suspected had been cut from a creature tracked by the owner. She smelled pine and polish and old leather. It was hard to imagine that a young man like Johann would know anyone who lived in this way; this was an old hunter's house.

Johann left the window shutters closed, and flicked on a gas fire filled with artificial logs. While she warmed herself, he found cut-crystal glasses arranged on a walnut drinks cabinet and poured out two brandies. 'Soon I think the snows will come,' he told her, 'even here.'

'And I'll have to go back home,' she admitted. 'The first part of my support money came through today. I was expecting more, but it's enough for me and Ryan to live on for a little while.'

'So why not stay?'

'It wouldn't last long if I did that. I have to go back to my flat in London. I don't have any wealthy friends like you do.' She looked around the shadowy lounge and drew her legs up, feeling the warmth of the fire on her skin.

When he kissed her, she tasted brandy on his tongue. It remained in her mouth as his lips moved down to her neck, his hands avoiding the swell of her breasts but slipping around her back in a tight grip, as if he was scared of ever letting her go, as if he might never be able to find her again. He removed his shirt without a thought, shrugging it from his shoulders as though the material was burning his skin.

He lowered himself on to his knees before her, taking her to the floor, moving smoothly, almost gracefully above her. His arms were tanned darker below the biceps, and she could discern a faint scent of sweat released by the warmth of his chest. He was so tender and careful that she wondered if he had somehow guessed her past suffering at the hands of men.

The intensity of her arousal surprised her, because it was caused by another's desire. She had not expected or even wanted this, but now that her need had been unmasked, she gave way to it. It was absurdly picturesque, making love on the floor of a stranger's house, lying on an animal skin before a fire, a scene made even more artificial by the fact that the flame effect was fake, but his anxiety to please her was real enough, and she relaxed, closing her eyes as he placed a hand at the base of her spine, raising her hips to slide down her jeans. Water dripped metronomically somewhere far above them. She heard the wind rising outside, and rain falling softly in the pines. Her senses felt heightened. A shudder of air passed between them, as if the spirits of earlier inhabitants were crossing the room.

He made love to her in silence, his smooth dry hands guiding, moving, pressing down firmly, as though every action had to be performed in a certain manner. The rain fell harder. The house creaked. The heat within her raised the pulse of her heart, shortening her breath. The steady rustle of leaves sounded like static. He held her gaze, never breaking the link he had established between them, holding her in place, the entire act controlled for her benefit.

Some time later, after he had pulled away from her, she felt cool air returning to the room as a diagonal bar of light widened across the floor, and a shower tap was turned on. It was an old man's house, where everything was within easy reach.

She sat up slowly, gathering her thoughts, looking around for her clothes. He had folded them neatly on the edge of the sofa while she dozed. She rose and dressed, waiting for him to finish, but the sound of the shower continued. He had folded his own clothes, too, topping them with the satchel she had never seen away from his side.

She had no intention to pry, simply wanted to understand more about him because he had told her so little, and then the satchel's flap was at her fingertips. Inside she saw nothing unusual at first: a wallet, small change, some loose scraps of paper with scrawled phone numbers, a small monochrome photograph of a stern old woman, a bundle tied with a rubber band and seated in an open envelope.

She took the bundle out and tipped it to the firelight.

Almost too frightened to look, she opened her fingers to see what she was holding. A French passport and a matching identity card bearing his photograph, two French credit cards, a chequebook, all in the same name, *Johann Bellocq*. She turned back to the passport and saw that it had been issued in Marseilles. Johann had been raised here in the Alpes-Maritimes, he had told her so himself.

She had faintly suspected from the outset that he might not operate within the boundaries of the law: his reluctance to reveal any hard information about himself, the clandestine way in which he seemed to move around, the changing cars, the borrowed houses – nothing added up. Johann kept his passport in his jacket at all times. He had shown it to her. This looked different. It had to be another one. In that case, whose identity was he carrying about with him?

A dropping sensation filled her stomach. Was Bellocq even his real name? He was . . . who? A liar? A thief? The credit cards were issued from two different banks. Suddenly his absence of character started to make sense. The betrayals had been small: a slip about his childhood, the corrected mention of a place, an interrupted recollection, the hasty dismissal of a memory, the constant guarding of his feelings – perhaps the only real part had been his desire for her. He saw something in her, some damage, some sense of kindred spirit . . .

A familiar rising panic sent her to the stack of photographs lying beneath the passport in the bundle. She flicked through them with widening eyes and horrified realization, image after image of such cruelty and disgust that she could scarcely trust her senses. Parts of bodies, women's bodies, so twisted and torn that they resembled flowers more than flesh. She suddenly became aware that the shower had stopped running. He would dry himself and come to find her.

She rose to her feet and desperately looked about for her purse, surprised to discover how shaky she felt. He would not be able to stop her leaving. Uncertain of what to do, she hesitated, listening as the shower door opened and shut. The upper half of the room was deeply shadowed. He had turned off the light, so that the false flames of the fire provided the only illumination. She would have to fetch Ryan and get out of the village. It was dangerous to stay a minute more.

For a second she thought she saw an outflung arm clad in brown wool, the palm turned up, fingers splayed, lying behind the sofa. Unable to look, she prayed it was just a log that had rolled from the fire. Whose house was this? No friend of Johann's. He must have stolen the car and found house keys, entered a stranger's home and come back for her. For all she knew he had murdered someone in their bed, made love to her while the corpse lay upstairs . . .

She had not meant to cry out, but she did, and he came

running for her. He sat beside her, gripping her hand. He tried to calm her fears, then told her of his childhood, how he had come to kill his mother, how even the local gendarmes had turned a blind eye because they had known what the old woman was like, and how he had then been sent away to the nuns for five long years, until he could come to terms with the weight of his crime.

For the first time in his life he was completely honest, telling her everything, because he loved her and wanted her to forgive him. Because he wanted to be with her for ever, no matter what she thought of his past, even though it meant telling her how he survived from day to day, moving from town to town, from life to life . . .

Then he stared into her eyes.

She knew all about his past even before he told her; for a certain kind of man, the problems always began with a bad childhood. She listened to his story very carefully, because she was afraid of him. He was an amalgam of every damaged soul she had ever met. She knew that if she managed to get away, she would have to tell someone about him, and his history would become part of her story.

As she sat before the great stone fireplace in the Villa de l'Ouest, shivering with fear and cold, listening intently, she forced herself to imagine how terrible his childhood had been, and tried to forgive him for what he had become, but found she could not. *Matricide,* she thought, *the ultimate crime against woman.* The thought of it, coupled with the knowledge that she had made love to him, sickened and shamed her. She remembered the photographs, and bile rose in her throat.

He had taken her hand and was saying something about her being the only woman he could ever trust with his burden, and never wanting to let her go. She tried to wriggle her fingers free, panic shortening her breath, terror soaring in her heart. But even as she tried to escape, she suddenly saw that she might never be free of him.

12

LACUNA

'Where on earth are we?' asked Arthur Bryant.

'You're the map reader, you should know,' suggested May, switching on the windscreen wipers. 'It's starting to snow. That could slow us down a bit.'

Bryant dug into his astrakhan coat and withdrew a crumpled bag. 'You're always going on about what a good driver you are. Now's your chance to prove it. Have a Milk Bottle. Or there are some pink sugar Shrimps.' He rattled the bag at May.

'No, thank you, they get stuck in my teeth. What was the last sign you saw?'

'Windlesham. Or possibly Bagshot. Hang on, there's one coming up on the left.' Bryant wrapped his spectacle arms around his ears and squinted. 'Hawley, Framley, Minley Manor, Hartley Wintney. The names of English towns are more like elocution exercises than real places. Listen to this: Tinkerton, Tapperton, Topley. Sounds like a ping-pong ball falling down a flight of steps. I say, look at that.' He pointed through the windscreen. 'Not often you see a green sky. Is that some kind of shepherd's warning, I wonder?'

'Not much traffic,' May noted in puzzlement. 'Turn on the radio.'

Bryant rolled the dial through a range of staticky channels, each less distinct than the last, but got a refreshing blast of Respighi on Radio Three and, on a local station, several women holding an urgent discussion about butter. 'This isn't Alma's original radio,' he explained. 'I had to buy it from an Armenian man in the Caledonian Road who ran away with my change. There was a time when being a police officer used to count for something.'

'I don't understand.' May took his eyes from the road, confused. 'What happened to the original radio?'

'Oh, it melted.' Bryant sucked his sweet pensively. 'I borrowed it from the van and wired it to a car battery for a party back in 1970. We were celebrating the anniversary of the Messina brothers being sent down. Remember them? Five Maltese racketeers who ran an empire of brothels and street-walkers across the West End after the war. The senior officers at Bow Street were full of stories about them running around armed with razors, hammers and coshes. The Messinas introduced the "short time" rule for London prostitutes, reducing their time with punters to ten minutes, working them from four p.m. to six a.m. until they were half dead. Eugenio Messina used to drive around Piccadilly in a yellow Rolls-Royce, checking that his girls weren't leaning against walls, not that the gesture made him a gentleman. He just wanted to make sure they were working hard.'

'I don't see what this has to do with your melted radio—'

'Some of the call girls heard we were holding a bash, and threw a Molotov cocktail through the window of the station-house kitchen to remind us that we had ruined their livelihoods.'

'So that's how the radio—'

'No, I'd put the radio on the cooker, not realizing the grill was on. We almost choked to death on the fumes. Oh, we had a laugh in those days.' He peered out at the passing fields. 'Look at the snow falling in the trees; it's so postcard-pretty out there. I'd forgotten how much I hate the countryside. All those rustic views and seasonal changes give me the willies.'

'That's because you've never spent time there,' May replied.

'Why would I? My family came from London. None of us

had any business out here. Rural folk think they're so superior, just because they have a village pub and a duck pond.'

May knew that his partner's antipathy to the countryside stemmed from the lean times his parents had endured following the war, when their only work came from long days spent hop-picking in Kent. Locals had hated rowdy East-Enders piling down to disturb the peace in their charabancs. 'The engine doesn't sound quite right to me.'

'I had it checked over only recently.'

'A fully qualified mechanic, I hope.'

'No, he's a fully qualified astrologer,' Bryant admitted.

'He must have thought you were born under the sign of the mug, charging you to tie string around the distributor. Do me a favour and call Janice, would you?' asked May. 'Make sure everything's all right.'

Bryant thumped away at his mobile and listened. 'Janice?' he shouted. 'Are you there?'

At Mornington Crescent, Sergeant Longbright had been expecting the call. 'You don't need to keep checking on us,' she said. 'Everything's fine. How's your trip?'

'Long motorways play havoc with a weak bladder, but we soldier on. I'll call you at regular intervals.'

'There's really no need, I assure you.'

Longbright replaced the receiver and looked back at Giles Kershaw. 'I didn't say anything. I know how upset you must be, but what good would it do to mention it now? Mr Bryant can't do anything from where he is. At least he didn't ask if I was still at the unit.'

'He could talk to Raymond about the matter; he could use his authority,' Kershaw replied, dropping his head into his hands and allowing his thin blond hair to run through his fingers. 'I can't believe Oswald would do a thing like this. He told me I was the best assistant he'd had in years. Why would he refuse to recommend me for the position?'

'He obviously doesn't think you're ready for it,' said Longbright. 'You know how demanding he is, you've been shadowing him for nearly a year now.'

'So Finch steps down on Friday, and Land appoints an outsider to come in and take over. Someone who's never worked with the unit before, and might decide to stay on for ever. Oswald led me to believe the job was mine. He can't do this to me. This is a specialist unit. All my training has been geared towards this work – where else can I go? You know it's not fair, Janice. My career's on the line here.'

'Leave it for forty-eight hours, until the boys are back,' Longbright suggested. 'Nothing will happen before then. I'll go in with them and see Raymond, but I warn you, Mr Bryant thinks you rely too much on technology and not enough on your natural instincts. He's told you that before. You'll need to convince him as well.' She checked her watch. 'You'd better go down to the Bayham Street Morgue. They brought someone in a few minutes ago. Caucasian female, early twenties, some kind of overdose, but she was found in suspicious circumstances. It's probably nothing, but Raymond wants us to take care of it.'

Kershaw puffed his cheeks in annoyance. 'The system's down now. I thought we weren't accepting any cases until the upgrade was finished.'

'It's not a referral; we're just lending a hand. Oswald will be down there, Giles. You're going to have to work alongside him without letting him know about what you've heard.'

'So I have to help the man who just stepped on my promotion. That's just great.' Kershaw picked up his folders and stormed out of the office.

Longbright went to the window and looked out at the grey-green evening. Her bosses were right to remain aloof from the everyday problems of the office; it allowed them space to think. Instead, everyone came to her with their problems, and then expected her to take sides. Since he had announced his retirement, Oswald Finch had managed to upset everyone in the unit. Could it be he simply regretted making the decision to leave? If he could no longer make himself useful, what was left for him?

It looked like it was snowing outside. She pressed her hand against the radiator and discovered it was cold. *No heat, no computers, no investigations, and now Raymond has decided not to let us go home after all,* she thought. *What else can go wrong?*

'It's snowing,' said Meera, clearing a patch of condensation from the curved window in her office. 'With any luck it'll cover the tramps and they'll freeze to death.'

'There's a touch of Margaret Thatcher in you,' Colin Bimsley pointed out. 'I love seeing snow; it freshens everything up. It even makes Camden Town look almost attractive. It's beautiful.'

'Not when you're standing out in it.' Mangeshkar remembered an incident from her childhood, when she spent the evening locked out on the balcony of the flats while her stepfather beat the hell out of her mother. She had been wearing a T-shirt and tracksuit bottoms, and the snow had fallen steadily enough to whiten her hair. Eventually a neighbour had taken the frozen girl in and warmed her beside the fire. She had not cried or complained, but never spoke to her mother's husband again, even after he begged her to forgive him. She had no love of snow. Watching Bimsley's goggle-eyed reaction to the weather merely convinced her that he was part Labrador. The fact that they expected her to work with someone so hopelessly optimistic and soft showed how badly they had misjudged her abilities. With a groan of fury, she stalked out of the office in search of Giles Kershaw, slamming the door hard behind her.

Raymond Land sat in his office and tipped back his chair, balancing his heels on the edge of his desk. This was how he liked it, so quiet you could hear mice scampering in the skirting boards and Crippen straining in his litter tray. He had been right to keep his staff on at the unit. It was time to stop treating them with kid gloves.

Only the angry traffic in the street below could remind him that he was still stranded here, in an ugly district of the city at a miserable time of the year. If only he had taken a post far, far away from the junkies and nutters of North London, some-where in the southern hemisphere, where the sun remained visible even in the depth of winter, and the locals smiled respectfully instead of waving two fingers at you. Actually, he would have been grateful to find the Agincourt V sign still in use, but few of the street traders in Camden could manage English and they only mustered a phlegmy expectoration as his officers passed.

He tipped his chair back further and placed his hands behind his head, savouring the first moments of what he fully expected to be the calmest three days of his career at the PCU. No tabloid-baiting lunatics to track down, no white witches, weepy clairvoyants or chanting necromancers to chuck out of Bryant's room, nothing but the gentle drift of a half-empty office running on a skeleton crew. Faraday had failed to close the unit down entirely, but at least both Bryant and May were out of his hair for the first time in many years. For once there was no one telling him what to do, or what he ought to have done, or completely ignoring him. Land felt in charge once more, and at a time when there was so little work on that even he could not be accused of making a mistake.

Smiling to himself, he stretched and tipped his chair just a little bit too far.

13

HUNTING

Madeline ran down the steep slope of the road, her trainers sliding on loose gravel. She knew that her head start would not last long.

In the time it would take Johann to dry and clothe himself, she could be back at the hotel. Steep staircases and flood gutters traversed the winding roads, allowing her to cut a path down the hillside to the palm-lined Basse Corniche. She reached sea level without a car passing her, and ran around the granite wall that lined the cliff in the direction of her hotel. Even though it was still not late, the village was dormant and lifeless. Only the occasional motorbike tore past her, waiters heading home from Monte Carlo to Nice.

She was shocked to discover that she still had the envelope with the passport and photographs gripped tightly in her hand, the proof of his guilt that would protect her from harm. What could she do now? He knew where she was staying, and there was nowhere else to go in a place as small as this.

She checked her watch and thought about the time it would take to rouse Ryan, pack and check out. She could not remember how the winter train schedule operated, and did not want to wait on the exposed station platform, which could be seen from virtually everywhere in the village. The only alternative was to find a gendarme and convince him that this man was dangerous, but she could imagine how that conversation would go: 'What were you doing with him in a house he'd broken into?' 'You made love to him while the owner lay dying in the upstairs room?'

She had already been warned about the local police treating outsiders with suspicion. He had not just stolen passports; he had stolen whole identities. Perhaps if she threw the photographic evidence away, into the bushes beside the railway track, he would leave her alone – but they were her only weapon against him.

Or he might ignore her, simply move on to another town and start again. How long had he been travelling about like this, burgling and killing? How many others had discovered his secret, and what had he done to them? He had shown gentility and thoughtfulness in her company. Or perhaps he had just been careful. Her husband had always demonstrated a capacity for violence, but Johann – or whatever his real name might be – had hidden his other self so completely that he had disarmed her natural inclination to suspicion.

She thought back to the day that Kate Summerton had shown her how to kill the moth, using only the power of her unconscious mind. When she had first visited the refuge, Kate had healed her and cared for her like any hospital nurse. It was what she had done for so many other women who had been bullied and beaten by their men. But later, the art of her healing had moved beyond salves and sticking plasters to something more spiritual, a personal-training programme that had allowed Madeline to understand why men had always troubled and deceived her. Yet it seemed that even Kate had not been able to prevent it from happening again . . .

Heavy clouds far blacker than the night were rolling over the edge of the Savaric cliffs, and the first fat droplets of rain had started to fall, drawing up the scent of pine and earth. She reached L'Auberge des Anges and walked through the bright, empty bar. Mme Funes and her husband usually stayed in the back watching television when there were no diners or drinkers to serve.

She unlatched the door of her room quietly and found Ryan folded up in the corner of her bed. She packed around the sleeping boy, shoving everything into two small bags, placing the envelope with the passport and photographs in her shoulder bag. It was twelve minutes past nine. She thought there was a train at nine twenty-two, but could not be sure. There would probably not be another for an hour.

Ryan remained heavy and unmanageable, drifting in a fugue state from pyjamas to sweater and jeans without fully awakening. She needed to leave without disturbing Mme Funes, who would keep her talking, and tell others that she had left. She could settle the bill by post at a later date. Getting out of the front door, on the other side of the bar, would be the tricky part.

'Ryan, I want you to be very quiet, OK? We don't want anyone to know we're going out.'

'Where's Johann?' the boy asked sleepily. 'Can he come with us?'

'No, he has to work tonight. We'll call him later.' She hoisted Ryan's bag on to her spare shoulder and led him down the stairs. The floorboards were covered in threadbare carpet, and creaked horribly.

'Where are we going?' he whispered.

'We have to catch a train. We can't stay here.' He was about to speak again, but she cut him off. He was at the age when he demanded explanations for everything. 'I'll tell you all about it once we're on our way, I promise.' She would provide him with some invented excuse; there was no point in scaring him further.

At the foot of the stairs, she stopped and peered back through the hatch to the Funeses' claustrophobically wallpapered lounge. She could hear the television playing, some announcer shouting *'Qui gagnera le grand prix ce soir?'* – Mme Funes was addicted to game shows. When she opened the front door, a blast of rainy wind blew in, and she heard the old lady rising from her place in front of the TV. Pulling Ryan through the door, she closed it firmly and headed out across the forecourt in the direction of the yellow radiance marking the railway station. Streetlights obscured by branches caused patches of shadow to waver across the road like flittering bats.

The station platform was deserted, a sign that the next train was not due for some time yet. The timetable was almost impossible to decipher, but it appeared that they had missed a train heading all the way to Marseilles. There was a connection to Nice due in fifteen minutes. Ryan's hand had grown cold in hers, and she knew he would soon start protesting. She was still deciding what to do when a crackle of gravel heralded the arrival of the stolen Mercedes in the station forecourt. Lifting her surprised son into her arms, she abandoned her bags and ran through the underpass beneath the track, climbing the staircase back to the main road.

Above them stood the village, its barred, unlit houses offering little refuge.

He saw her moving and reversed the car, but the parking area was too narrow to offer a turning circle. Not daring to look back, she carried on up the slope to the grand white houses cut in against the base of the cliff. All the villas had barred gates, automatic floodlights and entry-phones. Setting Ryan down, she tried the first buzzer she reached, but there was no answer. *Someone must be in,* she thought. *They can't all be summer homes; somebody must live here.* She ran from bell to bell, slapping them with her palm, but they rang in darkened dead hallways, and no lights came on.

Somewhere a dog began barking, the sound echoing around the hills, but every villa was shuttered and dead, ghost buildings in a village that could only be brought to life by the warmth of summer.

Behind them, the sleek Mercedes coasted a curve and began its unhurried approach. There was nowhere for them to hide; the cliff rose on one side of the road, and bare walls lined the other. On their left, an alleyway overhung with pomegranate trees led to a pair of small houses built on to the steps, the remnants of the original village. Ryan resisted as she pulled him up towards the first front door. There was no doorbell or buzzer for the property, so she rapped with her knuckles.

At the base of the alley, the Mercedes halted as Johann ducked his head and watched them through the passenger window.

Madeline was sure she had seen a curtain twitch from the corner of her eye, but no one came to answer her call. The sound of the car door opening propelled her to the second building, a lopsided two-floor house with peeling green shutters. She slapped at the door with her hand, calling '*S'il vous plaît! Au secours!*' but there was silence within. He was striding up the alley steps towards them now, calling to her, 'Madeline, I have to talk with you.'

The door before her suddenly opened, and a minuscule old lady peered up at her from the gap. 'Please, do you speak English?' Madeline asked. 'There is a man following us.'

'*Alors, vous devez entrer.*' She slipped the chain and widened the door as Madeline pushed Ryan forward. The old woman remembered the village as it had been before the arrival of the foreigners, when residents still took care of each other. For centuries these hills had offered refuge to smugglers, and old habits were slow to die.

'We don't want to get you into trouble,' Madeline insisted. 'Is there another way out of the house?'

'Madeline!' She heard the call from the street. 'I know where you are. I just want to talk.'

'*Est-ce votre mari?*' asked the old lady, squinting suspiciously from the window.

'No, he is a burglar,' she said, searching for her schoolgirl French. '*Un cambrioleur.*'

'*Je comprends. Venez avec moi, il y a une porte à l'arrière.*' She led the way through a small Provence-style lounge crowded with dark turned wood and overstuffed floral chairs. They reached the kitchen as Johann started hammering at the door. '*Allez-y avec votre fils. Je me débarrasserai de lui. Vite, vite.*'

Madeline found herself in the dark rear garden of the house

as the old woman closed the door on her. Gripping Ryan's hand tightly, she pushed into the wet hibiscus bushes, searching for the back gate. As they slipped along the side of the house she could hear Johann arguing with the old woman at the front door, and prayed he would not hurt her. He was swearing loudly at her now, and she was shrieking back. Ryan yelled at his mother, complaining that she was hurting his arm as they hurtled back down the steps to the road.

The train had left Cap-d'Ail and was already coasting the headland as they ran towards the station. The underpass to the correct platform was too far away. 'We'll have to go over the line,' she told Ryan. 'Can you run?'

'Mum, the barrier's down. I can see the train coming.'

She swung him up into her arms before he could think further, and ran across the track as the light from the double-decked train illuminated the pine trees around them. Their bags were still lying on the platform. The sight of Johann appearing on the other side was cut off as the carriages flashed past and the train came to a stop. She prayed he would not have enough time to reach the underpass.

They boarded the train without tickets and found their way to an upstairs seat. Madeline watched anxiously from the window as the train stayed at the platform, its door wide open. *Please,* she prayed, *let the doors close before he reaches us.*

As they finally pulled out of Eze-sur-Mer in the direction of Nice, she had no idea whether he had managed to board the train or not.

14

MORTIFICATION

At five to twelve on Tuesday morning, DS Janice Longbright pushed open the door of the Bayham Street mortuary and entered the musty passageway that ran beside the former school gymnasium.

She looked up at the narrow windows, paused, and took a slow, deep breath. Having resisted promotion from the status of Detective Sergeant for so many years, it now seemed that she was to have the responsibility of leadership placed upon her whether she liked it or not. An uncomfortable-looking Giles Kershaw was waiting for her outside the door. The young forensic scientist coughed loudly, but remained at the threshold of the room. He leaned around the doorframe, reluctant to enter.

'Giles, either go in or stay out,' said Longbright, more in puzzlement than irritation. 'What on earth's the matter?'

Kershaw looked sheepish. 'Oswald didn't want me here at all, so I'm not sure I should be intruding upon his turf.'

'Oh, don't be so sensitive and territorial. I don't understand what's so important that you couldn't talk to me about it on the phone.' The sickly look on his face stopped her. 'Tell me what's happened.'

'I think you'd better take a look,' said Giles, running a hand through his lank blond hair as he stepped back to admit her first. 'The door was locked on the inside. I had to use one of the spare keys to get it open. This is just how I found the place.'

She moved carefully into a room that was still more like a gymnasium than a morgue. Most of it was below street level, with five short windows near the ceiling framing a dusty view of passing ankles on the pavement outside. An old wood-and-steel climbing frame still stood in the corner, the last surviving remnant of the St Patrick Junior Catholic Boys' School gym. The bare brick walls had been painted gloss white, and the aluminium-cased strip lights that hung low across the steel desks added a forensic glare to a room which still smelled faintly of plimsolls and hormonal teens. The sprung wood basketball floor had been covered with carpet tiles. Longbright noted a folded pile of black micromesh sheets, a scuffed stainless-steel dissecting table, several glass-fronted equipment cabinets, Finch's old wooden desk and, at the rear of the room, a bank of four steel body drawers, but there was no sign of the pathologist.

She had expected to find Finch in his usual spot, seated on a bentwood chair beside one of the sinks, reading a gardening magazine. He was now past the age when he could spend much of his day standing. She looked about, puzzled. 'I don't understand. Where is he?'

'Look under the sink,' Kershaw instructed her. Longbright slowly bent over, apprehensive of what she might find. Finch was lying on his back with his papery eyelids shut, his bony death's-head face finally suited to circumstance. He looked for all the world as if he had decided to take a nap on the floor and then simply drifted beyond the vale of sorrow.

'Seems entirely at peace, doesn't he?' Kershaw voiced her thought. 'At a guess, I'd say he's been dead for at least an hour. The exact time might prove difficult to pin down, but I'll get to that problem later. There's no blood, no outward sign of the cause. The only anomaly I can see is the angled bruise on the left side of his neck, about two inches long, just above his collar.'

Longbright crouched beside the pathologist's body and gently touched her hand against his skin. 'Looks new. What do you think it is?'

'I don't know. I came here looking for Dan and found this instead. He's cold to the touch. There's a contusion on the back of his head, presumably caused by the fall. Ought we to call someone?'

'I'm not sure if he has any surviving relatives – there might be a cousin in Broadstairs.'

'I'd heard he was depressed. John told me he'd changed his mind about leaving the unit, but Raymond Land wouldn't take back his resignation. There's a clear handprint on the stainless-steel counter – Finch's own, because there's a band missing on the fourth finger, where he wears a ring. It would be consistent with him placing his left-hand palm down on the surface. It's the sort of thing you'd do to steady yourself. My first thought was heart attack, but what about suicide?'

'Surely a sudden illness is the most likely explanation,' said Longbright.

'Of course, that's the first thing Dan will be considering after his examination of the room. The door was locked from the inside, and the only key in the room should be on the hook behind Finch's desk, but it's not. The windows require a pole to be opened, and have no external fastenings.'

'There's another way into the mortuary,' said Longbright, looking up. 'The ventilator shaft.'

'Right, the cover's missing from the front of the extractor fan.'

'The pipe measures about forty-five centimetres,' said Dan Banbury, walking in beside them. 'So unless someone trained a monkey to come and attack him I think we can rule out that possibility.'

'Murders in the Rue Morgue,' said Longbright. 'How on earth do you know what the pipe measures?'

'You learn to make accurate measurements from sight-readings in this job,' said Banbury casually. 'My wife's a district nurse. She does the same thing when she's pouring me a beer, measures it out to the centilitre. Look further under the table.'

'What is that?' Longbright spotted the grey metal object, a double-ended aluminium fan blade.

'He'd been complaining for weeks that no one had come to replace the extractor cover.' Banbury pointed to the ceiling, and the framed end of the ventilation pipe. 'Looks to me like the fan blade worked itself loose and finally came off, falling down and striking him on the neck.'

'A bit unlikely, don't you think?' said Kershaw.

'You wouldn't believe the stats on accidents in the work-place. Employees have more than 1.6 million a year in Britain alone, impaling themselves on pens, getting electrocuted by ungrounded metal toilets, falling out of windows, choking on paper clips. University College Hospital had a woman last week who had managed to cut her throat opening a padded envelope. There's no sign of a forced entry, and this is a secure building. Even so, Finch had the door lock changed last month so that it could only be opened from the outside with a key. Apparently he was fed up with Mr Bryant wandering in and being rude to him all the time.'

'I don't think he could face retirement in Hastings,' said Kershaw.

'This is not suicide, Giles. He was strange, I'll admit, but he'd have to have been pretty bloody perverse to loosen the blade of an extractor fan and stand underneath it with his neck exposed, waiting for it to fall off. Besides, there's nothing to stand on in here. He'd never have been able to reach it in the first place.'

'I'm talking about finding some kind of malignant chemical in his body. Finch had a background in biology and chemistry. If he had really wanted to commit suicide, he'd have been able to access any amount of painless drugs for the purpose.'

'I know Arthur has always encouraged us to rank the most bizarre possibilities beside more obvious causes of death,' said Longbright, 'but isn't this going a bit far? Even if he did found the PCU upon that idea.' She studied the supine pathologist with sadness. 'Poor Oswald, he never did get to leave this place.'

Longbright rose and checked around the room. She couldn't smell alcohol on the body, and Finch had no history of drink or drug abuse. Clear-headed suicides usually tidied up before killing themselves. The pathologist's casebook and notes were scattered over the workbench. True, he had tried to rescind his resignation, and was probably mortified about his failure to do so, but depression was his natural state.

She wondered whether to tell her bosses and have them return to the unit, but decided against it. She understood their thought processes better than anyone, and could partially reproduce them if necessary. It was time for her to become more independent.

'What would John do next, do you think? Set up a common approach path, run a particle sweep, start swabbing for DNA?'

'The trouble is, neither he nor Bryant ever operated in the prescribed official manner,' said Banbury. 'Their methodology is as unpredictable as a wind before a storm.'

Longbright pinched a glossy crimson lip and studied the scene, trying to clear her head of preconceptions. Finch had been standing at his workbench, and had fallen on to his back. He was left-handed. If the fan had spun off and fallen on him, wouldn't he have heard the sound of it coming loose? What had absorbed his concentration so intently? She looked at the workbench and saw loose papers, an uncapped ballpoint pen, notebooks, a broken-backed toxicology manual – nothing out of the ordinary.

'What's the first thing you do if you hear a noise above you?' she asked Banbury. 'You look up.'

'Helicopters,' said Banbury enigmatically. 'That's what we used to call those seeds with little wings that fell from trees when we were nippers. They don't fall straight down, do they? The fan blade wouldn't, either. It's lightweight aluminium. Finch looked up, stretching his neck, and it could have come down at him from an angle, striking a blow from the side.'

'What, you think the blow to his neck caused a blood clot, some kind of internal haemorrhage? That seems no more likely than the idea of him killing himself.'

'I'm not going to perform an autopsy on him, Janice,' stated Kershaw. 'Not only would it be unethical, the idea of using Finch's own medical instruments to divine the cause of his death would be highly inappropriate. We'd have to falsify the paperwork.'

'See, that's the difference between you and Oswald. He would never show such squeamishness when it's a matter of doing the right thing.'

'I'm not squeamish.' Kershaw bridled. 'It's a moral issue.'

The detective sergeant was not one to see the world in shades of grey. 'You knew about the unit's habit of ignoring the boundaries of propriety before you came to us,' she warned him. 'If you want to prove yourself a worthy successor to Oswald, this is where you start.'

'At least it's not difficult sealing off the site,' said Banbury. 'As far as I'm aware, there are only four sets of keys into the mortuary, including Finch's own. Giles, can you see if he has a set on him?'

Kershaw flicked a lick of blond hair from his eyes and knelt beside the body. He carefully removed a pair of keys, one Chubb, one Yale, from the pathologist's pocket and placed them in a plastic bag. As the unit had no photographer of its own, Banbury photographed the body's position and marked it. All that remained was for Finch to be lifted on to his own table.

'Well, we've got an instrument of death, but I don't think this was quite the simple accident it appears to be,' said Banbury.

'What do you mean?' Longbright studied his face for clues.

'Giles, is it OK to pick up the fan blade?'

'So long as you've grid-marked it.'

Banbury raised the aluminium spinner by its fin. 'The central pin holding the propeller to the shaft has sheared. Looks to me like a slow stress fracture, and they take a long time to develop. You can see the thing was spinning anticlockwise because this edge' – he pointed to the top rim of the right-hand blade – 'is covered by a thick layer of dirt, like the opposite side of the other blade, so that was the direction in which it was travelling. There's a dent on the very end, which I'm willing to bet will match the crescent dent on the fan housing.' He pointed upwards. 'You can see the mark where it flew off from down here. So, let's piece the event together and find out what's wrong.'

Banbury had a commonsense attitude to police work that the others sometimes lacked. You could see cogs turning in his head. 'I know that the fan housing fell off some weeks ago – it's over there on its side, under Finch's desk, waiting to be reattached. Finch complained about it to anyone who would listen, and wasn't happy about having to operate beneath the uncovered blades. But I suppose he needed the air on whenever he was working. The pin finally snapped, and with nothing to stop it the spinning blade dropped, bouncing against the housing, which would have sent it down into the room still spinning, but at an angle. But Finch was standing right underneath – we know that by the way in which he's fallen – so how on earth could he get hit by a fan blade that was veering away from him? That's one point. This is the other.'

He indicated the two clean edges of the blade. 'If the blade was spinning anticlockwise, it would be one of the two dirty edges that would hit him. However, as you can both see, the rims of dirt on either blade have not been disturbed, nor is there a dirt-mark on Oswald's neck. So, although this thing is the only potential weapon in the room that is likely to have caused such a bruise, it seems it didn't do so. If Finch wasn't killed by a falling fan, what did kill him?'

He led them over to the door handle. 'The lock hasn't been forced. If someone came here looking for trouble without having the right keys, Finch would have had to let them in himself. For any assailant, the obvious weapons couldn't be more visible.' He pointed to the glass cabinets where an assortment of scalpels and knives stood in their racks. 'He always returned them there after they'd cooled down from the sterilizer. Suppose he somehow bashed himself on the furniture and suffered a trauma?'

'You're thinking he underwent a natural death in the form of a cardiac arrest? It would make life easier to think so, but there's no sign of cyanosis, no muscle tension, no dilation of his pupils.' Kershaw knew that once accident, natural death and suicide were ruled out, only homicide remained. It was a conclusion he would be reluctant to reach. 'So what was it?'

In the faintly humming room, beneath bleach-white lights, the three officers stood looking around, and wondered. 'He was argumentative and frail,' said Longbright. 'Suppose he fought with someone, and they lost their temper? All of us have wanted to thump him at one time or another. Some have more reason to do so than others.'

Both she and Banbury turned to look at Giles Kershaw.

15

MATRIARCHY

'I detest motorways,' Bryant complained for the third time as he attempted to realign his overcoat buttons. 'How on earth are you supposed to know where you get off?'

'There are several absolutely enormous signposts along the way,' May pointed out.

Bryant squinted through the windscreen. 'Did I miss Taunton?'

'You slept through Taunton and Exeter,' said May. 'We're about to come off the M5 on to the A38. Why this spiritualists' convention has to take place in such a remote corner of the country is beyond me.'

'It's an area perfectly attuned to the mysteries of the nether-world,' replied Bryant. 'You clearly have no historical appreciation of the countryside.' This was a bit rich coming from a man who usually only left central London to attend funerals, and complained bitterly every time he did so. 'There's not much traffic, is there?'

'The journey's taking longer than I thought. Sensible people have probably been listening to the weather forecast. The Devon and Cornwall Police have been issuing warnings to stay indoors for the past hour. Damn, I've missed a sign now.' May rubbed his forehead wearily. 'I was looking out for Buckfast and Ashburton.'

Snow had been falling fast and hard for more than two hours, blotting the pallid sky and sheening the grey, half-empty road. Across the light woodland, a village spire flickered through falling flakes.

'I'll map-read for a while.' Bryant dragged the ancient guide out of his overcoat and leafed through it without recourse to his reading glasses. 'I knew you would eventually need me to get us there.'

'I've been meaning to ask you for years, Arthur, but we so rarely get the chance to talk like this. When did your fascination with the occult and alternative religions start? I mean, all that stuff you believe in, psychogeography, pagan cabals, astromancy, witchcraft and predestination, where did it all come from? You're from sensible working-class East End stock. I'm sure your mother didn't have time for such things.'

'That's the paradox,' said Bryant, popping a Milk Bottle into his mouth and chewing pensively. 'East-Enders are a prosaic but superstitious lot. My father would never bring a budgerigar into the house or put his boots on the bed, or take photographs of babies, or hand a knife to a friend, or touch a Welshman . . .'

'Wait, what were those things supposed to signify?'

'Well, all house birds except canaries were considered bad luck because sailors left them at home while they were at sea. If they didn't return to claim them, the birds acted as reminders of lost husbands. Boots on a bed meant a death in the family, because that was how you chose the burial boots, by laying them out. Photographing babies was tempting fate when they were so likely to die before the age of two, and knives cut friendship.'

'And not touching a Welshman?'

'Oh, he just couldn't stand them. Take this next exit.'

'Are you sure? I thought we were supposed to stay on the motorway until it ended.'

'You wanted to bypass Totnes.'

'No, I said the A38 did that anyway.'

Earlier they had glimpsed the pale ribbon of the sea, but now to their right was the bleak vastness of Dartmoor, where the frosted roads dwindled into twisting corridors of hedge, and coasting winds could buffet snow into maze-like drifts. The dark hills had faded beneath unblemished whiteness, like freshly ironed tablecloths. Fat snowflakes almost blotted out the slate sky.

Bryant had been a good passenger for most of the journey by dint of the fact that he had been asleep, but now he was wide-eyed, aching and fidgety with boredom. 'It was difficult not to seek alternative meanings in our house,' he continued. 'My devout grandmother lost all three of her sons in the Great War, and my aunts lost their children in the flu pandemic that followed. Then, just when we all seemed to be recovering in the intervening years, my uncles were drowned at sea and we were bombed out of the family house in Bethnal Green. Where did our devotion to God get us? If you ask such questions as a child and don't receive any satisfactory answers, you start to look for other means of proof.'

'So you attend spiritualists' conventions. A bit outmoded, isn't it, all that table-rapping?'

'Every street in London once housed a woman with so-called special powers, someone to whom the neighbours would turn for traditional remedies and health predictions,' said Bryant, pensively sucking his sweet. 'It was a strictly matriarchal network, of course. Mothers brought their babies around and wives would ask for advice on aches and pains, allergies, sexual health and marital problems. Often the wisdom they received was based on sound psychological sense, and the kind of conservative values that required everyone to remain in his or her rightful place before the advice could work. Many of these superstition-based remedies were rendered nonsensical by the changing times, but some are still with us. And of course other, more alternative services were also offered: the psychic comforting that followed bereavement, predictions and palliatives linked by the searching-out of signs and symbols. My grandmother used to read tea leaves for the local ladies, and told them she saw angels. The tradition went back hundreds of years, and only came to a proper end in the 1970s.' Bryant paused for breath while his partner increased the speed of their windscreen wipers.

'Nowadays, increased awareness of mental and physical health means that the spiritual urban mother-figure has all but disappeared in Western society. Meanwhile, technology has supposedly given us the means to gauge psychic energy. I don't believe in the supernatural, just the untapped power of the mind. Look in the papers: we read about tiny women lifting cars off their loved ones and boat people surviving without water, and don't think it odd. Extreme situations can make heroes of us all.'

'Just because you trace your beliefs to your grandmother doesn't mean you should still believe what she told the neighbourhood.'

Bryant shrugged. 'I have to. She was so often right, you see, and she insisted that I, too, had her gift. Which I believe to this day.' He tapped his map. 'Next left.'

'I really don't think we're supposed to turn off yet,' May anxiously pointed out.

'The A38 takes us in a sort of horseshoe, but we can cut part of it off. We should be able to make up some lost time.'

It was against May's better judgement to take practical advice from his partner. Arthur's kaleidoscopic manner of determining complex solutions to simple problems could prove disastrous. Perhaps because he wasn't concentrating hard enough, perhaps because he was worried about the rapidly increasing intensity of the snowfall and reaching their hotel before night, he listened and acted accordingly, forgetting for the moment that Arthur was reading from a map printed before the assassination of the Archduke Franz Ferdinand.

16

INTERNECINE

'There's no blood,' the detective sergeant remarked, searching the spot where Finch had fallen. 'He must have given his skull a good crack.'

'An autopsy will show if there's been any cranial bruising or bleeding into his internal cavities.' Kershaw sighed and rubbed his hand across his face. 'If I didn't know better, I'd think he did this to test me. Did Raymond tell you who Finch's successor is to be?'

'I really don't think this a good time to have that conversation,' said Longbright. 'I'm appointing you in charge of this case, Giles. You knew him well, and you're familiar with his room.'

'I'm technically a forensic scientist, not a coroner.'

'I assume you're fully trained in pathology, otherwise you wouldn't have been applying for Finch's job. I heard you received the highest pass-grade in your year.'

'But I could be prejudicial to the findings,' Kershaw warned. 'In these circumstances, you're meant to appoint an outsider.'

'I'm not *meant* to do anything,' Longbright informed him. 'This is the PCU, not the Metropolitan Police, and you're now in charge. Call Bimsley in and keep him on site until you've got some preliminary findings. I don't want you left alone in here.'

'I say, that's a bit strong.' Kershaw rose and flicked back his hair, affronted, his public-school background drawn to the fore in any confrontation with someone he considered to be from an inferior class. 'I'm assuming you're appointing me because you trust me.'

'Yes,' Longbright admitted, 'but I also sent you down to visit the morgue earlier, which makes you a potential suspect with a strong motive, placed at a possible crime scene at the estimated time of death.'

For once, Kershaw was dumbfounded. 'Then I can't possibly be seen to be investigating my victim's murder. I can't find myself guilty.'

'You might try taking Mr Bryant's advice about thinking instinctively rather than putting all your trust in the circumstantial evidence. I want a report from you before we close tonight.'

Returning to the PCU, the detective sergeant found DC Mangeshkar at work in the office she shared with Bimsley. 'Why were you looking for Giles Kershaw this morning?' she asked. The forensic scientist had informed her of Meera's visit to the mortuary.

'I was going to ask him if I could help out with the unidentified female they brought in. I didn't think Finch would let me watch the postmortem; I just wanted to examine his case notes. I heard it had already gone down to Bayham Street, so I went there.'

'Did you take a set of keys with you?' Longbright asked, already knowing the answer.

'I had to, because when Finch is alone in the room with the door shut he keeps his headphones on and doesn't hear you knocking.'

'You found him, I take it.'

'Yes, but Finch told me to leave. He must have heard my key in the lock, because he opened the door before I could. But he wouldn't let me in.'

'Why not?'

'He was in the middle of an argument. Kershaw was asking

him why he'd changed his mind about something. I didn't hear Finch's reply but he sounded bloody angry, told Kershaw that he was immature and careless. I decided to leave them to it, and came back here.' Presumably Kershaw had gone specifically to complain to Finch about being passed over for his promotion, and the old man had given him a piece of his mind, after which Kershaw had left the coroner alone in the room.

A grim thought formed in Longbright's mind. Access to Bayham Street Morgue was restricted. The Met could arrange visits via its resident pathologist, as could members of the PCU. The room's tiny windows were all bolted, and its only door was locked. The good news was that all the sets of keys were now accounted for. Finch, Kershaw and Mangeshkar had been holding a set each, which left the final bunch of keys on the hook behind Arthur Bryant's desk, from where Banbury had borrowed them.

The bad news was that if Kershaw found enough reason to suspect homicide, the restricted access to the morgue limited the murder suspects to those in the Peculiar Crimes Unit itself.

'Meera, you'll have to stay here, too,' Longbright said.

Mangeshkar looked more furious than the detective sergeant had ever seen her. 'That's ridiculous. I've done nothing wrong.'

'Wait, let me think for a minute.' *Four sets of keys, four suspects*, Longbright thought, *but anyone in the unit could have walked into Arthur's office and taken them. If we have to suspect each other, all the trust we've built up over the years will be destroyed. Oswald's death could achieve something that none of our enemies has managed to do. It could divide us and bring about the end of the unit.*

17

BLOCKADE

'Ah, Devon,' said Arthur Bryant, thumbing through his ancient map book. 'A million people and only fourteen surnames.' The battered white Bedford van left the arterial route at a junction and coasted on to a snowy tree-lined road free of traffic. Low clouds beyond the hills reflected soft saffron light from a distant town. 'You see,' said Bryant, 'that's Plymouth to the right of us. Five miles at the most.'

But the road curved away to the left down a one-in-seven hill, dropping them into a valley surrounded by wind-blasted woodland. By now the last vestiges of daylight had faded, and the snow had bleached all remaining features from their surroundings. May turned the wipers up as high as they would go, but they could no longer keep the windscreen clear.

'I don't like the look of this.' He angled the heater nozzles so that they warmed the glass and provided him with some vague visibility.

The road ahead was as direct as desert blacktop, Roman in its refusal to deviate for the land's natural features. It cut over the far side of the valley in a perfect straight line, and was hemmed on either side by a hawthorn hedge. May felt the traction in his tyres give as he started on the downward slope. The rear of the van fishtailed on the hardening snow tracks left by the previous vehicle. He gripped the wheel tightly, struggling to keep the van from ploughing into walls of dense brush. The engine squealed as the tyres spun, gripped, spun again.

'I was just thinking about the *Malleus Maleficarum*, the Witches' Hammer,' said Bryant, who had clearly failed to notice that they were in difficulty. 'Have you ever actually tried reading the 1486 edition? I mean, it's intriguing that we vilify *Mein Kampf*, a volume with which it shares the same fundamental fear and hatred of anyone different, while most practising Christians still have the same beliefs that the Hammer puts forward, so that if you hold the contemporary view of piety that places Wicca on the opposite side of Christianity, you're aligned with the same witch-burning mentality that existed over five centuries ago.'

He watched as the headlights flashed across bushes, then road, then bushes again. 'I mean, even Galileo was considered heretical for thinking about the planets in terms of their gravitational fields rather than their holy design. I suppose what I'm really trying to say is —'

May never found out what Bryant was really trying to say, for at that moment the wheel spun out of his hands as the tyres locked into a set of frozen truck tracks. He fought to correct the trajectory of the Bedford van, then changed gear and applied the brakes when that failed. Bryant was thrown against the passenger door as they slipped sideways across the road and came to an angled halt against the hawthorn bank.

May flooded the engine trying to restart it. As the snow clouds briefly parted, he saw that there were at least half a dozen vehicles littering the road ahead. Opening his window and looking back through the spattering white flakes, he could see a Spar supermarket truck coming in behind him, and another vehicle pulling up behind that. If they blocked the road, nobody would be able to leave.

As he closed the window, the wind rose in an ear-battering bluster, and the flurries turned back into a blizzard. 'Well, that's it,' he said, sitting back in his seat. 'We're not going anywhere tonight. We'll have to wait for the emergency services to come and dig us out. You realize this wouldn't have happened if we'd stayed on the main highway.'

'Don't blame me,' said Bryant indignantly. 'You should have paid more heed to the weather report. We can't just stay here. I have to be at tomorrow's opening ceremony in Plymouth.'

'Well, I wouldn't suggest trying to walk there tonight, especially as you managed to forget your stick. The snow's getting deep, and you'd never get across the fields while it's like this. I think we're on the closest main road running beside the southern part of Dartmoor. Your shortcut appears to have taken us over the most inhospitable piece of land in the whole of Southern England.'

'It looks as though there are plenty of others in the same boat,' Bryant pointed out. 'At least we shouldn't have to wait here for very long.'

'I wouldn't bet on it. It looks as if the road is already impassable. They won't be able to get a snowplough down here. When this happened last year, the Devon and Cornwall rescue services had to send out British Navy helicopters to airlift over sixty drivers and passengers to safety. Their vehicles were flooded out when the thaw came.'

'This is exactly the sort of thing I always expect to happen in the countryside,' Bryant complained. 'You read about people falling into bogs and quarries, being trampled by cows and drowned in chicken slurry. You're better off getting mugged and stabbed in London. I read *The Hound of the Baskervilles*; I know about treacherous patches of quicksand lurking on the moors.'

May fixed him with an annoyed stare, but chose to remain silent.

'Look on the bright side, John. We've plenty of warm clothing in the back. You helped me pack all those outfits for the show.'

'If you think I'm sitting here dressed in a fig-leaf body stocking and a Protestant cleric's cassock, Arthur, you're sadly mistaken.'

Bryant huddled down inside his voluminous overcoat. 'It was

just an idea. We still have plenty of Alma's sandwiches to keep us going. We could probably feed everyone who's been stranded here. I wonder why triangular ones are considered posher than oblong ones?'

'Most of the cars in front look empty,' said May. 'It looks like their drivers had the good sense to get out and head for the nearest town before the blizzard started up again. At least we know that things can't get any worse tonight.'

Just then his mobile rang. The display told him that Janice Longbright was calling from the unit. With a growing sense of unease he tried to take the call, but the connection suddenly vanished.

18

MIGRATION

The train had been too crowded to risk talking to her. All he wanted to do was talk, and hear that she had understood his pain. She had left his satchel behind, the one that contained his own passport, so he could continue travelling, but in his confusion he had given her a head start.

It wasn't hard to predict where she was headed; her complaints about her flat in South London were tinged with a longing to return there. She would either catch the ferry from Calais or use the Channel Tunnel service, then find the fastest train to the city centre.

He imagined watching from the end of the carriage as she slept in her seat, her head tilting with the sway of the tracks, jean-clad thighs shifting with the roll of the train as it passed across points, and knew that he had to make her understand. The thought of never touching her again, or never finding anyone else to share his secrets, made him sick with fear. She was the woman who held the key to his continued survival. How had it come to this? Everything had been going so well between them. He was overcome with the need to explain himself. He had earned the right to do that, at least. Even now he felt safe and protected by her, knowing that she was unlikely to go to the police. He needed to watch her from a distance, until he could be sure. He would clear the path for the three of them, get rid of the stupid ex-husband and his brother, help her to see that he could build a happy life for them, because he had a strength few other men possessed, born from the day he had taken another's life. He had faced the evil within himself and overcome it.

She was a tourist, but he knew the system. He ran across the tracks and caught a fast train to Calais just as it was leaving, knowing she would miss it because the boy slowed her down. He arrived forty minutes before her train pulled in. As they alighted on to the platform and set off to purchase tickets for the P&O boat, he followed at a discreet pace, ready to intervene if she decided to find a police officer.

'It's too cold to be out here,' Madeline complained, gripping her son's hand tightly as he stood at the rail of the ferry. 'Let's go back inside.'

'Why did you leave my Spider-Man bag behind?' asked Ryan. His scarf and her warmest jacket had been folded away in it, but the bag had been left behind in their room in the rush to leave the hotel. He looked back out at the ice-grey channel and pointed to the sickly amber mist forming close to the water. Snow had begun to fall in thick flakes that stuck to his eyelids. He was a resilient child, but his mother's behaviour was increasingly confusing.

A steward tacked his way towards them. 'Can you go back inside, please? The deck's too slippery to be walking on. We'll be docking in twenty minutes.'

As she pushed Ryan towards the doors, Madeline glanced back at the sea and wondered if there was time to throw the incriminating envelope overboard. She no longer wanted to take it to the police; it tainted her, pulling them both back, a harmful omen that reminded her of the mariner's albatross.

She wanted to be home in Waterloo Road, where even her husband posed a smaller threat than the disturbing stranger who had invaded their life in France. She tried to imagine any circumstances that would present her discovery in a different light, but knew the truth in her heart: that he had killed and robbed and gone undiscovered, and would do so again if he felt threatened. She had learned to recognize the poisons that could fester and ripen inside him, knew it was her duty to warn the authorities, but feared they would bully and perhaps even implicate her. She could not find the energy within herself to set the process in motion. Instead, she was taking the coward's way out and running away. There would be no more confrontations with violent men. She had to think of her son's safety.

As the ferry lowered its great steel doors on the snow-swept dock, she waited with her hands on Ryan's shoulders, preventing the impatient boy from charging forward.

'Are we going to catch another train?' he asked, looking up at her. 'Can't we get a car?'

Suddenly driving seemed a better option; she would be able to hire a vehicle and take Ryan to the South-West. She had relatives there, and it would be a way of making up for her lack of judgement with Johann, to let him enjoy some of the wonderful places she had never been able to see as a child. They could drive back to London before the money ran out. 'All right,' she told him. 'We'll visit your aunt in Cornwall. We'll hire a car.'

At customs, her fingers closed around the packet containing Johann's other identity. Its secrets were burning her hand. She wanted to speak out, but the sour-faced young officer who checked her passport and waved her through showed no inclination to even acknowledge her presence.

As she made her way to the EasyCar kiosk, she felt that she was being watched. Most likely there were CCTV cameras trained on them, checking for aberrant behaviour patterns and warning signs among the new arrivals. Surely he would never come here, where so much public life was monitored by security systems? Yet he had seemed entirely comfortable in Monaco, the most heavily policed country in the world. He was so convinced that no one would ever be able to catch him that he had tested himself there.

She recalled the way he had kept looking for the cameras in

each street they entered, almost daring them to pick him out. How close had she come to placing herself and Ryan in danger? His victims had been chosen for the sake of expedience, so he could gain their identities. This fact alone made him mystifyingly complex; he was no serial killer, attacking for gratification. Instead, he seemed to view his actions as the mere removal of obstacles standing in his way. The pattern, she had learned, was classic.

'Mum, she's talking to you.' Ryan tugged at her arm, pointing to the car-hire lady.

'Did you want a manual saloon or an automatic?' asked the counter girl.

'Automatic. I need to drop it off in London.' While she filled in the forms, Ryan wandered to the glass wall and looked out at the falling snow. He was making patterns in the condensation when he saw Johann walking across the slush-scabbed forecourt towards the truck park. He opened the door and slipped outside.

'Johann!' he called, running after the man he had started to consider his new father. 'Wait, we're over here!'

Johann stopped in mid-stride and looked back. When he recognized the boy, he waved back unsmilingly.

'Can you come with us?'

'I'll be with you soon, Ryan, I promise.'

'Mum's taking me to Cornwall. She's in there hiring a car. Let me get her.'

'No, don't do that.'

'But you don't know where we'll be.' He hung on to Johann's arm.

'Don't worry, Ryan, I'll find you.'

Madeline was coming out of the car-hire kiosk, studying her receipt as she walked. Johann caught up with her in the snowy shadows of the dockside, the treacherous swell of ice-grey waves rising and plunging beside them.

'I don't understand you,' he said, seizing her arms, holding her close. 'You run away from me before I can explain, so I have to come after you. I know I am bad, I know what I have done, but you can save me, Madeline, you can make me good.'

'Leave me alone.' She was forced to shout because the wind was so strong in their ears. 'You're a murderer.' There were other words, but they were lost to the whirling sky.

'Yes, it is true, I cannot deny what I have done. But you—'

As she crushed Ryan to her side and ran from the quay, slipping on sea-wet concrete, she thought, *He means to kill us both. I'll never let him near Ryan, never. Whatever I do, no matter how terrible, it will be for the sake of my son.*

19

INTIMATIONS

DS Janice Longbright closed her mobile and perched on the edge of the desk, crossing her legs in a slither of caramel nylon. It was now quarter to six, and Giles Kershaw had returned with his preliminary notes on the examination of Oswald Finch's body. The shell-shocked members of the PCU had been gathered in Longbright's office, although no one had yet managed to contact Raymond Land, who had last been seen tottering back from an extended Masonic luncheon with his Home Office liaison man, Leslie Faraday, in Covent Garden.

'Have you spoken to John and Mr Bryant?' asked Dan Banbury, following the unit's odd tradition of referring to May by his first name and Arthur by his last.

'It's not necessary to raise your hand, Dan, you're not in school. No, I thought I'd call them in a minute, with all of us here. Giles, have you got a time line for us?'

'Hang on a mo.' Kershaw unfolded his spindly legs and rose to stand before the blackboard he had erected under the window. 'I'd usually PowerPoint my notes to you all, but we have no network.' He glanced accusingly at Banbury, who seemed not to mind. Bimsley had chosen to sit next to Mangeshkar, who had moved her legs as far away from him as possible. April sat at the back, watching intently, her arms folded protectively across her chest.

'The bruise on Oswald's neck wasn't the only one,' Kershaw explained. 'I found another, identical in shape and discolouring, on the left side of his chest. It would appear he suffered a thrombotic attack after getting thumped on the opening of his pulmonary artery and aortic valve, which prevents blood from reversing its flow back into the left ventricle of the heart. The convulsion interrupted the rhythm of his heart and stopped it. The whole thing happened very quickly, and was over in a few seconds. He was standing when this happened, and immediately fell down beneath the counter.'

'How do you know that?' asked Mangeshkar. 'How can you be sure he didn't simply suffer a traumatic episode due to the weakness of his heart? Why does it have to be linked to his bruises?'

'The marks go deep, Meera; they were made with great force. The one on his chest has actually torn several layers of the epidermis. They weren't caused by just bumping into the furniture, and they're fresh enough to have occurred at his time of death. There's a secondary contusion on his skull where he glanced against the table edge as he fell. His right shoe twisted, causing a faint spiral pattern on the flooring, and he instinctively put out his left hand to break the fall, so he still had consciousness at that point. Dan lifted a partial palm print from the floor.

'No instruments of any kind have been removed from the wall cases, and there are no prints on the blades of the broken fan, even though I had my money on it having been used as a weapon. It couldn't have simply spun down, striking him twice in succession. It's not a boomerang. But as a weapon it would have carried prints easily, so I was surprised that none showed up. However, when I examined the clean edges of one of the blades, I found a tiny skin impression that suggests it might have come into contact with Finch's neck.'

'If you're telling us that someone else was there – leaving aside that impossibility for a moment – and chose to hit him with a ceiling fan, surely you can run a DNA match on his sweat marks, and separate them out from any other prints in the room?' asked Banbury, whose love of technical wizardry made him want to press the human genome into service in the form of computer code.

'Dan, we have Finch's prints on file, and I promise you, there are no outsider prints at all. I dusted the place from top to bottom, and all we have are finger marks from other members of the PCU. I know that because you're all on file. So, our time line.' He produced a piece of chalk and began scratching away on the board, oblivious to the teeth-gritting noise it made. 'Finch arrived for work this morning at eight a.m. There was nothing booked on his schedule for the day, so it's hard to be totally accurate what he got up to. Dan, you checked the phone log.'

'No outgoings in that time, and the internals don't register, but we know he called Land to talk about his position here at the unit, because Land called Mr Bryant to discuss the matter further.'

'Then Sergeant Renfield came over from Albany Street station with a docket for the body that was delivered to the Bayham Street Morgue.'

'Finch had a case?'

'He'd agreed to help Renfield out. Young unidentified female, probably living rough on the streets of Camden, found dead in the doorway of the Office shoe shop this morning, corner of Inverness Street and Camden High Street – exposure combined with a drug intake. Colin, you rang around the hostels, didn't you?'

'No obvious candidates yet, Sarge. I'm waiting for the Eversholt Street Women's Refuge to call me back.'

'Did Oswald carry out an autopsy on her?' asked Meera.

'He's supposed to wait for hospital notes,' said Banbury, 'but he'd started some preliminary exploration, then locked her back in the body drawer. I just took a quick look at her, and now the cadaver can't be moved anyway, at least until Giles and I have finished in there. No one's come forward to claim her, and I don't suppose they will straightaway.'

'Did Oswald leave any notes?'

'Just an estimated time of death on the report form, which he set at five thirty a.m., an external description and some basic observations about her condition.'

'No other appointments or personal notes to himself?'

'Nothing that I can find,' said Banbury. 'There's no obvious point of entry for an intruder, and no way of gaining access. Giles, you checked Finch's body for long-term defects, didn't you?'

'He shows some symptoms of having had a weak heart,' said Kershaw. 'I took a look at an artery and found it pretty furred up. I don't suppose he'd have lasted very long in retirement, but I don't think he killed himself. There's a two-centimetre cut on the palm of his left hand, fresh and very fine. It looks like it was made with the point of a scalpel. He'd put a new blade in this morning and dropped the wrapper in his bin. I have to say that the position of his body suggests an attack. What if he was surprised, raised his hand in defence, was jabbed, and the attacker struck again with the handle? Of course, that raises more questions than it answers. Anyway, here's your time line.' He tapped the blackboard with his chalk.

'Finch enters the morgue at eight a.m. and locks the door on the inside, returning the key to its hook. He gets an immediate call from Renfield saying that he's on the way over with a case. Renfield turns up ten minutes later with someone, presumably a paramedic, drops off the body and they leave. Finch starts work, then stops when he realizes he won't get the hospital notes until later in the day – there's a bit of confusion about this at the moment – so he locks the corpse in one of the drawers and starts to write up his notes. We know that at around eight thirty a.m. he calls Land and tries to get him to rescind his resignation. Apparently he began to have doubts about leaving after talking to Mr Bryant yesterday. At nine forty-five a.m. I go to see him about his refusal to recommend me for the position of unit pathologist, and I admit it, we have a bit of a contretemps. While we're arguing, Meera turns up, wanting to sit in on the rest of the autopsy.'

'It couldn't have been very comfortable for you,' said Long-bright, 'having to confront the man who had just destroyed your chances of promotion.'

'I don't much care for your implication,' Kershaw said, bridling. 'I'll admit I wasn't *comfortable* about seeing him, but I'm a professional. I didn't let my true feelings show.'

'How long did you stay?'

'Only a few minutes. Oswald told me he was waiting for documentation to come through before continuing his case-work, so I left him to it. I don't think he's legally bound to wait for it, but that's what he told me.'

'We know he was in an argumentative mood. Did he seem different in any other way?'

'It's hard to remember.' Kershaw seemed so uncomfortable with the question that Longbright had the distinct impression he was holding something back.

'And to your knowledge he had no further visitors.'

'No, but we have no way of being sure because no one has to get signed in at Bayham Street. You can walk in from outside without being seen so long as you have the access code to the front door. The morgue is cold, and his body temperature may have fallen sharply. I say *may* because the thermostat's on the fritz and I can't tell if the heaters were on the whole time, but I assume he died between ten a.m. and eleven a.m.'

'By which time it was already snowing hard,' Longbright added, making a note.

'Yes, that's an odd thing,' Kershaw admitted. 'The morgue lights were off, and given the size of the windows it means that Finch must have been sitting in virtual darkness, which means that his killer – if a killer it was – attacked without needing much light. There's a street lamp outside, but the bulb is broken. And as I say, the key to the morgue door was still hanging on the hook.'

'I don't suppose we have a way of checking how many other keys were still in place at any time through the day.'

'I know they were there before, because I had to borrow one, and the remaining keys were all there when I returned mine an hour later.'

'There must be absolute secrecy about this while we conduct an internal investigation,' Longbright warned. 'If that Home Office hit man Kasavian finds out what's happened here, we're dead.'

'We won't be able to let John and Uncle Arthur know yet,' said April. 'They're only contactable on their mobiles until they get to their hotel, and the lines of communication won't be secure.'

'Then we'll have to work by ourselves for the time being,' Longbright told her. 'We have the only keys to Bayham Street, and we daren't admit anyone else to the investigation, so I'm afraid we have to consider ourselves all under house arrest here at the unit until we can get to the truth.'

20

SNOW-BLIND

'*Qanugglir*,' Bryant enunciated so carefully that his dental plate nearly fell out, 'snowy weather. *Kanevcir*, first snowfall. *Kanut*, crusty snow. *Anymanya*, a snowstorm. *Igadug*, a blizzard. *Qaniit*, feathery—'

'All right,' May interrupted. 'I know you know all of the Inuit words for snow – '

'Sixty-seven,' said Bryant absently, staring out of the windscreen.

' – but it's really not very helpful. In fact it's rather annoying.'

The blizzard showed no sign of abating. The wind had risen to a roar, lifting the snow that had already fallen, swirling it into bleached dunes. The high hedges were buried beneath sculpted white plumes, the sides of the roadway banking into an immense channel, its centre half-mile packed with marooned vehicles, anchored in undulating spines of snow. A nearby tree appeared to have been hung with crystal pendants.

Visibility had fallen to around six metres. The vehicle in front of them, a green designer SUV sold on its ability to bounce bounty hunters across rugged terrain but generally owned by middle-class mothers who insisted on driving their fragile darlings to school, had been hastily abandoned, and was subsumed to the top of its wheel arches. The Spar truck behind was starting to look like a Rachel Whiteread sculpture. Looking in his rear-view mirror, May could see the driver arguing into his mobile phone. In the last few minutes, one or two passengers had attempted to alight from their vehicles, only to be driven back by the pounding winds.

'How long can this keep up?' asked Bryant, smudging a clear patch on the windscreen with the back of his woolly mitten.

'It's Dartmoor,' replied his partner. 'Normal weather rules don't apply out here. We have a full tank, but we'll be in trouble if the engine dies. We can't stay in this cabin without heat.'

'It's a marvellous thing, snow,' said Bryant wistfully, appearing not to hear his partner's concerns. 'As much as six feet can fall in a single day, and the volume is ten times that of the equivalent moisture in rainfall. I remember snowfalls in the East End that were so heavy they pulled down the overhead telegraph lines, temperatures so low that sheets of ice slid like guillotine blades from the roofs of cornering taxis.'

In the last few years, Bryant seemed not to concern himself with common fears. He made his way through the world in a state of blithe cheerfulness, leaving a trail of concern and distress behind him. Others fretted for his welfare far more than he did himself, and May had been pressed into service as a professional worrier for everyone's well-being.

'We cannot stay here,' May reiterated. 'People die stranded on Dartmoor, Arthur. It happens almost every winter.'

'Can I light my pipe?' Bryant's watery blue eyes rolled up at him beseechingly. 'It would help me think.'

'No, you cannot. I daren't open the windows. We'll freeze to death.'

'A lot of mysterious goings-on on Dartmoor, you know,' said Bryant, digging in the glove compartment. 'I was reading about them in my guide book. Hound Tor is haunted by the spirit of a hanged woman, and Okehampton Castle is positively alive with the ghosts of slaughtered nobles. And apparently you should never drive on the B3212 between Postbridge and Two Bridges after dark because a pair of dismembered hairy hands are liable to wrench the steering wheel from you, sending you careening into a bog. Then there are the Piskies, who are the unbathed children of Eve, exiled by God from the Garden of Eden and sent to Devon, who are said to contain the souls of dead babies, and of course witchcraft is still practised today across Dartmoor, especially near Ringastan. That's a stone circle excavated in 1903 that was found to have had a false floor in it, filled with coils of human hair.'

'Really, Arthur—'

'Oh, I know all this seems like old hat, but during the winter solstice of 2005 the police at Moortown found half a dozen sheep with their necks broken and their eyes torn out. Their corpses were arranged in occult patterns. Seven more dead sheep were found arranged in the shape of a heptagon at an ancient pagan sacrificial altar in the shadow of Vixen Tor. Perhaps we've been stranded here for a reason.' Bryant rolled his blue eyes meaningfully as the wind moaned around the van.

'This is ridiculous. I'm going to call Janice and see if she can find out what's happening with the emergency services.' May speed-dialled her number on his mobile and listened.

But Bryant had started having morbid thoughts; he looked out at the ferociously blank landscape and wondered what it would be like to die outside, a painless numbing of the senses accompanied by a shutting out of light, kinder than drowning or even fading in a hospital bed; a sort of suspended animation that held the possibility of being reversed. Snow White and Sleeping Beauty had both slipped into comas, only to be revived by the heat of another human life. He felt something – a faint tremor, a flutter of the heart, a fleeting premonition that beat overhead like a death's-head moth and vanished with the intrusion of May's voice.

'Well, what are they suggesting? Of course we're going to stay put, we don't have much of a choice. Call me back, then.'

May was staring oddly at the phone, as if trying to understand what he had heard. 'What's the matter?' asked Bryant, suddenly concerned about what he had missed.

'I don't know. She sounded very strange. I think she wanted

to tell me – I don't know, exactly.' He shook the idea from his head. After working for so many years with each other, they had developed certain intuitions that went beyond their voiced opinions. 'She says the whole of South-West England has been hit by blizzards. They're trying to mobilize snow ploughs and marine emergency helicopters, but all rescue vehicles have been grounded until the high winds abate. Traffic's at a standstill everywhere, and there's worse weather to come. We have no choice but to stay put here.'

'I wouldn't worry; it won't take long to clear the roads, and meanwhile we have food and water and heat. Apart from Alma's surplus sandwich mountain, there's a hamper in the back. I was taking it down for the raffle.'

'We should check on the other drivers, warn them to stay in their vehicles, try to make sure they're all right.' May opened his window and peered out, trying to see, but the blast of icy snow that burst into the van cab forced him to quickly reseal it. He dropped back in his seat, frustrated. 'I knew I shouldn't have left London.'

Several hundred metres behind them on the road, Madeline and Ryan sat inside their stalled Toyota clinging to each other as the temperature plunged. Snow had soaked a length of stripped cabling and shorted out the vehicle's ignition. 'Don't worry,' she told her son. 'The snow ploughs will come and get us. They're prepared for storms like this.'

'Why doesn't the heater work without the engine running?' Ryan asked. 'It's not like it uses petrol.'

'No, but it runs on electricity. Here.' She had found a red emergency blanket in the boot of the vehicle, but it wasn't wide enough to go around both of them, so she tucked it in around her son, hoping he wouldn't notice that her teeth were chattering. 'When we get home I'm making you hot chocolate and buttered crumpets with melted cheese and Marmite, and you can watch all the TV shows I don't let you watch normally.' Ryan had trusted her and the new man who had come into their lives, only to be betrayed. The least she could do was let him watch some unhealthy television once they were safe and warm again. She hugged him close to her, sensing his fragility through the rough blanket.

'Mum, I can't breathe, you're squashing me,' he called from within the folds.

'Don't worry,' she said, convincing herself, 'everything's going to be all right.'

'Where's Johann? Why can't he come with us?' said the muffled voice.

She closed her eyes and tried to avoid imagining the dangers that might lie in wait for them both.

'We ain't going anywhere in this.' The van driver smelled of rolling tobacco and cabbages. His name was Danny, and he was transporting cartons of counterfeit cigarettes to his supermarket in Cornwall. He had offered Johann a lift from the port because he felt the police were less likely to stop trucks with co-drivers. Johann had watched the silver Toyota setting off ahead of them, and had created an absurd story about needing to keep within sight of his ex-wife because she was worried about breaking down on the motorway.

Danny had heard worse, and dutifully stayed within ten vehicles of the Toyota. It wasn't difficult; driving conditions had rapidly become atrocious, and no one was overtaking or speeding. He'd expected to cut off the edge of the A38 and make a stop outside Plymouth, where he had promised to deliver some whisky to his business partner, but the traffic had slowed to a crawl, and had now stopped altogether.

'I've never seen weather like this, man.' Danny tapped out a Romanian Rothmans and lit up. 'It's as far as we go until the ploughs get here.'

'Don't worry about it,' Johann told him. 'I can see my wife's car from here.' He opened the passenger door and swung himself down into the snowdrift. 'Thank you for the ride.'

'But I didn't get you there,' Danny called after him.

'You got me as far as I needed to go,' Johann shouted back, but his words were torn up by the driving gale.

*   *   *

'They're stranded in a blizzard somewhere at the southern edge of Dartmoor,' said Longbright. 'April, try to get an update on conditions from the Devon and Cornwall police. Tell them we've got a couple of senior officers snowed in, see if we can get them out and brought back here. Colin, you'd better try and track down Raymond Land. We'll have to tell him what's happened. Dan, you come with me to Bayham Street and give me a walk-through.'

'What about me?' asked Giles Kershaw, rising from his seat.

'You stay here, Giles. You had both motive and opportunity. Out of all of us, you're most under suspicion of murder. Meera, make sure he doesn't go anywhere and remember you're under suspicion as well. Neither of you are to use a phone or a computer until I return. You're on your honour. Don't make me have to enforce this by calling in the Met.'

My God, she thought, running down the steeply angled stairs to the street, *if we really have a murderer inside the unit, there's no one I can rely on to help me.*

21

LOCKDOWN

As a child, young Oskar Kasavian had shopped his mother to the police for smoking a joint at a Belgravia embassy party held for King Zog of Albania. This had been a serious matter because his parents both worked in the Foreign Office, and the family were in the middle of delicate negotiations with the Italians. It was only his father's status as a politically appointed diplomat that prevented severe repercussions. Relations soured between Kasavian and his mother, to the point where she disowned him on her deathbed, but Oskar didn't care. By then he knew how to operate within the complex ecosystem of interdepartmental government politics, and used the knowledge to his full advantage.

By the time he had been promoted within the Home Office to handling matters of national security, he knew how to step on time-serving ministers like Leslie Faraday and gently squash them until they carried out his instructions without ever realizing they had lost control of their own departments. The middle managers of Whitehall lived in fear of him, and even his superiors felt a sense of relief when he left the room. Only Arthur Bryant had managed to bloody his nose over the investigation of the prankster-murderer the newspapers had nicknamed the Highwayman. Kasavian's relationship with a married tabloid editor had been exposed, and the PCU had blackmailed him into dropping his assault on unit funding in return for their continued silence about his affair.

Now, he felt, it was time to take revenge.

Her Royal Highness Princess Beatrice of Connaught, who performed no public duties and was known to the press as 'Princess Poison', was the Baroness Katarina-Marchmaine von Treppitz, Viennese daughter of Baron von Treppitz and the Countess Alexandria Spenten-Berger, and was usually in the headlines for the wrong reasons. She had allegedly told a group of Chinese diners in a Chelsea restaurant to 'go back to Chinky Land', and had been accused of everything from expressing pro-Nazi sympathies to living in a Regent's Park apartment subsidized by the Queen. Her office also had occasion to correspond with Oskar Kasavian, and she had been persuaded, in the interest of public relations, to make a rare royal visit to a government law-enforcement unit representing experimental policing techniques, namely the Peculiar Crimes Unit.

Kasavian's plan in arranging the trip was ostensibly connected with the princess's desire to take more of an interest in government-funding initiatives. She had a reputation for being outspoken and litigious, something journalists rarely forgave, but had seemed perfectly charming on the few occasions that Kasavian had dealt with her. He reasoned that, as his hands were still tied in the matter of closing down the PCU, which he considered a ridiculous squandering of resources, he would get someone else to do it for him. When Princess Beatrice saw the chaotic shambles that existed above Mornington Crescent Tube station, he felt sure that her acerbic comments would bring the harsh spotlight of attention on to the PCU and provide him with the ammunition he needed to shut its doors once and for all. Then he would be able to re-allocate funding to a new unit under his personal supervision.

When the Princess's office confirmed that the conductor of the Vienna Boys' Choir had slipped and broken his baton wrist outside a Salzburg McDonald's, the sudden cancellation of his royal performance allowed her to schedule a brief visit to the unit in its place, which meant that she would be stepping daintily from her limousine on to the mean streets of Mornington Crescent this Thursday afternoon at five. Kasavian quickly informed Leslie Faraday, who sent a protocol package to Raymond Land, who was in the middle of opening it and reading the contents with a dropping jaw just as Janice Longbright walked into his room.

'He can't do this,' Land murmured. 'He can't send a royal visitor around at such short notice, not here, not now – not *her*.' He had always known that the unit's victory over Kasavian would be temporary, and that he would come back fighting, but this was more underhand than he had imagined. 'They're heading here for an inspection in less than two days' time. Our computer system is down, there are cables and equipment boxes and God knows what all over the floor and our two chief detectives are away on some kind of bizarre winter holiday.' Well, the last part was perhaps a blessing, as Mr Bryant could not be trusted to avoid controversial topics, and had expressed his cynicism about certain members of the royal family a number of times in the past. 'Hello, Janice, what do you want?' Land eyed the strangely garbed sergeant with suspicion. *Why is she sporting that outlandish hairstyle and wearing a pencil skirt?* he wondered. *Would it kill her to dress normally?*

'Sorry to be the bearer of more bad news, Raymond. Oswald Finch has been found dead in the Bayham Street Morgue, a heart attack brought on by blows to the neck and the chest, and our lads think it looks like murder.'

'In our own pathology centre?' Land all but squeaked.

'I'm afraid there's worse, because it looks like an inside job. On that basis, we're conducting an internal murder investigation with our own staff as suspects.'

'Good God, woman, does anyone else know about this?'

'No, sir. Not yet, at least. Thought I'd better tell you.'

'Then for heaven's sake don't tell anyone else. If word of this gets out, it will kill us. You'd better get Bryant and May back here at once. They'll know what to do.'

Longbright chose to ignore the snub. 'I can't, sir. They're stuck in a snowdrift on the edge of Dartmoor on their way to a spiritualists' convention. I haven't told them what's happened yet. Do you want me to call them?'

Having to make spot decisions without the advice of a superior was the kind of situation Land dreaded. He worried a nail between his teeth, trying to think. If he turned down Faraday, the minister would be instantly suspicious, and would probably send Kasavian around to the unit to sniff out trouble.

'We daren't tell them what's happened,' he said finally. 'The Home Office is sending Princess Beatrice of Connaught here for a full demonstration of the facilities. Kasavian's doing it to embarrass and discredit us, but he doesn't know the half of it. He thinks Arthur will be here to make a mess of things. Imagine how thrilled he'll be when he discovers the truth. They're expecting to be shown a crime lab, not a crime scene. We can't turn them down; it would be admitting defeat. There's only one thing for it: Oswald's investigation must be concluded before the princess arrives. There must be no sign of anything untoward having happened.'

'I'm afraid that's going to be a little difficult, sir,' Longbright informed him. 'Access to the morgue was strictly limited to those of us inside the unit, and you know what Finch was like, he pretty much upset everyone in the course of last week, so our own staff members will have to be kept here under house arrest.'

'Suffering Jesus, if Kasavian finds out we can't even solve a murder taking place on our own property, involving our own staff, he'll make damned sure we'll get shut down instantly, so that he can reallocate his funding elsewhere. To think of the things I've survived here, from Bryant blowing up the building to carpenters falling through the floor – you have to sort out this mess.'

'I've already grounded everyone at the unit until we have a clearer picture of what happened,' she informed him.

'Good.' He rose to leave. 'Well, I suppose that's a start. You can fill me in on the rest in the morning.'

133

'I'm afraid that means you as well, sir. You also had access to the morgue keys.'

Land's eyebrows rose to where his hairline would have been had he still owned hair. 'That's outrageous! Oswald and I were old friends. My wife went crown green bowling with him.'

'You refused to take back his resignation. Did he threaten you in any way? Place you in a difficult position?'

'I will not be interrogated by my own staff sergeant!' Land roared, clearly mortified. 'And you have no right to keep me here.'

'I'm afraid I do, sir. I've been appointed acting head in Mr Bryant's absence – he inserted the clause in my contract when you renegotiated it – so you'd better make yourself comfortable, because I think it's going to be a long night.'

Longbright left the spluttering department head and returned to her office to call the detectives.

May answered on the second ring. 'Things are pretty bad here, Janice,' he said before she could speak. 'I don't know how long it's going to be before we can get free.' There was a hesitation on the other end of the line. 'You're holding something back from us. What's happened?' He knew instinctively that something was wrong.

'It's Oswald,' she told him, explaining the circumstances of the pathologist's death. 'This is starting to look like an internal problem. I think I know what to do, but I need your advice on how to go about it.'

'You'd better tell us everything Giles and Dan have found since the body was discovered,' said May. 'Poor old Oswald. I'll see what we can do to help. After all, it's not as if we're going anywhere.'

Just then, Banbury stuck his head around the door.

'Call him back,' he told Longbright. 'I need to talk to you right now. I think we have a lead.'

22

CONFRONTATION

'Poor, poor Oswald,' said Bryant, shunting down into his overcoat and ruminatively sucking the last of the Humbugs. 'What a terrible thing to happen.'

'You two spent decades being vile to each other. Don't tell me you've had a change of heart.'

'No, of course not; he was perfectly disgusting and managed to upset everyone he ever met, but that doesn't mean I'd wish him dead. They can rule out suicide. Oswald had last-minute regrets about his retirement, but he'd paid off his mortgage and was about to buy a new car. I know, because I lent him the deposit. That's not the action of a man about to kill himself.'

'Come on, Arthur, you know that room. If the windows are sealed, there's no other way in or out except by the main door.'

'Then someone borrowed a key and copied it, which makes his death a premeditated act. The corridor outside is secured at the main entrance by a code panel, but you'd only have to watch from the road to see someone key in the numbers and memorize them. Or you simply go in as someone else is entering and wait in the toilets until the coast is clear. Kids do it all the time. Oswald used to complain about them leaving lager cans in the hall. No, access to the building isn't the issue; it's motive.'

'You said he upset everyone.'

'Yes, but you don't plan someone's death just because they were a bit grumpy with you. I'm talking about a real motive, and I can think of at least three. One, he might have been attacked by somebody trying to get back at the unit. Two, he could have surprised someone in the act of stealing drugs. Three, there's the possibility that his death was the result of action taken by a disgruntled member of the public.'

'I don't understand.'

'What did Oswald do for a living? Pronounce upon the dead. Anyone who sets themselves up as a public judge will always have enemies. We should try the more obvious routes first. Tell Dan to run an inventory and check to see if anything is missing from the room. It would have to be something worth killing for. Of course, there's another explanation . . .' He clattered the boiled sweet around his false teeth, shrinking ever further into his coat. May waited patiently for him to resume.

'Well?' he asked.

'Oh, you wouldn't like it,' said Bryant annoyingly. 'I was thinking of Edgar Allan Poe. Let Janice and the others go through the obvious routes of investigation first. It'll do them good to try and sort this out without our help.'

'Our help?' May repeated. 'Should I remind you that we are marooned in the middle of nowhere? We're not placed to offer anyone our help.'

'Rubbish,' countered Bryant. 'We have mobiles, satellites, cameras and the Internet, don't we? All those technological marvels you're forever banging on about. Now's the time to put your money where your mouth is, matey. Let's see how wonderful they really are.' Bryant folded his arms with a smug smile. 'You've got your PDSA on you, whatever it's called, your Raspberry; let's see you use it.'

'You mean my PDA. The PDSA is the People's Dispensary for Sick Animals. And it's a BlackBerry.'

'You can start by giving them a tip,' said Bryant. 'Tell Janice there's an old lady who lives opposite the entrance to the Bayham Street Morgue – number thirty-five I think, first floor. She's in a wheelchair and hardly ever goes out. She'll probably be able to provide a list of visitors for the entire day. Then you can give me the keys to the back door of the van. Given the circumstances, I think we might open the hamper and make a start on the veal-and-egg pies.'

Johann pushed forward through the drift in the direction of the marooned Toyota. In the few metres he had progressed, the snow had burned his cheeks and silted against the front of his blue nylon windcheater. His actions became automatic, the raising and lowering of each leg in turn, pushing against an icy force field of wind, his sense of survival bypassing reason.

He could no longer recall his purpose in confronting Madeline. The part of him that wanted to reassure her of his devotion was fast giving way to something more primal. Although he longed to believe that she would understand what he had been through – what he was still going through – and would somehow forgive him, he suspected she was going to react as women always reacted, by shutting him out and regarding him with fear and hatred. He knew, at that point, he would have to surrender her. It seemed his life was destined to be nothing more than a series of dashed hopes and false starts.

He looked behind him, and saw that his footprint trail had already been obliterated. The sight was a confirmation of his invisibility. He longed to be seen by those who sat in judgement of him. Madeline had trusted him because he had encouraged her to do so, but sooner or later everyone was faced with a test, when meaning well was no longer enough, and now it was his time to be tried again. He wanted the corridor to open to the sky once more, but the snow-laden clouds blocked the stars from sight.

At first when he knocked on the snow-crusted window, there was no response. Then a gloved mitten wiped an arc through the ice ferns, and he saw her frightened face. She started and immediately grappled with the door lock, but he was too fast for her, wrenching open the rear door and sliding himself in beside the dozing boy in the red blanket.

'I just want to talk,' he said quickly. 'I need to tell you about myself, about how I survive.' He put his arm around the boy, knowing that she would not dare to leave without him. It was cruel, but the only way to make her pay attention.

'I know what you are,' she replied, turning to move his hand from Ryan. 'Get away from my son. What are you doing here?'

'You don't understand, Madeline, I meant everything I said. There are things—'

'Why are you doing this to us?' She tried to stare him down through the car's aquarium light, shaming him. 'Everything you told me was a lie; you're not who you said; you wanted me to trust you and I did. I don't know what you are, you're worse than all the others because you're—' She stopped short, knowing that Ryan lay between them. The car's interior was icy; she could see her son's breath, and the sight made her fear for him. 'I want you to get out and leave us alone. I won't go to the police, I won't say anything, but you can't be near my son.'

'I had to follow you, but I am not crazy, Madeline, I just need this one chance to put things right, I need you to believe in me.' His breath came with difficulty; since childhood he had been prone to fits of panic. He fought to keep his emotions under control. 'Please, Madeline, we're stuck here, there's nowhere else to go. You're the only one who can help.'

'What do you expect from me, Johann – I don't even know what to call you, because that's not your real name. You think we're going to be together after what I know about you? You think I can save you from yourself?'

'Yes,' he said, softly and sincerely. 'I do believe that. We both live beneath God's watchful eyes but you are as alone as me. We can help each other.'

During the conversation she slowly reached across the seat, closing her hand over the envelope that contained the proof of his guilt. So long as she had this weapon against him, she could feel safe. 'Ryan, it's OK, darling, just come over into the front,' she instructed.

The waking boy looked at her in confusion. Johann remained motionless, but finally moved away as Ryan scrambled over into the passenger seat. 'You have to get out now,' she told Johann.

'Mum, you're frightening me,' said Ryan. 'Stop it.'

'You ran from me in France, Madeline, but I needed to talk.'

'I ran from you because you'd broken into that house in the hills, just like you'd stolen the car. Nothing you told me was the truth, Johann. I left an old man dying on the floor above. I don't know what you did to him, but I—'

'I didn't do anything, Madeline. God took him away, so I could use the house.'

'Just like all the other people in the passports you've stolen?' she asked, knowing the answer. 'I saw all the photographs you kept – the women's bodies, their battered faces.'

He seemed dumbfounded by this, and she knew at last that he had run out of lies. Ryan was drawing closer to her. She kept her eyes on Johann's face, sure that if she glanced away now he would guess her intentions. She had learned how to deceive violent men in the course of her marriage. So many conversations with her husband and his brother had turned into cat-and-mouse games of guilt and fabrication.

It was growing dark inside the car as the night and the blizzard cocooned it. She tried to recall which way the door lock opened. 'What do you want with me, Johann?' she asked. 'When do you reach the point where your love for me switches over to hatred, and all you want to do is smash my head in?'

'Mum, no, please – '

For a moment the snow clouds scudded apart, creating a pale pathway to the fading light. The interior of the car grew brighter.

Turning to the window, Johann flinched from the jaundicing snowscape. It was a moment that could not come again; Madeline threw her weight against the driver's door as she unlocked it, hauling Ryan out with her. She was on her feet and braced before he had managed to open the rear door. When he did so, ducking his head to come out, she slammed it back against his skull, catching him hard and crushing his unlowered right leg.

With Ryan pressed against her jacket she turned to run, but her trainers refused to grip against the powdery drifts. She found herself floundering and sliding, her progress confounded by an elemental force that seemed intent on pushing them back. Ahead, the blanched channel of the road appeared and vanished. The tracks between the stalled vehicles had been obliterated. No one was out on the road. Passengers and drivers alike were heeding the police broadcasts to remain inside their cars. Once more, she could expect no help.

She tried to see in through the car windows. There was no time to stop and check each interior. She heard only the bluster of the gale and the thrum of engines.

'This one,' said Ryan suddenly, dragging her over to the passenger door of an abandoned white Vauxhall van, buried in the shadowed drift of a large Spar truck. He tried to turn the handle, but it was either locked or frozen solid. Pulling his mother back to the rear door, he tried again, but this time she helped him and it twisted open. Madeline climbed inside the icy dark vehicle and fell back while he attempted to close the door without dislodging its crust of snow. The door could not be locked, so she made him hold it shut between them, their breath blurring together in grey clouds as they gripped the handle. There was no rear window, and no way of knowing whether he would pass them by.

All they could do now was hang on to the freezing metal and wait.

23

OBSERVATION

'CCTV camera,' said Banbury. 'There was someone in the morgue corridor prior to the time period of Finch's death. He was captured on the hard drive of the security system at Bayham Street. I need to check it out.'

'You're not to leave this building unaccompanied,' said Longbright. 'I have to come with you.'

'I'll need Giles. We work as a team. We'll achieve more.'

'Then bring him as well.' The young forensic scientist's impetuosity might have angered Finch, but proved useful when a quick eye was required at crime scenes. He and Banbury fired ideas and hypotheses off each other and could reach conclusions others missed.

'Getting a positive ID from a piece of blurry monochrome camera footage is going to be a challenge,' warned Banbury as the trio dodged the slush and traffic in Camden High Street. 'But it'll give us the exact moment he appeared, and that's a starting point.'

'Arthur says there's an old lady who lives opposite the mortuary entrance. If we're patient, she might get us a description.'

'If someone else managed to enter that room, there should be evidence of a forced entry, and the lights would have been on,'

Kershaw was muttering. 'Do you think the old lady can tell us that? And how do I really know if anything has been taken? Finch never showed anyone what he kept there. He certainly never catalogued anything properly. None of his ledgers are up to date. He stored most of the important information in his mind. If someone was trying to get back at the unit, there are a lot of easier ways than breaking into a locked room and resealing it to appear as though it was never entered.'

'Mr Bryant thinks we don't need him to sort this out,' said Longbright, but she did not pass on everything Bryant had told her. *Watch Kershaw*, he'd said. *The boy is clever but lacks understanding. He needs to develop his emotional responses.*

She listened to Kershaw and Banbury arguing together as they headed into the Camden side streets, and wondered if it was possible that either of them could have caused the elderly pathologist's death. Finch had been more frail than he pretended; it could have been an accident. At best, a lie. At worst, manslaughter or murder. The DS knew she could not afford to let either of them out of her sight.

Back at the unit, Mangeshkar and Bimsley had taken Bryant's advice literally, and were seated across from each other, trying to solve the puzzle of the medical examiner's death by themselves.

'We know how they think, sort of,' Colin told his fellow DC. 'We should be able to make a positive contribution. Apart from anything else, think how it would help our careers.'

'Bryant would start by looking for some kind of supernatural influence,' said Meera scornfully. 'He probably thinks Finch was cursed by witches, or placed under an evil spell that made him punch himself in the heart.'

'He just uses the process as part of what he calls "Open Thinking", Meera. You don't suppose he really believes all that stuff?'

'I don't? Then come and look at this.' She grabbed Colin's sleeve – his hand would have provided too much contact – and led him to Bryant's room. 'Does this look like the headquarters of London's most advanced crime think tank to you?'

She had a point; on the mantelpiece was Bryant's chased-silver human skull, which had been smuggled out of Tibet by dissident monks and now oozed rank-smelling algae from its brainpan. Beside this, wax from a pair of wonky black candles belonging to a satanic cult had dripped over his copies of *The East Anglia Witches: An Investigation into the Nature of Evil*, *The 1645 Omens of the Apocalypse*, *Grow Your Own Hemp* and *The Beano Christmas Annual 1968*. On the wall, a drawing of a fractal pentagram with a Scraperboard print of a goat's head pinned at its centre was signed 'To Arthur – Happy Winter Solstice, love Maggie.'

'You knew his methods were weird when you were transferred here,' Bimsley reminded her. 'You've also seen the results he gets.'

'Yeah, he almost got John's granddaughter thrown off a roof, didn't he? They managed to hush that one up. He may get results, but only by putting others at risk. I've been based with dodgy units before, but at least I knew what I was dealing with on the problem housing estates. I was thinking of transferring out of here anyway, before this happened. The whole idea has been a mistake. Everyone in the unit is infected with the same weird mind-set. I was taught structure, responsibility, a chain of command; instead I'm surrounded by anarchists and nutters.'

'You don't really want to leave,' Bimsley told her.

'Really? You know that, do you?'

'You're still holding my sleeve.' Bimsley grinned at her.

'At least it's not your hand.'

'It is now.' He pressed his slender fingers into her palm.

'And you – you're the worst of the lot!' She threw his hand aside as if it were a tarantula and stalked from the room.

'You're just playing hard to get,' he called after her. 'I won't wait for ever!'

Eleanor Newman's room had been decorated by her husband in the late sixties, but he had died of a stroke just after laying the last piece of swirly amber carpet, and the place had never been touched again. Longbright felt completely at home in an apartment that resembled John Steed's set from *The Avengers*. She had been sporting the bleached-blonde Ruth Ellis look for long enough now, and felt it might be time to move forward a decade into the Emma Peel era. As Longbright sank back into a black leather Eames chair, Banbury showed Mrs Newman footage of the mortuary corridor from the hard drive, loaded on to his MP3 player.

'Dear me, he looks like a drab grey duck,' said Mrs Newman, rolling her wheelchair a little closer, 'with the hoodie, the baseball cap and the baggy trackie bottoms, the universal dress code of the socially impoverished male. It's not the lack of money, it's the paucity of imagination I find so depressing.' Although her face was densely lined, she still had the bone structure of a model and the posture of a dancer. She examined the images with a keen and careful eye. 'I miss less from this window than your cameras.'

'This is the footage shot from the far end of the corridor,' Banbury explained. 'The lighting isn't very good, but you might be able to tell if this was the boy you saw. It's like regular film footage, just on a little screen. Can you see?'

'Is there any particular reason why you're addressing me as if I'm a five-year-old? I was a camerawoman at Pinewood Studios for thirty years, young man. I may be old, but I probably have a better visual grasp than you. The only difference is that I can afford more memory than this piece of rubbish. Won't they at least buy you a sixty-gig iPod?' She gave the plastic screen a desultory flick with her nail. Kershaw suppressed a laugh as he caught Banbury's disgruntled glare. 'I wasn't at the window when this boy entered the building. The nurse must have been running my bath. No details on his face, but he's got rather a nice bum. It's not the equipment you need to concentrate on; it's the lighting. You say you work for Arthur?'

'That's right, ma'am.'

'I met him in 1968, you know. What a year of riots and revolutions; it felt as if we were on the brink of a reborn world, a wonderful time to be young and idealistic. I tried to get him to go out with me. I suppose that was before either of you was born. Wait, run that back. Any chance of you enlarging the image without it pixelating too much?' She felt for a pair of glasses on her side table and fixed them to her nose. 'The badge on his sweatshirt – I recognize it. Camley Road Canoe Club. It's a ten-minute walk from here along the canal. Funded by Camden Council to keep problem kids off the streets. Upload the shot on to my computer and I'll print you off a screen-grab.'

She indicated the mock-Gothic cupboard behind her. Banbury opened it and found himself looking at twenty grand's worth of state-of-the-art kit. 'I can't get out to the world any more,' Mrs Newman explained, 'so now the world comes to me.'

The Camley Road Canoe Club was a trapezoid of stained concrete perched over the edge of the Regent's Canal. It was surrounded by an estate of neat redbrick dolls' houses with fake lead-light windows and white plastic drainpipes, the architectural equivalent of an Essex girls' hen night. The clubhouse appeared to be shut, but a bored-looking girl with hoop earrings and a dangling fag divorced herself from two male friends and buzzed them in when she saw that they weren't about to go away. 'It's shut,' she told them. 'Ain't open till the weekend.'

'Why's that?' asked Longbright, who had already noticed that she was wearing the badged club sweatshirt.

The girl studied the sergeant's perfectly coiffured Ruth Ellis hair in amazement. 'Shuts early in the afternoons. Council cutbacks, innit.'

'Do you work here?'

'Why?' The girl grouped herself defensively against the youths at her back.

'We're looking for this lad. Wondered if he'd been in recently.'

'Don't know him.' The girl spat smoke, barely bothering to look. One of her friends, a skinny Indian boy with spiked hair and the posture of a boomerang, peered over her shoulder. 'That's Dizzee,' he said firmly. 'He don't come here no more. Got kicked out, innit.'

'Shut up, Pravin,' the girl snapped, clearly not happy about sharing her knowledge with strangers.

'But he was a member of the club.'

'Yeah.' A grudging admittance as she examined the end of her cigarette.

'Then they'll have a record of his address here.' Banbury headed for the reception computer, addressing the Indian boy, who obviously wanted no trouble. 'What's Dizzee's real name? Dylan?'

'Mills,' said the boy. 'Owen Mills.'

'Dylan Mills is the real name of the hip-hop singer Dizzee Rascal,' Banbury explained to the mystified Longbright. 'This kid is smart enough to wear a hood, but dumb enough to wear a badge.' He seated himself behind the reception desk and typed for a minute. 'Here you go, 105 Disraeli House – that's on the Crowndale Estate. Call it in.'

Forty-five minutes later, a very nervous Owen Mills found himself sitting in the interview room at the Peculiar Crimes Unit.

'Welcome to the PCU,' said Longbright, offering a hospitable smile. 'How would you like to help us solve a crime?'

24

REMOTE

She should have felt safe, but knew she was still in danger, even though it seemed Johann had lost them. She sensed him out there, prowling along the straggling line of stalled vans, grocery trucks and half-buried cars. She wondered how long their hiding place would remain safe. The gale had whipped the snow to such a blinding intensity that he was probably in danger of losing his bearings. She had bruised his leg and forehead, but were his injuries and the adverse weather conditions enough to protect them?

Johann felt no pain in the sub-zero temperature as he limped beside the traffic. Some vehicles had come to a stop after sliding from the icy camber of the road into the gorse and hawthorn, and proved impossible to climb around. Some had been abandoned to elemental forces, and were mutating into molten white shapes. Others showed vague dark figures huddled within.

He had not come dressed for this kind of weather; England was supposed to enjoy mild winters, not suffer arctic conditions. He felt as though everything was starting to slip from his control. In France he had enjoyed freedom to do what he pleased, but now a real threat hung over him. He had managed to outwit the local police before, but if he was captured here, where police technology could identify him in an instant, his past would count against him. It was no longer about the passport she had stolen; it was about his love for Madeline. If he could win her back and save her from herself, he knew she would never betray him. If he failed – well, she was English, and would do the right thing by going to the police to make sure he was locked away.

The boy was her weak spot, and she knew it. Wherever Ryan hid, she would always be close by, somewhere here in the quarter-mile column of blocked traffic slowly being obliterated by the narrowing white valley, surrounded by treacherous moors. He swore under his breath, shaking his head in bitter laughter as he trudged through the thickening drifts, his trainers soaked, his leg aching, his feet wet and numb. *What a fix, what an idiot. This is what happens when you let a woman in.*

He knew that if he didn't protect himself from the blizzard, he would gradually succumb and freeze to death. In the mountain schools they taught you all about subacute hypothermia, and how your metabolism got damaged if your body temperature fell below thirty-two degrees centigrade. It was important to keep checking for warning signs: rapid breathing, confusion, forgetfulness, blue fingers, difficulty swallowing, unsteadiness, the need to urinate. He had been in snowstorms far worse than this, but never without shelter or the right clothes. Nothing looked familiar. The cars had become organic and mysterious, dying creatures whose steel carapaces were rimed with ice. He turned around and tried to shield the snow from his eyes. That was when he spotted Danny's frosted-over Spar truck, twisted across the road at a perilous angle. He made his way back in the direction of his ride and hammered on the passenger window.

Danny leaned across and grinned, flicking open the door. 'Blimey, you picked a good evening to go for a walk, didn't cha?'

'I can't find my friend.' Johann pulled himself into the warm cockpit of the cab and stamped snow from his numb feet.

'Thought you said she was your wife. Course, that's your

business. Nobody's going anywhere in this, mate. You're better off in here with me. There's a generator in the back, and cans of spare petrol, loads of grub. I do this trip every winter, and I've been caught out before. The wind comes off the moor and builds drifts across the road. Never seen it this bad, though.'

'You think everyone is still here?'

'What can they do but stay put? The nearest village is six miles away, and there are rivers and ponds all over the place. You wouldn't want to fall into one tonight. I spoke to my missus in Guildford, and she says it's nearly as bad there. Biggest temperature drop ever recorded in a single day, she reckons.'

'Then we must wait together, where we are safe,' said Johann, as he began to regain the sensation in his limbs.

'Princess Beatrice of Connaught?' Bryant pulled a horrified face. 'How typical of Faraday to think that sucking up to a minor royal is more important than tackling a murder investigation.'

'This is Kasavian's doing,' said May. 'Raymond Land has a hold over him that prevents him from personally closing the unit –'

'– because he knows about the minister's affair with a married woman.'

'Exactly, so Kasavian is craftily getting someone else to provide the ammunition for him while we're stranded here.'

'Can't you turn the heater up? My nose is turning blue.'

'I'm rationing our energy. Those veal-and-egg pies you ate should keep you warm for a few hours. I don't know where you put it all. Besides, you've got plenty of blankets.' May plugged his phone charger into the cigarette lighter. 'I wonder how they're getting on at the PCU.'

'I need to be there,' muttered Bryant. 'I've failed poor old Oswald. I can't be of any use stuck in a snowdrift without my walking stick. Ironic, isn't it? My greatest field of expertise is completely wasted here. There's nothing I don't know about the streets of London. I know where the iron from St Paul's railings came from, and who haunts the Rose and Crown in Old Park Lane, and what went on in the Man-Killing Club of St Clement Danes and the Whores' Club of the Shakespeare's Head Inn, and how to play Mornington Crescent without cheating, and why there was a London craze for electrifying yourself in the mid eighteenth century, but I know *absolutely nothing* about the countryside. Here I'm simply a very, very old fish out of water. If you opened that car door right now and shoved me out, I'd simply lie there and die in the snow. I don't know how to make a bivouac out of curlews' nests or how to tell whether sheep have got conjunctivitis. I can remember only one old country saw, and that's relating to the sighting of one-legged ducks: *Mallard with less than two good feet, rainy day and then some sleet.* I can't look after myself in the open air. In fact, the very term "open air" is anathema to me. I come from a city of closed air.'

'Just as well we don't have to do anything except wait for the emergency services to come and dig us out, then,' said May. 'I suppose I might try one of your boiled sweets.'

'You won't like it,' Bryant warned, watching as his partner popped it in his mouth and pulled a face.

'What flavour is that meant to be?' May asked, tentatively moving his tongue about.

'It's either gooseberry or Bovril. They've been in the same bag for the last five hours, so they probably taste of both. Put me out of my misery and call Janice, would you?'

May speed-dialled the number and spoke to the sergeant. 'Your hunch with the old lady paid off, Arthur,' he said, after listening to her report. 'They've found their witness. A seventeen-year-old West Indian kid called Owen Mills. They're interviewing him now.'

'What time was he sighted leaving the morgue corridor?' asked Bryant.

'Hang on. Janice, Arthur wants to know what time the boy was seen leaving the corridor . . . nine–oh–five a.m.'

'So unless Giles's estimated timings are off, he didn't kill Oswald. How did he get inside?'

'Arthur wants to know how he got in,' May asked, then turned to his partner. 'He just pressed the buzzer.'

'That means Finch admitted him. I wonder why he would have done that. Can you ask her—'

'God, you ask her,' said May, thrusting the mobile at him. 'I can't keep relaying the conversation.'

'Janice, the boy wasn't just loitering; he went there with a specific purpose. Ask him what it was. Act like you know why; you're just seeking confirmation. No, I'll wait.' He rattled the sweet bag at May. 'Want another one?'

'No, thank you.' May spat the brown-and-purple drop into a tissue.

Bryant returned to the phone. 'Just passing by? Well, he's lying. He'd seen someone punch that code and repeated the action to speak to Oswald, who would never have let him in without a very good reason, so the lad must have thought about what he was going to say. Keep trying, I need to talk to John for a mo.' He turned to May. 'What's the one thing that was different about the morgue this morning?' he asked.

'There was a fresh cadaver in it,' said May as an idea dawned.

'Precisely. I'm betting Mills knew the deceased, which was why he went to the morgue: to see the body. Why won't he admit it? Because she was found dead in a shop doorway, and he's frightened of being implicated.'

'So he probably knows she died of an overdose, and that means he might even be the one who supplied or administered it.'

'Possible, but not quite what I'm thinking. If he suspected he'd killed her, he'd be reluctant to walk into a Metropolitan Police compound. Janice: Renfield's overdose case, you need to quiz Mills about his relationship with the girl. He may be able to confirm an ID. OK, I'll call you back.'

Bryant replaced the mobile in its dashboard cradle and briskly rubbed his hands together. 'I think perhaps this could work, crime investigation by remote control. I could do this from the comfort of my armchair at home and never have to visit any more crime scenes. It would be interesting if the boy's appearance at the morgue had some direct influence on Oswald's death, wouldn't it? It might mean the dead girl held a secret worth killing for.'

He picked up the mobile once more and redialled. 'Janice, I know you don't want to let the others out of your sight, but I think it's important that Dan and Giles work together at Bayham Street. I think they've missed something. Yes, I do have an idea but I'm not going to tell you what it is, because this is your chance to prove yourselves. Get them to call me back.' He grinned at May. 'We'll have this whole thing sorted before Princess Poison sticks her royal nose around the door, trust me.'

May knew it was the worst possible declaration Bryant could make, because in his experience a remark such as this usually heralded the arrival of the moment when everything started to go horribly wrong.

25

CONSTRICTION

'I don't know what we're looking for,' said Banbury, flicking on the tic-inducing neon overhead. 'God, it's freezing in here.'

'Oswald never turned up the heating because of the bodies, although he was supposed to keep the place at eighteen degrees centigrade,' said Kershaw, pulling on plastic gloves. 'He completed his training prior to public refrigeration. Everyone revered him as the perfect medical examiner, but he had his peculiarities, just like everyone else. And I can't tell if the thermostat was raised this morning, so we have no exact time of death yet.'

'Stay within the markers.' Banbury pointed at the pathway of yellow tags he had attached between the doorway and the steel dissection table.

'If I do that, I won't find anything new. If there's something to be seen, it'll be found at closer quarters. Bryant was eager to release us. He knows there's more to this than meets the casual eye.'

'How can he? He's stuck in a snowdrift four hundred miles away.'

'They were old friends, despite all those tricks he played on Oswald. He knows what he was likely to do or not do.' Kershaw carefully unlocked the medical cabinets that ran along the rear of the converted gymnasium. 'It looks like we do have something missing here. MEs are required to list everything they keep on their shelves. I thought you checked them.' He pointed to a laminated card placed in a pocket of the door. 'According to the register there's supposed to be a bottle of naltrexone in this space.'

'What's that?'

'It's a type of naloxone, an opioid antagonist. It's a fast-acting drug used to reverse the effect of strong narcotics like heroin and morphine. Addicts often have it as part of their emergency kit. And it's not here, which means Finch must have used it recently. Don't touch the hazard bins, they'll contain sharps. Let me do it.'

He rooted about in the yellow plastic bin-liner for a few minutes, but turned up nothing. Pulling open the body drawer where he had stored the medical examiner, he bent over Finch with a halogen torch.

Banbury wasn't keen on watching his partner study the corpse of a co-worker, and kept his distance beyond the end of the drawer. He was more comfortable examining the circum-stances of crime; dead faces bothered him. 'What are you looking for?' he asked.

'Needle marks. It occurs to me that Finch might have been a user.'

'You think he was a drug addict?'

'No, but we know he suffered from heart disease and plenty of other age-related illnesses. He was a very private man. If he was in pain, he might have covered up the fact and taken something to quell it, like morphine. It's the kind of traditional opiate that would have appealed to him. You take it in tablet form as well. Cancer patients can ingest it as a syrup. It would have made him lethargic, though, and I haven't heard any reports of unusual behaviour on his part. If he'd accidentally overdosed, he would have had reason to use the naltrexone.'

'I thought you already checked his body.'

'I only had time to carry out a preliminary survey before I was accused of murder by the unit's resident Diana Dors.

Besides, Finch's skin tone was naturally jaundiced, and I had no reason to look for opiates.'

'We haven't got much in the way of prints,' said Banbury, disappointed. 'I think Finch was in the habit of frequently cleaning the surfaces with sterile wipes.'

'What about the floor?'

'Sprung wood flooring sealed under a polymer – I might get something more from the carpet tiles, or in the corridor. By the time visitors reached here, their shoes were clean.' His mobile suddenly played the first seven bars of the overture to *Utopia, Limited*. 'Sorry,' Banbury apologized. 'I lent it to Mr Bryant and it came back playing Gilbert and Sullivan. Hello?' He listened for a moment. 'I don't know. Hang on. Giles, the body of the unidentified girl – where are her clothes?'

'Finch probably tagged and sealed them – is that Bryant?'

'Yes, he says to go through everything she was wearing. He thinks Mills might have come back to take something from her.'

'Tell him I'll have a look.' Kershaw tried the steel file cabinets beneath the sink and found what he was looking for. Removing the clear plastic envelope, he unzipped it and shook out a floral miniskirt, black tights, knickers, dirty white Nike trainers, a stained green T-shirt, a man's belt, a grey long-sleeved sweat-shirt and a bra. Everything smelled of alcohol. 'Cheap brands, well cared for but worn for too long. Colour fading from overwashing. No bag.' He upended the packet and found a handful of beaded arm bracelets, the kind sold on every stall in Camden Market.

'There's not much there to tell you about her life,' said Banbury.

'Actually, there's quite a bit,' Kershaw contradicted. 'She started drinking hard and thieving in the last year of her life. A drug user but not dependently so. Probably got kicked out of her parents' house, did some sofa-surfing in old school friends' flats.'

'You can tell that from her clothes?'

'She was a size ten when she bought these things. Everything here was fashionable about a year ago, and the trainers are worn out. Even taking into account the fact that women tend to buy their bras and pants a size too small, Finch's notes suggest she died at a heavier weight than that indicated by her clothes. Hard drugs are appetite suppressants, so that couldn't have been her problem.'

'How do you know she was a thief?'

Kershaw poked his finger through matching holes in the sweatshirt and T-shirt.

'She shoplifted them with the tags intact, then was forced to tear them out. No rings, no money, no purse, no jewellery of value. Either she was robbed on the street or she sold everything she had. If this kid Mills really knew her, he was probably her only friend. What do you think sparked the change in her behaviour?'

'I'm not good with people,' Banbury admitted. 'I stick with surfaces, software and stains.'

'You techies have no soul,' muttered Kershaw, sniffing a trainer. 'She washed, kept herself nice. There's perfume and soap beneath the alcohol; I think it's a Donna Karan brand. Strange that she'd have an expensive perfume but no money to buy clothes.' He set down the training shoe. 'You think you know how children grow up. It's just biology. But something happens: unmentioned damage, a private passion, the shock of lost innocence; the points change and the train gets diverted. How does that work? I wish Bryant and May were here. They're so good at understanding this sort of thing. What would they do now?'

'The only lead is the boy,' said Banbury, 'so they'd ask him what it was he came to take.'

Kershaw stared thoughtfully at the sad little bundle of clothing. 'I thought you said Finch did a preliminary on her?'

'He did. At least, he told several people he was working on the case, and he always made notes as he went along using the Waterman fountain pen Mr Bryant gave him for his birthday.'

'That's what I thought. He's jotted down her height and weight, but that's all.' He held up the ring binder Finch kept on his work table and flipped it open. 'The pen's here with its cap off. Apart from that, his last entry in the book is dated six days ago. No other notes. Why didn't he make any?'

'Maybe he didn't feel they were conclusive enough to set down just yet.'

'If he'd been suffering from the effects of morphine, he wouldn't have been thinking clearly,' said Kershaw. 'You may not want to stay around for this, Dan. I have to perform an autopsy on Oswald.'

'Have you done one before?'

'Plenty of times, at college, but this will be my first live corpse. I'm going to find proof that he was murdered.'

'You're supposed to keep an open mind about the cause of death until you uncover defining evidence.'

'Bryant thinks he was killed.' Kershaw reopened the drawer containing the medical examiner's body. 'That's good enough for me. I'd like to hear what Owen Mills has to say for himself.'

The unheated institution-green interview room was supposed to appear bare and depressing, somewhere witnesses could deliver concise statements before fleeing as quickly as possible. While she waited for Mills's next monosyllable, Longbright thought about pinning up a few movie posters, Ava Gardner and Gregory Peck, perhaps. The boy didn't seem very bright, and was having trouble dragging up any kind of plausible story. First he told them that the street door to the mortuary had been left open and he'd simply walked in. Then he tried to suggest that he and Finch were friends, but could not seem to recall where or when they had met. As for the girl lying dead in the morgue drawer, he had never seen, heard of or met her.

The sergeant knew that when suspects chose to hide the truth, they were better off sticking with very simple statements. The ones who offered too much detail tried so hard to convince that they were rarely believed. While DC Mangeshkar took over the questioning, Longbright slipped outside and rang the senior detectives.

'We're not getting anywhere with him,' she admitted. 'I could really do with your help.'

In the misted cabin of Alma Sorrowbridge's transit van, Arthur Bryant held his hand over the mobile and gave his partner a look of concern. 'John, I have need of your technical knowledge. Is there a way I can get some close-up pictures of the dead girl's body?'

'That should be easy. Let me get Dan Banbury on my phone. If he's still at the morgue I'll have him take digital shots and get them sent to this mobile, but you'll have to specify exactly what you're looking for.'

Bryant rang off with a promise to call back, waiting while Banbury sent through photographs of the dead girl's ankles, her wrists and the back of her neck. The elderly detective raised his bifocals and studied the images. He only needed to search for a few moments. 'Ask Mills to return her neck chain, and while you're at it, ask him what he's done with Oswald's notes.'

'What did you spot?' asked May, puzzled.

'A bit of a long shot. She'd put on weight recently, so I thought we might be able to see if the lividity of the body would point to her wearing a chain that had grown a little tight. With the cessation of circulation, the blood settled gravitationally, but at that point she was still wearing the chain, so it left a white line around the back of her neck, see?' He showed May a photograph of a blotched red neck with a pale thread traversing it. 'The next assumption we might dare to make is that the chain could identify either her or Mills. Perhaps it was engraved with an inscription. He really doesn't want to be linked to her. The constable on Renfield's beat would have searched her and the surrounding doorway for regular forms of ID. Someone should check with him to make sure he didn't remove anything. My guess is the boy holds all the keys to her identity.'

Longbright was beginning to wonder if Owen Mills was only dumb in the sense that he was refusing to talk. He lounged in his chair, legs crossed at the ankles, and stared in silent insolence at the detective sergeant. With time being of the essence, it was too risky to merely wait him out. There was enough evidence to hold him for trespass on government property, but not much else. Mills's pockets were empty; he might have taken the chain and disposed of it.

As the silence in the room stretched into its seventeenth minute, Longbright discreetly checked the time and tried to think of a way to break the deadlock. 'OK,' she said finally. 'Owen, I'm not going to ask anything more about your presence at Bayham Street. We're not getting very far, are we? I'll let you go home for now.'

Mills's deadpan expression glitched with a trace of satisfaction, and he swung lazily to his feet.

'Wait – show me your left hand.'

Reluctantly, the boy opened his fist and raised it. A tiny blue curlicue stained his palm.

'What is that?' Longbright held his wrist and examined the mark. A fragment of mirror lettering revealed the familiar spikes of Finch's strange handwriting.

'You had his notes after all. You crumpled them up with your sweaty palm and transferred the still-wet ink from his fountain pen.'

Longbright rose and walked behind Mills, gently teasing her fingers down the collar of his sweatshirt.

'Hey!' Mills attempted to squirm away, but the DS was too quick for him. She extracted the cheap gold chain from under his shirt and hauled him back to the chair.

'I think you'd better sit down and tell us what you did with the papers you took,' she said, permitting herself a smile. 'Then you can explain why you stole jewellery from a dead girl.'

26

ERADICATION

'I spy, with my little eye, something beginning with S.' Bryant looked out through the frosted windscreen with cheery wide eyes. His white fringe was standing on end, an effect of the lowering temperature. He looked like Jack Frost's grandfather.

'I'm not even going to dignify that with an answer.' May sighed.

'Can't we call them again?'

'You said yourself that they need to stand on their own feet. We won't always be around, you know.'

'I certainly won't be around for much longer if you continue to ration the heater.' Bryant tapped ineffectually at the radio. 'The bulldozers should have been here by now. All they keep saying is that the driving winds are keeping rescuers at bay.'

'This isn't the only road blocked. Presumably the snow's affecting every major route for miles around, and there's more on the way. We're going to be here overnight, so we should try to get some sleep.'

The props in the back of the van were wrapped in old blankets, bubble wrap and plastic bags to protect their edges. Keeping warm would be easy enough, but Bryant worried how the passengers in other vehicles were faring. He knew they should really go and check, but stepping outside now would place them both in danger. Neither man was equipped to face sub-zero temperatures.

They put the heater back on, and were dozing in its desiccating warmth when the fist at their window made them both start. All John May could see was a pair of alarmed brown eyes peering through the furry tunnel of a green hood. He rolled down the glass.

'Thank God,' said the man. 'Nobody else will open their windows. There's been a terrible—'

'Wait,' May shouted. 'I can't hear you. Go round the back.' He climbed out of the van and plodded around it, cracking ice from the frozen rear-door handle. The man in the green parka clambered up and shook down his hood. He was young, Chinese, frightened. If he noticed that he had been seated next to a gigantic gold-painted statue of Ganesh the Elephant God, he chose not to comment. 'I'm in the Honda Civic back there. My engine stalled and the heater died,' he explained. 'I needed to keep warm but didn't have any other clothes in the car with me. There was a truck behind me – I could vaguely see the driver in my rear-view mirror – so I thought I'd ask him if I could sit in his cabin. The truck's side windows were covered in snow and I couldn't see in, so I tried the driver's door. I'm sorry—' The man fought down a wave of panic. 'I need to call the police – my mobile has no battery left, I just needed to tell someone—'

'It's all right, you've found yourself a pair of police officers,' said May.

'He's dead, lying across the seat; someone's cut a hole in his throat. It must have only just happened, because blood is still pouring out. I tried to stop it, but didn't know what to do.' He held up a crimson left hand.

'Was he alone? Did you see a passenger?'

'No, but the door was swinging open. It hadn't been properly closed. I must have only just missed him.'

'It's probably a good thing that you did. You'd better stay here while I go and look.'

'I'm coming with you,' Bryant called from his base deep within the passenger seat.

'It's freezing out there, Arthur. You're better off staying in here.'

'Don't be ridiculous. My blood is so thin I'm virtually reptilian. I haven't felt anything in my extremities since I slipped over and landed on my arse in the Princess Diana Memorial Fountain. Besides, you need my help. You're not as steady on your pins as you once were.'

'I resent that,' muttered May. 'Come on then, just for a minute, but do your coat up properly.'

With the wind trying to whip the handle from his grasp, May had trouble closing the van door until their witness reached out to help him pull it shut. The detectives padded back along the column of stranded cars to the grocery truck, but any footprints that might have been left around it had already been obliterated by the gale. Snow coated their ears and eyes in feathered clumps. The mere act of breathing stung their noses and throats. The sky, the hills, the wind itself: all were white. The moorlands had been transformed into a blanched ice-desert, the trees bent low in frozen peninsulas of frost. May needed gloves and proper boots. His leather town shoes had become soaked in seconds. As he fumbled with the driver's door, he realized he had already lost all sensation in his hands.

'Oh, let me do it,' said Bryant. 'There.' The door came open in a spray of crystal shards.

The driver's body was splayed across the seat on its back with one arm draped across a distended stomach, the mouth agape, as in the throes of a nightmare. The interior of the cabin had been darkened by snow building up across the windscreen, but there was enough light to reveal the hole beneath the driver's chin. In the freezing exposure of the cabin, blood had quickly coagulated and darkened across the upholstery.

'Penknife or scissor wound,' said Bryant. 'Interesting.'

The dead man appeared to be in his mid-forties but was probably younger. He wore the blue overalls provided by his company. A badge read Bentick's – We Deliver. 'Dreadful skin, looks like he hasn't had a drink of water in years,' sniffed

Bryant. 'Subsisted on a diet of cigarettes, coffee and bad motorway food, no doubt.'

May had forgotten to pack the Valiant, his trusted old cinema torch, but he was enough of a pessimist still to carry a pencil flashlight in his jacket. He shone it into the pale wash of light and picked up blood spots on the steering wheel, a streak across the base of the windscreen, a still-wet smear on the dashboard. 'No struggle here,' he told Bryant, 'just surprise and collapse. He was attacked by someone who posed no threat. Someone he probably thought was a friend.'

'The passenger. A hitchhiker, you think? He fled the scene pretty quickly. Blood on the passenger-door handle. He won't last long out there in the blizzard.'

'Not unless he's climbed into one of the other stranded vehicles. Someone else could be in danger. We need to get a description of him somehow. I can't get much from the crime scene in these conditions.'

Bryant looked up at the windscreen. 'I don't understand. This window is snowed over. How could your witness have seen the driver through the glass?'

'You don't think that's our man?' asked May. 'Why on earth would he have come to us?'

'I don't think he faked looking that terrified, John. We can't trust what we see. Snow and wind can do anything to this landscape.'

'OK, let's get back to the van. You're starting to turn blue.'

They trudged back through the white valley of stranded cars. The rear door of the van stood wide open, and without its heater running the Bedford had started to ice solid. Their witness was nowhere to be found. May took his mobile from the dashboard and got connected to the Plymouth constabulary.

'They can't get anyone to the area,' he informed Bryant. 'The Highways Agency has stopped all traffic because the winds are expected to stay at gale force tonight. They're saying that as long as no one's in imminent danger we should just sit tight. They've got GPS and mobile tracking equipment, so they have a rough idea of how many people are stranded here. They're going to try and drop in emergency supplies the moment the wind lets up.'

'A snowbound murderer,' said Bryant with relish. 'It's almost too good to be true.' May shot him a cold look. 'From an academic viewpoint, I mean. We know he's stranded here with us, but what is he doing?'

Outside in the white corridor of the arterial road, twenty-seven drivers and passengers were marooned in their vehicles, spread over half a mile of inundated road. Johann moved among them, silent and trackless, prepared to pass from one warm haven to the next, desperately searching for a mother and her son.

27

THE ANCIENT CORONER

Dissecting the body of his former colleague not only felt unethical, but was a profoundly depressing experience. Kershaw pushed his hair from his eyes and set aside the scalpel, flexing his slender fingers. He looked down at the splayed body on the steel table. Even though the temperature in the converted gymnasium had fallen to around ten degrees centigrade, he was sweating. Finch would never have lived to see much of his retirement; the parts of his arteries that had not hardened were bubbled with developing embolisms. He must have suffered painful side effects, certainly enough to encourage the use of powerful painkillers. All the talk about finally being able to relax in his fishing hut in Hastings had been bravado, nothing more. The pathologist had known he was dying.

The thought recurred to Kershaw: might he have arranged his own demise? If so, to what end? Bryant would doubtless suggest he had done it to annoy everyone.

He looked down at the old tyrant, laid out on the very dissecting table he had used for so much of his working life. Kershaw had once read that the body weighed infinitesimally less after the spirit had departed. The ancient coroner's life force had clearly evaporated now, for he had been reduced to a papery dry shell, the cocoon husk of a departed creature.

Facially, he resembled an etiolated Boris Karloff. His arms were traversed with a tangle of partially collapsed veins and blossoms of broken blood vessels, but there were no recent marks of violence other than the ones on his neck and chest, nothing else to suggest that a struggle had taken place.

Finch had admitted his attacker in good faith, thought Kershaw, only to be surprised while his defences were down. If it wasn't someone from the unit, it had to be Mills. Finch must have trusted the boy enough to turn away from him. The old man had never married, never mentioned emotional attachments of any kind. Was it possible he had a secret; could he have found the seventeen-year-old attractive, and acted inappropriately? He tried to recall any rumours he had heard about the pathologist, but came up with nothing untoward.

Kershaw rang the detective sergeant. 'Are you still with Mills?' he asked. 'Think he's on drugs?'

'Absolutely not. Normal pupil dilation, clear speech, fast reactions, completely normal as far as I can tell. At least he's talking now.'

'Any idea how tall he is?'

'About one metre sixty-five centimetres,' Longbright replied. 'Why?'

'Five five – he's too short, Janice. Apart from the disparity between his visit and the time of death, the bruising angle is wrong. I don't think he killed Finch. You didn't find a small brown plastic bottle on him?'

'Nothing in his pockets, but we know he took Finch's notes, even though he won't admit it. They may still be on site. He's wearing her neck chain, says she gave it to him. A piece of cheap gold plate, but there's a name engraved on it: Lilith Starr. Sounds made up. Mills says she inhabited a squat on the Crowndale Estate, where he lives.'

'You think he's just some opportunist thief who saw a girl he knew, followed the ambulance and plundered her dead body? Doesn't that seem a little odd to you?'

'Come on, Giles, there are crime victims in Camden Town who are stripped before they hit the pavement.'

There was a knock at the door. 'Have you finished?' asked Banbury, averting his eyes. It was bad enough that Bryant had asked him to photograph the deceased girl's neck, without him having to see the dead face of a former colleague.

'Pretty much. You can come in now.' Kershaw pulled a Mylar tarp over the body and clipped it in place. 'I tested for naltrexone and morphine. There's none in his body, but he must have been suffering periodic bouts of pain. He would only have lasted a matter of months.'

'You think he knew that?'

'He should have done – he was a biologist, although they're notoriously neglectful about their own workings.'

'Can I take another look around?'

'Knock yourself out,' said Kershaw, rubbing his eyes. 'It's gone eleven. I'm just about done here.' He looked about the sparse room. 'I don't know – there's some trace evidence we've missed . . .'

'There's always something more.' Banbury peered out from behind a locker. 'You can't be expected to pick up on everything.'

'That was Finch's main criticism of me. He said I rushed things, missed obvious opportunities. I don't want to make that mistake now. This is my chance to put things right.'

The empty space on the drug shelves nagged at him. He had seen the bottles lined up on them often enough, knew how much of a stickler the old pathologist had been about them. There could be other explanations; he might have accidentally broken the naltrexone bottle, or forgotten to get it replaced after use.

'Giles.'

The young forensic scientist turned around and saw what Banbury was holding up in his hand. 'Where did you find that?'

'Your missing bottle. It had rolled right under the desk. It's been used recently.' A syringe could be inserted through the plastic cap of the naltrexone to maintain sterility, but the bottle had not been completely emptied, and a small amount had leaked out. 'When I photographed her, I noticed that the girl in the drawer had track marks on the back of her left leg. You don't suppose he experimented on her by injecting this stuff?'

'It wouldn't react on inert tissue. You need circulating blood to carry chemicals into the system. The only other explanation is that the boy came here with the specific purpose of stealing drugs, and that he somehow used it on himself, but that makes no sense. So we have a fresh mystery.'

'There's something else,' said Dan, unlocking the body drawer and pulling it out. 'I think Mills came here to ensure that his girlfriend's identity remained secret.'

'Why do you say that?'

Banbury gingerly felt inside the body bag. 'He took her neck chain and swiped Oswald's notes. Suppose he followed her to the morgue for the express purpose of protecting her, even beyond death? Because there's this.' He pulled out Lilith Starr's left arm and indicated a paler, scarred patch on the inside, just below her elbow. 'She had a tattoo removed in the last year, not with a laser either.' He pointed to a faint red-and-blue mark on her skin. 'You can just see the edges of the original design.'

'Something traditional. Looks like it might have been a heart with a banner,' said Banbury, peering closer. 'We'll need to check the local tattoo parlours. I think there's one right on the edge of the Crowndale Estate, and there are several basement joints in Camden Town, not all of them legal. Many of the artists have signature patterns. Maybe one of them will recognize it. Meanwhile, Mills has to remain our main suspect. If Oswald discovered who she really was, maybe it was a secret worth killing to protect.' He answered his ringing mobile, then passed it over. 'John May for you. He tried calling yours but couldn't get through.'

'I thought they were going to leave us to handle this,' said Kershaw. 'Anyone would think they were still at the PCU, not stuck in a bloody blizzard.' He took the call, mainly listening to instructions. 'He wants us to take a shot of Lilith Starr's face and send it on to Colin and Meera. A job for you, I think. I'll tell you what, though. Those old boys aren't in charge of this investigation. It's not something that can be handled from long distance. We're right here, on the ground. They won't be able to take the credit if we're the ones who manage to sort it out.'

'They're not after credit, Giles,' said Banbury. 'They were already working with Oswald when you and I were at primary school. They want to do something for him. Show some respect for once.' He was embarrassed by his colleague's display of ambition. 'I'll get the shot.'

28

FORTITUDE

Princess Beatrice's social secretary, Rosemary Armstrong, was an astonishingly angry woman. Among the things that angered her were socialists, untidiness, public transport, modern architecture, poor handwriting, economic migrants, curry houses, scruffy people who refused to better themselves, council flats, the residents of London, all of whom were rude and wanted something for nothing, foxhunt saboteurs, litter, shop assistants who spoke badly and people who didn't carry fresh handkerchiefs. Most of all, she was angry about existing in a substratum of upper-middle-class folk who had not attained the higher rank of lords or ladies. To be so close to the well-born and find the station forever out of reach was like a corrosive poison rotting her soul. To temper this pain, she indulged herself in things she liked, which included dinner parties, pearls, life peers, limousines, Victorian teddy bears, holidays in Barbados, decent society, big hats, matching luggage, flowers, traditional English cooking and Pulling Yourself Up By Your Own Bootstraps.

Perusing the schedule for the Princess's visit to the PCU with distaste, she wondered if there was any way she might be able to get the trip cancelled, before recalling that the Princess was Oskar Kasavian's second cousin once removed. The unit was apparently some kind of left-wing experimental think tank, and the thought of mingling with the personnel there made her hackles rise. Princess Beatrice had made some unfortunate remarks about the quality of British police recruits in the press, and it was to be hoped that her public appearance would repair some of the bad feeling, but Kasavian was on the record for having voiced his hatred of such organizations; she wondered why he had been so insistent about fast-tracking the Princess on a visit.

She decided to give Leslie Faraday a call.

'Mrs Armstrong, how delightful to hear from you.' She could tell Faraday was wetting himself with excitement to receive a call from a lady positioned so close to royalty. 'I well remember our meeting at the Café Royal Metropolitan Police Benevolent Society Dinner in September 1998, when my wife had the good fortune to win a year's subscription to the *Tatler* on the tombola—'

Rosemary Armstrong hated being called a 'Mrs' when she should have been a Right Hon, and had no time for obsequious chitchat. She steamrollered over the minister's pleasantries, cutting him off in mid flow. 'The Princess Royal's visit to this police unit, I see it has been scheduled for Thursday afternoon from five until six. The Princess is attending a dinner in Kensington at six forty-five, so I think we can shave half an hour from her appearance, yes? So five to five-thirty, yes? And no formal presentations to staff, only the division heads, yes? We'd prefer not to have lilies or tulips in the presentation bouquet, best to stick with a small-bud pastel English arrangement. Get your florist to take a tip from Sissinghurst, which the Princess patronizes. Still water and a selection of China teas during the photo opportunity; I'll fax you a full list of requirements, yes? No "Meet the People" walkabouts, no presentation on the future of national policing, just a few opening pleasantries, a tour of the refurbished offices, "This is the operations room", a quick demonstration of the latest technology, et cetera, photo opportunity and out, yes?'

'Well, I suppose we can squeeze the schedule down to half an hour,' said Faraday, who had no idea just how unprepared the unit was to receive royal visitors, 'but I do think it's a shame when—'

'Jolly good, that's all settled, then, yes? We shall have a chance to chat further on Thursday afternoon, no doubt.' *Over my dead body, you ghastly little man*, she thought, replacing the receiver before he had a chance to reply.

In the white Vauxhall van, Madeline lay awake, clutching the jammed door handle. Ryan was buried under her arm once more, snoring lightly, untroubled by the cold.

We could die here, she thought. *At the rate this snow is falling, we'll be buried beneath the drifts soon.* For a split second the idea seemed almost appealing, to slip away into the frozen darkness and have all her problems resolved. Then she glanced back at Ryan's calm features and knew she would fight to protect him, whatever the cost.

How far was it to the nearest town? Those who had been equipped for such an emergency had long ago set off on the road, before it had become entirely impassable. Now it was too late, deep into the night, and all they could do was wait for the rescue services to arrive. Her breath blossomed in misted arabesques. She could hardly feel her lips.

At least the glittering signatures of frost on the windows prevented Johann from seeing in. Judging by the noise of the maelstrom outside, he would be too concerned with his own safety now to try and find them. Kate Summerton had warned her that psychically sensitive women could develop extraordinary connections to the men with whom they made love. She felt a growing sureness about their bond now; within a few hours it would be light, and he would come to track her down once more. He wanted no salvation, only protection from exposure, but she was determined not to surrender the incriminating packet of horrific photographs.

It would be important to keep up their strength. She remembered there was a bar of chocolate in her pocket; it was better than nothing. And perhaps others were still trapped in their vehicles. Surely someone would be able to help her. She pressed her eyes shut and concentrated. *Whoever you are, wherever you are, I'm sending out a message for help.*

With the collar of her padded jacket pulled over them both, she shifted Ryan closer to her breast and tried to sleep.

29

CONNECTION

Janice Longbright had asked everyone else to leave the room. Once the door closed, she turned down the light a little and sat beside Owen Mills. She knew that he would only ever view her as the enemy, even if he had done nothing wrong. Sometimes, though, it was possible to lower the barriers set in place by age, race, gender and authority just a little, enough to allow common gestures of grace to pass between two lives.

'Owen, I want to talk to you, not because my job demands it, but because I want to understand a little more. It's hard to imagine this as neutral territory, isn't it?' She looked up at the glaring light panels. 'I hate this room as much as you do. Probably more, because I see it nearly every day. God, it's depressing in here.' She moved a little closer. 'Seeing that we have to talk, would you rather be somewhere else?'

'Whatever. The quicker I can get away.' He threw her a sullen glare.

'Let's see how we get on. I can wrap this up more quickly if you give me an answer. Silence implies guilt, you know? At least if we talk, we can clear the air. How did you come to meet Lilith Starr?'

'Saw her around on the estate.'

'You probably see a lot of people on the estate, but you don't have to talk to them. What made you choose her?'

Silence. Mills folded his arms defensively.

Longbright narrowed her eyes, thinking. 'You asked her out?'

Nothing.

'You dated her?'

'*Dated*. What is that?'

'All right then, *went out with*. You went out with her.' She stopped and watched him. 'You were still going out with Lilith Starr.'

Silence, she saw, was starting to mean yes.

'How long have you been going out with her?'

Downcast eyes. A sigh, a refolding of the arms. 'Seven, maybe eight months.'

'You still at school?'

'They got nothing to teach me.'

'You went to St Ormond's, Camden? I've been there a few times. Can't say I'd blame you for leaving. A real dump.' The room had grown cold. April brought them take-away coffees. Beneath his padded nylon sweats, Owen was small. He had the look of a boy who had been teased, then bullied and finally ostracized by those around him in class. In Camden, kids sometimes killed each other for living in the wrong postcodes. 'I guess you and Lilith looked out for each other. A private thing. We all need someone who'll do that, Owen. The streets can be pretty bad, especially in winter. Did you think she was going to stay out all night on Monday?'

'No, man, she had a crib. The place was fine.'

'So it came as a surprise when she didn't return.'

No answer.

'She had a tattoo removed. Didn't she like it any more?'

'No.' Emphatic.

'What was it, the name of an old boyfriend?'

No answer.

'I was thinking of getting one once, a picture of Sabrina – an English glamour model from the fifties with a tiny waist and a big bust, you won't have heard of her. I changed my mind when I discovered that her real name was Norma Ann Sykes.'

'*Bust*. You use weird words.'

'Everyone needs to find the language they're comfortable with, Owen. I haven't seen this removed tattoo, but apparently it's a real mess. How did she get rid of it?'

'Cut it off with a penknife. It was going to cost too much to take care of it.'

'When did she do that?'

'Soon after I met her.'

'Was it because of you? Did you ask her to do it?'

No answer.

'Where did she go to get it done? That place in the market?' Janice looked up at the ceiling, thinking. 'Lilith Starr. If I was planning a career in show business, it's the kind of name I'd pick. What made her choose that one?'

'I'm not telling you anything more about her. You didn't know her.'

Longbright kept her voice soft and low. 'I know she went out last night meaning to come straight back, then maybe met a couple of friends, maybe had a drink, got a little high, got wasted, forgot the time. She suddenly felt tired, arms and legs really heavy, dragging at her so she just wanted to rest, and sat down to get her breath back for a moment, but the night turned really cold. She meant to get up, knew you were waiting, didn't want to let you down, just five more minutes, you were already looking for her, but by then it was too late. The temperature fell so suddenly. Five minutes made all the difference between living and dying. You could have saved her if she'd let you, you're really angry that she could have been so damned dumb. Five minutes to save a life, who wouldn't be angry? It had happened before, her staying late somewhere, but this time was different. She wanted to chill and she really *chilled*, so much that she died. The whole thing could have been avoided. Just bad circumstances.' She looked across and saw a silver thread on his cheek.

'Finish your coffee, Owen,' she said gently. 'I'm going to let you go home soon. I hope this doesn't have to go any further. You've been through enough, kid.'

*   *   *

It seemed that, whether they liked it or not, Colin Bimsley and Meera Mangeshkar were destined to be yoked together during their hours of work, even out of the office. Colin thought they should make the best of it and at least try to get on, but Meera was still fighting him every step of the way.

As they walked along the balcony checking door numbers, she found herself fascinated by her partner's inability to pass plant pots or bicycles without tripping or becoming entangled. He was so determined to follow in his father's footsteps and become a detective that the natural barrier of sheer inability did nothing to deter him.

Banbury's photograph of Lilith Starr had come through to Bimsley's mobile. The picture showed a puffy-faced girl with fiery red hair, a rather flat nose and small eyes, pouted lips and a formative double chin. She reminded the DC of Marilyn Monroe's morgue shot. Photographs of the dead were never flattering; as the muscles relaxed, gravity dragged at the face to produce alarming effects. Neither of them was sure why Bryant and May had been so keen to get the photo sent.

'Number seventeen is just here,' Bimsley called, stopping before a red council door with a chipboard square fixed across a missing glass panel. 'Looks as if she was squatting.'

He prised the loose wood from the window and reached in, opening the door. The flat was clean and bare, with strings of red plastic Christmas lights taped around the edges of the ceilings. The kitchen held a portable electric ring and an ancient microwave oven. A grubby sleeping bag and a chair covered in bright polyester undergarments indicated the bedroom. The few pieces of furniture looked as if they had been scavenged from the street, but several – a bedside cabinet, a sofa, a coffee table – had been amateurishly restored to good condition. What was missing was any clue to the identity of the squatter.

'There must be something here,' said Meera, wrenching open a wardrobe door and pulling tiny T-shirts aside. 'Everybody leaves a few signs behind.'

'Be careful with her belongings,' warned Colin. 'She took

the trouble to press her clothes and hang them up.'

'She's dead, Colin; she doesn't care what happens to this stuff any more.' She kicked aside a pair of worn high-heeled boots and rooted about in the back of the wardrobe. 'Nothing of any value here. There never is. White-trash clothes and junk jewellery. Crack whores will try to sell their family photo albums for drug money.'

'You have a pretty ugly view of people, you know that?'

'I don't go around with my head in the clouds, if that's what you mean. Last summer, over in Parkway above the Adidas shop, two junkies kept an old woman tied to a bed for three weeks while they systematically emptied out her bank account and tortured her to death. When she was gone, they put her body in a bin bag and threw it into the Regent's Canal. You think my view of them should be something other than ugly?'

'It's just that we don't know anything about this girl, except that she probably split from home and came here nine months ago. Looks like she tried to keep this place decent.'

'She'd need to, if she was turning tricks on the premises.' Meera spoke over her shoulder while she was trying the second bedroom door. The Alsatian mongrel that leaped out had been maddened by starvation and confinement. Mangeshkar yelled in surprise as the dog sprayed spittle, twisting its head to bite her throat, knocking her to the floor.

In the next second Bimsley reached the animal, forcing his elbow into its jaw, bringing his other arm around to grip it in a headlock. 'Hold the door open,' he shouted, lifting the thrashing animal from its feet. 'Then get out of the way.'

He struggled along the hall and hurled the Alsatian on to the balcony, where it regained its feet and charged the front door, but was unable to reach them through the narrow gap.

Bimsley returned to the bedroom and pulled Meera to her feet, checking her neck and face. 'You all right?'

'A bit shaken, that's all.' She brushed herself down and looked at him. 'How's your arm?'

Bimsley checked his elbow. 'I'm good. Padded jacket, no broken skin.'

'I guess she locked it in there before she went out.'

'Someone will remember the dog, even if they don't know her.'

'I suppose I should thank you.'

'You don't have to. What's that?'

Mangeshkar had knocked the sofa back as the Alsatian bowled her over. She held up the library book revealed beneath it. '*Women Who Can't Stay Faithful*, by Felicity Bronwin. Lilith Starr was into self-help books. Incredible how people can delude themselves.'

'What do you mean?'

'Come on, Colin, she overdosed in a shop doorway. She had bigger problems than staying faithful.' Meera threw the paperback on to the sofa. 'Let's get out of here.'

'Wait.' Bimsley picked up the book and stared at the back cover, turning it around for Meera to see. 'The author's shot looks a lot like her, don't you think? Family resemblance?' He took out his mobile and thumbed open the image of Lilith Starr in the morgue. In death it had become almost identical to the photograph on the book. 'Looks to me like Felicity Bronwin might be her mother. This is probably why she changed her name.'

It was one fifteen on Wednesday morning, and DS Janice Longbright was fighting to stay awake. She had drunk two Red Bulls and a Starbucks grande latte with an extra syrupy shot, but her eyelids were succumbing to forces beyond her control. She would sleep on John May's sofa tonight, but not until she had written up notes of the day's events, something Arthur Bryant always insisted upon doing before going home.

She was puzzled by Owen Mills.

The boy had finally admitted that, yes, Lilith Starr was his official girlfriend, and that they had argued the previous night. She had left his flat a little after four a.m., heading for Camden High Street, where she expected to score hash and cocaine. When she had failed to return, Mills had walked over to the spot on the south side of the canal bridge, at the entrance to Inverness Street Market, knowing that dealers always congregated there. After wandering around the area for what seemed like hours, he had finally found her lying in the doorway. He didn't think she was breathing, couldn't find a pulse, so he called the emergency services, refusing to give his name, and watched from the opposite corner while a constable checked her out, then had her loaded into an ambulance.

He knew she was dead because the ambulance had driven away in silence, without its lights or siren. And he knew that she'd be taken to the Royal Free or UCH, because those were the two hospitals where all A&E cases were taken. But he'd called both, and nobody in admissions had checked her in. So then he had called the morgue at Bayham Street, because she wasn't the first dead junkie he had seen removed from the pavements of Camden Town.

Longbright had looked into his wide brown eyes and seen a strong intelligence cloaked with a mistrustful attitude. She had no reason to disbelieve his story, but felt sure there was something that he had decided not to tell her about their relationship. She thought back to their final exchange about his visit to Oswald Finch, just before she allowed Owen to leave the PCU.

'I didn't argue with him, didn't hurt him. I didn't know him, hadn't ever seen him before. He was OK about letting me see her. Unzipped the body bag, explained why she died. He showed me the notes he was writing. I must have put my hand on them, and the ink came off. He was using this old pen. But I swear I didn't take them. I was there five minutes, that's all.'

'You wanted something to remember her by,' said Longbright. 'You took the neck chain. Can I see it?'

Owen had clutched the chain tight to his throat. 'It's all I got of her now.'

She knew she should have persisted, keeping him longer at the unit, but the PCU made its own rules, and those were set by the two old men she had always relied upon to make all her decisions.

Now, until they were safely back in London, the responsibility for everything that happened in the following hours would rest with her.

30

HUNTERS

'We have to warn everyone who's still stranded,' said Bryant. 'He could attack anyone.'

'How do you propose we manage to do that?' snapped May. 'We don't even have any proper shoes. I haven't been this cold since I fell off the pier in Cole Bay when I was twelve. I can't feel my buttocks. Even my teeth are cold. It's below zero and the wind is strong enough to knock you off your feet – God knows you're not steady at the best of times. You think you're going to wade through the drifts banging on car windows shouting "There's a killer loose"? All we can do is report the death and wait for someone to turn up. Have you any idea what's going on in other parts of the county? There are sixty people trapped in a supermarket in Canterbury because the roof has collapsed under the weight of snow. We're not going to get priority. This sort of thing happens almost every year on the moor.'

He looked across at his partner and softened. Bryant's white fringe was now sticking up around his ears in stiffened tufts, like stalagmites. His watery blue eyes peered up above his travel blanket. 'Try to get some sleep, at least until it's light. We'll figure out what to do in the morning.'

They awoke into a strange new world of opalescent

whiteness. The sky was a vulgar shade of heliotrope that reminded May of a Maxfield Parrish painting. The undulating snow dunes were as shiny as vinyl, and extended to the tips of the lowest trees. The road had been transformed into a sparkling white canyon. Some vehicles had been twisted and tipped by the snowpack that had shifted down from the surrounding moors.

Bryant peered sleepily out from his blanket. 'What time is it? My back's killing me. I feel as if I've slept on a bag of spanners.'

'Seven fifteen,' said May. 'I've just spoken to the Highways Authority emergency services. They're hoping to get a supply helicopter out this morning if the wind speed stays low. Do you want something to eat?'

'No. I need to venture outside and perform my ablutions, but the thought of lowering my trousers in these temperatures is a trifle unappealing. Give me a minute, then let's get into the back of the van and see if there's anything in there that can help us.'

When he returned, they dragged open the great canvas bags that Alma and Arthur had wedged behind the props and flats for the convention performance, and checked their contents.

'What kind of a show were you planning to stage?' asked May, pulling out a grotesque crimson papier-mâché devil's head with an axe in its skull and bloody eyeballs on springs.

'They're not just our props. There are all kinds of activities taking place throughout the convention. I agreed to take down equipment for other attendees. There are lots of indoor and outdoor events planned, ceramics, divination and crystal healing, bungee jumps, potholing, all kinds of extreme—'

'Don't tell me you've got equipment bags for potholers here. Where are they?' May pulled at an immense backpack covered in Hello Kitty stickers and opened it, releasing a pile of blue Gore-Tex all-weather suits covered in pockets.

'They belong to the Women's North Wales Potholing Team,' said Bryant, 'but they're pretty big lasses, so we could probably fit them, although the flies do up on the wrong side.'

In minutes, the pair had zipped themselves into ungainly but practical outfits, although they had been forced to roll up the legs and stuff spare socks into the toes of the boots. They clambered from the truck like spacemen, and stopped to examine the road. Snow was still falling, but now the flurries were light and manageable. The exact number of stranded vehicles was hard to determine, but the jewelled spine of traffic snaked around the next bend in the valley like the bones of a great dinosaur.

'Let's start with the cars nearest the spot where we found the dead Bentick's driver,' said May, hauling his floundering partner out of a deep drift. They reached the abandoned truck, but were unable to open the frozen door. Scraping ice from the window, May saw that the body had frozen solid. 'At least the temperature will preserve it until we can get it to a morgue,' he said. 'I think our murderer must have gone back. I haven't seen anyone pass us. No sign of the witness either, and we'll need his statement. Let's start with the cars behind.'

They approached a blue Nissan and scraped at the window. 'Empty,' said Bryant. 'Next one.'

A black BMW and a red Fiat were both abandoned, but in a silver Mercedes saloon they found a young couple fast asleep, warm and safe beneath all-weather jackets. A straggle-haired businessman still dressed in a tightly knotted tie mouthed at them through the window of his Vauxhall Signum, indicating that he could not open the door. May ran the edge of his penknife around the edges, but it made no difference. Ice had frozen the wet seals as firmly as if they had been welded shut.

'What's he saying?' asked May, trying to read the driver's lips.

'He's from Kettering,' said Bryant.

'I'm in catering,' said the driver, opening the window an inch before it stuck. 'I've got plenty of food to last, so don't worry about me. The same thing happened two years ago. To be honest, it made a nice break from the wife. You might take an Eccles cake back to the lady behind me. It's all I can pass through the window.' He slid the cake through the gap. 'She looks very upset.'

The detectives trudged farther back. A grey-faced woman in

a green Barbour jacket watched them anxiously. The door of her Volvo saloon was iced shut, but she could open one of the rear passenger windows. 'We're police officers,' Bryant explained, tapping the glass. 'Don't open this to anyone else. Have an Eccles cake. Do you need anything else?'

She shook her head miserably. 'I've been listening to the radio. There are people much worse off than me. I manage a farm outside Holbeton. My husband knows I'm here. There was a man outside a while ago, just after dawn. He tried to get in, but couldn't open the door.'

'What did he look like?'

'I'm sorry, it was dark and snowing, I really didn't see.'

'At least the ice is preventing him from entering other cars,' said Bryant as they made slow progress up the hill.

'He'll be able to get into trucks, though. Their cabins are built to withstand extreme weather.'

'If this fellow knows there was a witness, that Chinese chap will be at risk. I wish he'd stayed with us. Any one of these stranded motorists could be the person we're looking for.'

'Given the circumstances, he'll be hiding in plain sight. My concern is over our situation here. There's no back-up, no threat of legal retribution we can invoke. The man we seek will probably be younger and fitter than us.'

'My dear chap,' said Bryant, '*everyone* is younger and fitter than us. What have we got on our side? Decrepitude, mid-afternoon narcoleptic attacks and ill-timed lapses of memory. Although being the oldest, I am of course less afraid of dying and therefore liable to do anything, no matter how uncalled-for and dangerous.'

May eyed him warily. 'Thanks for the warning.'

'Now, we need to enlist some aid and organize a search. There are plenty of others trapped out here. It's no use just waiting for the authorities to turn up. Let's do what we've always done at the PCU, and get some civilians to help us.'

A quarter of a mile from the detectives, in the half-buried Vauxhall van, Madeline's thoughts were also turning to her nemesis. *He took me to the huntsman's villa in the hills,* she remembered, standing watch over Ryan while he peed circular traces in the snowdrift beside the car. *He knew its owner was lying dead on the floor. Why would he have taken such a risk?* 'Finished?' she asked aloud. 'Let's get back inside.'

'Can't I play for a while?' Ryan peered up at her over the folds of his scarf.

'No, it's not safe. In you go.'

'All this snow and I can't build a snowman – what else is it good for, anyway?'

It keeps us trapped here, she thought. *He's from a village in the mountains; he knows how to get around in weather like this.*

'I'm hungry,' said Ryan. 'How much longer are we going to be here?'

'It won't be long now.' The van and its engine were frozen into a single solid, but Madeline and Ryan's combined body heat, together with the warmth from an extra blanket they had discovered under the rear passenger seat, had guaranteed their survival. There were patches of brilliant blue in the sky, and although the wind still seemed high it felt milder than the previous day. She could hear trees creaking and dripping. Perhaps Johann had decided to leave them alone, and had struck out in the direction of the nearest town. Perhaps the worst was over.

The envelope with the passport and the photographs lay on the floor of the van, behind her legs. This time, she knew, she would do the right thing, and have him stopped before he could hurt anyone else. She laid her head back against the seat rest and closed her eyes, just for a moment, not meaning to fall asleep.

Johann's leg still hurt, and the icy wind bit deeply into his chest and thighs, numbing them further. He had slept the night in an abandoned carpenter's van which had, at least, supplied him with some useful tools, but he needed to find weatherproof clothes. This, he felt, was to be his greatest test, a battle fought with the demons that had pursued him all his life, the same demons that pursue all lonely men. *If I can't convince her to see the truth, I have nothing left,* he thought. *I know no one else in this terrible country. She has to be here somewhere. All these cars look the same now. She even has nature working on her side.*

He could see drivers hunched across their seats, vague organic shapes huddled down in positions of protection, barely recognizable as human beings. They had been reduced to rudimentary life-forms with the most basic requirements: shelter, food, warmth. The adverse conditions could work in his favour, he decided. He was free to rise above them, to prove his fitness and strength, against them all.

He knew that Madeline would never come back to him; that was no longer the issue. Part of her had retreated too far to be reached. He had behaved stupidly, impulsively, and saw nothing but uncomprehending hatred and the madness of maternal protection in her eyes. He would make her understand, then take back the packet and go on his way, lose himself in the empty coastal towns, never returning to the fierce light of southern France, where he would be forced to exist as a failure beneath God's ever-watchful gaze.

He seated the carpenter's tools more firmly in his back pocket and trudged on, searching each of the vehicles in turn. He felt he was close; the corridor of snow had locked them in at either end of the stretch of road. He could escape across the moor, hoping that the break in the weather held. In the mountains of his childhood, storms could arrive within seconds, trapping unwary climbers. He had watched clouds roll over the cliffs like the fallout from some great explosion. Was it the same here, in these deceptive woodlands? And the people; he had always considered the residents of the Alpes-Maritimes to be a suspicious, private people, but they were nothing compared to these faceless shapes sealed in their cars. What would it take to prise Madeline from her hiding place?

31

LOST CHILD

The roads surrounding Camden Market had been severed by its network of sepia railway lines and canals, but also by the bombs that had removed so many Edwardian yellow brick houses, allowing them to be replaced by sixties buildings distinguished only by their paucity of imagination. In the high street, the area's boom-and-bust arc was most pronounced. Ground floors had been converted into shops selling household items, then art deco antiques, then shoes and thrash metal T-shirts and finally magic mushrooms, drug paraphernalia and tattoos. It was into this last parlour that Banbury and Kershaw now stepped.

The store was called Tribe, and had proved popular with the gentle, literate Goth set. With a Chelsea haircut, cable-knit sweater and corduroy trousers marking him as a member of the upper middle classes, the medical examiner looked hopelessly out of place, but with their superiors still stranded in the West Country and all leave cancelled at the unit, he had little choice but to help out wherever he was needed.

'I can't believe anyone in England would allow themselves to be tattooed with that,' he told Banbury, pointing to a design of a flaming skeleton riding a Harley. 'Don't they consider how bad it will look when they're sixty?'

'No one looks their best at sixty,' said Banbury absently. 'Check these out.' He pointed to a series of photographs tacked on to the wall. A fat bare back adorned with a gigantic red spider, wide chrome studs pinning a spine from neck to sternum, a horned devil with hands like crab legs spread across a woman's back. A centipede wrapped around a man's pale chest, its claw-feet ending in hooks that actually pierced the skin. Beyond the examples of the tattooist's work were photographs of more extreme scarification: multiple bolts through cheeks, steel horns inserted into foreheads, rivets through scrotal sacs . . . Banbury looked as if he'd accidentally stepped on a three-pin plug in his socks.

'Anyone home?'

A scrawny, sallow man who resembled an old-time fair-ground barker stepped out from behind curtains adorned with tarot symbols. Above his shaven eyebrows the word SATAN was spelled out in naked women. 'Help you?'

'Police officers,' said Banbury. 'Do you know this girl?' He showed the tattooist the image he had taken on his mobile. 'She would have asked for a tattoo on her left arm.'

'I'm registered,' said the tattooist. 'Everyone's kept on file with proof of their age and details of what they want done. I don't work on anyone under-age. I can't tell from this picture.' He handed back the phone.

'She would have come back to you about seven months ago to try and get the thing removed, but she was refused.'

'That narrows it down. Give me a minute.' He checked the ancient Dell computer on his counter, refining his search. 'I remember this one. She wanted it taken off, had a real go at me because I wouldn't do it. I'm not licensed for laser removal.'

'Recall anything else about the day she came back?'

'Let me think. I've a pretty good memory for the difficult ones.' He scratched absently at a demon in a flaming hot rod. 'We did the original tattoo in two sessions, and both times she was alone. When she returned for its removal she was with a little black dude, the new boyfriend I guess. They were holding hands. Don't often see that these days.'

'After she left you, she went ahead and carved the tattoo from her arm with a penknife.'

'That's not my responsibility. Be easier to find more details if you had an ID.'

'Lilith Starr, but that's unlikely to be her real name. Try Bronwin.'

'No, she's here under Starr, and it was a real traditional job, red-and-blue heart with an unfurled name panel.'

'Do you have a picture of the design?'

'Sure. I always take a picture once it's complete. Sometimes they get the design altered somewhere else, then come back to me for a repair job, so I have to keep the original as reference.' He turned the screen around. Lilith had pulled down her slash-neck T-shirt sleeve to reveal the tattoo. Her round face and snub nose were instantly recognizable, but her beautiful red hair had been raggedly cropped. Her small, freckled breasts appeared barely more than pubescent. She appeared ill at ease before the camera, frowning into the flash with dis-comfort.

Beneath her photograph was a copy of the design: a plump red heart with a banner wrapped around it, upon which was written a single word. The tattoo was almost as wide as her arm.

'"Samuel",' said Banbury. 'She must have been pretty serious about him to get that done, yet she wanted to erase his memory very soon after meeting Owen Mills.'

'Happens a lot,' said the tattooist. 'They fall for someone else and try to get the name changed, but she just wanted it taken off.'

'Maybe Owen told her to get rid of it,' replied Kershaw, raising an eyebrow.

'You think that's why he came with her to get the thing removed? To make sure she did it? He doesn't look the dangerous type.'

'Difficult to know,' said Kershaw. 'Women see something in men that we hardly see in ourselves. We don't find him threatening, but she might have been terrified of him.'

'Or terrified of Samuel,' said Banbury, thinking of the tattoo's ragged remains.

DS Janice Longbright was not good at handling people like Felicity Bronwin. The author was a well-preserved woman in her mid forties with all the assurance of someone who was used to being right, and clearly expected others to agree with her opinions. Her apartment was on the third floor of a polished-brick mansion block that provided a graceful lacuna within the arbitrarily imperial architecture of Knightsbridge. Its décor was county-woman-in-London: traditional, floral, cluttered and cold.

Felicity sat before the sergeant in a brown woollen skirt, legs neatly crossed at thick ankles, and exuded impatience, despite having just been informed that her daughter was dead. Her husband was little more than a ghostly presence in the room, grey in moustache and suit, washed-out, silent, keen to be among trees once more. He sat in the chair behind her, watching his wife intently, as if waiting to edit or censor her words.

The detective sergeant had asked if she could take something belonging to Mrs Bronwin's daughter. With reluctance, Felicity had handed over a pink furry diary Lilith had left behind on her last visit.

Janice carefully leafed through the pages. 'Your daughter—'

'I have no daughter.' Mrs Bronwin's voice was toneless, uninterested. 'What I have is a misfit who sought only to hurt me at every possible turn, and who died some while ago, as far as I or my husband is concerned.'

'You don't seem very surprised,' Longbright ventured.

'I've been expecting it for some time now. That's what drug addicts do, isn't it, repeatedly let you down before killing themselves?'

'When did you last see Lilith?'

Mrs Bronwin winced, as if the very mention of her child's name was objectionable. 'Last Christmas, at our home in Somerset. Not a good idea to walk into the village pub with

pink hair and torn tights. The place was full of our land-
workers, and it makes them lose respect. Turned up here with a
young man in tow, obviously on drugs.'

'What did you do?'

'We argued and they left.' She sighed. 'The endless rebellions,
the pleas for attention, it's all so drearily predictable of the
young these days. The rules and traditions of country life are
too boring for them, I suppose.' *For a woman who writes about
understanding the female mind-set,* thought Longbright, *she
doesn't seem interested in understanding her own daughter.*

'Do you remember the boyfriend's name? Did he look like
this?' Longbright showed her Owen Mills's photograph.

'God, no, he wasn't black.' She tried, but failed, to hide her
distaste. 'Fair, possibly ginger, with shaved eyebrows. But
definitely not a – not black.'

'You don't remember his name?'

'Luke,' said Mr Bronwin, speaking for the first time.

'Matthew,' said Felicity, glaring at him.

'Did you ever hear of your daughter going out with someone
called Samuel?'

They exchanged glances. 'No,' they agreed, rather too
quickly.

'She never said anything about dating him? We have reason
to believe they were seriously involved with each other for a
time, up until she met Owen Mills.'

Mr Bronwin appeared about to speak, but changed his mind.

'You show me a picture of a withered, bleached corpse,' said
Felicity Bronwin, 'and I'm supposed to unfold our family
history before you, just so that you can file away a report? I'm
sorry to disappoint you. This pitiful creature you found frozen
to death in a shop doorway bears no resemblance to my
beautiful child any more. Why should I feel any pain now, when
I said good-bye so long ago?'

'Because the death of a child is always a tragedy,' said the
sergeant hotly. She had met women like Mrs Bronwin too many
times before. 'Perhaps you don't believe someone can still be a
child at seventeen. But your daughter suffered a pauper's death

in the middle of one of the world's richest cities, and I'm afraid you must bear some of the responsibility for that.' Furious with the parents, but even more annoyed with herself for losing her impartiality, Longbright rose to her feet. 'I'd like a recent photograph of Lilith, if you can spare one.'

'I'm not sure we have any,' said Felicity.

'Yes, we do. I'll get it for you.' Mr Bronwin shot his wife an angry look and left the freezing room. He returned with a photograph showing the pale, scowling redhead standing in a corner of the Bronwins' lounge, beside a gigantic Christmas tree. She was dressed for midsummer, in the standard Goth outfit of a black sleeveless top decorated with skulls, skintight black leggings and studded boots.

Who are you? thought Longbright, studying the picture. *You were the last case Oswald ever handled. What did he discover about your life that was worth dying for?*

32

SUB-ZERO

'They spoke about something serious and personal shortly before she died, I'm sure of it,' Longbright told him.

'What makes you say that?' asked Bryant, holding the mobile tightly to his frozen right ear.

'Because I've been talking to Owen Mills again, and I'm sure he's hiding something about their conversation that night. He's more astute than I first thought, but he's still holding back. Lilith had broken up badly with her former boyfriend, even going so far as to cut his name from her arm with a penknife, possibly at Owen's request. Her drug-taking stems from around the time she took Samuel home to meet her parents.'

'They admitted meeting this chap?'

'As good as – I think they were trying to disguise his name but couldn't agree on a new one for him. Matthew or Luke. What I don't understand is, if she was so in love that she had him tattooed on her arm, why did she end up hating him so badly that she would put herself through agony? And why did Owen Mills let her?'

'It sounds to me as if there were three of them in the relationship,' said Bryant. 'You know about the lives of two of the participants, Mills and the girl, but you won't get any answers until you have more information on the third.'

'Do you think I'm tackling this the wrong way?' the sergeant asked, despondent. 'It's such an indirect approach. Perhaps I should be thinking more about Oswald, rather than the boy who came to see him.'

'You said yourself that Owen Mills was Finch's only visitor. I don't suppose John would agree with me, but in the absence of any other leads, it's what I'd go after. The girl is dead, Oswald is dead, the ex-partner remains a blank, so you have to take aim at the last person to see Finch alive: Mills. Use everybody in the unit if you have to, but you must also keep an eye on Kershaw. He makes mistakes when he feels threatened, and I imagine he's feeling pretty threatened right now.'

He was about to ring off, but came close to the mobile again. 'I'm afraid I have to go. We've a murderer of our own to track down here.' He shut the phone before Longbright had a chance to ask him what on earth was going on.

The detectives had reached a dogleg in the road, and could see across the valley to the darkening moors beyond. 'It looks as though there's another volley of snow coming in,' said May. 'We should get back to the van.'

'Let's check out a few more, just another hundred yards. I'm fine, I assure you.' Bryant made his way up to the next vehicle.

This time, a young man opened the door of his Rover to meet them halfway. 'You should stay inside your vehicles,' he told them. 'It's not safe outside.' He explained that he was a staff nurse at Exeter General Hospital, and had been further along the road calling on those still trapped in their vehicles.

'I'm Jez Morris, pleased to meet you.' He shook their hands with grave formality. 'You're really police officers?'

'We're attached to a special unit in London,' explained Bryant, without revealing anything. He knew he might be facing the man who had murdered their truck driver. 'How many more are back there?'

'Thirteen by my count, including a couple of kids. I treated an elderly couple for early symptoms of hypothermic shock, but surprisingly there's been nothing too serious. People in these parts are pretty tough. They know they're taking a chance if they go against a blizzard warning. How many in your direction?'

'We counted eleven,' said May. *And one no longer alive*, he thought uncomfortably. They left Morris with a promise to check in on him within the hour. Behind the nurse's car, a snow-weighted beech tree had collapsed across the road, and a narrow pantechnicon had been thrown on its side. The cabin was empty, but as May called out, the lower rear door was pushed up and a young black man in a store uniform looked out.

'Hey, no sign of the rescue workers yet?' he asked. His accent placed him from South London. 'Are you stuck here, too?'

May explained. 'What happened here?' he asked.

'I came around the bend and saw the cars across the road. Braked too hard to avoid the tree and my load shifted. Over she went.' The driver introduced himself as Louis. 'I'm supposed to deliver to Derry and Co. in Plymouth by nightfall. Won't make much difference when I get there now; the stock's pretty messed up.'

'Are you warm enough in there?' May asked.

'I'm carrying bed linen as well as crockery, so that's not a problem,' said Louis. 'But some of the geezers behind me aren't doing so well. I opened a few of the boxes and gave blankets out to the cars. My manager will go crazy, but I'll tell him it's good publicity for the store. I don't want to lose my job, but I couldn't just leave people freezing while I've got all this stuff, you know? Do you know what's happening? My battery's flat, so I've got no radio.'

May was about to answer when the bulky chop of helicopter blades displaced the air above them. Everyone looked up.

'Is he attempting to land?' asked Bryant.

The red air ambulance was trying to set itself down on the narrow ridge above the road, but great gusts of wind caught at its blades and threatened to flip it. After searching for other spots to land, it hovered beside the road and a crew member threw out supplies sealed in Day-Glo orange plastic packs that tumbled down the hillside trailing plumes of snow. The helicopter swung away in the direction of Plymouth.

'Some good people out here,' said May, watching the chopper depart. 'They can keep an eye on the other drivers, but we can't tell them who to watch out for. We haven't seen this fellow clearly ourselves. What we need to do—'

His mobile rang. He checked the number and saw that Longbright was calling.

One of the orange supply packs lay in deep snow on the other side of the sallows and sycamores that lined the road, no more than a hundred metres from the Vauxhall in which Madeline and Ryan were sheltering.

Madeline scraped at the window and tried to locate it through the trees. Their padded jackets afforded protection against the sub-zero temperature, but neither of them had eaten more than a few squares of chocolate since the previous day. Ryan's teeth were chattering; he needed something to restore his body's energy. 'It must be easy to open,' she said, searching for a gap in the branches. 'People can't be expected to carry penknives on them.'

'We've got a Swiss Army knife,' Ryan remembered.

'I left it in France, in your Spider-Man bag.'

An hour had passed without her catching sight of Johann. Heavy snow clouds were reappearing above the trees. It would take longer to bring supplies back in another blizzard, and it would be harder to spot him if he decided to attack. 'I'm going outside for a few minutes,' she told Ryan. 'I want you to lock the door as soon as I've gone, and don't unlock it for anyone except me.'

She picked up the envelope containing the evidence and slipped it inside her jacket, then climbed out of the van. Their rented Toyota was five cars ahead. Keeping low, she moved quickly between the vehicles until she reached it, then dropped to her knees behind the car. The picture packet wedged easily under the wheel arch, and could not be seen from any angle.

Satisfied that no one else would know it was there, she set off towards the supply carton.

It proved trickier than she'd expected getting through the icy thicket above the roadway. The branches sprang up as stalactites broke from them, scratching her face, but she pushed ahead until she found herself standing in a field of flawless white with graceful bargellos of wind-sculpted snow crossing its edges.

The case had come to rest in the ditch that ran beside the trees. She tried to right it, but it was too heavy to shift. A nylon cord ran the length of the pack, beneath a perforated section of the plastic, and tore the wrapper open when she pulled it. Inside were meals that heated themselves in aluminium cans, blankets, a flexible-frame tent, light sticks and an array of tools. She wrapped the ready meals and hot-drink packets in a blanket, and retraced her steps back to the thicket. Snow had started to fall once more.

A dark figure was standing in the shadows on the other side.

She stopped, her breath growing shallow. Pushing back through the branches would instantly reveal her whereabouts. She could see Ryan inside the van on the other side of the trees. The only answer was to go around to the first space between the low hawthorn bushes that surrounded the tree trunks. She moved as quickly and quietly as she could, but the crust of the snow kept breaking, sinking her into the ditches and furrows of the field.

She reached the gap and ventured a backward glance. He had not moved. He had no need to; she would have to come back up the road and pass near him to reach the van. She stayed on the far side of the vehicles, taking care not to slip in the frozen tyre tracks. When she looked back up, he had disappeared.

He came for her when she was not expecting it, seizing her left hand, pleading in a low voice, causing her to drop the blanket, which opened, spilling its contents across the road. Johann's face betrayed no emotion. He seemed hardly aware of his actions, as if he had decided it wasn't worth bargaining with her any more.

Her hand slipped free of its glove, and she used the moment of surprise to run, back to the driver's side of the van. She threw herself inside and punched down the door lock as Ryan screamed. 'It's all right,' she told the frightened boy. 'He can't get in.'

Johann's fist slammed a tattoo of frustration on the side window, but the glass held. He lowered himself to look inside, and gestured with an open palm. *Give it back to me.* She shook her head, shrinking from the window. He ran at the van, and seemed about to try and kick his way in when he suddenly froze and turned away.

'What's going on?' asked Ryan.

'Stay over here.' She pulled the boy closer.

'You dropped the food.'

'I know, baby, I know.' They looked out at the red blanket, which had splayed across the snow like a bloodstain, the cans and packets lying there beyond reach, and Johann, crouched beneath the overhanging branches, vulpine, waiting for them to emerge.

33

RENFIELD

'We've rather got our hands full here, Janice,' said John May impatiently. 'What can we do for you now?'

'I'm sorry, John, it's just that I've never had a problem like this, and I couldn't phone Arthur again. I know you wanted us to sort out the investigation without your help, but if we don't find a solution to Oswald's death before the Home Office descends on us with their royal patron, we're finished. I thought it would help if I could talk to you.'

'Tell me what's on your mind.'

'Deportment,' said Longbright. 'Lilith Starr was taking a course in it. She put the appointments in her diary.'

'Deportment? I presume you don't mean getting thrown out of the country?'

'No, I mean walking around with a book on your head, carrying yourself well, learning how to sit. It's a very old-fashioned approach to being finished. Girls in the sixties were packed off to Swiss schools to learn social skills befitting the high-born. Essentially, they learned how to make themselves attractive to men and serve them well.'

'I don't understand. Why would a doped-up girl living in a Camden squat want to do that?' asked May. 'You don't think she was entertaining some fantasy about becoming a high-priced call girl?'

'That's just what I wondered,' replied Longbright. 'She would have to have been introduced into an organization – the ones in Mayfair and the Edgware Road that provide girls for hotels and wealthy clients are very tightly run these days. Mills wouldn't have the right connections.'

'Which leaves the former boyfriend, Sam. You think he pimped for her, was maybe grooming her? It might go some way towards explaining why she fell out with him.'

'Exactly.'

'Perhaps you'd better pay her "finishing school" a quick visit.'

'If I can arrange it in time,' Longbright agreed. 'That's the one thing I don't have. Arthur thinks that Owen Mills is the key to all this, but we've got no further with him.'

May thought for a moment. 'Are Giles and Dan *absolutely* sure that Oswald Finch was murdered?'

'They're unshakable. It means he was killed about an hour and a half after Mills left.'

'What if Mills is lying? He lied about his girlfriend, didn't he? He could have come to the morgue and picked a fight with Finch, giving him a couple of smacks in the neck and chest, bringing on the thrombotic trauma.'

'He's sullen, but I can't see him slapping anyone about,' said Longbright.

'All right, even if he didn't kill Finch, what if he found him already dead, and closed the door behind him as he left, leaving the room sealed?'

'Again the timing is wrong, and besides, there's no reason why he would do that. Arthur always says there's a rational motive at the root of everything.'

'Not since the Highwayman case, he doesn't. The outcome of that investigation shook him up badly. He says he no longer understands the young, so he certainly wouldn't know what to make of Mills.'

'All right, using another criterion of Arthur's, I'd say it just doesn't feel right. I don't think the boy lies, so much as he simply omits the truth.'

'Mills has to be the link, Janice. Without him you have nothing. What about the dead girl? Renfield brought her in; have you spoken to him yet?'

'*Renfield.*' Longbright shuddered.

Sergeant Renfield had no interest in what anyone thought of him, which was just as well, because nobody thought much of him at all. Bitterness is an unattractive trait in a middle-aged man, and his stemmed from the fact that he had been passed over for promotion with such consistency that he could only imagine there was a conspiracy against him. There was not, as it happened; only vague dislike for a misanthropic, charmless desk sergeant who believed in guilt without proof and punishment without conditions. He performed his duties with a certain solid thoroughness, but seemed so lacking in human understanding that it was a mystery why he had decided on a career in the police. Renfield suspected everyone of breaking the law, especially the innocent, but was prepared to look favourably on his own men whenever they behaved badly. This moral blindness bestowed upon him a small team of loyal acolytes, but had also earned him an unsavoury reputation. His redeeming feature, a loyalty to the letter of the law, was the same quality that held him back. He was particularly disliked by women, who sensed that his leering eye would probably be accompanied by a roving hand if he thought he could get away with it. Renfield was considered by the PCU to be a throwback, low, wide and hairy-shouldered, too set in his ways and too stubborn to learn better behaviour, and yet, perversely, there was a broad streak of decency buried within him.

'I wonder what you're here for, Longbright,' he mused without looking up at her. He had a cold, and was surrounded by wet balls of tissue. 'I hear your bosses are stuck in a snowdrift. You lot must be running about like headless chickens without someone to tell you what to do.'

'I was just passing, and thought I'd check on that girl you

took around to Mr Finch on Tuesday morning.' As far as she knew, the unit had successfully hushed up news of Oswald's demise, but someone was bound to notice that something was wrong when they found the doors to the Bayham Street Morgue locked.

'I thought Finch would be on the blower with some kind of report by now.' Renfield blasted another tissue apart and set it aside. 'Poor old sod shouldn't still be working at his age. He'll peg out on the job one day, wait and see.'

'He doesn't have to report to you, Renfield.' Longbright wondered, *Has he heard something?*

'No, but he never misses a chance to give my lads a hard time. I told him she was just another Camden junkie, but he started arguing with me.'

'What do you mean?'

'He reckoned she didn't show the classic signs, or fit the mould or something. You know how he goes on, you stop listening after a while. Told us we should have been more thorough. It's all right for him, with one weirdo to deal with each week; he should try keeping up with our quotas—'

'I don't understand,' said Longbright. 'Thorough about what?'

'He wanted us to go back to the scene and check for proof of an overdose, but by the time we got there the street cleaners had been along.'

'You didn't cordon off the site?'

'Don't you bloody start,' Renfield complained as he miserably dragged another tissue from the box. 'We did everything by the book. It's all laid down in black and white so that my lads don't have to keep stopping and working things out for themselves.'

That's exactly the problem, thought Longbright as she left Camden Town Police Station. Good officers were like good doctors, relying on their innate morality to clear a path through restricting rules. The PCU took that approach to some kind of *ne plus ultra. Well, it's time to raise the stakes,* she thought, flipping her collar against the falling sleet. *I'd rather break the law than see the unit taken away from us now.*

34

IMPEDIMENT

'Where on earth is everybody?' Raymond Land asked April when he arrived on Thursday morning. 'I thought they were supposed to be working through the night.'

Outside the PCU, the overnight snowfall was turning to tobacco-coloured slush as the temperature rose above zero. Wet boots were lined up by the hall radiator, and Crippen was guiltily wolfing the lardy remains of Bimsley's breakfast burger because Bryant wasn't there to feed him.

'They *have* been working, sir,' said April. 'Mr Banbury and Mr Kershaw are running some further tests at Bayham Street. PCs Bimsley and Mangeshkar went to talk to Owen Mills's neighbours. Detective Sergeant Longbright has gone back to Camden Town nick –' She checked the hurried notes she had made half an hour ago. *Lie to Raymond if you have to, but hold him off and keep him calm,* Longbright had told her. *And Arthur wants to know if you can do anything to get today's ridiculous royal visit cancelled.*

'Meanwhile, my star detectives are building bloody snowmen somewhere near the English Riviera,' Land snapped. 'What am I supposed to say to the Princess? "I'm sorry, your Royal Highness, we're not quite ready for your visit, seeing as one of our best men has been murdered, possibly by another member of staff, and as they're all under house arrest we haven't had time to nip out and purchase your bouquet." What are you doing?'

'I'm holding the fort,' said April, feeling useless.

'Then you'll have to meet up with the Princess's social secretary at noon,' warned Land. 'This Armstrong woman wants to go through protocol to make sure everyone knows exactly how to greet Her Magnificence and what to say if she deigns to speak to them. You'll have to nip up to the Esso garage and buy flowers and refreshments. And get this place looking decent. And hide anything unsavoury from the royal view. You might start with Mr Bryant's office.' Here, Land was thinking specifically of the marijuana plant Bryant kept beneath his desk 'for his rheumatism', the reeking Tibetan skull on his shelf, and some of the more outré and explicit books with which he surrounded himself.

'Sir?' April raised a timid hand. 'Mr Bryant asked me to warn you about the petri dishes he keeps in his cupboard. He's been growing some virulent bacillus cultures, some experiment he's conducting into plague transmission in the Middle Ages. I accidentally knocked over one of them yesterday. I don't want to worry you, but do you think it's wise to expose the Princess to a possibly dangerous virus? Perhaps we should cancel her visit.'

'Don't try to bamboozle me, girl,' snapped Land. 'Bryant's had those pots and dishes for donkey's years. He made us all as sick as dogs in '85 after using one to serve cocktail sausages in at the Christmas party, but they're inert now. I even saw Crippen eating from one of them. We have to do something about that cat. He smells quite indescribable when he's wet. Bryant's just attempting to get the visit postponed, but it won't work.'

'There's another problem,' April blurted. 'The network cabling. The carpenters have had to tear the floorboards up, and they can't guarantee they'll be able to put everything back in time. Surely you don't want the Princess falling through our floor.'

'Then I'll put a rocket up them, you watch,' snapped Land. 'They'll finish the job by lunchtime if I threaten to withdraw their pay.' He stamped out of the room, slamming the door behind him.

You can't say I didn't try, Uncle Arthur, she thought. Checking her watch, she saw that it was quarter past nine. They had less than eight hours to solve the mystery of Oswald's death before Oskar Kasavian presented the unit for public ridicule and closure.

35

AMELIORATION

Janice had marked the page in Lilith's diary with a Post-it note. Strap-hanging in the Tube on her way along the Piccadilly line, she re-read the entries, virtually the only ones Lilith had bothered to make: a series of appointments over the last three months at a Knightsbridge beauty salon, including several training sessions in deportment. The entries had immediately struck her as being incongruous. Here was a girl who had mutilated her arm to please her new boyfriend, who was taking drugs and behaving irrationally. Why would she attend the kind of expensive salon usually frequented by wealthy middle-aged women? *Everyone has their dreams*, she thought, *no matter how disillusioning they may turn out to be.*

As she ventured through the doors of The Temple, at least three pairs of women studied her before turning their heads and whispering to one another. Longbright realized it was because she was wearing a standard-issue black padded police jacket and what appeared to be men's boots, the continuing inclement weather having finally forced her to abandon her usual array of exotic outfits.

As Longbright passed through, she had the all-too-familiar feeling of being looked down upon, because she was a woman in a man's job, because she had a job at all, because she was large and unusual. It took extra effort to hold her head up and march past these pampered, supine women who were more like pets than adults.

The Temple was a hip take on the ladies' salons of the 1950s, but now the red flock wallpaper patterns were finished in shocking retro pinks and crimsons, and for the price of a full day's body treatment you could once have bought a car in Knightsbridge. On the salon's faux-marbled wall was a photograph of a man in sunglasses with a bouffant hair stack, a shark-skin suit and a narrow black tie. Beneath it ran a caption: *Monsieur Alphonse attending the Cannes Film Festival, 2006.* She understood now: it was a postmodern joke, the kitsch fifties set-up that aped a dozen British films from the period, usually starring Peter Sellers or Norman Wisdom – the archetypal gangster-turned-hairdresser, all phony French accent and camp mannerisms. How knowing, how droll, his customers would think as they handed over their gold cards.

'I would like an appointment with Monsieur Alphonse,' she told the receptionist, a lacquered raptor who had been exfoliated and plucked to a life-threatening degree.

The receptionist flicked through her suede-edged address book with a crimson claw, avoiding Longbright's gaze. 'Let's see, we could fit you in at the beginning of March. Are you here for our extreme skin-care rehabilitation programme?'

'No, I'm not,' said Longbright, affronted. 'I always wear a heavy foundation. I'd like to see Monsieur Alphonse right now.'

The receptionist performed a double-take that nearly dislodged her from her perch. 'Monsieur Alphonse can't possibly take short-notice appointments. I'm afraid such a request is completely out of the question.'

Longbright flicked her badge on to the counter and gave her a hard smile. 'Oh, it's not a request.'

Monsieur Alphonse was, to her surprise, not a South London wide boy with a dodgy Parisian accent, but a Chelsea footballer from the mid-nineties called Darren Spender who had stumbled upon a way of extending his brief claim to fame. According to the tabloids, running The Temple was his way of making a fortune while searching for his next ex-wife, although Longbright could tell from his patronizing attitude to women that, like so many men of rudimentary maturity, he had bypassed monogamy in favour of indefinitely sustained states of sexual tension. Unlike his customers, he preferred nothing to be cut and dried. As a consequence, he had been photographed leaving bars with a wide variety of pneumatically enhanced exotic dancers in the back pages of *Heat* magazine, as well as padding out On-the-Town features in brick-thick monthly glossies written by and for the brick-thick. None of this celebrity exposure cut the mustard with Longbright, who regarded him as one would a spider in the bath.

'It's not good for business having the police come in here,' said Spender, inviting her to sit and twinkling moodily at her. 'I haven't done anything wrong, have I?'

'Not to my knowledge,' said Longbright. 'At least, not since that rubbish penalty you took against Aston Villa. Know this girl?'

If Spender was surprised by Lilith's picture, he betrayed no sign of it. 'I wouldn't have any idea,' he said. 'We have a high turnover of clients, as you can imagine. I don't deal with them all personally, you know. This is a business.'

'Your name is in her diary for three of the five appointments, so I assumed you were acquainted.'

'There's a sliding scale for my second-, third-, and fourth-level assistants.'

'Her name was Lilith Starr, and I'm using the past tense because she's dead.'

'I'm very sorry to hear that.' He didn't miss a beat. 'How can I help?'

'One of the things we have to do in a situation like this is establish her movements during her final days. She came to see you forty-eight hours before she died, hence my need for this visit. Lilith lived in a squat in Camden Town. What does it cost to cut someone's hair?'

'It depends on which stylist the client books. Let me call

someone.' Using an old-fashioned desk intercom, he rang his outside office. 'Can you get Sonya in here?'

A tall blonde in her mid-thirties, dressed in an iridescent pink trouser suit and heels, entered and seated herself beside Spender. Longbright passed her the photograph and waited for a response.

'How much do you charge for a consultation, Mr Spender?' asked Longbright.

'My personal rate starts at five hundred pounds an hour.'

'I remember this girl,' said Sonya, tapping the picture.

Longbright turned her attention to the Barbie woman. 'How much did Lilith pay for your services?'

Sonya attempted to show that she was analysing the question, but the effect merely looked guarded and secretive. 'I believe we gave her a very healthy discount rate,' she said finally.

'I don't understand. Why would you do that? You're a beautician, not a philanthropist.'

Sonya gave a quick, insincere smile. 'She was getting a full makeover. Skin care, dietary control, hair, manicure, body-wrapping, make-up, deportment, speech therapy, one of our best tailored lifestyle packages. She wanted to shed her origins. I remember when she first came in with one of our New Talent flyers. One glance at her told me she couldn't afford us, but it also told me that she had the look.'

'What look?'

'Lilith had almost everything it takes to be a great model except height, and that's only important if you're doing catwalk work. Anyone can be pretty these days. She had something more elusive and mysterious, a quality that set her apart. A touch of the street. You invest money in girls like these and they repay you when they start to get press coverage. We make the money back in sponsorship contra-deals alone.'

'We're about to launch a talent agency and our own line of cosmetics,' Spender explained. 'This is the period when we need to make a lot of friends, some of whom already have high profiles, others who are just starting out.'

'I wouldn't normally have picked someone quite so raw,' said Sonya, 'but sometimes you have to take chances.'

In the brief silence that followed, Longbright decided to ask an indelicate question. 'Was your relationship with her more than just professional, Mr Spender? Were you sleeping with her?'

'No, that would have been a violation of our customer-relationship policy,' said Spender without a flinch.

Oddly, the sergeant believed him. *But you were planning to,* she thought, *once you'd finished making her over into the image of your ideal sexual partner.*

'She was your type, though. I've seen the similar look of the girls on your arm who are always in *Heat.* I mean the magazine,' she added hastily. 'Why did she come here? There must be plenty of less expensive places.'

Sonya took over, glancing at her boss. 'I think she realized that the first step towards becoming a successful photographic model was looking and behaving like one. We agreed to bankroll her at the salon for three months, at the end of which time we would assess her and decide whether to sign her with our agency.'

'Did either of you know that she had a drug habit?'

'No, of course not. Although I noticed that she had some problems with her skin.'

'So you never saw the state of her arms or the backs of her legs?'

Sonya looked blankly at her, a pose she had perfected. 'I don't think so. She told me she was from a good part of Fulham. She spoke nicely. I thought she was probably from a decent middle-class background. Goths often are.'

'And of course that would be important.'

'This isn't some shitty little Hackney hairdresser's,' said Spender sharply. 'We have high standards to maintain. Our ladies come here for lifestyle amelioration.' Longbright felt he had learned the phrase especially for this use.

As she took her leave, she walked back through the salon and stopped beside the receptionist's counter. 'I like your hair,' Longbright told one of the passing stylists. 'What colour is that?'

'Amaretto Latte,' the girl told her, touching the ends lightly. She was used to compliments. 'I'm planning Cappuccino highlights with a biscuit finish.'

'Sounds fattening.' Longbright looked about. 'Pretty exclusive place. They don't just cut hair here, do they?'

'Oh, no,' said the girl, whose badge proclaimed her to be Lavinia. 'We do diet and exercise, spa treatments, stress management, life training—'

'What's that?' asked Longbright.

'Some of the ladies –' she lowered her voice in confidence, '– have recurring issues with portion control, so they get enrolled in Mr Spender's club, Circe. I can get you a brochure if you want.'

'Yes, I'd like that.'

Lavinia returned with a copy and slipped it to Longbright. 'I'm not really supposed to give them out to casual visitors,' she confided. 'But seeing as you had a private meeting with Mr Spender, I'm sure it's all right.'

As Longbright walked back past Harrods towards the Tube station, flicking through the brochure, she decided to call Kershaw. 'Giles, is it legal to employ a private doctor to offer advice to your customers?' she asked.

'Bit of a grey area,' the forensic man told her. 'Pharmacies allow their shop assistants to recommend products. The government's more relaxed about it than they used to be.'

'This guy's offering lifestyle courses to women "under the expert guidance of trained physicians", it says here. I can't help thinking that our dead girl is the key somehow, and I need a key to her.'

'Got any names for me from that brochure?'

'Hang on.' She scanned the page. 'Dr R. Martino MD BMA, Dr P. Ranswar MD BSA.'

'Give me about ten minutes. I'll get back to you.' He rang off.

Longbright loitered outside a coffee shop. Aproned waitresses were hunched in its marbled doorway, sheltering from the sleet and guiltily dragging on cigarettes as if half expecting to be charged with armed robbery. Her phone rang.

'No record of them on the BMA register,' said Kershaw. 'Neither is licensed to practise in the UK.'

'You mean they've been struck off?' asked Longbright.

'No, it could mean they were originally licensed in non-Commonwealth areas, or that they qualified with quasi-medical diplomas, possibly in homeopathic sciences, and are calling themselves doctors. It wouldn't necessarily stop them from offering advice, but they wouldn't be able to issue prescriptions.'

'I want to go in there, Giles. There's a session starting at noon.'

'If you think it's a lead . . .' Kershaw began.

'The problem is, I'd have to go in undercover because they've seen me at The Temple, and the Circe Club wants three hundred and fifty pounds for the first session. Can we afford it?'

Kershaw had taken to organizing the unit's finances because no one else wanted the job. 'Absolutely not. You'll have to find another way of getting in if you think it's that important.'

Lately, Longbright had come to accept her role as the unit's undercover mistress of disguises on the condition that it came with a decent clothing allowance. For the visit to Circe, she called in a favour from the manager of Typhoon, for whom she had once unravelled a massive credit-card fraud. She had reasoned that more might be achieved if she showed sensitivity to the salon's wealthy clientele, and besides, she had been longing to dress glamorously this winter, but her threadbare social life had been such that an opportunity had not presented itself.

Fifteen minutes later, she exited the store in a fake-leopardskin coat with a red woollen two-piece suit, artificial pearls and patent-leather heels. *If Catherine Deneuve ever makes a wildlife documentary, this is what she'd wear,* thought Janice. *Not good for Mornington Crescent, but appropriate for Knightsbridge.*

The club was discreetly tucked away in a Victorian terrace, above and behind the main salon. *Why am I doing this?* she wondered, waiting for the door to be opened. *Because Arthur would have me follow the same lead if he was here.*

The steel lattice swung slowly back before her, admitting her to the club's inner sanctum. Bryant believed that when a case offered no likely scenarios, it was necessary to plunge from the beaten track of police investigation. The difference this time was that Longbright had just six hours left before their grace time expired for ever.

36

THE CORRIDORS

Johann had disappeared in the night.

Numb and aching, Madeline uprighted herself. She could see the remains of his footprints trailing off into the briars above the bank. Ryan peered up at the clearing dawn sky. 'It's stopped snowing,' he told her. 'Can we go outside and get the food now?'

'No, Ryan, stay in the car.'

'But we're going to starve to death if we stay here.'

'Don't exaggerate.'

'I'm cold and I'm thirsty. I want my Game Boy. And I need to go to the toilet again.'

'You went a little while ago; what's wrong with you?'

'It's the cold weather.' Ryan had heard his father say it.

Despite her fears, she couldn't help smiling. 'I'll have to see if the coast is clear. Take a look out of the back.'

Ryan scrambled over the seat and cleared the window. 'I can be really quick. I won't even stop to get a snowball.'

'No.' She thought of Ryan left alone in the car. Perhaps that was what Johann was waiting for. 'Maybe we should go together.'

She reached down to the door handle and pulled it out. The door needed a shoulder to unstick it, and opened with a pop.

Taking her son's hand, she stepped gingerly on to the ice-crusted road, pulling him with her. The sky had returned to a fierce cyan, but the respite felt temporary, as if they were in the eye of a hurricane. He had run while the storm had abated, she told herself. He had reached the decision to leave them alone and make his escape, just as he had engineered his first meeting with her. He had probably moved her handbag that day in order to make her thank him for finding it.

'Don't try to take everything,' she told Ryan, 'just some water and snacks. We'll be on our way soon.' The boy had reached the blanket and was already loading packets into his coat. 'Come on, Ryan.' She pulled at his sleeve. 'Leave it.'

'But it'll just go to waste. There's crisps and stuff.' He was crouching now, checking labels and looking for something other than plain water. She jerked him to his feet and turned to go, then saw Johann bending inside the van. He had waited for them to leave so he could search it for the envelope. Where the hell had he been hiding? She froze, slipping a protective arm around the boy, tightly muzzling him with her hand when he went to speak.

She started to back up along the line of abandoned cars, carefully placing one boot behind the other, dragging Ryan with her, but the crunch of hard snow in the blue stillness was enough to alert him, and he stared up at her through the windscreen.

Their sight of each other was like a static shock. Like it or not, she had a connection with him, and in that moment they both recognized the subterfuge. This was no longer about the envelope, which was still tucked inside the wheel arch of the Toyota, but about something unfinished between them.

Sweeping Ryan into her arms, she abandoned caution and ran.

'A clear sky, perfect landing conditions for air rescue,' sniffed Bryant, squinting into the iceberg-blue of the morning. 'Why don't they come?'

'I don't know,' May admitted. He and Bryant had headed

back to the truck to take another look at the driver's corpse. 'Perhaps they only just reached base and have to refuel before returning. We can't wait any longer to tell someone about the body, Arthur.'

'By the time they send out locals to investigate, our man will have gone.'

'Where? Where can he go?' May waved a hand at the silted landscape. 'There are no tracks in any direction other than up and down this road, and the only fresh footprints are ours. He can't run across the moor without risking his life. He has to be in one of the cars.'

'Then we conduct a proper search, from one end to the other.'

'And do what, exactly? Does it occur to you that he might be stronger than either of us? We don't know what we're up against. We have no power here. We can't involve innocent drivers without placing them at risk, and although I hate to bring up the subject, you're too old to tackle murderers.'

'We can still out-think them, even if we can't outrun them,' Bryant muttered. 'I know you dread the idea of acting your age, tinting out your grey and sucking in your stomach whenever you talk to attractive women, or even hideous ones; I've seen you.' Bryant looked about the cabin. 'I know one thing. He's a young French hitchhiker, possibly from a mountain region.'

'What makes you say that?'

'He was sitting here in the passenger seat with his feet on the dashboard. Nobody over twenty-five ever sits like that. He boarded the truck in wet snow and his boot prints dried out, see? He's wearing Merveilles, a brand of French ski resort trainer you can only buy in Alpine regions; he's probably quite at home in the snow. There's a customs clearance form in the glove box. The driver's details are printed on the customs form. My guess is he picked up our man as a hitchhiker.'

'That is pure supposition, Arthur. We don't have any real information. And I don't think we should spend any more time in this cabin wrecking the crime scene. You look frozen.'

'We have to keep searching the cars,' said Bryant. 'For all we know, he's moving from car to car, preying on the innocent without fear of capture.'

May did not wish to stress his partner's lack of suitability for a search conducted in inhospitable conditions. He knew how Bryant would react to the subject of his own mortality. 'Then stay in the car and let me conduct the search,' he said. 'There's no need for both of us to freeze. We should have stayed in those potholers' outfits.'

'I could barely walk. The crotch was around my knees. And what if something happens to you? You could die out there all alone. Don't be ridiculous.' Bryant snapped his scarf around his neck and pushed out of the cabin, dropping up to his knees in a snowdrift. He fought to maintain his balance for a few seconds, then tipped over on to his face.

'That's exactly the kind of thing I'm talking about,' said May, helping him up and dusting him off. Linking arms, the pair of them set off like children in the dark, wading past the column of vehicles.

Half an hour later, Bryant was puffing like a kettle and showing signs of distress. A gleaming crust had formed across the snow, levelling the drifts over potholes and ditches, making walking perilous and exhausting. May knew that they had come too far to turn back now, but he needed to find shelter. The wind was rising once more. Fresh flurries blew across the sparkling ridges of ice like sand skittering over dunes. Several times Bryant nearly fell, but was hauled back to his feet. He weighed nothing. Against the blinding snow, he appeared like a character from a Dickens Christmas, a dark bundle of over-sized clothes topped by a tonsured head and a bulbous blue nose.

'We're too old for this sort of thing,' May puffed.

'What you mean is I'm too old.' Bryant beat snow from his coat for the twentieth time. 'I know right now I look like something that belongs on the wall of a second-rate cathedral, but I'm stronger than I appear. Our family is a hardy breed. My mother was an usherette for twenty-two years, and then cleaned the same cinema until she was eighty. We're used to standing about in the cold.'

'Why tempt fate?' asked May. 'Divine providence isn't going to intervene and lend a hand. There's no one within a hundred-mile radius who can help us.'

'Don't be so sure,' said Bryant, raising his hand. 'Look.'

'Oh, no – tell me I'm dreaming.' May gave his forehead a theatrical smack of the hand. 'What on earth is she doing here?' He stared back at the painted army truck and read the unfurled purple and yellow pendant on the side: *Coven of St James the Elder (North London Division) Prop. M. Armitage (Grand Order Grade IV White Witch)*.

Just then, a hatch in the rear door opened and a dyed crimson head poked out. 'I thought that was you, Arthur,' called Maggie Armitage, dubious doyenne of the London witch world and occasional helpmate of the Peculiar Crimes Unit. 'I didn't expect to see you until the convention. We took to the B roads because Maureen is our designated driver and she suffers from tunnel vision, so she tends to rely on the advice of her spirit guide, Captain Younghusband, and he's not at all trustworthy when it comes to overtaking. He died long before the motorcar was invented, you see, so he's a bit surprised whenever she goes over twelve miles an hour, and she drives quite fast because the situation with her waterworks is such that she requires a comfort stop every twenty minutes.'

'I thought I told you, John,' Bryant explained with a pleased grin. 'Maggie is booked to perform the Opening of the Ways ceremony on the first night. It grants spiritualists unparalleled access to the Netherworld for the duration of the convention.' He made it sound as though she was selling tickets for a fairground ride.

'I brought some of the coven members with me in the truck,' said Maggie, her smiling eyes closing to mascara'd crescent moons as she beckoned them. 'The convention centre called Wendy, our organist, to ask if she would protect the entrances to their car park from Cornish spirit-suckers by casting runes in salt and chalk – apparently the little buggers like to nip over the border and torment believers. Wendy can speak Piskie, and made us stop on the moor to commune with them, but they stole her jump leads, stranding us here. Come on in.'

The army truck had been filled with crimson cushions, divans and heavy velvet drapes. Crystal pendants, joss-stick burners and animal bones hung from the crossbars, lending it an air of decadence. 'We've been using it as a mobile pagan temple,' Maggie explained. 'A place of spiritual fulfilment.' Its stuffy incense-filled atmosphere reminded May of an unhygienic brothel he had once visited in Tangiers, strictly in the course of an investigation. 'May I introduce Dame Maud Hackshaw . . .'

A middle-aged lady with improbable mauve hair and tele-scope-dense spectacle lenses eagerly clasped their hands. 'Hello, ducks,' she said. 'Charmed, I'm sure.'

'She's a true force for positive energy,' said Maggie. 'She's predicted so many births that the spiritualist newspapers nick-named her Madame Ovary. Over there, Junior Warlock for our north-eastern branch, Stanley Olthwaite. He came to our Win-ter Solstice snack 'n' spells party to help with the washing-up, and ended up staying on.'

A skinny young man in wellingtons and a patched tweed overcoat eagerly removed his flat cap. "Ow do.'

John May started to feel as if he had wandered into an old Will Hay comedy. Something was making him itch. He resolved not to touch anything unusual.

'Maureen you've already met. Don't get up, love, it's not worth the risk. And Wendy, our organist.' Looking at the outrageously buxom, slender-waisted Wendy, rising to greet them as much as her tight spencer would allow, May under-stood why Stanley Olthwaite had elected to stay.

'Vicky said they needed a hand, like, at the centre,' Olthwaite told the detectives. 'I came out of the army with nowt; I'd done tours of duty in Northern Ireland, Kosovo, Basra, and ended up working as a bloody security guard in Newcastle.'

'Then he heard the call,' said Maggie, clasping her hands over her bosom. 'These are spiritually lean times, and we needed someone who could manage heavy lifting. Plus he had his own spade and socket set, you see. Actually, we were just in the middle of a séance, but I put it on pause when I saw you coming, a little trick I learned from my new book.'

'A volume of invocations?' asked Bryant.

'No, it's the instruction manual for my DVD player, but the principle's the same. I'm glad you're here, because funnily enough your name came up just as Maureen started her spirit writing. Grab a seat.'

'Well, we really can't—' May began.

'No, I think this is important because there's something very strange going on out here. We've been picking up some disturbing signals. The indications suggest we are in the presence of death. Snow elementals like to provide mortals with signs; it makes them feel useful.'

How could she know? thought May. *How does she always know?* Whether one was a believer or not, the cheerful little witch possessed a talent that had been tempered in adversity. She had never exploited her skills, but had dedicated her life to helping those left in pain and confusion by loss. May suspected she was more of a natural psychologist than most people, and this gave her abilities others ascribed to supernaturalism. Certainly, she had a phenomenal success rate in helping the PCU, even if her advice often seemed somewhat tangential to the investigation at hand.

Stanley helped the detectives inside, and Maggie closed the rear door. Bryant's watery blue eyes had trouble adjusting after the blinding glare of the snowscape. As he found himself in the middle of a circle lit by a pair of paraffin lamps, it seemed as though he had stepped back into some dim-remembered past. The scene reminded him of a chiaroscuro painting by Wright of Derby, the flickering amber uplighting the faces of the group, the whispering drapes casting twisted shadows, the rising wind creaking against the struts of the truck walls. No matter how many times his partner had tried to dismiss the coven of St James as an anachronistic absurdity, the conviction of its members drew them both towards belief in the unthinkable. The strange intensity of those within the circle had the power to siphon off cynicism and breed conviction in the unknown.

'What form do these indications take?' asked Bryant.

'There is a dark vibration in the air that can be read with a mind trained to such fluctuations of the spirit,' said Maggie. 'Maureen and I have both felt it very strongly. It could mean that someone has died as the result of being trapped in these freezing temperatures,' said Maggie, 'but I don't think so. Different types of death elicit different readings. The quiet ebbing away of a life force is very different from the sensations created by an act of violence. One might compare these feelings to seismic readings, the former a series of gently undulating waves, the latter jagged and tightly packed. I should have known you were here. The signs always grow stronger in your presence, Arthur. Your life is so often at risk. Now they will read the signs for you.'

At the centre of the circle, perched beside a folding card table and preparing for the impromptu séance, sat Maureen, a fleshy, sallow young woman in a brown roll-neck sweater and jeans. Her right hand rested lightly on a ballpoint pen, at the centre of a dozen sheets of foolscap. Her head had fallen forward and was partly obscured by a curtain of lank brown hair. She might have been asleep. The pen moved with almost imperceptible slowness, but picked up speed as Bryant approached. As neat letters formed – too neat to have been drawn freehand with one's head bowed – the coven members read aloud. The intense concentration of the group would have impressed the most staunch nonbeliever.

The woman's pale hand drifted across the sheet, leaving behind a letter C. The pen jumped, forming an R, then an O. Bryant felt the tiny white hairs on the back of his neck begin to prickle.

'Crow,' said Wendy.

'Crotch,' said Stanley Olthwaite.

'Cormorant,' said Maggie.

'Crossroads, she's trying to write crossroads,' said Dame Maud. 'The unholy spot where the guilty were jeered by the mob, then hanged and buried alive in punishment for their sins.'

Another O appeared on the paper.

'Or perhaps she's missed an episode of *Coronation Street*,' said Dame Maud.

'No, it's corridors,' said Stanley softly, as if deciphering a crossword clue that had been eluding him. The pen moved again, but no ink appeared. With head still bowed, the spirit writer suddenly jabbed the tip into her left palm until it bled. Using the tiny pool of blood as a reservoir, she continued to scrawl in an unbroken flow. Not a word this time but a drawing, childlike and unfocused, caused by the difficulty of writing without ink.

The face which formed was thin and young, with high cheekbones and sunken eyes where the blood spread into hollows, but it could have been anyone. Now Wendy had rocked back on her knees and was chanting something too softly for Bryant to catch beneath the moaning of the wind.

At that moment, the gusting stopped and the air became silent and still, revealing her whispered words. 'Four pathways, two leading directly to death and two leading to salvation. Between God and Mephisto stand the white corridors.' She fell forward, and was caught by Olthwaite, who gently set her to sleep on a stack of pillows.

'White corridors always spell danger because they represent conduits through which evil can pass,' whispered Maggie. 'Do you have any way of interpreting this, Arthur?'

'I think I may be able to shed some light,' said Bryant, catching his partner's eye. 'We are looking for a murderer who has struck among the passengers trapped here. I think you'll find that the first white corridor is right outside, the snowbound roadway on which we find ourselves marooned. The second is the corridor leading to the London mortuary where our friend Oswald Finch has been found dead, a crime we are equally prevented from solving.'

'Then what are the other two?' asked May. For once he felt no desire to ridicule Maggie and her colleagues.

'The readings are not always literal.' Maggie watched her friend as she wiped her bloodstained hand with a cloth and fumbled with her hair band, as disoriented as a patient emerging from anesthetic. 'You have to look beyond the corporeal to find another interpretation. These corridors might represent states of mind. They are perhaps intended for you to find a path through disorder. Or they may serve to remind you of something only half remembered, some signifying event that you have tried long and hard to bury deep within your subconscious. There are other times and places than those our bodies lead us to.'

Outside the army truck, the freezing brightness of the snow and the glaring white sky broke the spell that had held May for the past few minutes. Blinking in the light he felt foolish, ashamed that age and doubt had led him to believe the things he had ridiculed in his youth.

'There is help on the way, but your lives will be endangered before it can arrive,' Maggie called. 'Pass safely. The message was personal, and directed at you both. We shouldn't leave the truck now that Wendy has cast her circle of protection around us. But we'll be here if you should need spiritual help.'

She watched them totter off through the snow arm in arm, and worried for their safety. Removed from the protection of the PCU, they looked so small and frail. 'You must understand the meaning of all the corridors in your life, not just this one,' she shouted after them, pointing to the obliterated road with its cars marooned like fishing boats in a frozen tide. 'You must look into your hearts. Only then can we help you further.' But her anxious words of warning were lost in the rising wind.

She knew the ways of men, knew that anger was clouding his mind in a raging fire. He would shove on through the snow, smashing his fists against the vehicles that imprisoned him here, scattering shards of ice across the road. She had hidden his new passport, his disgusting photographs. He would be looking in the fields and on the road, but would have sensed that neither

Madeline nor her son were to be found outside, which meant they were sheltering in another vehicle. He was thinking that the roads were still impassable, so she had to be here within reach. All this she knew about him.

He would become more systematic in his hunt for her. He'd told her he had once gone hunting with his grandfather, and had killed a mountain boar from the safety of a hide. That was what he needed now, a vantage point from which he could watch their movements.

Madeline felt a kinship with her hunter. She knew he would find an abandoned truck and climb up on to its roof where, lying on his elbows, he could watch the entire column of cars. They had taken the food from the emergency blanket. Tracks led forward from it, towards the head of the traffic jam. He would count the vehicles in which she might have taken shelter, and check them one by one. Then, armed with a stolen weapon, he would slip down from the truck roof and make his way inexorably towards them . . .

'The motorway and the mortuary I can understand, but where are the third and fourth corridors?' asked Bryant, struggling through a particularly deep drift. 'My toes feel like they belong to someone else. Is that frostbite, do you think, or are my boots too tight?'

'We're not meant to take any of that literally,' said May. 'Why is it that oracles are always so lacking in specific details?'

'How quickly you become a doubter again.' Bryant sighed. 'A return to brightness is all it takes to dispel the shadows created by belief.'

'You have to admit, it's pretty far-fetched that a bunch of tree-hugging spirit-chasing madrigal-chanters in the back of a truck can locate a murderer.'

'They didn't say they could do that, only that they could provide psychological signposts. You discuss cases with fellow officers who are barely qualified to hold all the facts of an investigation in their heads, men and women for whom anything but the most logical and direct progression of thought is anathema. Here, you are doing the opposite. Those people in the truck spend much of their lives in a dream state.'

'You're just confirming my worst fears by saying that, Arthur.'

'But don't you see? It qualifies them to aid us in other ways. They can restore the logic of childhood with simple symbolism we must learn to read.'

'All right, I'll try,' said May, struggling with the idea. 'Perhaps the third corridor lies in the house where the killer grew up. Perhaps it is the key to his aberrant behaviour.'

'And the fourth?'

'I have an idea about that, too. But it's not one I wish to entertain at the present.'

In all the time they had worked together, there had been few subjects that May had been unwilling to discuss, but Bryant now felt he had stumbled on to one of them. He sensed a sudden veil of secrecy descending between them.

As the detectives made their way back around the road to Alma's stranded Bedford van, they saw two hunched figures weaving and hopping through the drifts towards them.

'Thank God,' Madeline gasped. 'We thought there was no one else out here. Can you help us?'

37

INEXPLICABLE

Madeline told them the full story, omitting no detail. There was something about these elderly gentlemen that encouraged her to do so without hesitation. She felt safe in their company, although she could see that they would hardly be able to provide protection against Johann. Everything tumbled out as she sought to end the burden of her secret. The tall elegant one scribbled notes as she talked, asking her to expand on details, while the elderly white-haired gentleman squatted on a roll of bubble wrap with his hands buried deep in his pockets and his wrinkled head all but consumed by his gargantuan overcoat. They, in turn, saw a nervous thin blonde with large eyes and a graceful neck, who was clearly in a state of distress.

'When he killed his mother, he said a shaft of sunlight opened to Heaven, and he showed his defiance to God. It's what he still watches for whenever he kills, a corridor through the clouds to God. I know it sounds insane—'

'And this Johann—'

'That's not his real name; I think it's the name of one of his victims, but I have nothing else to call him.'

'But you're saying he behaved normally towards you until you confronted him at the villa?'

'That's right. I trusted him. He was very charming. Ask Ryan.'

'You liked him as well?' May asked the boy.

'He was nice. And he had a great car. Like my dad.' Ryan was more intent on examining the interior of the van, which smelled of leather, rust and peppermint.

'You think he followed you here for no other purpose than to prevent you from exposing him?' asked May. 'May I see your evidence?'

'I have it in an envelope, or rather I've put it somewhere safe, in the car we rented – I can go back and get it for you.' She tried to set her handbag on the dashboard but it slid off, her book and purse falling out on the floor. Bryant shovelled everything back in and handed it to her. As he did so, he studied her eyes for clues to her state of mind, and saw a mother determined to show strength for the sake of her child.

'Perhaps we should get it later. Tell us about the contents of the envelope.'

'The passport of one of the men he murdered, and a set of photographs, terrible photographs—' She pressed a hand to her face, lowering her voice to a whisper. 'Women whose faces he'd disfigured with some kind of tool; he takes their picture afterwards and keeps them on him. Why would a man do something like that? I had no idea how dangerous he was, until – he moves about in the snow like an animal, and I think he carries a hunting knife. He chased us through the village, and came to find us when we got off the ferry to hire a car. We were barely able to escape with our lives.'

'The issue-point of the passport could give us some idea of the trail he's leaving,' said May. 'There have been killers operating in Europe who have assumed the identity of each of their victims before moving on. It's not difficult to do when you're crossing so many borders and states.'

'I took something from the envelope, just to carry with me.' She handed the detectives a single sheet of paper.

May unfolded the page and examined the names scribbled on it. He read: *Pascal Favier, Patrice Bezard, Johann Bellocq, Edward Winthrop, Paulo Escobar, Pierre Castel.* 'What's this?'

'I think they're names he's copied from other passports, people whose identities he has assumed,' said Madeline.

'And you say one of these names belongs to the old man you saw lying dead in the villa he took you to?'

'That's right, but I didn't see him dead, I just thought I did. Johann told me he had left the owner upstairs, dead.'

'And he insisted that his name was Johann Bellocq, so perhaps he had taken the identity of this latest victim. Which means you have no idea what his real name might be.' May glanced up at the frozen woman and her son. 'Look, we have food in the cabin. Make yourself at home while John and I think this through.'

'Why?' said Madeline. 'He just needs to be stopped, can't you see that?'

'Yes, but it's not the way we work,' said May apologetically.

'We need to know where the sequence of victims begins.' Bryant studied the page of names. 'I have some people I can contact.'

'I hope they're in the Sûreté,' said May.

'Not exactly. Do you remember the members of the Panic Site?'

'That website set up by Dr Harold Masters, the academic who runs the Insomnia Squad? Arthur, they're all completely loopy, if not actually dangerous.'

'Obsessives perhaps, but occasionally quite brilliant.' Masters's group of rogue intellectuals stayed on-line through the night to argue about everything from Quakerism to corn deities, before returning bleary-eyed to their jobs in the capital's museums and art galleries. 'They're affiliated to a bunch of expatriate crime fans based in Nice, most of whom are former coppers. Janice put the number in my speed dial.'

'Can you give them a call?'

'I'm afraid I have absolutely no idea how to use that particular function,' Bryant admitted.

'Give me your mobile. You think they'll know someone who can run a check on these names?'

'Bound to, old sock. I told you we were looking for someone

from a mountain region. Mrs Gilby is right, he's probably adept at moving about in extreme weather conditions. If he's a tracker, he'll run a sweep from car to car, narrowing down the search until he finds her – and us.'

They settled Madeline and Ryan in the rear of the van and locked them inside, then returned to the cabin to call Dan Banbury, who was better positioned to find out the status of the rescue services. 'They're waiting to try again with the chopper,' he told them, 'but it looks like there's one more really big squall on the way. It should hit you in the next hour or so. After that, you'll have to hope that the northeasterly wind drops and makes way for rising temperatures. The Devon and Cornwall police say there's little chance of the snow ploughs breaking through until daybreak tomorrow. Part of the road outside Totnes has collapsed, and there have been avalanches large enough to block nearly all of the major routes.'

'Then we really are alone,' said May, dismayed. 'Except for a few frozen salesmen, a terrified woman, a handful of practising pagans and a murderer.'

'Who are you calling now?' asked Bryant.

'A friend of mine at the International Bureau of Investigation. Before you start trying with Harold Masters, let me run the list of names past them. We need to see if any of these have been reported. If we can place them in the right order, starting in the French Alps and plotting a path to Dover, they might even give us a clue to his real identity. Don't worry, I'll fall back on your friend Dr Masters if I have to.' *And if all normal paths of investigation fail first*, he caught himself thinking.

'Edward Winthrop,' said Bryant, tapping his dashboard. 'The name rings a bell. It sticks out from all the others on that list. I've definitely heard it before.' He dug a battered alligator-skin address book from his overcoat and flicked through it.

'What have you got in there?'

'Missing persons, murder victims, suspects, Alma's shopping lists, key witnesses, and people who have generally annoyed me,' said Bryant. 'It runs into several notebooks, as you can imagine, especially the last category. Here we are. Edward Winthrop, a London lawyer murdered in Marseilles in 2004.'

'Why would he be of interest to you?'

'Because he was killed in a police station,' said Bryant with some satisfaction, 'by the young man he had come to represent. It was in all the papers, sparked an extraordinary court case. You have your starting point, I think.'

May connected his laptop to his mobile and began composing e-mails. 'I know nothing about the movements and motives of serial killers,' he admitted. 'So many other terrible crimes go unreported, it seems they get a disproportionate amount of publicity through books, films and television, yet there are only really a handful.'

'A handful who get caught,' Bryant corrected. 'We have no way of knowing how many others are cunning or merely lucky enough to get away with their crimes. Roberto Succo terrorized the South of France in the 1980s, slaughtering anyone who got in his way. He was a twenty-five-year-old Italian who'd been locked in a mental institution for stabbing his parents to death. A supreme egotist – nothing mattered to him, not life or death. He saw himself as already dead, and was so confident that he operated right under the noses of the police. How do you catch someone like that? Andrei Romanovic Chikatilo killed over fifty women and children in Russia. He showed no remorse or even any understanding of his cruelties.' He settled himself into his seat. 'Most of the murderers we've faced have been desperate men and women who've killed to cover their own weaknesses, not murdered indiscriminately. I've done a bit of reading in this area and have some statistics here somewhere.' He pulled a handful of black leather notebooks from his pocket and blew the fluff from them.

'Hang on,' said May. 'Exactly how many of those do you own?'

'Forty-six,' Bryant answered matter-of-factly. 'I was going to quote from a few during my convention speech.' He riffled the pages. 'Ah, listen to this. Did you know that seventy-seven per cent of all serial killers are American citizens, and only sixteen per cent are European? Eighty-four per cent are white, sixteen per cent are black. Ninety per cent are male heterosexuals. Sixty-five per cent of the victims are female, and ninety per cent of all victims are white. A quarter start killing when they're teenaged, half start in their twenties, the remaining quarter begin in their thirties. But then we have the anomalies, like the elderly Dr Harold Shipman, the world's worst serial killer, with at least four hundred attributable deaths to his name, who injected lethal doses of Pethidine into vulnerable English ladies who loved and trusted him. He fitted the pattern of being arrogant and violent-tempered, but many of his crimes remained undiscovered for decades. His wife Primrose supposedly never guessed the truth. Dozens of questions about him remain unanswered, and the authorities are still not sure if they've found all the victims.

'A lot of serial killers are boring, mentally subnormal and inadequate as human beings, which rather contradicts the image of the superior intellectual usually portrayed in films. We've never really dealt with psychopathic brutality before. My wits can't protect me against such an opponent, and this hostile environment makes me realize how vulnerable I've become. How do you find, let alone stop, someone like this? The PCU isn't equipped to locate such people. There are special units to deal with them, I remember, because I took Alma to see *The Silence of the Lambs*. If I were to speculate on how such people are created, I'd guess that geography plays a part, just as much as family upbringing and rogue chromosomes. Europe can be just as lonely as America. Think of all the desolate landscapes that are barely populated for most of the year, places where no one remembers you.'

'But the same things happen in cities, where alienation and hardship are just as rife,' argued May. 'Look at London, and how conducive its society has been to cruel practices. Children are raised in a paradoxical environment of decadence and restriction. How many of them truly learn to think and behave like rational adults? What are we breeding in our schools and on our streets now that traditional society has been so radically transformed?'

'For once I must agree with you,' said Bryant. 'I think the science of rationality is being pushed aside to make way for new superstitions. Look at the move to teach the mysteries of God's will beside Darwinism under the term "intelligent design", the reliance on discredited homeopathic drugs to treat cancers we know to be caused by poor diet and cigarettes, the rise of pyramid-selling religions sold under the guise of lifestyle-improving courses. We've substituted opinions for expertise. It's obvious when you think about it. Through the proliferation of clutter, our access to hard information is being radically reduced. If you take away knowledge you create myth – not the old myths that help to underpin and elucidate the human condition, but ones with the more sinister purpose of increasing commercial gain.'

May shook his head sadly. 'I thought the Internet would transform the world, but half the time it's just another method of spreading disinformation. This isn't our field, Arthur. Look how the Highwayman had us fooled, simply because we refused to believe the truth that was right in front of us.'

'Some changes in society are too painful to accept easily,' Bryant admitted, his eyes downcast. 'The power of the human mind remains inexplicable.' He was thinking of May's guarded reaction to the spirit writing. 'Where does that leave us now?'

'We may be isolated in a hostile environment, but we have a world of help at our fingertips. He's just one man working alone in a limited space, and we will catch him. Now, you call Harold Masters, and I'll call the Bureau.'

38

HEART OF OAK

'There's something I have to tell you,' said DC Meera Mangeshkar. 'Let's grab a sandwich.' Meera and Colin were returning from a fruitless visit to Owen Mills's neighbours, who had treated the officers with a mixture of disdain and mistrust. 'My sister Jezminder works here.'

Bimsley noted the family resemblance the minute he saw the girl behind the counter of Café Nero in Camden High Street. Jezminder was older and taller than her sister, more graceful of limb, more downcast of eye, although, he noted, she wore Meera's trademark toe-capped boots and men's baggy jeans. They ordered tea and toast as Meera circled sections of her copious notes. 'That girl on the top floor fancied you,' she remarked with studied casualness.

'The one with the blond plait?' He folded a whole piece of toast into his mouth and couldn't speak for a minute while he chewed. 'I didn't notice,' he finally managed.

'Oh, come on, all that guff about why you weren't in uniform and where you go in the evenings. She didn't answer any of your questions properly, and kept watching you from the corner of her eye.'

'She didn't know Owen Mills.' Bimsley dunked his second piece of toast in his tea, filling the saucer. 'She was just a time-waster.'

'Then you shouldn't have kept on asking her questions. If you fancy her, you can go back there on your own time, not the unit's.' Meera pointedly tore the girl's interview form into quarters.

'I don't know what's wrong with you,' he complained. 'I can never do anything right.'

'Let's just drop it.'

'Is this what you wanted to talk to me about? Or did you just want to have a good old go at me somewhere warm, where your mouth could work properly?'

'No, it's about Finch. You know I admitted I was there on Tuesday morning.'

'I heard. You wanted to sit in on the autopsy.'

'Yeah. Actually, I had a bit of a row with him. He wouldn't let me stay, said it violated the privacy rights of the victim. Started going on about dignity in death, and how I didn't have the proper qualifications. I answered back, you know how I do, and he virtually started pushing me towards the door. It wasn't like him. He was agitated, sweating and red in the face, really angry, and the room was really warm, like he'd had the wall heaters going full blast, but he always says how much he hates the heat in there.'

'Why didn't you tell Raymond all this?'

She looked sheepishly down at her mug. 'I was upset. I get treated like the office junior even though I've got years of experience in some of the toughest cop shops in London. Even May's granddaughter gets more respect, and she's got no formal training. I didn't go for sergeant because it would have meant I couldn't stay at the unit, with Janice already occupying that position. I just want to be taken seriously.'

'For what it's worth, I take you seriously,' said Bimsley. 'You're a true professional, Meera. You're just too hard on yourself. All you need to do is lighten up a bit. But you need to tell the others about arguing with Oswald.'

'I've a feeling some of them suspect me,' she said miserably. 'I haven't exactly made friends at the unit.'

'It's never too late to start,' said Bimsley, giving her an encouraging smile.

He thought about the young Indian detective constable while she went to speak with her sister; perhaps the fault had lain with him. He had assumed that her anger was an issue connected with race and class, some kind of attitude she was working through. Now he saw that she simply wanted to be accepted as a team player.

His thoughts were interrupted by the sound of raised voices at the counter. Glancing up, he saw an emaciated young man with a shaved head attempting to grab Jezminder's arm as Meera warned him off. Bimsley instinctively pushed back from the table and made his way over.

'Let go of the lady, mate,' he warned.

'I've told him,' said Jezminder, 'he can't come in here while I am working.'

'Who is he?' asked Colin.

'He used to be her boyfriend,' said Meera with a grimace of disapproval. 'Jake, she's told you before about turning up here. She doesn't want to see you any more.' He was half as tall again as the little detective constable. Meera was prepared to take on anyone, but even she stepped back as he tried to slap her with a bony fist.

'I'm her man, not yours, all right? So I've got the right to—'

It took barely a second for Bimsley to assess the situation. The boyfriend was chasing cash, and he could see why; the urgency burned fiercely within his hollow eyes, robbing him of rationality. Heroin addicts were usually wheedling, pathetic, needy, but this one was dangerous. He grabbed at Jezminder's bag, breaking the strap as the two girls tried to push him away.

Colin had trained for six years at the Hoxton Boys' Boxing Club until his instructor had warned him to stay away, not because he lost his matches or failed training, or even because he lacked the essential hand-eye coordination of his profession, but because his reach was too short and his wildly swinging fists were potentially lethal.

He unleashed one now, the right, and listened as it connected with Jake's jaw. There it was, the sound he remembered hearing at the gym, the tearing of jaw muscle as Jake went down.

'Ganesh!' said Meera, watching as he slammed on to the tiled floor, for her mother had taught her to invoke Indian gods rather than swear like a navvy whenever she was surprised. Jake was out cold.

'Do you want him in rehab, or do you just want him gone?' asked Colin, sitting his opponent upright and checking his jaw.

'Gone,' whispered Jezminder.

Back on the street, Meera looked at him warily, as if seeing a new side of her colleague.

'What?' he asked, not liking to be stared at. 'I'm sorry about that. I'm usually a bit of a pacifist. I didn't mean to hit him so hard.'

'Never mind.'

'Then don't stare at me. You make me uncomfortable.'

'I was noticing. You have a heart of oak,' she said finally. 'Probably got a head to match, though.' She saw that the knuckles of his right hand were scraped, dripping dark sap.

'I'm fine,' he told her. But he could sense that something had changed between them. For the first time, she was looking upon him with kindness and, unless he was imagining it, something altogether more interesting.

39

CIRCE

The fake-leopardskin coat scratched her neck, the red woollen two-piece suit was too tight across the bust, and the patent-leather heels pinched, but DS Janice Longbright looked good and knew it. *This is no way to run an investigation,* she thought, strutting across the illuminated green glass of the causeway that acted as a catwalk into Circe, *but I know it's what Arthur would have made me do.* She strode up to the counter and asked to see the woman whose name was on the card she had been given. She had decided to pay her induction fee by using the credit-card details Raymond Land had asked her to acquire for his wife. Leanne Land deserved to pay for having an affair with a golf caddie behind her husband's back.

'I'm afraid Miss Grutzmacher is taking a class at the moment, but you can see someone else about induction suitability,' the receptionist told her, picking up a modular white trim-phone and smiling vacantly into the middle distance.

Juan-Luis was a ponytailed young Spaniard with more than a hint of the flamenco dancer in his movements. He shook Longbright's hand so lightly that she felt touched by an angel, then led her to a white room bordered by recessed blue lights and deep-purple seating before flopping down beside her. 'You say you were recommended by Monsieur Alphonse for one of our rejuvenation courses?' he said, checking his PDA.

'I won't be on the system yet,' said Longbright. 'I only just saw him this morning. You come very highly recommended. A friend's daughter has been receiving treatment here, a girl called Lilith Starr. I wonder, how is she doing?'

Clearly, the conversation had taken a turn for which he had not been prepared. A momentary fluster occurred in his composure before he returned to form. 'I'm not sure I know who you mean . . .'

'You must do. She was personally recommended by Mr Spender.'

'Well, that wouldn't be my area. I only handle induction. Besides, our client details are confidential.'

'But if you conduct all the inductions, you must have seen her.'

Juan-Luis sighed. Clearly, the subject was not going to go away. 'I think she is no longer with us.'

'Really? I find that surprising, as she was singled out for special attention.'

'I heard the treatment proved unsuitable for her. A medical condition . . .'

'Surely your treatments don't require a doctor's intervention?'

'Everyone has to fill out an approval form, and she omitted to tell us about certain – ah – medications.'

'You mean not just prescription drugs but others associated with –'

'– lifestyle choices. That's correct.'

So he knows about her habit, thought Longbright. 'But I thought she came to you for several treatments. My friend said—'

'Look, as soon as we discovered she had filled the form in falsely, we cancelled her appointments.'

'Why would you do that? I mean if she had made her own choices—'

'Because there are diets, exercise regimes and supplements we prefer our clients to take, and obviously we can't risk their health.'

Or the lawsuits, thought Longbright. 'So what was wrong with her?'

Juan-Luis could see she would not rest until he had provided satisfactory information, and he badly needed to hit this week's client quota. He set aside his PDA and lowered his voice. 'Apart from the recreational drugs she chose to use, she had been taking Haldol since she was a child. It's a drug formerly used to control behavioural problems in children.'

'You mean her parents had it prescribed for her?'

'I imagine so, but it should have been stopped, because it has long been known to pose health risks, like low blood pressure and even cardiac arrest, and there's potential cross-reaction with other chemicals that makes it unsafe at any dosage. Unfortunately, Haldol can also be addictive.'

'Do you prescribe drugs for your patients? Anti-ageing potions, anything like that?'

'You're a police officer, aren't you.' He offered the statement as a matter of fact. 'Listen, it's not my company, I have no vested interests here, but I can tell you the rules are strictly adhered to. We provide our clients with medical supervision in the form of advice and, in certain cases, dietary aids. We never suggest they can stave off illness and live for ever just by changing their diet and exercising more, like some clubs promise, but we show them how they can live healthier, more active lives for longer.'

'But in your brochure you recommend homeopathic remedies.'

'We make no claims that they'll perform miracles, but I admit, sometimes women want to believe more than we can promise.' He shrugged. 'It's up to them.'

As she left the clinic, Longbright tried to make sense of what she had learned. It was possible that Lilith had not died as a direct result of her drug use, in which case someone else might have felt responsible for her death.

She returned to the unit and sought out Giles Kershaw. An idea had begun to form in her head, but it was one that could lead them all into trouble, for it meant lodging an accusation against a fellow officer.

40

PERFORMING THE IMPOSSIBLE

'I feel like I might be heading down the wrong route with this,' Longbright told the pathologist. 'We *have* definitely discounted the most likely causes, haven't we?'

'I told you that,' said Kershaw, falling in beside her as they headed through the unit. 'The primary blow to his chest is the one that initiated the seizure. The neck bruise is secondary.'

'Then I need to run something by you.'

'Try me.'

'Suppose someone other than Mills came to the mortuary to check on Lilith Starr, and ended up arguing with Oswald Finch about her cause of death? By that time, Finch's notes had already been removed, although Mills still insists it wasn't him. What if Finch set down the true cause of her death, and it laid the blame at someone else's door – God knows, Oswald was never afraid to accuse others. That would place Mills in the clear, but who would it point to?'

'Not a member of the PCU staff,' Kershaw remarked, 'because none of them knew the victim. What about her parents?'

'Highly unlikely, don't you think? Our pugnacious Sergeant Renfield was the one who brought her in. Finch might have threatened to report him for some minor transgression. He had the power to do so. A lot of senior officers in the Met held him in the highest regard. Plus, Renfield and Finch had always hated each other.'

'Renfield prides himself on playing by the book. He would have been mortified to be reported by a man he considered his enemy.'

Longbright felt she was finally on the right track. 'I think Renfield returned to the mortuary for some reason, and found Finch writing up a report that accused him of failure to carry out correct procedure.'

'The sergeant certainly has the right temperament,' Kershaw admitted.

'Wasn't he once placed on a month's paid leave for attacking another officer? Finch would probably have goaded him. You know how he liked to wind people up. Suppose he realized that the girl could have been saved if Renfield had acted differently? What was he doing accompanying a body to the morgue anyway? If Lilith Starr wasn't just another Camden overdose after all, Renfield should have noticed something and called in medics at once. Imagine Finch spotting that. He challenges the sergeant, the limit of Renfield's patience is reached, and he gives Finch a little happy-slap . . .'

'But the pathologist is old and infirm, and the effect on him is more drastic than intended.' Kershaw seized on the idea, taking it further. 'He collapses on the floor. Renfield panics, looks about the room, sees the loose ceiling-fan cover and decides to make it look like an accident. He leaves the room, closing the door behind him.'

'You realize what will happen if we try to take him in as a suspect,' warned Longbright. 'All these years we've spent attempting to heal the rift between the PCU and the Metropolitan Police. We'll have to fight them head-on.'

'The Princess Royal's visit is scheduled to commence in precisely five hours, but I see little sign of preparation for her appearance,' said Rosemary Armstrong, the royal appointments secretary. Upon her arrival she had glanced about the unit with a vaguely horrified air before flicking a handkerchief over the chair April had offered her. A search for a teacup had commenced, but April had only been able to produce a clean mug bearing the shield of St Crispin's Boys' School, which Bryant had swiped in the course of their last investigation.

'We are a working unit,' said April, 'and today is especially busy. We're short-staffed, and—'

'Yes, yes.' Armstrong impatiently waved the thought aside. 'I'm sure we all have lots of work to do, yes? But by this evening the Princess will be quite fatigued, and in no mood for a poor show. Last night she had to sit through a performance of *The Marriage of Figaro* that could, with the utmost charity, have best been described as pedestrian, and today she is required to unveil a plaque dedicated to the Dagenham Girl Pipers before attending your presentation. Few people can imagine the stamina required to handle her responsibilities.' She rose and peered from the corner window overlooking the road. 'What on earth is that down there?'

'It's Camden High Street.'

'What a pity. Does it always look like that?'

'I'm afraid so, yes.'

'With all those people milling about? That won't do. I thought we'd decided on barriers.'

'The mayor was against the idea, I'm afraid.'

'That ghastly little Trot? Well, I suppose these things can't be helped. I assume you can assure me that the building will have been thoroughly cleaned and tidied, with the fresh-cut flowers I requested in place throughout the offices by five o'clock, yes? That everyone will be in their places, and that the royal protocol brochures will have been read and digested? We cannot risk breaches of etiquette simply because some members of staff have failed to observe a few painfully simple rules.'

'We'll certainly do our best to ensure that the princess has a pleasant and informative visit,' said April.

'Hmm.' Rosemary Armstrong looked as if she did not believe it for a minute, but the girl was sweet enough and seemed eager to please. 'I shall be with the Princess for the rest of the day, and as she does not approve of mobile telephones, mine will be switched off, so if there are any problems, you'll simply have to sort them out yourself. Oh, and one other thing – ' She waggled her fingers at the air. 'There's a most peculiar smell in here. It seems to be emanating from that cat. The Princess has allergies, and is very sensitive to a lack of freshness. Make it disappear, would you?'

'What a dreadful woman,' said Raymond Land after the royal secretary had wafted from the building in a haze of old English gardenia. 'What are we going to do when they return expecting a full complement of staff? April, it's your job to look after the unit, can't you think of something?'

'What about a bomb scare?' she suggested. 'We could get the area cordoned off, have the visit cancelled. It would be nobody's fault.'

Land was too worried to hear her. 'If she doesn't come here and assess our operation in a positive light, we risk losing all of our remaining funding. It's absolutely imperative that she approves and reports back to Kasavian. How did we ever get into this mess? It's Bryant's fault, trotting off to a ridiculous spiritualists' convention and taking our best man with him. We're for the high jump, there's no way out of it this time. Obviously we can't get them back here by five, but we have to release the rest of the staff from house arrest, and that means finding an explanation for Oswald's death.' He checked his watch. 'We've got a five-hour window. Surely it's not asking the impossible?'

It seemed to be a rite of passage at the PCU that the performance of the impossible was required from every member of staff at least once during their tenure. April had already risked her life for the unit, as her mother had done before her. Only weeks ago she had almost been thrown to her death from the top of a building during the unmasking of the Highwayman. Now, she realized, with her grandfather out of action and everyone else trying to solve Oswald Finch's murder, their survival might be in her hands alone.

41

DIABLE

'We've had a call back, Arthur,' said John May, checking his messages. 'You were right about the London lawyer, Edward Winthrop. He was sent to Marseilles to attempt the extradition of a young man named Pascal Favier, but Favier managed to attack him in an empty courtyard, knocking the lawyer un-conscious and stealing his identity. Winthrop died of a fractured skull. Favier was never caught.'

Bryant's eyes lit up. 'Then the police must have been tracking him ever since. Why haven't they been able to catch him?'

'Who knows how efficient these people are?' May replied. 'I don't suppose the local police were notified properly. All kinds of communication breakdowns occur between the regions. It sounds as if he's been travelling through the southern provinces of France, adopting the identities of those he has assaulted and left for dead. Hang on, another positive ID coming in.' He played back the rest of the returned calls, listening intently. 'There's a Johann Bellocq registered as the owner of a villa in Eze-sur-Mer, which ties in with Madeline's story. We can get the local gendarmes to go around there now.'

'It still doesn't help us with the real identity of this maniac who's out there in the snow, unless they can find a link which proves that Pascal Favier and Johann Bellocq are one and the same. I feel so hand-tied, stuck in here.' Bryant threw himself back in the passenger seat, frustrated.

May checked through his notes. 'Madeline Gilby said Johann confessed his past to her. He said that his beloved grandfather had died, leaving him alone with his mother, and that he murdered her. He spent just five years in a church which operated as the local mental hospital, run by nuns – apparently there were mitigating circumstances surrounding the mother's death – but the reprieve did him no good, as he became a member of something called Le Société du Diable, some kind of neo-Nazi organization run from Jean-Marie Le Pen country. After leaving there, who knows where he went? Presumably this was the period in which he committed the crimes that landed him in trouble in Marseilles. After his escape he went off-radar again, living somewhere in the Alpes-Maritimes area, until killing this Bellocq chap.

'So, somewhere in that history there must be records revealing his movements, and we can provide the identities he adopted. What's the point of having satellite tracking systems if they can't keep tabs on people like him? I mean, it's little use knowing where he's been. We need to know what's making him strike now. If we understand what drives him, perhaps we can stop him. Luckily, we have an expert right here who may be able to help us.'

May saw how his partner's mind was working. 'Don't tell me. Your white witch – she'll know all about satanic groups.'

'Exactly. I have to go and talk to her.'

'No, let me do it,' said May. 'You can't take any more cold. Stay here in the warm with Madeline and the boy. Just tell me what you want to ask her.'

'He's followed Mrs Gilby here for two reasons: he wants what she took from him, and he's developed an obsession with her. She says he believes that only she can redeem him. He can give the authorities the slip every time he changes identity, but if they get a fix on him he's sunk. She has the passport of the last man he killed, and he needs it back. He might try to contact other branches of this Société du Diable, and use their members in some way. Ask Maggie if they also operate from somewhere in the UK. Find out if they've heard from him, and warn them that he's dangerous. These groups are notoriously private. Contrary to what the newspapers would have us believe, they rarely try to recruit innocent members of the public. But they must be made to inform us if he gets in touch. It would be helpful to know exactly what it is they believe in, and if he's operating in accordance with their doctrines.'

After May had plunged off into the diamond drifts once more, Bryant called the Plymouth Emergency Services and tracked down their Severe Weather supervisor, who informed him that they had abandoned the use of helicopters and were still working hard to clear the railway tracks. The first train was setting off in a few minutes, and would reach them in just over an hour.

Bryant was both pleased and dismayed by the news. He looked forward to being able to feel his extremities again, but knew that a train might bring those who would take the case away from him. He sat back and thought about Johann Bellocq's missing passport, and the young woman who had hidden it. Bellocq needed his past identities in order to stay free, but he also saw a chance of salvation in Madeline. Why, though? What was he planning to do once he had found her again?

She feared him because she needed to protect her son, but there was some other reason why he had tracked her all the way to another country. Bryant understood from the few textbooks he had read on the subject that most serial murderers operated within a tight radius of their homes. Something wasn't making sense.

The detective's ears, nose, feet and brain were frozen. His neural impulses had slowed until they were as faint as fogbound harbour lights. Breathing on the windscreen, he drew lines in the condensation, as if trying to trace the connections in his mind. It was too easy not to think.

The two investigations, one far away, one close at hand, both immediate and pressing, overlapped each other in his head like architectural drawings on tracing paper. The icy air felt like the long-expected touch of death, destroying his cells and removing his senses. He considered the story of Johann's childhood, recounted by the woman he was hunting. Johann continued to brutalize because he had been able to kill his mother without remorse. He had even waited until his grandfather's death to act.

He had been raised in a land of devout Catholics, but had finally chosen a far stranger path to God. Had his mother been so strict that she had drawn out a monster from within her child? In his experience, even those who renounced the confines of a constricting religion never truly forgot the primal fears they developed as children. How did Bellocq reconcile those terrors with his embrace of the darkness?

How could he find the permission to kill within himself?

Why would he track a young woman and her son all the way to another country, just to protect his last identity, when he could surely commit the same crime and gain a new persona, find a new redeemer? Was there any point in even attempting to understand what went on in his mind?

Yes, because if you understand it, thought Bryant, *you understand the man. And then you own the key to catching him.* An alarm bell rang in his head, faint and persistent. The driver of the van with whom he had hitched a ride still had his own passport tucked inside his jacket. Why had Johann not taken it and simply started again? Why did he need the one she had stolen from him?

Because that's not why he followed her here, Bryant decided. *The passport has nothing to do with it. Only Madeline Gilby thinks it does. In that case, he just wants the photographs back, even though by the sound of it they won't directly incriminate him. They're pieces of circumstantial evidence that might place him at the scenes of the crimes, but they also have personal significance to him; that's why he took them, and why he needs to retain them.*

Bryant turned to the rear of the van and saw that mother and son were curled in the shadowed storage compartment, asleep beneath the moulting goatskin rug he had set aside for the Eden scene.

When his mobile rang, he tried to stifle the sound, so as not to wake them.

'Arthur, this is weird,' said May. 'I'm with Maggie right now, and she says that Le Société du Diable isn't a meeting group at all. It's a cybersite.'

'You mean it only exists on the interweb thingie?'

'That's right. It's just a forum used by teenaged Goths and lapsed Catholics to moan about their lives and discuss death-metal music; it's not a proper satanic site at all. She's most disparaging about such organizations.'

'I don't understand. Why would he have bothered to lie to Mrs Gilby? Besides, he's not a lapsed Catholic. According to her, he's such a believer that he thinks God watches him whenever there's a clear sky. I don't like the sound of this, John; something is not right about the man's life. I'm starting to think we've been mightily had.'

'I'm coming back,' said his partner. 'My battery's nearly dead, so I'll get off the line. Don't do anything reckless.'

'I need to go and find the envelope Mrs Gilby took from her attacker. We have to expose him. Is there any way of getting its contents transmitted?'

'I can upload digital shots and send them back to the unit in seconds, but what if you have an accident out there? Wait in the vehicle and I'll collect it.'

'She put it under the front passenger-side wheel arch of her rented blue Toyota,' Bryant explained. 'It's about ten cars in front of us, around the curve.'

'I'll go after it now.'

May bade farewell to Maggie and her group, and set off along the road until he reached the bend, where it banked steeply. The snow had started to fall heavily once more, and was rapidly obscuring the way ahead. *If Johann thinks God is watching him, he could strike whenever the clouds hide him from view*, thought May. *That's now.*

A new sense of urgency drove him on, but the route had

scabbed over with gem-hard ice, and the going was difficult. When he heard the rumble, he thought that a train must have finally managed to break through, but upon looking up at the side of the hill he saw what appeared to be rocks disappearing in the great plateau of white smoke.

A plain of snow the size of a football pitch was slowly gaining momentum. It gathered speed as it slid down towards the road, bursting between the trees and spraying over the bushes. When it hit the valley of cars, it raised and shoved them gently, silently, to the far bank, burying several completely. May fought to keep his footing, but the avalanche was fracturing the ground in a pattern that reminded him of the partition of ice floes, shaking and finally tipping him over on to his back.

As he clambered back to his feet, May saw that the other half of the traffic corridor had been cut off and that he was completely separated from Bryant, without any way of reaching him.

42

CULPABILITY

Giles Kershaw agreed to join Longbright for the interview. She had been planning to take Banbury in with her, as he was the burliest officer they had apart from Bimsley, but no one knew where the detective constable was. The pair of them peered through the window before they went in.

Sergeant Renfield was squirming about on an orange plastic chair as if he had been tethered there. He was so furious that he had changed colour. His ears were white, his cheeks were a deep crimson, his nose almost blue. If his face had been rounder he would have looked like an archery target. He had once told Longbright that the Met was run like a doctors' surgery and the unit behaved like a bunch of alternative therapists, and his detention today confirmed this belief. He had always fancied his chances with the detective sergeant, but now he was displaying the bitterness of a man who knew that he had been irrevocably rejected.

'What the hell do you think you're doing, bringing me in here?' He spat the words at her as she entered.

'I wanted to keep this more informal, but the heater's broken in my room,' she told him. 'And it's less public in here.'

'You've lost the bloody plot, Longbright. I knew you lot were hopeless without your bosses around, but this is a bloody joke.'

'No joke,' said Janice. 'You went back to the mortuary to see Oswald, didn't you?' She knew she was chancing her arm with this supposition, but needed to provoke a reaction. If he decided to call her bluff and demand evidence, she was lost.

'I didn't have much of a choice, did I? Finch phoned me and accused me of screwing up. He told me he'd put it in the report if I didn't come over and sort it out at once.'

'So you went back to Bayham Street and had it out with him.'

'Finch hadn't been out in the field for years; he had no idea what it's like on the streets: the chavs, the drunks, the endless aggression. The Camden junkies are worse than their dealers, because they're either whining excuses or angling for a fix, by which time they're little more than animals. I'd seen that girlie on the street before, or if it wasn't her it was someone damned well like her.' Renfield was eager to explain his side of the story. 'Anyone who tells you that rehabilitation works is a liar. They'll swear to God they're clean, and you can lift the gear out of their pockets while they're talking to you. No matter what they say, you know you'll see them again, shooting up in a toilet or a shop doorway. That's what we did when we picked up the girl; we dealt with the situation.'

'Then why did Finch call you back in?' asked Longbright.

'Listen, I'd been on duty all night, and she looked like another dead junkie.' Renfield's body language proclaimed him guilty without the need to speak.

'You bypassed the hospital and sent her straight to the morgue, didn't you?' said Longbright. 'That's why you went yourself. You didn't call the paramedics.'

'I saved everyone a docket. You think you have the monopoly on unorthodox procedure? *If it improves the situation for all parties concerned, do it without thinking twice.* Bryant himself told me that. Finch was a doctor, he could have signed her off easy enough, but instead he had to make life difficult for everyone. My boys were coming to the end of a long shift; they were knackered.'

'What did Finch tell you about Lilith Starr?' asked Longbright.

'He said the girl was in ana – ana—' Renfield stuttered.

'Anaphylactic shock?' asked Kershaw.

'Yeah, that's it.'

'It's an extreme allergic reaction to a particular substance,' the young forensic scientist told Longbright. 'Her immune system would already have been compromised because she was a junkie. Under anaphylaxis, the system decides that some alien substance poses a danger, and overreacts by creating huge quantities of the antibody immunoglobulin E. The body releases an excess amount of histamine and the throat closes up, making it difficult to breathe.'

'What happens after that?' asked Longbright.

'All sorts of problems can occur,' said Kershaw, 'but mainly, immunoglobulin E expands blood vessels, causing a drop in blood pressure, which leads to loss of consciousness.' As if to avoid letting Renfield off the hook, he added, 'There are usually visible signs a paramedic would immediately notice. Swelling and rashes on the skin, or on the lips and tongue if it was something ingested orally.'

'Even Finch didn't know what had set her off,' snapped Renfield. 'It's a mistake anyone could have made. He said it could have been any number of things.'

'That's right. Nuts, drugs like morphine or X-ray dye, dental painkillers, something in the dope she'd taken,' Kershaw confirmed.

'Finch's competence in diagnosing her isn't the matter at hand,' said Longbright. 'I want to know whether he made you so angry that you attacked him.'

'Of course not. God, he'd made me angry often enough in the past. You think I couldn't take it from him? He had a go at me, and I left.'

'Then why didn't you tell us when we first talked?' Longbright demanded.

'Because he and his lads dropped off a woman at a morgue who wasn't dead,' said Kershaw disgustedly. 'He didn't turn up at Bayham Street with a paramedic, just one of his constables. When they'd found her in the doorway, her body was cold to the touch and showing signs of cyanosis. They couldn't find a pulse, so they made an assumption, when a hospital might have saved her life.'

'It wasn't you who found the body, was it?' said Longbright. Renfield was too experienced to have made such a mistake.

'My PC is nineteen years old, Longbright. The kid's in shock; it's his second week on the beat. She would have died anyway, if not this week then the next. Finch didn't care about that. It was my call, but he told me he was going to report the boy.' Renfield looked miserable. 'He never let anything go. That's why he wouldn't support your promotion, Kershaw. He didn't trust you not to make the same kind of mistakes.'

'So before you left the mortuary, you waited until his back was turned, then tore the pages out of his report and destroyed them.'

Renfield shook his head violently. 'No, I never saw any report. I didn't think he'd had time to write it up, and wouldn't have touched it if he had.'

Longbright left the interview room in a bad mood. Whatever else Renfield was, he wasn't a liar. She went to Bryant's desk and sat down behind it, rubbing her eyes, hoping that being in his tobacco-stained room would somehow provide her with inspiration. On the chart before her was the time line of Finch's final hours. All the question marks and gaps she had left were now filled in, and they were no closer to the truth.

She checked the clock on the wall: two forty-five p.m. Two and a quarter hours left before the Princess turned up with her entourage to find the staff under arrest and the place in a shambles. She could almost see Kasavian and Faraday rubbing their hands with glee.

There was still one loose end to tie up. The missing boy, Lilith's former lover, Samuel. She was considering the problem when Kershaw knocked and stuck his head round the door. 'Can I let Renfield go, Janice? He's kicking up a fuss.'

'Apply the same restrictions I've applied to everybody else, then get back to the morgue. I want you to test out something for me. It's a ridiculous idea, but it's the only one left. This is my last shot before we're out of time.'

'What do you want me to do?'

'Assume Finch was in pain, on medication, not thinking clearly. He knew he wouldn't live to enjoy his retirement. I want you to see if it's at all possible . . .' She wondered if she could even bring herself to say the words. Kershaw waited obediently. 'Could it have started with an accident? Knowing that he was dying, could he have pulled the ultimate practical joke on his old nemesis? When the fan blade came loose and fell on him, you don't think he could have decided to commit suicide and make it look like murder, just to get the most bitter last laugh of all on Arthur?'

43

IN PLAIN SIGHT

Longbright looked around at Arthur Bryant's memorabilia. On the opposite wall was a sampler stitched in gratitude by the Oregon Ladies' Sewing Bee after he had solved the Chemeketa Rain Devil case for them in 1963. It read *The Greatest Secrets Are Hidden in Plain Sight.* It was a favourite sentiment of Bryant's. What was hidden in plain sight here?

She missed him looking over her shoulder, discoursing on any bizarre subject that took his fancy. She missed the stagnant reek of his pipe, his furtive watering of the sickly marijuana plant beneath his desk, the tottering stacks of mouldy books he dumped on her, the impossible requests, the childlike innocence in his eyes whenever she suspected him. *You'd know what to look for,* she thought. *You've shown us how a thousand times over. Why can't I work out what to do now?*

She studied the books on the shelves, trying to imagine Bryant in the room, arguing with John about methodology. He'd be stepping off on a tangent, refusing to follow the obvious routes of detection, leaving the doorstepping and data-gathering to others while he blew the dust from volumes of ancient myth and folklore. It was amazing how he managed to reach accurate conclusions by examining the case from the wrong end, and no matter how often he explained the process to her, it still didn't make sense. She read the spines on the opposite shelves: *Victorian Water Closets: A Social History, Sumerian Religious Beliefs & Legends, Colonic Exercises for Asthmatics, The Adventures of Captain Marvel, Mend Your Own Pipes, The Complete Works of Edgar Allan Poe, Pornography and Paganism, Courtship Rituals of Papua New Guinea, Code-Breaking in Braille.* How on earth could any of these help?

Lilith Starr had suffered an allergic reaction to something other than the chemicals in the recreational drugs she had taken, but what? Longbright took down A *History of Vivisection* and idly thumbed through it. Samuel, Lilith's former boyfriend, had disappeared, but Owen Mills was still around. Even though he wasn't with her when she died, he was still the only person who could shed some light on her condition. She decided to give him one last try, but found that his mobile was switched on to voice mail.

She looked up to see April dashing past with a bowl of wilted nasturtiums. 'What are you doing?' she called.

'The Princess is going to be here with half of the Home Office in two hours, and we've fulfilled none of the requirements on Rosemary Armstrong's list.' April looked as if she could do with some help.

'A few crummy old garage flowers aren't going to make any difference to our future now,' said Longbright despondently.

'No, but until I can come up with something better they will have to do,' April replied, not pleased at having to shoulder the responsibility alone.

'April, what did you do with that photograph of Lilith Starr? The one her father gave me?'

'It's on your desk in the file. Want me to get it?'

'Please.' Longbright placed herself in Bryant's seat, spreading her hands on his desk, amid the perfumed aroma of exotic rolling tobacco and the weird aftershave he favoured that no one had sold for forty years. April returned with the photograph and handed it to her.

She examined Lilith's face, her clothes. Her arms. Digging in the desk drawers, she found Bryant's horn-handled magnifying glass and passed it over the print. Lilith had still had the tattoo when the picture had been taken. *Samuel.* It was clear on her left arm.

Hidden in plain sight. She looked back at the volume of Poe, and thought of *The Purloined Letter*, with its clue hidden right under the noses of the police. 'She must have removed it soon after this photograph was taken.'

'Maybe that's why she got rid of it,' said April, peering over her shoulder. 'The tattooist spelled her boyfriend's name wrong.'

'What are you talking about?'

'Look again. That's an *a*, not a *u*.'

Longbright stared at the bare arm once more. *Samael.* 'Maybe it's right. Kids spell their names in a lot of crazy ways these days. Check with the tattoo parlour and see if he remembers.' She rose and collected her jacket.

'Where are you going?' asked April.

'To get the truth out of Owen Mills, even if I have to throttle it out of him,' said Longbright. 'He's the only one who's left alive to tell us what might have happened. Don't worry, I'll be back in time for our royal visit.'

Kershaw took Banbury with him to Bayham Street, hoping that the crime-scene manager might spot something he had missed. He looked around the room in which he had spent so much time expecting to become the unit's next medical examiner. Part of him was perversely pleased that Finch had failed to recommend him. If he couldn't understand what had happened here, he would not consider himself worthy of holding the post. Today his career would live or die by the decisions he made.

Finch, found dead in his own morgue. Why had the blade of an extractor fan been used as a weapon? Because it had fallen, because it was there. 'If you meant to kill or at least wound someone, you wouldn't strike them with a piece of lightweight aluminium, would you?' he asked Dan. 'I mean, a child could tell it's no good as a weapon.'

'When you're desperate, anything will do,' said Banbury, pulling his head out of Finch's instrument cupboard. 'I've heard of pens, stereo speakers, coat hangers, candles and laptops all being used as assault weapons. Everyone knows that if you attack a burglar with a torch you're likely to get off, because it's an item you're likely to be carrying. You don't think Renfield clouted him?'

'I should imagine the good sergeant's training in the Met would have taught him not to leave marks,' said Kershaw. 'The business with the empty bottle of naltrexone still bothers me. Finch didn't use it on himself. There was nothing in his system.'

Banbury rose slowly to his feet and stared steadily at his colleague. 'My God, he used it on the corpse,' he said, heading for the cabinets. 'You heard Renfield. Oswald knew that the sergeant's boy had got it wrong; he realized she wasn't your usual Camden overdoser. He was trying to revive her when the sergeant reappeared. He must have been furious with him. He'd already had Owen Mills turning up in a state just after the body had been delivered, trying to understand why his girlfriend was lying on an autopsy tray, and it sowed doubt in his mind, so he pumped in the naltrexone and called Renfield back to have a go at him.'

Kershaw was already helping him to slide open the drawer and ease out the body bag containing Lilith Starr's cadaver. 'This is my damned fault. I was so preoccupied with Finch putting the blocks on my career that I didn't run the obvious checks. I'll bet he had doubts about the cause of death from the moment he saw the body. He'd have found obvious signs of cocaine and heroin use, but would have known the levels weren't enough to put her into a coma, so he tried to pull her out of it. When that didn't work, he started searching for something else, probably testing for the most common causes of anaphylactic shock. And either before or after Renfield returned, he discovered something, stopping to write it down.'

'Wait, that can't be right,' said Banbury. 'Renfield insists he didn't destroy the report, so Mills must have, but Mills arrived first, when Finch could only have just started working on it. So why would he have ripped it out?'

'You have a point, old chap. You don't think someone else was here?'

Banbury looked up. 'Who?'

'There is only one other person left: our missing man, the former lover – Samuel, the man with no surname.'

'Blimey, it seems like the morgue was busier than Camden Market on Tuesday morning.'

'An appropriate blasphemy,' said Kershaw excitedly. 'Blimey is supposedly short for God blind me, something that's been happening to all of us in this investigation. We've been blinded from the outset. Think, what else did you find here?'

'I've got Finch's handprints, Mills's trainers and Renfield's boot marks, but no fingerprints on your supposed weapon, the fan blade. Exactly where am I supposed to look for this invisible man?'

Meanwhile, Longbright had found Owen Mills in the very first place she looked – Lilith Starr's claustrophobic flat on the Crowndale Estate. The front door was ajar, and Lilith's belongings stood stacked in cardboard boxes in the hall. Mills was sitting cross-legged on the floor of her bedroom, sorting through a pile of drawings and photographs.

'Owen?' Longbright took a further step into the shadowed room. When he turned to her, she could see he had been crying, but he hastily wiped away the evidence with the tips of his fingers. 'I'm not going to go away, you know,' she told him. 'Not until I've heard the truth. You see, I've been wondering about your last night together.'

'That's nothing to do with you.'

'How was she? You spent the evening here, right? How did she seem to you?'

Mills thought for a moment, caught by the question.

'Owen, I'll help you, I promise. I have the power to do that. If you care about her, you have to tell me how she was.'

'All right, she was kind of weird. Vague, you know? Not all there. She kept saying she had a chest pain. But she'd said that before. I don't want to talk about her.'

'I'm not here to disrespect your relationship with Lilith,' Longbright insisted. 'I think you've been through enough in the last two days. I know how much you cared for her, but I want to rule out your involvement in the death at Bayham Street.'

'Then talk to me about something else.' Part of him seemed anxious to tell her more.

'All right, let's talk about you. How are you coping?'

'OK, I suppose.'

'What's your family arrangement?'

'I got three other brothers, two sisters. I'm the oldest.'

The detective sergeant seated herself on the floor beside him. 'Get on all right with your parents?'

'I don't know. I guess.'

'Did they meet Lilith? What did they think of her? I mean, you were serious about her, right?'

'She wanted me to marry her, I guess that's serious.'

'Did you introduce her to your mum and dad?'

'Yeah. Yeah, they met her once. They thought she was nice.'

'And to your brothers and sisters?'

'No.'

'Why not?'

'They respect me. They look up to me.'

'What, you didn't think Lilith was respectable enough for them?'

'Not that.' The wall of evasion Mills used as protection had suddenly reappeared.

'Owen, I'm going to need two answers from you about Lilith, then I'm out of your way. Can we make that a deal?'

'I don't have to answer anything.'

'I know, but you must be as anxious as I am to put the subject to rest. I'm convinced you took Finch's notes. Just tell me what you did with them.'

'I told you, I didn't take anything.'

'They were there before you turned up, and gone immediately after. He didn't tear them out himself, or we would have found them. If you're only prepared to tell me one thing, make it this. I won't ask anything more of you.'

'I didn't take them; he burned them. It was like, one page, OK? He did it for her.' His voice was toneless.

'You mean Oswald Finch burned his own notes? Why would he do that?'

'You don't need to know. It has nothing to do with your investigation.'

'I understand why you asked him, to protect her,' said Longbright. 'I know that. You didn't want her drug use to come out on the report that would be sent to her parents.'

'She hated her parents, but she felt like she'd hurt them enough. She said there was no point in kicking them beyond the grave, asked me to clean up behind her if anything bad ever happened, like she was expecting it.'

'Where can I find her former boyfriend?'

'Why do you need to know?' asked Owen wearily.

'I have to eliminate him from the investigation.'

'Well, you can do that, all right. He's dead and buried, innit. Gone for ever.'

'When did it happen?'

'Eight months ago. That's why she took his name off her arm.'

'What happened? How did he die?'

Owen gave her a crooked smile. 'It was a knife wound.'

'Who did it?'

'Nobody you know.'

Getting answers from the boy was like pulling teeth once more. In the peculiar manner of most of the kids living around this estate, he had answered her questions without explaining a single thing. Longbright checked her watch and saw that it was three fifteen, which left just one and three quarter hours before the slow-motion car crash of the unit's destruction concluded. More frustrated than angry, she rose and left Mills to his grief and his photographs.

Crossing the sleet-slick paths of the estate, she tried to shake the feeling that she had been tricked. Somehow, Mills had told her everything she needed to know while simultaneously hiding the truth in plain sight.

44

IN THE DRIFTS

A grey veil of rain descended over the grime-crusted gas lamps of Old Montague Street, where the 'light of heaven' brought safety to the pavements Saucy Jack had walked only fifty years earlier.

The rolling amber fog that dripped down walls and slicked the cobbles was pierced with fiery mantles that burned until the break of dawn, when daylight dissipated the miasma. Another fifty years passed, and now the wrecking balls swung into row after row of mean terraced houses with a chink and clatter of brick and mortar, tearing down Durward Street, Buck's Row, Hanbury Street, blasting so much brightness into the dark canyons that no shred of London's shape-shifting history remained. Now there was only the roar and glare of the approaching future . . .

Arthur Bryant awoke with a start, wondering where he was.

In 1930, his father had photographed the spot where 'Polly' Nichols had fallen with her throat slit open from ear to ear. He had kept the little sepia print of the dingy kerbstone in his trouser pocket, using it to frighten young Arthur whenever he was bad. Reeking sourly of stout, his father had staggered from The Ten Bells in Commercial Street, the public house where

Mary Kelly had ordered her final drink, and collapsed in the road, where he was found dead by his terrified son . . .

Why had Bryant dreamed of such a thing now? Nothing in the past could truly be repaired. Remembrance of his father only came when the cold hand of his own mortality pressed upon him. Disoriented, he shivered and tightened the collar of his coat.

He knew it was dangerous to fall asleep, but increasingly his body was defending itself by pulling the plug on his consciousness. A freezing draught was coming from somewhere behind him. Freshly fallen snow had darkened the windscreen of the van, cocooning the cabin. It was like being trapped inside an icy pillowcase.

Bryant checked his watch and realized that his partner had been gone for over an hour. May had called to say he was returning . . . surely he should have arrived by now?

He twisted in his seat and pulled back the curtain to see if Madeline was awake. The rear door had been opened; he could see snow drifting through the gap. There was no sign of mother or child, and several props had been overturned. The remains of a plaster vase lay smashed on the floor of the van, and a Hieronymus Bosch backdrop had split where it had fallen, imps and devils let loose to spread chaos in corners.

No, he thought, *you idiot old man!* He tried ringing May, but there was no answer. Checking his own mobile, he saw that there were three missed calls: one from May, two from Longbright.

The clearing sky placed Madeline in danger. Johann could act without fear of guilt, for his corridor to the eyes of God would open again, and he would once more attempt to show defiance before his Maker. Bryant's muscles protested as he opened the door of the cabin and eased himself out.

The wind took his breath away. He bundled his scarf around his head and set off for the rear of the van, but even this small distance proved hard going.

The chaotic scuffle of footprints beneath the open rear door was difficult to read, but two clear shoe sizes indicated that mother and son were now outside and exposed. The tracks were fresh and deep; they could not have gone far, especially if they were being dragged unwillingly. Bryant returned to the cabin and pulled a page of his battered old map book from the dashboard. Their hunter would have to be taking them to the shelter of another vehicle, unless he was planning to leave them to die in the snow. Bryant punched Maggie Armitage's number with a frozen digit, and found that his partner had already left her.

Bryant glanced back through the stranded traffic and realized that a massive block of snow had cascaded across the road, just beyond the bend. No wonder May had not come back; he'd been buried beneath the fall, or at least had been stranded on the wrong side of the valley.

'The silly old fool,' he muttered beneath his breath. Pulling his coat tighter around him, Bryant started to follow the prints leading from the van. They cut away from the road, through crystalline bushes that glittered like chandeliers, in the direction of the hill and the railway line where the other stranded travellers had headed at the start of the storm.

He squinted at the map and tried to determine how closely the barred line of the railway twisted past the motorway, but it was difficult to read in the glare of the snow. If they reached the tracks, he would not be able to follow them further. With a sinking heart, he realized that the line ran across the steepest point of the hill. He knew he would not have the stamina needed to follow it for so long. At least the deep snow now kept him upright as he walked; in London he would have needed his stick.

Reaching a sheltered hollow formed by some thorny gorse, he checked his mobile for a signal, then returned Longbright's call with numb fingers.

The DS sounded desperate. 'I'm sorry, Arthur, I didn't want to bother you again, but we're no nearer closing up the Finch investigation, and I'm almost out of time.'

Bryant forced his mind to switch tracks, something he never had much trouble doing. 'Have you found out anything from Mills since I last spoke to you?'

'I talked to him again, but every time I got close he shut up on me. And we wanted to get DNA tests done on skin flakes found in Bayham Street, but there isn't any time—'

'I'm not talking about forensic evidence, but something you've missed. I told you, the answer lies with Mills. Did you remember to do what I asked? Did you talk to him about his family?'

'It was as you said. He's the oldest of six. I think the others look to him for guidance. The parents met Lilith, but his siblings didn't. Why did you want to know?'

'Omissions,' said Bryant. 'Of course he has no desire to bare his private life to anyone he perceives to be in a position of authority, and who can blame him? It will always be your job to fill in the gaps. I take it you didn't find out anything more about the former boyfriend?'

'According to Mills, he's dead, killed by a knife.'

'Yes, that fits.'

'It's so hard to get at the truth,' said Longbright despairingly.

'The only evidence you have that the boyfriend ever existed is in the photograph of Lilith's tattoo, is that correct?'

'Yes, and even there his name is spelled wrong.'

'What do you mean?'

'With an *a* instead of a *u*. Samael.'

'And you just discovered this? Remind yourself about the health club Lilith joined – what was it called?'

'Circe.'

'The owner, this fellow Spender, wasn't he involved in some kind of scandal about a year ago?'

'That's right, he got caught cheating on his wife and she left him.'

'I remember now. Well, good heavens, woman, you've got the whole thing spelled out right in front of you, what more do you want? You can still close the investigation to everyone's satisfaction, but I'm not going to do it for you. John and I won't always be around to help.'

'This is no time for playing games, Arthur. If you don't tell me what you know, we'll lose the unit.'

'All right, I'll give you one last clue. Go to my office and look on the shelves behind my desk. Take down the volume called *Sumerian Religious Beliefs & Legends*. You'll find what you need about half a dozen chapters in, if memory serves, which it usually doesn't. Read it over carefully with Giles Kershaw, then do what you have to do.'

'What do you mean?' asked Longbright. 'Why can't you just tell me? Am I supposed to make an arrest?'

'There's no arrest to be made. Look at the names, Janice. The moment you understand, take everyone out of house arrest and get the unit up to scratch in time for inspection. I have to go now.'

He closed the mobile and leaned back against a tree trunk. He would not finish the job for her, whatever happened, he decided. There would come a day when he would no longer be there to sort out the unit's problems. It was time Longbright and the rest of the staff started using his methods to think for themselves. Only then would the unit have a secure future after his death.

He turned and squinted up at the hill ahead. Tugging his scarf tighter around his ears so that he looked like an exhausted elderly rabbit, he trudged on, following the tracks on to the dazzling white slope of the mount.

John May had never welcomed meetings with North London's mystic coven leader, but for once he was glad to see her toiling through the snowdrifts towards him. As she approached, wrapped in red shamanistic folk blankets and looking for all the world like a Russian doll come to life, Maggie Armitage waved her arms frantically towards the valley of stranded vehicles.

'I left the safety of our truck to bring you a warning, John,' she called. 'Arthur's not in the van. He told me to tell you he was going after the mother and her son, says they've been taken up towards the railway line. There's a rescue train on its way. But there's something else, another sensation I'm getting that his crisis moment is about to arrive. He is in terrible danger,

John, because of something he knows, or perhaps is about to find out. I see him lying helpless in total darkness.'

'Thank you, Maggie. Here, take my arm.'

'I'm very much obliged,' puffed the white witch. 'This kind of elemental turbulence is tricky to negotiate.' She was carrying a round walnut box that she now stopped to consult.

'What are you doing?' he asked, irritated.

'It's a spirit tracer,' she explained, hitching up her blankets and peering over the top of her roll-neck. 'Inside there's a chased silver ball containing variously treated herbal extracts and seeds, some of them more than a century old, a few which are even extinct. The item is a great rarity these days, and of enormous talismanic value. I've been worried about Arthur lately, so I had him keep the ball in his pocket for a month. It picks up a sort of spiritual imprint that can be used to find someone. The ball starts to shift in its casket when we come within range of its human marker, so we can use it to locate him.'

'You're pulling my leg, aren't you?' said May. 'I can't even get him to wear a pager, and yet he happily spends a month leaving his spiritual imprint on some kind of mystical GPS device. Even by your extreme standards, such a thing is patently absurd.' He peered over her shoulder. 'Is he within range?'

'I thought you weren't a believer, Mr May.'

'I'm not,' said May, 'but I have no better way of finding him.'

The pair trudged on around the iridescent blocks of snow and ice that had dammed the valley, looking down at the shunted cars and trucks, hoping to see signs of life. 'I told him to stay put, but no, he had to go off on his own. The simplest instruction always becomes a challenge.'

'You care about him very much, don't you?' said Maggie. 'When I think of the arrests you two have made over the years, it's amazing—'

'We've certainly had our share of excitement,' May admitted.

'I was going to say it's amazing nobody's had you both shot.'

May narrowed his eyes at her, unable to decide if she was being honest or merely rude. 'Are we near him?'

She peered into the box. 'Nothing yet. He shouldn't be out in this. When are the pair of you going to retire?'

'We've some unfinished business to deal with before we think about that,' May said testily.

'We're none of us getting any younger, you know. It's different for me, darling, I'm at the end of the line. The next generation isn't interested in the mystic arts. They just want to keep their heads down and make money, and you don't need any spiritual leanings to do that. They're far too interested in personal wealth. But someone has to take care of all our invisible needs, don't you think? That's what you and Arthur do. We're the gatekeepers to the nation's soul. What happens when there's no one left to heal the secret wounds we all bear? We'll never be able to set the world upright and end all of its inequalities, but each of us can make a small difference until they add up to something more.' She paused for breath, stretching her back. 'You know, I've spent my life forcing myself to believe in the innate goodness of people, but it never gets any easier. This creature you're after is spiritually tortured, and people like that are unpredictable. They can't be healed by being thrown in jail. A process of understanding must first take place.'

May knew that the white witch was as interested in psyches as she was in souls. As she fell silent and they pushed on through the drifts, he thought back over the last few hours, knowing that she, too, sensed something was not right. He had experienced this phenomenon before, when his daughter had walked into the trap that had led to her death. Arthur wanted to believe that the world possessed unseen dimensions, but paradoxically it was May who most often experienced these momentary shifts.

He was feeling it very strongly now. Maggie pointed into her spirit tracer box. The ball inside was gently rolling in an ellipse, but he could not tell whether it was really being guided by unseen forces or whether she had simply tipped it away from her.

'He's close,' she announced, then abruptly changed direction, heading up towards the railway tracks that ran across the hill.

Above them, the sky was turning an ominous shade of apocalyptic pink.

'What is that?' asked May. They watched as a muscular black shape loped through the snow searching for cover. 'Are there wolves in Devon?'

'Maybe it was just a big fox,' said Maggie uncertainly. Overhead, a crackle of black wings batted against the white sky, as crows were shocked into flight from the glassy branches.

'Something's startled them.' Maggie looked around, then narrowed her search to the hill ahead. 'This way. We have to go faster. You feel it as well, don't you?'

'I think so,' May admitted. 'Arthur's made some kind of misjudgement that's put him at risk. And don't ask me to explain, because I don't know how to, OK?'

Maggie kept silent, but smiled to herself as they climbed. Seemingly psychic instincts were learned through experience, habit, and the passing of time. The detectives had developed a link they could not see or understand, but it was obvious to anyone with the slightest sensitivity that it existed. There was nothing supernatural about the development of such an ability; parents and children quickly grew bonds, twins inherited them genetically. People who spent a great deal of time in each other's company became automatically adept at guessing the actions of their counterparts, in the same way that animals were attuned to tiny vibrations of movement and changes in air pressure. She had a fleeting image of a moth in a jar, fighting to free itself, then the image vanished.

Maggie loved the idea that the detective was becoming corrupted by his latent spirituality; if someone as rational as John could succumb, it gave her hope for the rest of humankind.

'Of course, having some smidgen of psychic ability doesn't single you out as special, you know,' she puffed. 'Everyone has it to a greater or lesser extent. I can usually feel it when I meet people. That lady and her son, they knocked on our truck earlier, did you know? We offered to shelter them, but she decided to head back to her own vehicle.'

'She never mentioned that to Arthur and me,' said May, surprised.

'No, I don't suppose she would have done. Why would she? She doesn't know that you know me. She was attracted by the sign on our truck, you see. Latched on to my arm and told me she had some kind of psychic gift that allowed her to see the true nature of men, but of course I saw she didn't.'

'What makes you say that?'

'I asked how she knew, and she gave me the name of her mentor. I clearly made her uncomfortable, because she refused our help. There are so many frauds operating in London. Often they just crave attention, but end up draining money from those who are desperate to believe, the vulnerable ones who've had difficulties in the past.'

'The world is full of natural victims,' said May.

"And natural predators,' replied Maggie. 'I'm afraid Kate Summerton is rather well known in South London. She's been jailed a couple of times and isn't legally allowed to practise any more, not that it stops her. The odd thing is, I think she genuinely means well. But it's unethical to use a refuge for battered women to recruit clients for spiritualism courses.'

'God, I forgot,' said May suddenly. 'I have to go back down there.' He pointed to the buried road that lay below them.

'Back? What are you talking about? We're past the worst part of the fallen snow.'

'Exactly. We were passing near Madeline Gilby's hired car. I promised to collect something from it. Stay under the shelter of the trees. I can see the blue Toyota from here. It'll only take a minute.'

John May half ran, half tumbled towards the inundated vehicle. Snow had covered the wheel arches and half of the bonnet. He looked around for something to dig with, settling on a broken branch. After a minute or two he was able to reach under the vehicle's front wing. He forced his arm deep into the snow and groped around, closing frozen fingers over the envelope. It had stayed dry within the impacted drift. He wanted to stop and open it, but there was no time to waste.

He began cutting back in Maggie's direction. The witch was standing with her hands cupped about her eyes, watching for trouble.

A burning sensation in his heart caused him to stop and regain his breath. He took advantage of the respite to call the unit from his mobile. 'Hello?' He could barely hear against the buffeting wind. 'Who's that? Meera? I need you to check something out for me. Quick as you can.'

'What's the matter?' asked Maggie when he finally reached her side. 'You look as if someone just walked over your grave.'

'It's been preying on my mind ever since I saw the list of victims Madeline Gilby showed me,' said May. 'The names on it were vaguely familiar, but I didn't know why.' He turned his attention to the phone.

'I can see someone,' said Maggie, pointing to a figure standing on the railway tracks ahead. 'We must get up there as quickly as possible. I think Arthur is about to face his moment of truth.'

45

ENGAGEMENT

Arthur Bryant could see the faint impression of the double railway track indented through fallen snow; no train had been able to pass here since the blizzard began, but now the gale had blown the top layers clear, and with the thaw setting in it appeared that the line might become passable.

The black tracks wound over the hill towards the dark mouth of a tunnel. The cut was still inundated beyond this, so the rescue train would have to back up the line after collecting stranded travellers.

As he forced himself to concentrate on the fading footmarks in the white expanse of the hill, he could not help but wonder if his own tracks would disappear like snow prints from London's history.

I've dedicated my life to something that now seems less tangible and more pointless than wood-carving, he thought, *the resolution of criminal mysteries that pass entirely unnoticed by the general public.* It was hardly surprising that the Home Office no longer wished to fund such a division when they gained no benefit to themselves. The PCU acted as a magnet for embarrassing publicity, and Bryant knew that his own irascibility made matters worse.

In a world where so few people are willing to become

involved, we have to set an example, he thought. *And so we will pass the way of censorship bodies and experimental science labs, in the same manner that Bletchley Park, the Propaganda Unit and the Mass Observation Society were no longer needed after the war. And May and I will pass, too, becoming just another quirky footnote to the capital's strange history, along with other abandoned ideas like the GLC's Regent Street Monorail and the 1796 plan to straighten out the Thames, and therefore perhaps that is how it should be. But for now, and until we are all ejected from our premises in Mornington Crescent, I still have a public duty to perform.*

Any further musing on the past was stopped when he saw the boy.

Why is he standing there? Bryant wondered, before spotting the red handkerchief that tied his wrist to the briars of a hawthorn bush covered in icicles like cracked prisms. He lowered himself down to Ryan, whose tear-streaked cheeks were already starting to freeze. His jacket had been pulled down over his shoulders to impede his movement. 'What happened?' Bryant asked, shielding him from the bitter wind as he tried to unscramble the knot with numb ringers.

'He came for us and took my mum away,' said the boy tonelessly. 'He's going to kill her on the railway line because he hates ladies.'

'Well, we're certainly not going to let that happen.' The knot was too small and tight, and Bryant could not tear the cloth. 'Can you slip your hand out for me?'

'He wants to hurt ladies,' said Ryan again, as if trying to remember something he had seen or heard elsewhere. He struggled against the material but could not pull free. His efforts seemed halfhearted, as though he had given up any thought of escape.

He's in shock, thought Bryant. *He's not reacting normally.* 'Wait,' he said, 'let me see if I have something that can help.' He produced a bunch of keys, selected the sharpest-looking one and began sawing at the handkerchief. 'In which direction did they go?'

'Over there, into the tunnel,' said Ryan, pointing with his free hand at the black hole cut into the side of the hill.

Bryant's heart sank. The sub-zero temperature had already slowed his mind and body. The thought of entering the hillside to look for Madeline and her captor cruelly exposed his defencelessness. *If I stay here with Ryan she may die*, he thought. *But if I leave the boy . . .*

He dug out his mobile and tried May once more. This time it rang and John answered. 'I'm up at the railway line. He's headed into the tunnel with the mother,' Bryant told his partner. 'I don't want to go in there alone. It feels like some kind of a set-up. She said he only kills when he's in a shaft of light, where God can witness his defiance.'

'So he's the third of Maggie's four white corridors.'

'Apparently so, but if he's hidden in the darkness of the tunnel she'll be safe, surely? It's a contradiction.'

'Arthur, I'm on my way. You're right, it's a trap. There is no—'

A shrill scream, distortingly high like the shriek of an excited child, sounded from the shadowy entrance of the tunnel. Without thinking, Bryant snapped the phone shut and headed off into its mouth as Ryan shouted behind him.

After all these years, it's too late not to stay involved, Bryant thought, stumbling over the bared brown railway sleepers. *I can't stand on the sidelines any longer, even if it means taking my own life in my hands.*

46

OMISSIONS

Janice Longbright rose before Bryant's bookcase and pulled down the dust-encrusted volume entitled *Sumerian Religious Beliefs & Legends*. Seating herself behind his leather-topped desk, she thumbed forward to the sixth chapter and began to read.

In the primeval mists of Sumerian legend there first exists a heavenly ocean called the Abyss, from which gods, the ZU, emerged. Their servants were the Abgal, seven wise demigods who emerged from this ocean.

The detective sergeant shifted uncomfortably on her chair. *I should be doing something of practical use, not sitting here wasting time,* she thought. *This is hopeless.* But with no other course of action left than to heed Bryant's recommendation, she read on.

One of the most legendary night spirits was the benevolent Lilith, who was associated with guarding the gateway between the spiritual and physical realms. Her figure could be found on most Sumerian temple doorways. Lilith is usually represented holding the Rings of Shem, proof that she gained immortality by traversing the Underworld to gain sacred wisdom from the Tree of Knowledge. As the guardian of the Temple Mysteries, Lilith was the original 'scarlet woman', the term originally referring to menstrual blood and another symbol of divine power, fiery red hair. Ancient cultures often believed that red hair denoted one whose ancestors had intermarried with fallen, i.e., demonic, angels. Because she connected two worlds, the dazzling Lilith was regarded as a goddess of transformation. Other goddesses of transformation included Hecate and Circe.

Longbright tapped a crimson nail against her teeth. *Circe*, she thought, *the health club that creates beautiful women. What are you getting at, Arthur?* She turned the page.

Many Sumerian traditions were inherited by the Greeks, whose legends correspond accordingly. Their divine nymphs brought about physical and spiritual regeneration in the form of sexual rites, from which we derive the term 'nymphomania'. Jews subsequently transformed the Sumerian Lilith into the consort of the Angel Samael.

'So she was a bit of a Goth,' said Longbright aloud. That wasn't so unusual in Camden Town; there were so many that pubs painted with angels and demons specifically catered to them. She returned to the chapter.

The lovers Samael and Lilith passed their knowledge of the Angels to man and created a dynasty via intermarriage with humans, resulting in Lilith being punished by being turned into an essence without form. Lilith was said to appear in the natural world as a seductive spirit, confronting men who slept alone. Among recent variations and additions to this myth is one particularly prevalent among students of mythology who regard Samael and Lilith as warring parts of the same human being, having been born as one creature incorporating both male and female genders. In this popular version of the legend, Lilith and Samael simultaneously love and hate each other. The battle for supremacy within this 'male goddess' can only be resolved when Lilith triumphs over Samael and transforms him into a complete woman. In this we can see the age-old struggle between male and female—

Longbright closed the book and carefully replaced it on the shelf as revelations tumbled through her mind.

No wonder everyone had been so guarded about admitting the truth. Lilith's parents had not lied; they had, in a typically English manner, hoped their omissions would speak for themselves. They had borne and raised a redheaded son, Samuel, who had escaped from his stifling upbringing and come to London in order to change his life. It explained why his mother had been loath to find old photographs of the boy. Samuel had discovered the legend of the scarlet woman, the goddess of transformation, the woman in a man's body. He had proudly changed the spelling of his name, even going so far as to have it tattooed on to his arm.

But the hormonal war being waged within him had only just begun, and it had been fought as it had between the ancient gods, with Samael finally being subsumed into the persona of Lilith.

Longbright thought, *What did he do next?* On completion of his own spiritual transformation, he had symbolically killed off his former self, removing the tattoo, undertaking lessons in everything from deportment to make-up with the aid of the helpful, unscrupulous Spender. There was nothing, after all, like a model with an outrageous press-friendly history, and The Temple's new cosmetic lines needed publicity . . .

Sam Bronwin had come to London hoping to define his identity, and had been preyed upon. He had been fed hormones, had taken drugs . . .

She needed air. Standing at the opened crescent window, she thought about Owen Mills. Lilith had met him on the

Crowndale Estate and had fallen deeply in love. What's more, her love had been reciprocated, despite the fact that Lilith had been born a male, despite the fact that she took drugs to deaden her painful memories, despite the fact that she had possibly even turned tricks to pay for—

Longbright ran back to the desk and picked up the phone. 'Giles, you're still at Bayham Street?'

'I was just about to leave.'

'Stay there until I arrive. And don't touch anything.'

Longbright ran through the alleyway slush, darting between trucks and motorbikes on Camden High Street; the home-going rush hour had already started. At the morgue, she found Kershaw seated at Finch's desk, resigned to the coming conversation, calmly awaiting her arrival.

'Giles, did you have any reason to examine Lilith Starr's body?' she asked, catching her breath and looking around.

'I saw her when I first came to the morgue,' he replied guardedly. 'Why?'

'I mean, did you make a full examination of her corpse?'

'No, there was no need. Finch had already conducted the preliminary examination.' Kershaw looked unnerved.

Omissions, she thought suddenly. *He's not telling me something.*

'But you're the one who found Oswald's body. What did you do before you called me? I'm not saying you did anything illegal, but you did do something, didn't you?'

'Look, Finch collapsed and died before he could put Lilith Starr's corpse away, so I did it for him. You know the new regulations specify that they must be kept locked in the drawers when the room is occupied by non-members of staff.'

'I'm not doubting that you meant well, Giles, but as a consequence nobody else checked her after Oswald's death. You have to open the body bag all the way and tell me what you see,' she said.

Kershaw slowly rose to his feet, 'OK, but—'

'Just do it.' She waited, pacing the floor.

He unlocked the drawer and pulled it out, unzipping the body bag to the bottom. 'Well, yes.' He sighed. 'What do you want me to say, Janice? Lilith had had an operation, such a neat one that it's pretty hard to spot.'

'She was born a man, Giles, born with the name Samuel Bronwin. I know gender reassignment has come a long way in the last few years, but you'd think that would be the first thing Oswald noticed during his examination, wouldn't you? The first observation he'd write down in his report book? Owen Mills came to see Finch, to explain that he had made a pact with Lilith. He wanted to make sure that no one found out the truth about her in the event of her death, so of course he followed her to the mortuary that morning. It wasn't just for her sake, either, but for his. Mills has brothers and sisters who look up to him as a role model. Check her breasts for me.'

'I don't have to; I already know they've been enhanced,' Kershaw confirmed. 'I noticed it straight off when I first saw her lying there, but so many girls have augmentation these days that I doubted anyone else would think twice about it.'

'I think she had a spill. Mills said Lilith was vague and acting strangely on the night of her death, complaining of a chest pain. One of the implants split and the slow leak, in combination with what was already in her system, sent her into anaphylactic shock. I think we'll find that her transformation was all part of Circe's service. Gender change is a process conducted after exhaustive psychological profiling. It's planned in distinct stages, but she was rushed through the entire procedure by Spender, who was working to the timetable of his product launch.'

'Why would Mills go to such efforts to hide the truth about her?' asked Kershaw.

'Are you kidding? Think, Giles. The boy was raised in an old-school Baptist West Indian family, not exactly a culture known for its compassionate views on transgendered males. Mills had already been bullied at school; if anyone found out he'd been dating a transsexual he would have been ostracized by his siblings, his peers, his community. Even if we imagine they could have accepted it, he acted for a much simpler reason.

He loved her, and wanted to do right by her. He pleaded with Finch not to reveal the truth, and Finch probably refused to help him. Arthur knows the truth about Oswald's death, but he wants us to work it out.'

'So what's the sequence of events?' asked Kershaw.

'You're the one who wants Finch's job,' snapped Longbright. 'You figure it out.'

Kershaw sat defeatedly at the morgue bench. 'I should have been more careful,' he said. 'I thought I could help him.'

'We're running out of time. Let's go back and fill in the gaps.' Longbright seated herself opposite the young pathologist. 'First on the scene after Finch arrives for the day's work are Renfield and his constable – not a paramedic at all – with the body of Lilith Starr, presumed by his boy to be just another dead junkie. Renfield has covered for his PC and skipped procedure because he's in a rush; Finch is tired and taking painkillers. The ventilator cover is still where he left it, unrepaired, and now the fan itself has fallen down. We knew that the mortuary ceiling was too high for anyone to get up there and tamper with it. So, Finch picks up the fan blade that has dropped down in the night, and sets it on the counter. As soon as Renfield has gone, Oswald starts work and immediately writes out his primary observation: the true gender of the person on his table.

'He begins his examination, making a note that his victim has undergone a rushed sex-change. Owen Mills buzzes the door, blagging his way in as the partner of the deceased, and argues with Finch, begging him not to report what he knows. Being a stickler for the truth, Finch turns him down, and Mills is incensed – we know he slaps his hand down hard on Finch's notes, leaving the imprint on his palm – but he leaves.

'Rattled, but ever the professional, Finch returns to work, and now he makes a secondary observation, based on instincts honed across decades of dealing with human organisms: that there's a slim chance the girl on his table may not, in fact, be dead after all. The distraction with Mills has lost him valuable time, even though it only lasted a few minutes. Having to guess at what might work, he quickly prepares the naltrexone and injects it as part of a cocktail of stimulants, but there's no response. To prevent spasms he adds another drug, a muscle relaxant, vecuronium, which was also found in her system. What he doesn't know is that the drugs are indeed taking effect.

'Angered by Renfield's failure to involve the hospital when she might have been saved, he calls the sergeant to berate him. Now things should be quiet, but you turn up to talk about being passed over for the position of unit pathologist.

'And surprisingly, Finch is receptive to your case. He likes you – he's always liked you – so he asks for your help. He's been thinking about Lilith Starr, and has realized that all it would take is one little omission from his notes to prevent a young man's life from being ruined. He no longer wants to report her case as a male undergoing gender reassignment, something that, according to Mills, has already caused her own family to disown her. That's why he gets you to tear up his notes – at least he won't have to lie himself – it's just a few lines on a single page, which you destroy for him. You didn't argue with him at all – that little shouting match was staged for Meera's sake when she arrived at the morgue.

'And that should have been that. But the drugs Finch injected have now had time to cause an interaction. They can take longer than two hours to work, even longer in a cold room, and this one was warm. But the resuscitation goes horribly wrong.

'Lilith Starr wakes up in a state of shock, in terrible pain. The last thing she remembers is falling asleep in a shop doorway. Now she suddenly sits up on a steel table to find herself stripped to the waist, breasts exposed, with a horrible old man standing over her. Instinctively she fights him off – Finch is probably just as startled as she is – her hand seizes on the nearest object, the fan blade, and she strikes him hard in the chest with it, then lashes out a second time as he backs away. Oswald collapses, but the appalling shock to Lilith's system is just as great, and she falls back. This time, she really is dead. The discrepancy in her time of death is hard to spot because her body has *already had time to cool*. That's why there were no fingerprints on the blade; she wasn't producing any sweat. And nobody else left or entered the locked morgue. So, after years of investigating similar crimes with the PCU, Finch becomes a victim of his own perfect murder.

'Except that we would have found Lilith's body on the table, not in the drawer, wouldn't we, Giles? I know you came back to Bayham Street because you called me from there at eleven thirty-five a.m., and I arrived ten minutes later. Another omission.'

Kershaw rubbed his face with his long fingers. 'I was taken aback when Oswald asked me to help him. He was a scientist who believed that ethical issues had little relevance to his work. But Bryant was always going on to him about discovering a moral dimension to crime. And now he had come face-to-face with a genuine moral dilemma: to respect the wishes of the dead and thus help the living, or to stubbornly stick to the letter of the law and hurt everyone. I had never seen him so confused. I went out for a coffee and came back at eleven twenty to reassure Oswald that he was doing the right thing, and instead I found him dead. It didn't take me long to see what had happened, and I knew that anyone else arriving would quickly figure out the truth. So I put Lilith Starr's body back in the drawer and locked it. We would assume, rightly, that Finch had suffered heart failure. Attention would be drawn away from the girl he had decided to protect, and I would have honoured his final wish. But as soon as I saw the bruises coming up on his neck and chest, I was faced with a dilemma of my own: to conceal them and start compounding the lie, or to report the facts and let everyone else decide what had happened. I thought about Finch's professional opinion of me, and knew what he would have expected me to do. I didn't obstruct, Janice, I just omitted. Now I've failed to carry out his wishes, as well as destroying my own career.'

Longbright reached out a tentative hand in sympathy. 'No, Giles, you behaved honourably, and I know Arthur will consider that to be your saving grace. He worked the whole thing out while he was four hundred miles away, sitting in a snowdrift, but he wanted us to decide what action to take.

I think I can answer that now. We'll continue to honour Oswald's wish, and close the case. You see, it was me who refused to countersign your application for Oswald's position. But now, I think I'm ready to recommend you.'

'Thank you, Janice.' Giles raised his head and smiled ruefully at her. 'I won't let any of you down, I promise. What amazes me is how Arthur figured out the truth.'

'Oh, he'll have read the answer in some dusty old book,' said Longbright, smiling to herself.

47

THE CONSPIRACY OF MEN

Arthur Bryant stood at the dark tunnel entrance and listened. The reflected light from the snow only lit the first five feet of the track, and he had left the Valiant, May's trusty cinema torch, on the dashboard of the van. He looked back at Ryan, still anchored to the bushes, and slowly advanced into darkness.

He heard dripping water, a click of flint. There was a scuffling sound somewhere ahead of him, a brush of material against rough brick. He was now moving in total darkness. By sliding one foot before the other around the edges of the sleepers, he was able to avoid the rails, staying close against the right-hand wall of the tunnel.

'I know you're there,' Bryant called gently. 'And I think I know the truth about you.'

There was a fresh sound of displaced gravel, much closer now. He stopped and listened to someone else's ragged breathing. He was wondering whether to go further, and suddenly realized that he was afraid. Not for himself – death had long since ceased to hold any terrors – but because something was very wrong, and had been for a while now. *This*, he thought, *is my hour of reckoning, the descent of my black angel.*

He took a step forward, then another, still feeling for the edges of the sleepers. The bitter blanket of blackness pressed in on him, for it was even colder in the tunnel than it had been outside. It seemed that he could smell the cuprous tang of metal and coal-soot, although no steam trains had passed through here in decades.

His right boot pressed against something soft. Lowering himself to a crouch, he reached forward and felt around. The body lying beside the track was still warm to the touch, but there was no longer a pulse in its wrist.

'What are you doing?' asked May as Maggie snatched the mobile from him.

'Come on, we both feel it,' she told him. 'A deviant force is at work, trying to fool us into making a mistake. We can't fight it alone, two elderly men and a crazy lady of a certain age coping with her psychic senses and a hip replacement; we need help, so that's what I'm going to get us.' She punched the number of the PCU. 'Hello, dear, to whom am I speaking? Well, if it's a wrong number why did you answer the phone? Anyway, it's not; get me April on the line, would you? John May's granddaughter – yes, I suppose that does make her name April May. Well, she probably never told you because she was embarrassed.' She pursed her lips at the phone. 'This is no laughing matter, young man, put me through at once!'

'Got her,' said April, running down the list of names on her computer with the phone propped under her chin. 'Kate Summerton went to jail on seven counts of fraud the first time in 1998, second time for receiving stolen goods and intent to deceive in 2002. Address, 24 Cranmere Road, Greenwich SE10, and there's a phone number. We'll get someone to call her right now and put the frighteners on her. No, not literally, Maggie, it's an expression I heard on the telly.'

'That's good,' said Maggie. 'I thought you were referring to shape-shifters.'

April jotted down the number, tore off the strip of paper and passed it to Bimsley. 'I hear Uncle Arthur managed to resolve our investigation at Bayham Street. Perhaps we can return the

compliment and do the same with his. Colin, we need everything you can get on a Madeline Gilby, she's a client of this
woman.'

Meera came into April's office with a folded page in her
hand. 'Your grandfather wants a check run for these names on
your ICDb,' she explained. 'He's on the line, waiting for an
answer. They're all supposed to be victims of the bloke they're
looking for on Dartmoor. Can you do it right now?'

April looked at the piece of paper. 'This is an Indian take-
away menu,' she said.

'Other side.'

April turned the sheet over and entered the names into the
International Criminal Database: *Pascal Favier, Patrice Bezard,
Johann Bellocq, Edward Winthrop, Paulo Escobar, Pierre
Castel.*

She took Meera's phone and transferred it to a speaker while
she typed. 'Easy, Granddad, they're coming up on my screen,
all well-known cases by the look of it. Johann Bellocq was born
in Marseilles, then moved to the family home near the village
of Roquebrune, Alpes-Maritimes, charged with manslaughter
for beating his mother to death. The judge commuted his
sentence to a stay in a mental hospital due to the extenuating
circumstances of the case, which he called "devastatingly sad".
Bellocq was released five years later. Bezard was executed in
Normandy for the murder of his wife in 1945, likewise Escobar
for the same crime in Paris in 1958. Winthrop was a lawyer
murdered by his client, Pascal Favier, in 2004 in Marseilles;
they never caught Favier. Castel was jailed for the murder of his
mother in La Rochelle in 1976. They're all in a book, *Famous
French Trials of the Twentieth Century* by Edith Corbeau,
published in France two years ago by J'ai Lu, currently
available here in paperback.'

'My God,' said May. 'I've just seen that book. Madeline Gilby
had a copy of it in her handbag.' He broke the connection,
pocketed the mobile, and turned his attention to opening the
envelope Madeline had left in her Toyota's wheel arch.

He found himself looking at Johann's old passport, its expiry dated for August the previous year, and ten colour photographs, scenic postcard views of different gardens in bloom at the Villa Rothschild. 'She lied to us,' he said. 'There are no murder victims here.'

'No, she didn't lie. I think she genuinely believed she could see them,' said Maggie. 'I told you, Madeline is convinced that she has the gift of second sight. Her reality is not yours or mine.'

'Then Arthur is in the gravest possible situation.' May grabbed Maggie's hand, pushing on towards the distant tunnel.

The ringing telephone pierced the stillness of the terraced Edwardian house. There was a creaking of the shabby leather armchair, a shuffling of tartan slippers. A hand reached for the telephone.

'I'm afraid Mrs Summerton is not here at present. Can I help? I'm Roger Summerton, her husband.' He listened for a minute. 'Yes, blonde, very attractive, I remember her well. She's often here. First came to the refuge after her husband beat her up, but she went back to him a couple of times before finally deciding on a divorce. Oh, she has a history of trouble. I think the same thing happened to her own mother, but I'm sure Mrs Summerton will be able to give you more information; she'll be back soon.'

Bimsley scrawled down the details and passed them to April, who called her grandfather back.

John May stopped dead on the great white hill below the railway line. 'I'm getting a message,' he said. 'My trousers are vibrating.'

Maggie looked delighted. 'I knew we would make a believer of you eventually.'

'No, a text message.' He pulled out his mobile.

'Honestly, you get more calls in the middle of the English countryside than you do in your office,' the white witch complained. 'I'm surprised anyone can ever get hold of you. And you're slowing us down.'

'I can't move any faster than this,' May replied. 'If you were a real witch you'd take us up there by broom. Let me read this; I'm being sent important information.'

'While your partner is risking his life,' she tutted, pulling on his arm. 'For heaven's sake, come on.'

Arthur Bryant rose with creaking knees and carefully stepped around the body. He felt disembodied, faintly unwell. There was no point in remaining inside the tunnel now. Pressing his left hand against the wet wall, he slowly made his way back towards the dazzling disc of light.

When the body dropped on him with its arms locked around his shoulders, the air was crushed from his chest, and the sudden weight threw him down on to the track. The grip tightened around his neck. Bryant knew there was little point in resisting, but twisted over on to his stomach, forcing his attacker to roll on to the line.

'What are you doing, Madeline?' He breathed with all the calmness he could muster. The flints that surrounded the sleepers were cutting into his chest. 'Are you going to kill me as well? You can't take revenge on the whole of mankind.'

She was shocked to hear him address her by name, but remained silent, her hands clasped tightly around him. He wondered what she thought she was doing.

'You shouldn't have picked the names from your book, Madeline. It's called *Famous Trials* because that's exactly what they are to anyone in law enforcement. And you shouldn't have got Ryan to lie for you. Children are always so obvious when they've been asked to lie for their parents. They simply can't look you in the eye.'

They remained locked in position on the track, although she was trying to pull him further in. Bryant's hand gripped the freezing rail. He dug his boots in against the sleeper, determined not to budge.

'The French boy whose throat you just tore open with the scissors from the Swiss Army knife you keep in your bag really is called Johann Bellocq. And a small pair of scissors is a woman's weapon, you should know that.'

Bryant raised his chin so that he could speak more clearly. 'In his own way, Bellocq paid for the crime he committed. He never hurt anyone but his mother, and that was after years of being locked away and tortured by her. He was a petty thief, and had borrowed cars, although he usually returned them. It's true that when an old hunting friend of his grandfather's died Bellocq borrowed his house, but there was no real malice in him. Nor was there any dead body in the villa – the local gendarmerie has had a chance to visit it; in your hysteria, you merely thought you saw one. You were furious about being lied to once more, and thought that your pattern with men was starting to repeat itself all over again, but you only saw what you wanted to see. When Johann told you about his past, he was opening himself up to you because he genuinely loved you. He wanted you to know everything about him, but in your panic you shut him out and ran away, embroidering his history with lurid scraps culled from your own warped imagination.'

She was lying rigid now, breathing hard behind him, her legs wrapped around his. He tried to turn his head, to make her hear. 'When you found the truck driver who'd given him a lift, he told you how desperate Johann was to find you, how much he said he loved you, but to you it was just further proof of the conspiracy of men. You shut out the truth, even going so far as to shut him up, slashing out at him. Do you even know that you killed him? Of course there are bad men in the world who'll seek to harm you, Madeline, but they're not all alike. Who made you believe they were?'

He suddenly realized why she was so still. She was listening, not to him, but to the tinging of the approaching train through the steel tracks.

From the corner of his eye he saw two silhouettes appear in the bright tunnel entrance, but before he could call out, her hand pulled hard on his scarf, tightening it over his mouth and throat until he could no longer draw breath.

I've forced her to realize the truth about herself, he thought. *She's decided she has nothing more to live for. And the trouble is, she's going to take me with her.*

48

LAST EMBRACE

As John May and Maggie Armitage reached the mouth of the tunnel, they threw away caution and began calling for their friend. Their voices returned unanswered from the curving walls.

'He has to be inside,' said May, 'his tracks lead to the entrance. Stay out here and look after the boy. I'll go in.'

As he stepped into the blanket of the dark, he heard it, the distant ring of the approaching train. 'Arthur, are you hurt?' he called. 'Listen to me carefully. Madeline Gilby is a very dangerous woman. The man she insists is hunting her is Johann Bellocq, and he's actually trying to stop her. There are no pictures of murder victims, no forged passports. Arthur, answer me!'

He could feel the weight of the train on the tracks, the steady displacement of air at the far end of the long tunnel, the faint crackle of electricity. A dim light appeared on the wall of the first bend. As it slowly increased in brightness and moved down, he saw what appeared to be a bundle of rags lying across the tracks. As he watched, it flinched like an animal caught in the coils of a snake, and he realized that he was looking at his partner, trapped with Madeline Gilby's limbs twisted around him. Bryant's boots kicked out in a burst of gravel, and he twisted his head to look plaintively around for help.

May dropped to his side and pulled at an arm, but Madeline's clutch tightened, rolling Bryant further on to the centre of the track. 'You'll kill us all,' May told her. 'We can get you help, Madeline. It doesn't have to end this way.'

Ahead, the lights of the train grew brighter as it coasted the bend, sparking steel. In the claustrophobia of the tunnel, it seemed to be approaching with surprising speed.

He tried to prise open her hands, but the muscles in her fingers and arms had locked with steely rigidity. Bryant kicked and wriggled, but was rapidly losing strength. Gilby was on top of him now, knotted around his body in a deathly grip that nothing could loosen. Braced against the track, May pulled at them in vain.

'Let me,' said Maggie, hopping across the tracks and grabbing Bryant's attacker from the other side. Madeline Gilby let out a sudden piercing yell and threw out her limbs as wildly as if she had been electrocuted. Released and able to breathe once more, Bryant let out a gasp.

May pulled hard, dragging his partner across the rail and up against the wall. He reached out a hand to Madeline, shouting for her, but she crawled further away, turning to face the explosion of light and noise.

May caught sight of Madeline's pale face one last time; her widening eyes were staring into the long white shaft of light that emanated from the front of the engine in the darkness of the tunnel. She looked quite calm, as if she was glad to be finally faced with the prospect of meeting her Maker.

A moment later, the duo watched as the flashing yellow panels raced past them, and the carriages started to slow with the braking of the train. When it had finally passed, there was no trace left behind of Madeline Gilby. Blinded by snow-light, the driver had failed to spot her.

Maggie Armitage had flattened herself against the opposite wall of the tunnel. Her arms were splayed and her hair had been shocked into a vermilion sunburst around her head, like Struwwelpeter.

'What did you do to make her let go?' gasped May as he pulled the shattered Bryant to his feet. 'Stick her with an evil enchantment?'

'No, a hatpin,' replied the white witch breathlessly. 'Every bit as effective. At least she didn't have to go towards the light. It came to her.'

'The final white corridor,' said May, taking her hand. 'Come on, you two. Let's get out of the dark.'

49

ROYALTY

They stood neatly in line, the seven of them, Meera Mangeshkar and Colin Bimsley, Dan Banbury and Giles Kershaw, Raymond Land, April May and Janice Longbright.

Meera had decided to work on an expression that could not be construed as a scowl, and had loosened her tied-back hair so that it glossily framed her face. Longbright had shown her how to administer lipstick, although teaching her to stop flinching as it was applied had proved tricky.

Colin had polished his shoes and was proudly wearing his father's old police tie. The legendarily clumsy PC was under strict instructions to keep his hands by his sides and not attempt anything more complicated than taking one pace forward or back.

Dan was dressed in the too-tight grey Ben Sherman suit he always wore to work, but his wife had forced him to don his only white shirt that took cuff links.

Giles was wearing his Eton tie, a lurid red carnation he had filched from April's garage flowers and a baggy blazer that made him look like a Henley Regatta captain.

Raymond Land had ditched his cardigan and opted to stretch a yellow striped shirt across his paunch, slicking back his receding locks with his son's hair gel so that he resembled a provincial advertising manager, or possibly a pimp.

Having escaped from the storeroom in which he had been shut, Crippen threaded his way through Land's legs and thought about taking a pee, but wisely decided against it.

April wore a simple black dress and matching shoes, with pearl earrings and a single strand of black pearls that had been bequeathed to her by her grandmother.

Janice Longbright was sporting a pair of high-heeled court shoes that had once belonged to Alma Cogan, the fifties chanteuse, and a seashell hair slide in the style of Dorothy Lamour. She was still wearing the red woollen two-piece suit she had borrowed to infiltrate the Circe Club earlier that day.

They had all done what they could to look smart, and the net result was appropriately peculiar. But on this afternoon, at this moment, they all felt part of an alternative family, the invisible connections of friendship joining them to one another more surely and steadfastly than any blood tie. For once, they were individuals united as one.

The offices of the Peculiar Crimes Unit had never looked clean, but at least all of the unfinished cabling, Bryant's dubious personal belongings and Crippen's litter tray had been shoved into storage cupboards. April had indulged her passion for neatness, placing fresh-cut flowers on every desk and arranging every file, every chair, every pen and piece of paper in pristine symmetry. The unit wasn't quite fit for a queen, but it would do for a princess.

April coughed nervously. Colin checked his breath and dug for a mint. Giles stole a surreptitious glance at his watch. Dan adjusted his boxers through his trousers. Janice pushed an errant coil of hair back in place and peeked at the opening door. Crippen rolled over on to his side and fell into a light doze. It was so unnaturally quiet that they heard the central heating thermostat turn itself off.

Rosemary Armstrong entered in a display of stiff hair and thick ankles, dressed in a peculiarly *Tatler*-ish arrangement of floral silk scarves that made her look like an ambulatory sideboard centrepiece from one of the less beloved National Trust homes. In an attempt to put everyone at ease, she sported an official smile that made even the cat wake up and move away.

Longbright leaned back into line with the others, disappointed to see that it was the Princess's assistant and not her bosses. The last she had heard, Arthur Bryant and John May had been collected by train, then transferred to a Royal Navy helicopter, to get them en route to Mornington Crescent for five o'clock, but it was now twelve minutes past and they were cutting it very fine indeed.

'The Princess has just arrived,' said Rosemary, cautiously sniffing the air. 'Everything shipshape here, yes?'

Longbright peered out through the sleet-stained crescent window and saw the black Bentley parked in the cordoned-off street outside. As she watched, Leslie Faraday and Oskar Kasavian alighted on to the strangely clean pavement in tight black suits and narrow ties, looking like agents of Beelzebub.

Raymond Land spoke out of the side of his mouth. 'It's gone five, Janice. Where the hell are they?'

'I don't know, sir. I spoke to the pilot and he swore he could get them here in time.'

Land had arranged for the Princess to be shown some of the unit's case histories before meeting its most senior detectives. He would lead her to his smartened office, in the company of Rosemary and several other palace heavies, to a display they had prepared for the BBC some months earlier. She would not enjoy it, he had been warned, but she would at least give the semblance of being interested. There were pictures; it would be easy to follow. The unit had very little in the way of expensive new equipment that could be demonstrated. Its history was by nature anecdotal, ephemeral and at times downright vague, but it was woven into the very fabric of London's colourful history, and was probably more interesting than opening a swimming pool or being shown around a pumping station.

Kasavian leaned into the room with his arm outstretched and ushered in an immaculately coiffured blonde woman whose wealth had mitigated the imprints of age. She raised the faint ghost of a smile as she was introduced to each member of staff, as if dimly recalling a happy moment from her childhood. Armstrong stood with her hands clasped over her skirt like a footballer on the ten-yard line waiting for someone to take a penalty. She displayed the level of boredom rich people showed when being told about the lives of the poor. Occasionally she glanced in the direction of whoever was speaking and nodded, but her mind was dwelling on old slights, recent snubs, and pastel place settings.

Faraday was ignored and virtually dismissed from the room as Kasavian took charge of the Princess's passage, rather like a tugboat drawing an elegant old steamship into a tricky harbour. Longbright could see that he was also glancing furtively around the room while he distracted the Princess's attention, looking for something embarrassing with which to collapse this house of cards. He needed to reduce the royal personage to a state of mortification, or even mild shock, so that he could race back to Whitehall and place his observations on file before the mortar of his outrage had a chance to set. He had decided that the best way to do this was to lead the Princess to the office that Bryant and May shared and loudly announce them, opening the door with a flourish, only to reveal a pair of empty leather armchairs.

He already knew what he would say: that it appeared the unit's most long-serving officers of the law had not seen fit to be here on the most auspicious occasion in its history, and had, he'd been told, chosen to attend a spiritualists' convention instead of further inspiring the Princess's keen interest in modern policing procedure. How disappointing, he would tut to Land, shaking his head sadly, how terribly rude, more than a mere breach of protocol, a defiantly thumbed nose from a precious coterie of leftie liberals to the reigning monarchy and its hardworking national law-enforcement network. Such an act could not be allowed to pass without repercussions.

With the unit's line-up fully introduced and murmured to in tiny hushed phrases that required no answer other than *Yes, ma'am*, the Princess and her flotilla drifted on towards Bryant and May's office.

'And this, your Royal Highness, is the nerve centre of the

unit,' said Oskar Kasavian, twisting the door handle before her. 'Mr Arthur Bryant and Mr John May are the longest-serving detectives in the London Metropolitan Police force, and the Peculiar Crimes Unit owes its existence entirely to their efforts. Through their presence here today, I'm sure they are anxious to express their feelings about the unit's royal patronage.' Barely able to suppress a smirk of victory, he opened the door to the empty room.

Except that it wasn't empty.

The two detectives were exactly where they usually were, in place behind their respective leather-topped desks. Admittedly, their suits were a little crumpled, their ties slightly askew, and they both looked as though they had been caught doing something mischievous, but they were as presentably arranged as they were ever likely to be for a meeting with royalty.

They had entered via the emergency exit from the Tube station. Kasavian was lost for words. His mouth opened, then closed again. He stared back at Faraday as thunderclouds extinguished the light in his amber eyes.

John May rose from his chair with a creak and stood respectfully at attention. Arthur Bryant followed suit, coming around from behind his desk, grinning with his big white false teeth as he stuck out both hands and clasped hers, shaking her arm vigorously. The Princess looked faintly alarmed, and glanced back for help.

'Most fabulously pleasurable to meet you, your highly royal ladyshipness,' he enthused. 'If you would care to step into our humble abode, perhaps we might be permitted to reveal to you some of the extraordinary secrets of our mysterious profession. Don't be scared, we're not mad or anything.' And with that he kicked the door shut, stranding Rosemary Armstrong, Faraday, Kasavian, Land and everyone else out in the corridor.

They looked at one another in confusion, then watched the closed door, waiting for it to open again. When nothing happened, they coughed politely in their fists and waited in silence like party guests queueing for the toilet.

After four minutes had passed, Rosemary Armstrong

ostentatiously checked her watch. 'The Princess has an incredibly tight schedule,' she told Kasavian, managing to make the statement sound vaguely gynaecological.

He studied her with compressed lips, then tentatively tried the door, only to find that it would not budge.

'What's the matter?' asked Rosemary.

'They've locked it,' said Land, always happy to state the obvious.

'Why would they do that?' asked Kasavian. 'Do they have something to say to her in private?'

Nobody answered. As the minutes stretched by, the group shuffled closer to the door, and whether they realized it or not, listened intently. They heard the sound of ice tinkling into glass, then a shriek of laughter, then something that resembled a spring being stretched and released, then an old Billie Holiday recording played on a Victrola gramophone, then more muted laughter and finally a blast on something like a naval foghorn.

When the door was finally unlocked and swung open, the Princess emerged with her immaculate blonde hair askew, glassy eyes and a strange smile on her face. She was also humming to herself. As she passed Kasavian, ignoring them all, the Home Office security supervisor caught a distinct whiff of tobacco and gin.

When the others had followed her out, Kasavian stormed into the smoky room and slapped a skeletal white hand on Bryant's desk. 'What the hell was going on in here?' he angrily hissed under his breath. But Bryant merely smiled and shrugged.

Princess Beatrice did not speak another word to anyone until long after she had left the unit, and when Bryant and May finally emerged from their room they refused to divulge to anyone what had taken place. However, while she was clearing up, Sergeant Longbright found some candid photographs of the British royal family taken at a party in Cowes in 1953, an empty bottle of Gordon's Gin and something that looked distinctly like the remains of a joint under Bryant's desk. There also appeared to have been a small fire in the bin.

When Oskar Kasavian rang Rosemary Armstrong two days

later and enquired by periphrastic means about the Princess's visit to the unit, he was harshly warned never to mention it again. Furthermore, when he ventured to suggest that the Princess might have an opinion concerning the possible future of the Peculiar Crimes Unit, he was told in no uncertain terms that if anyone's future was at all in doubt, it was most likely to be his own.

50

OLDER AND WILDER

'You're probably wondering why I called you here,' said Arthur Bryant as Giles Kershaw approached him through the traffic-blackened slush on Waterloo Bridge. Above them the sky had cleared but for a single blossom of cloud. Along the river, the arms of cranes drifted back and forth, as if the buildings were sprouting limbs and trying to rise.

'I know this is where you and John usually take a stroll of a summer evening,' said Kershaw, flicking back his hair in what had lately become a nervous tic, 'but I rather thought you'd be fed up with being outside in the cold by now.'

'Oh, we've been out in the cold for years,' replied Bryant cheerfully. 'We always like to come and look at all of this.' He waved his walking stick over the London view, nearly poking a passer-by in the eye. 'After Dartmoor, Waterloo Bridge is like the Bahamas. Besides, I don't trust the countryside, all mud and methane. I suppose you want to know the outcome of your reappraisal for the position of PCU pathologist.'

'Actually, before you say anything I want to apologize.' Kershaw looked down at the kerb, contrite. 'When I moved Lilith Starr's body, it never occurred to me that she might have been the cause of Oswald's death. I should have stopped to think about what had happened before acting. Instead, I was everything that Finch accused me of being. He was right to turn me down for the position. I wasn't ready to handle the job.'

'Perhaps not,' Bryant agreed, 'but I think you are now. You acted for Oswald's sake, instead of merely obeying the letter of the law.'

Kershaw was not entirely convinced. 'Renfield acted for the sake of his young recruit, but now he'll always blame himself for that girl's death.'

'We have no way of knowing if she could have been saved, Giles. It was Oswald who came up with such a drastic way of reviving her. In an ideal world, Owen Mills would have been able to tell everyone about his love for Lilith Starr, and who she really was, but sadly that's not how real life is, and you recognized that. You protected all of them. Which is why John, Janice and I have decided to recommend you for the position of unit pathologist. Here, I have a little something for you.' Bryant dug into the vast pocket of his disintegrating overcoat and produced an extendable radio antenna. 'It belonged to Oswald. He used it in every lecture he ever gave me about causes of death.'

'Oh, er, thank you.' Kershaw accepted the antenna with some puzzlement.

'My pleasure. Now buzz off, there's a good chap. I'm meeting John for a pint of bitter at The Anchor. But do come and chat to me anytime. My door is always open.' Bryant clasped his hands behind his back and faced the stone balustrade, watching the boats below.

Only he could turn Waterloo Bridge into his office, thought Kershaw, smiling to himself as he headed back towards the sooty canyon of the Strand.

Bryant found his partner ruminatively rooting inside a bag of crisps in the riverside bar of The Anchor. Although it was late afternoon, the pub was unusually empty. Brackish light filtered into the saloon as if passing through an emulsifier.

'Ah, there you are,' said May. 'I was beginning to think you'd stood me up. Did you talk to Kershaw?'

'You realize that by promoting him, we're reducing the size of the PCU by one?' said Bryant. 'You don't suppose Kasavian will allow us to recruit someone if I promise to tell him what went on with Princess Beatrice, do you?'

'Would you tell him?' asked May.

'Oh, of course not, I'd just make up any old rubbish. It's worth a try, although I don't suppose he'll stop now until he finds a way to shut us down for good.' He irritably tapped a coin on the bar. 'I say there, any danger of getting some service?' He turned to May. 'They can't get the staff, either. The barmaid who used to work here had a face like a rhino's right buttock but by Godfrey she knew how to pull a decent pint. What flavour are those?' Bryant pulled a crisp from the packet and held it to the light. 'Pea and ham? How disgusting. You know, I was thinking about poor Johann Bellocq on the way here.'

'Oh?' May waved at the arriving barman.

'He came to a sticky end after a brief lifetime filled with misery, didn't he? I wonder if he felt he was fated to be betrayed by a woman, and willed his destiny upon himself? He'd had old-time religion hammered into him to the point where it drove him to commit the ultimate sin of matricide. True, he eventually earned his forgiveness at the hands of nuns, but the trauma clearly haunted him, overshadowing any chance he had of forming normal relationships. He'd drifted from town to town, getting involved in petty crime, because in his heart he knew there could be no end to his torment. And so he contrived to meet a woman so damaged by her own beauty that she could only confirm his deepest fears. Makes you think that the great tragedies of our lives are built into us as surely as DNA, and proliferate quietly and inexorably, like cancer cells.'

'Perhaps,' May conceded, looking out through lead-light windows at the Hesperian sky. 'But if you follow the line of fate further back, you get to Kate Summerton, who spent her life trying to heal abused women, only to step across the line that divides good intentions from harmful influence. You might argue that Madeline Gilby was searching for someone who would confirm her neuroses. Bellocq suffered at the hands of women, Gilby suffered at the hands of men, and the pair were drawn into a relationship that destroyed them both. These tangles seem to lie in every one of our lives; we rarely have the self-knowledge to cut them free until it's too late. I'm afraid young Ryan will be the next to deal with his demons.' He passed Bryant a beer. 'Looks like we're going to get a rather lurid sunset.'

'It's nice having a free Friday to ourselves,' said Bryant. 'Although I wouldn't want many of them in a row.'

'Oh, I think we still have work ahead of us yet,' said May, glancing around the almost deserted saloon. 'Tell me, do you ever regret not finding another partner after Nathalie?'

'Oh, don't worry about me, there have been plenty of ladies whose company I've enjoyed,' said Bryant finally, creaking back on his stool, 'but never enough to marry. I always knew I would prove a disappointment to them. Very few men make perfect husbands, let alone policemen. Women secretly like partners they don't have to worry about all the time. You hardly ever talk about your own marriage, you know. It's obviously a painful subject for you.'

'Our family tree had poisoned roots,' said May enigmatically. 'Madness and death followed us like shadows.'

'I know how your daughter Elizabeth died, of course, but you never talk about what happened to your wife.'

'One day I'll take you to meet her,' said May, sipping his beer thoughtfully. 'Then you'll understand.'

For once, Bryant had been caught by surprise. He stared at his partner as if seeing him for the first time. 'Oh' was all he could manage.

'Do you believe in the afterlife?' asked May suddenly, turning to him.

'Me? Good Lord, no.' He smiled sadly at the thought. 'I suppose the worst thing isn't that there might be nothing after my death, but that there might be nothing before it. That's why I stay busy. There are always regrets, of course. But you have to try and make a difference without hurting anyone along the way, so that you can reach a final state of grace without shame.'

'That's fair,' May agreed. 'Look at that, one of Maggie's white corridors is back. I wonder how she'd interpret this one.'

'I'm not ready to look my Maker in the eye just yet,' said Bryant, shaking his head. 'Let's ignore it and have another pint.'

Outside, beyond the bridges of London, the dying scarlet sun appeared beneath the last dissipating snow cloud, to split corridors of saffron light across the ruffled grey river.